GRIFFON—TRAPPED!

"Down!" Wallie yelled, but the sailors were already dropping to the smelly gratings while the docks filled with the sounds of chaos, familiar from Ov—horses screaming, people yelling, wagons overturning...

From the deck Wallie bellowed for Nnanji and began to fumble inexpertly with the ropes. "Tack!" he shouted. Tomiyano started to argue—then waterspouts reared all around, and the *Griffon* staggered.

Wallie shivered convulsively as the River boiled around the little ship and the awful truth dawned—they had sailed straight into the sorcerers' trap!

By Dave Duncan
Published by Ballantine Books:

A ROSE-RED CITY

The Seventh Sword
THE RELUCTANT SWORDSMAN
THE COMING OF WISDOM
THE DESTINY OF THE SWORD

SHADOW

WEST OF JANUARY

STRINGS

A Man of His Word
MAGIC CASEMENT
FAERY LANDS FORLORN
PERILOUS SEAS
EMPEROR AND CLOWN*

HERO!

**Forthcoming*

THE DESTINY OF THE SWORD

Book Three of *The Seventh Sword*

DAVE DUNCAN

A Del Rey Book

BALLANTINE BOOKS • NEW YORK

A Del Rey Book
Published by Ballantine Books

 Published in the United States of America by Ballantine Books, a division of Random House, Inc., New York, and simultaneously in Canada by Random House of Canada Limited, Toronto.

Library of Congress Catalog Card Number: 88-91967

ISBN 0-345-35293-9

Manufactured in the United States of America

First Edition: December 1988
Sixth Printing: October 1991

Cover Art by Romas

This book is
dedicated
by a grateful protégé
to a peerless mentor
VERONICA CHAPMAN
editor of the seventh rank.

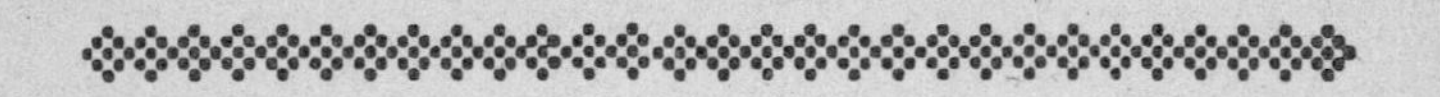

CONTENTS

First your brother you must chain.
And from another wisdom gain.
When the mighty has been spurned,
An army earned, a circle turned,
So the lesson may be learned.
Finally return that sword
And to its destiny accord.

The riddle of the demigod—
his instructions to Lord Shonsu

PROLOGUE:
A TRYST HAS BEEN CALLED

A tryst had been called in Casr and the Goddess had blessed it. Now any boat or ship that carried a swordsman might find itself arriving at Casr.

The swordsmen would then disembark and went in search of glory. The vessels would then be returned by Her Hand to their home waters, where the crews and passengers spread the word: A tryst had been called.

In the villages, the cities, and the palaces of the World, Her swordsmen heard the summons. They heard it in the steamy jungles of Aro and on the windy plains of Grin; among the orchards of Allia and the paddies of Az. They heard it in sandy Ib Man and under the glacier peaks of Zor.

Garrison swordsmen heard it in corridors or busy streets. Free swords heard it on hillsides or on shabby village jetties. They sharpened their blades, they oiled their boots and harnesses—and they headed down to the River.

Garrisons were in turmoil as excited juniors sought out their mentors, demanding to be led to Casr or released from their oaths. The seniors had then to decide—to stay with their comforts, their sinecures, and their families, or to heed the call of honor and the entreaties of their protégés. Some chose honor and others contempt.

The wandering bands of free swords had no such problem, for they were on Her service at all times. In many cases they did not even discuss the matter—they merely rose to their feet and went.

Yet the Goddess could take but few of Her swordsmen, or She would have left Her world without law and without order. Many an eager company embarked, and sailed, and soon found the light changing, the weather altered, the scenery shifted, and Casr coming up ahead. Others no less eager, and apparently no less worthy, embarked and sailed and were disappointed—the River did not change for them. No true swordsman would believe that he was undeserving . . . There was argument. Argument led to recrimination, recrimination to quarrel, quarrel to insult, insult to challenge, and challenge to bloodshed. The wounded went to the healers, the dead to the River. The survivors disembarked, re-formed in other groupings, and tried again in other ships.

Not only swordsmen heard the call. Behind them came their wives, their slaves, their concubines, and often their children. Came, too, the heralds and the armorers, the minstrels and the healers, and also moneylenders and cobblers and hostlers and cooks and whores. The youth of the World followed the swordsmen onto the ships and waited to see where the great River would bear them. Not for centuries had the Goddess summoned Her swordsmen to a tryst. Such confusion and disruption of the social order were unknown in the memory of the People.

On reaching Casr every swordsman asked the same question: Why had this tryst been called, who was the enemy?

And the answer to that was—*sorcerers*!

BOOK ONE:
HOW THE SWORDSMAN WEPT

†

For a swordsman of the seventh rank to hide—from anyone or anything—was unthinkable. Nevertheless, Wallie was being deliberately inconspicuous, to say the least.

He had spent the morning on deck, leaning on the gunwale and witnessing the tumult and bustle of the docks at Tau, but he had unclipped his swordsman ponytail, letting his thick black hair fall free to his shoulders. He had removed his harness and sword and laid them on the deck at his feet. The side of the ship concealed his blue Seventh's kilt and his swordsman boots. Passersby would therefore see only a very large young man with unusually long hair, unless they came close enough to note the seven swords on his brow. The dock was low in Tau; it would take good eyes to do that.

Two weeks of uninterrupted sailing from Ov had left *Sapphire* with stores depleted and much unfinished business. Mothers had herded children off to seek dentists. Old Lina had tottered down the plank to haggle with hawkers for meat and fruit and vegetables, and also flour and spices and salt. Nnanji had taken his brother to find a healer and have the cast on his arm replaced. Jja had gone shopping with Lae. Young Sinboro, having been judged to have reached manhood, had strutted off with his parents in search of a facemarker—there would be a party on board that evening.

Normally Brota sold the cargo and Tomiyano scouted for

another, but now the sailors were fretting about ballast and trim, so the roles were reversed. Big fat Brota strapped on her sword, took Mata along to wield it if necessary, and waddled away in search of profit. Tomiyano ordered two bronze ingots laid at the foot of the plank, stood young Matarro beside them, and headed back on board to attend to other business.

He was not left long in peace—traders arrived and Matarro fetched the captain. As a bargainer, Tomiyano was very nearly as shrewd as his mother. Wallie eavesdropped happily from his post on the rail while the discussion raged below him. Eventually the price range was narrowed, and the traders came on board to inspect the main cargo in the hold. Wallie turned his attention back to the dock life.

Tau was Wallie's favorite among all the cities of the Regi-Vul loop, although to call Tau a city was to stretch the term to its limit. As in most towns and cities, the dock road was too narrow for its duties, cramped between the bollards, gang-planks, and piles of unloaded cargoes on one side and the traders' warehouses on the other. The sun was unusually warm for a day in fall and it shone on a scene of loud and colorful disorder. Wagons rumbled and clanked, pedestrians milled, slave gangs sweated, hawkers pulled carts and shouted their wares. There were no rules—traffic went wherever it could find a space. The clamor of wheels mingled with oaths and insults and abuse. Yet the People were a good-natured race, and in the main the tumult was without rancor. The air smelled of horses and dust and people.

Wallie enjoyed watching the horses of the World. They seemed so mythological—the head of a camel and body of a basset hound. They smelled Earthlike enough, though. During the morning he had observed a herd of goats being unloaded. He had been amused to learn that goats had antlers, not horns. Goats smelled very earthy.

The backdrop for all this noisy confusion was a façade of two-story warehouses that fascinated him—dark oak wood-work and beige parqeting like a movie set of Merrie England; diamond-paned windows and beetling roofs of fuzzy thatch. Yet, however medieval or Tudor the architecture might seem to him, there were no farthingaled damsels or beruffed Elizabethan gallants strutting this stage. The dress of the People was simple and plain—kilts or loincloths on the men and wraps for the women, with the elders of both sexes decently concealed in robes. Youngsters ran naked. They were a brown-skinned, brown-haired folk, lithe and merry, and brown also was the dominant shade of their garb, the color worn by Thirds, qualified artisans of the three hundred and forty-three crafts of the World. The yellow of Seconds and the white of Firsts brightened the texture, with the rarer orange and red and green of higher ranks scattered around in the surging, scurrying throng.

A skinny youth in a white loincloth ran past Wallie and dashed down the plank to go racing and dodging off through the crowd, narrowly avoiding death under the wheels of a two-horse wagon. He was one of the traders' juniors, so he had undoubtedly been sent to fetch help. That meant that Tomiyano had made a sale. In a few minutes the captain emerged on deck and saw his visitors off. The smile that he then allowed himself told Wallie that the price had been more than satisfactory.

Tomiyano was an effective young man, aggressive and muscular, weathered to a dark chestnut, with hair approaching red, although not as red as Nnanji's. He wore only a skimpy brown breechclout, plus a belt and dagger to show that he was captain. Craftmarks of three ships were marked on his forehead, but he was a very competent sailor, who could have qualified for much higher rank had he wished. The scar on his face had been made by a sorcerer, and Wallie now knew that it was an acid burn.

Yet Tomiyano was a mere stripling alongside Wallie. Swordsmen were rarely big, but Shonsu had been an exception—very big. The sailor had to tilt his head back to meet Wallie's eyes. He did that now, and his face was full of astonishment.

"Hiding?" he demanded.

Wallie shrugged and smiled. "Being cautious."

The captain's eyes narrowed. "Is that how swordsmen behaved in your dream world, Shonsu?"

It was only within the last couple of weeks that Wallie had taken the crew of *Sapphire* totally into his confidence, explaining that he was not the original Shonsu, swordsman of the seventh rank; that his soul had been brought from another world and been given the body of Shonsu, his skill with a sword, and his unaccomplished mission for the gods. Tomiyano was a skeptical man. He had learned to trust Lord Shonsu—learned with difficulty, for the crew of *Sapphire* had little liking for swordsmen—but he still had trouble accepting so incredible a story. And tact was not the captain's most conspicuous trait.

Wallie sighed, thinking of plainclothes detectives and unmarked patrol cars. "Yes," he admitted. "They did this quite a lot."

Tomiyano snorted in disgust. "And last time we came to Tau you were screaming because you couldn't find a swordsman. Now the place is full of them."

"Exactly," Wallie said.

That was what he had been studying—swordsmen. Their ponytails and sword hilts made them conspicuous as they strode through the crowds, and sane civilians made way for swordsmen. They walked in twos or threes, sometimes fours or fives. Brown kilts were the most common, of course, but Wallie had seen several Fourths, two Fifths, and even—surprisingly—one Sixth. He had counted forty-two swordsmen in the last hour. Tau indeed was full of them.

Tomiyano looked down at the busy street for a while and then said, "Why?"

Wallie leaned his elbows on the rail and attempted to put his concern into words. "Work it out, Captain. Suppose you're a swordsman. The Goddess has brought you to Tau and you're on your way to Casr. You have a protégé or two with you. You're a Third, or a Fourth, maybe. There must be hundreds of swordsmen in Casr now . . . What's the first thing a swordsman will want when he gets there?"

Tomiyano spat over the side. "Women!"

Wallie chuckled. "Of course. Anything else?"

The sailor nodded, understanding. "A mentor?"

"Right! They're going to start banding together. Every one of them will be looking out for a good senior to swear to."

"And you don't want an army?" Tomiyano asked.

Wallie grinned at him. "Have you room on board?" There

would be few Sevenths around, and some of those would be getting old, for only rarely could a swordsman reach seventh rank before he was thirty and already at his peak, although Shonsu had obviously done so—Wallie had frequently studied his face in a mirror and decided he must be somewhere in his middle twenties. He was young, therefore. He was big and steely-eyed. If he were to stand at the top of the gangplank with his blue kilt visible, he would be fighting off would-be recruits in no time.

"No!" the captain said firmly. The thought of a few dozen swordsmen on his beloved *Sapphire* would be enough to loosen his teeth. He smiled faintly and muttered, "Considerate of you!"

And that, Wallie thought, was almost another miracle in itself.

"Look there!" he said.

The swordsman Sixth was returning and now he marched at the head of a column of ten. A Fifth leading two Thirds passed them, and sunbeams streaked from blades as salutes were exchanged. Civilians dodged, doubtless cursing under their breath.

Tomiyano grunted and went off to attend to business, while Wallie mused that his explanation to the captain had been less than half the truth. The juniors would be seeking mentors, true, but the seniors would be even more actively recruiting protégés. Followers brought status. Status would be a much sought-after commodity in Casr now.

Which raised the possibility that perhaps he *ought* to be recruiting an army. He bore the Goddess' own sword, he was Her champion . . . maybe he was supposed to arrive at the tryst with some status of his own. It would not be difficult. He could accost that Sixth and take him over, together with his ten flunkies. If he balked, Wallie could challenge—no Sixth had a hope against Shonsu. Afterward the man could be bandaged and sent out to round up more.

Might that explain why the Goddess had delivered these particular swordsmen to Tau instead of directly to Casr?

The thought held no appeal for Wallie. The whole tryst held no appeal. He still had not decided whether he was going to collaborate or not. So he let the green-kilted Napoleon continue his parade along the docks unmolested. If the gods wanted that man to swear to Lord Shonsu, then neither of them would be able to leave Tau until they cooperated. Their ships would merely return to Tau instead of going on to Casr.

Casr was a monstrous thundercloud on Wallie's horizon. He did not know what he wanted to do there, or what might be awaiting him. He knew that the original Shonsu had been castellan of the swordsmen's lodge in Casr, so Wallie must expect to be recognized when he arrived. He might find family or friends—or enemies. Nnanji, for one, was convinced that Shonsu was destined to become leader of the tryst. That might be the case, for certainly he knew more about the sorcerers and their un-Worldly abilities than any other swordsman. But he also knew enough to believe that the tryst was a horrible error. He was almost more inclined to try to block it than to lead it.

Tomiyano had rounded up his men. Holiyi, Maloli, Linihyo, and Oligarro—two cousins and two cousins by marriage. They were taking off the hatch covers and stacking the planks out of the way. Up on the poop deck the remaining children were playing loudly under the watchful eye of Fia, who wielded the unarguable authority of a twelve-year-old.

A wagon drew up alongside and unloaded a slave gang. The trader, a plump Fifth, began shouting unnecessary orders in a squeaky voice, and the derrick was swung out and put to use. Wallie watched as the bronze ingots from Gi were borne away. He wondered idly which one of those ingots had saved his life from the sorcerers' muskets in Ov.

Slaves wore black and little of it, for no one wasted cloth on a slave. They were a cowed and smelly bunch, that slave gang—skinny men in skimpy loincloths, working like fiends, streaming sweat while their bony rib cages pumped. Their backs were scarred. They ran, not daring to walk. They strained at the windlass handles until their eyes popped. Wallie could hardly bear to watch, for it was slavery more than anything else that brought home to him the faults of this barbaric, iron-age World. The thatched warehouses might teem with rats and the people with fleas, the alleys smell of urine and the streets of garbage . . . those he could tolerate, but slavery tested his resolve. The slave boss on the wagon brought out a whip and cracked it a few times to increase the pace. He did not recongize the danger looming above him at the ship's rail. Had he made one serious stroke—just one—he would have found himself lying on the cobbles, being mercilessly flogged . . . but he did not know that and he did not find out.

The wagon was filled and departed. Another took its place. Some members of *Sapphire*'s crew came wandering back from their explorations and paused to talk with the big man in the blue kilt. Tau was a turbulent place, they reported. Two hundred swordsmen had passed through on their way to the tryst, plus several times that many followers. Tau was a small town. The natives were restless.

Tomiyano went down to the dock and began weighing the traders' gold. Wallie continued to survey the scene, noting that the swordsmen were bunching as he had predicted. Couples were very rare now. A Fifth had collected seven, and later the triumphant Sixth paraded past again with fifteen.

Then Katanji returned, a snowy new cast on his damaged arm outshining his white kilt. He seemed smaller than ever, his face a paler brown than usual, and his wide, dark eyes not as sparkly—perhaps the healers had hammered a little too hard when removing the old plaster. His hair was beginning to reach a more respectable length for a swordsman's, but it curled up in a tiny bun instead of making a ponytail. He wore no sword, of course. Barring a miracle, he would never use that arm again—but miracles were not uncommon around Shonsu.

He managed an approximation of his normal pert smile, white teeth gleaming in dark face, while his eyes noted with surprise Wallie's unarmed, undressed state.

"Where's your brother?" Wallie demanded.

Katanji's wan smile became a smirk. "I left him to it, my lord."

He need say no more. Nnanji was still in a state of witless infatuation over the lithesome Thana, but it was four weeks since he had been ashore for recreation.

"The girls have been busy, I imagine?" Wallie inquired.

Katanji rolled his eyes. "The poor things are worn out, they told me." He scowled. "And they've raised their prices!"

Innocent little Katanji, of course, had seduced Diwa, Mei, and lately possibly Hana on the ship, and his need would not have been as great as his brother's. It would take more than a woman to make Katanji lose his head.

Wallie nodded and went back to his spectating. His mind began to wander, reverting to its ever-present worries about Casr and the troubles that must await him.

Tomiyano came striding back on deck, swinging a leather bag. He grinned happily at Wallie, jingled the bag gloatingly, and then went to peer down into the forward hatch and hold a shouted conversation with Oligarro and Holiyi, who had gone below to inspect ballast. The slaves had completed their work and were dragging their feet back down the gangplank.

Then . . .

Damn!

Wallie forgot sailors and slaves. Two swordsmen were striding across the road, obviously heading for *Sapphire*. The vacation was over! With a muffled curse, he ducked down out of sight and scrabbled for his sword. He was still on his knees and frantically fastening harness buckles when boots drummed on the gangplank. The two swordsmen came on deck and marched right by him.

Tomiyano spun around as if he had been kicked. In two fast strides he moved to accost the newcomers, feet apart, arms akimbo, and face thrust forward aggressively, his anger showing like a warning beacon.

Wallie noted the swordsmen boots with surprise: tooled leather, shiny as glass. Above them hung kilts of downy wool, of superlative cut and texture, the pleats like knife edges—red for a Fifth and white for a First. His eyes strayed higher. The harnesses and scabbards on the men's backs were as opulent as their boots, embossed, and decorated with topazes. Higher yet—the sword hilts bore silver filigree and more topaz. The hairclips were of silver also.

Well!

He rose silently to his feet, scooping back his hair and clipping it with his own sapphire hairclip, while he analyzed these strangers. They were not free swords, obviously, for the frees prided themselves on their poverty. They might be garrison swordsmen, but few cities would willingly clothe their police like that. Could any swordsmen come by such wealth honestly?

Wallie twitched his shoulder blades, tilting his sword to the vertical so that its hilt was behind his head. Then he leaned back with his elbows on the rail and waited to enjoy the fun.

The Fifth was trespassing. That might be from ignorance, but he knew enough to salute the captain as a superior and to refrain from drawing his sword on deck. He used the civilian hand gestures: "I am Polini, swordsman of the fifth rank, and it is my deepest and most humble wish that the Goddess Herself will see fit to grant you long life and happiness and to induce you to accept my modest and willing service in any way in which I may advance any of your noble purposes."

No titles or office mentioned? He was a tall, rangy man, probably in his early thirties. His voice was cultured and resonant. On first impressions and restricted to a rear view, Wallie was inclined to approve of this Polini. Tomiyano was not. He waited a long, insulting minute before speaking, his eyes slitted. Then he made the ritual reply without sounding as if he meant a word of it: "I am Tomiyano, sailor of the third rank, master of *Sapphire*, and am honored to accept your gracious service."

The First was a mere kid, slim and slight and much shorter than his mentor. Lowranks were not normally presented. He stood rigid and silent on Polini's left. Maloli and Linihyo drifted unobtrusively closer to fire buckets, whose sand contained knives. Tomiyano must be able to see Wallie in the background, but he was keeping his eyes on the Fifth.

"Permission to come aboard, Captain?"

Tomiyano pursed his lips. "Seems to me you already have."

Wallie knew from experience how Tomiyano enjoyed provoking swordsmen.

"Captain," the Fifth said, "I wish passage on your ship for my protégé and myself."

Tomiyano hooked thumbs in his belt, his right hand close to his dagger. "This is a family ship, master. We carry no passengers. The Goddess be with you."

"Two silvers for you, sailor! If She wills, you should return within the day."

Oligarro and Holiyi floated out of the fo'c'sle door. They, also, edged close to fire buckets. The children on the poop deck had fallen silent and lined up along the rail to watch. Sounds of wagons and horses drifted up from the dock.

"Jonahs, are you?" Tomiyano inquired. "Where did She drag you from?"

The back of Polini's neck was turning red, but he kept his voice calm. "From Plo. Not that you will have heard of it."

The captain still refrained from looking at Wallie, but his reply was meant for him, also. "Of course I have heard of Plo. The most beautiful woman I have ever seen came from Plo. Far to the south, I understand."

"Plo is famous for the beauty of its women," Polini agreed.

"But not for the manners of its men."

Very few swordsmen could have taken that from a civilian, very few. The youngster made an audible gasping sound, and Polini's sword arm twitched. Somehow he kept himself under control. "That was not itself a good demonstration of manners, sailor."

"Then go away frowning."

"I have told you that we wish passage. I shall be generous—five silvers and I shall overlook your impudence."

The captain shook his head. "The garrison of Tau is organizing a ship for the swordsmen, due to leave tomorrow. Yesterday one reached Casr within an hour, by Her Hand."

"I am aware of that."

Tomiyano's eyebrows shot up. "Doesn't want to go to Casr, huh?" There was a strong implication of cowardice in the way he spoke. Wallie expected the explosion.

It did not come, but it was close. Polini's voice dropped an octave. "No. I do not plan to go to Casr yet, if She wills."

"And I do not plan to visit Plo, in spite of its women."

The swordsman's fists were clenched. Wallie prepared to intervene. It was fun, but very dangerous fun.

"Your insolence becomes tiresome. Swordsmen serve the Goddess and are owed your help. Do not provoke me further!"

"Get off my ship—before I call on my friends!"

Incredibly, Polini still did not draw, although the First was staring up at him in stunned fury.

"Which friends, Captain?" Polini asked contemptuously, glancing at the other sailors.

"That one for a start." Tomiyano nodded at Wallie. The First wheeled around. The Fifth, suspecting a trap, did not.

The First squeaked, "Mentor!" and then Polini turned. He gaped in horror—blue kilt, seven sword facemarks . . . and a bigger man than himself, which must be a rare surprise for him.

For a moment no one spoke. Wallie was enjoying the effect, but also feeling rather ashamed of himself. Polini was obviously noting his battered boots, his shoddy kilt, and the contrast of the magnificently crafted harness. Then the Fifth recovered and saluted.

Wallie made the response. It was his privilege to speak first, and the captain would expect him to send this impudent interloper off promptly with his tail down; but Wallie was now very curious, and not without admiration. Polini had a craggy, honest-looking face. The First was being impassive, but he blinked and Wallie caught a glimpse of his eyelids. Aha!

"My congratulations, master," Wallie said with a smile. "Not many swordsmen keep their tempers when dealing with Sailor Tomiyano."

"Your lordship is gracious," Polini replied stiffly. "I see that I unwittingly erred in choosing this vessel. Obviously it is bound for Casr." He would be thinking of Tomiyano's imputation of cowardice, probably suffering a thousand deaths at the thought of a Seventh having heard it and likely agreeing. "With your permission, my lord, I shall depart."

Wallie was not going to let him escape without an explanation, but first he must get in character for a Seventh. "No, master," he said. "You will share some ale with me. I owe you that much for playing tricks on you. Sailor—three tankards of the mild!"

Tomiyano's jaw dropped at the tone, and he lost his smirk.

Wallie gestured to the aft end of the deck. "Come, Master Polini," he said. "And bring his Highness along, also."

††

The minstrels of the World sang ballads and epics of brave heroes and virtuous maidens, of monsters and sorcerers, of generous gods and just kings. Nnanji loved the heroic ones and could quote them endlessly, but one hero was conspicuously absent: Sherlock Holmes. Wallie's remark almost caused Polini to draw. Tomiyano made the sign of the Goddess, then relaxed when he saw that Lord Shonsu was merely up to his tricks again. The boy paled.

"No, no sorcery, Master Polini!" Wallie said hastily. "Just a good swordsman's eye—observation."

Polini glanced suspiciously over his protégé and back to this strange Seventh.

"Observation, my lord?"

Wallie smiled. "Few mentors would dress a First so well. Fewer Fifths would even take a First as protégé, and you yourself are obviously garbed as a man of high station. But I can go further: I note that his facemark has healed, yet he is so young that his swearing must have been recent. His hair is long enough to make a good ponytail, so his induction to the craft was decided at least a year ago, and only swordsmen's sons can normally count on becoming swordsmen. Yet his parentmarks show that he is the son of a priest. Elementary, Master Polini."

Royal houses were usually founded by swordsmen, but kingship was a dangerous trade. No swordsman could refuse a challenge, whereas a priest was sacrosanct. Kings' sons were mostly sworn to the priesthood.

Polini considered this and bowed his head in agreement. He caught his protégé's eye and said, "Learn!" The boy nodded and regarded the Seventh with awe.

Confidence having now returned, Wallie directed them smoothly to the far side of the deck, which was marginally farther from the hubbub of the dock. The aft hatch cover was still open, and the planks had been stacked in a neat pile, a low wall

that would suffice as a bench. But before he sat down...
"Present him, master."

"Lord Shonsu, I am honored to present to you my protégé, Arganari of the First."

Where, Wallie wondered, had he heard that name before?

The boy reached for his sword, remembered that he was on a ship, and turned the gesture into the start of the civilian salute. His voice was childish and curiously unmusical, making the statement a question, "... any of your noble purposes?"

Wallie solemnly assured him that he was honored to accept his gracious service. He bade his guests be seated, placing himself on a fire bucket beside the steps up to the poop. That way he was facing them and could also keep an eye on the plank. Above him, a line of youngsters peered down curiously.

The boy was even younger than he had seemed earlier. Wallie thought of the other two swordsman Firsts he knew. Matarro was one of the crew of *Sapphire*, a water-rat swordsman, and hence a sailor in all but name. Yet he took his craft very seriously, truly believing that to be a swordsman was a great honor. Then there was nipper Katanji, whose skeptical cynicism would have suited a man four times his age. This lad had neither of those qualities. He must surely be excited, for the Goddess had moved him halfway around the World, from far south to far north, and he was very near to the first tryst in centuries. Yet he was displaying only a solemn wariness, unsuited to his years.

The visitors sat stiffly on the planks, awaiting the Seventh's pleasure.

"You have a problem, Master Polini," Wallie said. "Perhaps I can help you with it?"

"It is a trivial matter, Lord Shonsu, but near to my honor." *I'm not going to talk about it.*

"Then I shall guess!" Nosiness was a prerogative of Sevenths. "You have come from the temple?"

Polini half rose, again almost reaching for his sword. He sank back uneasily, staring.

Wallie smiled cheerfully. "You are right to suspect sorcery. The sorcerers can change facemarks, so any man or woman may be a sorcerer. I, however, am not." He wondered if they had noticed the damnable feather mothermark that the god had placed on his left eyelid. That was going to be a serious problem. "I was merely speculating what a man of honor would do in what I suspect to be your situation." Polini had an honest face. He had been chosen as the most suitable member of the palace guard to be mentor to a prince—a strong tribute to his character. The lad's worshipful attitude seemed genuine. "For some reason you had cause to embark on a ship. You would have many swordsmen in your entourage if you were guarding a prince. The Goddess wanted them for Her tryst, so here you are."

Polini and Arganari both nodded, speechless at such acuity in a swordsman, making Wallie feel smug.

"So you find yourself in a dilemma of honor—your duty to the Holiest and your duty to the prince. Your decision was to send the rest of the swordsmen on to the tryst and seek to take the boy home. In that situation I would go to the temple and beseech Her to let me return him safely, making solemn pledge that I myself would come back here immediately afterward. I should throw in a promise to enlist more swordsmen, I think."

Polini looked down at the boy, and then they both smiled.

"A kill!" the Fifth said.

"Your perception is suited to your rank, my lord?" said Arganari.

Again that curious questioning? And a very flowery speech for one of his age.

Then Tomiyano himself appeared with a tray, placing foaming tankards on the planks beside each of the visitors, bowing low to offer the tray to Wallie—who should have been suspicious at once.

"May She strengthen your arms and sharpen your eyes!" he said, raising his tankard in salute.

"And yours!" the others chorused, and all three drank.

Wallie gagged and gasped and spluttered. His beer had been generously salted. He turned to glare at Tomiyano's retreating back and saw the grins on the other sailors standing beyond—that would teach him to pull rank on the captain in front of strangers! Wallie hurled the tankard over the side, wiped his mouth, and shamefacedly explained his performance to the others, who were again giving him very puzzled looks.

"You know that the water-rat swordsmen teach fencing to sailors?" he asked.

Polini scowled. "So I have heard, my lord. It is an abomination!"

"No," Wallie assured him, "there is a sutra that excludes sailors from the normal run of civilians. I just wanted to explain why I put up with my insolent friend over there. On his own deck, that man is at least a high Fifth or even a Sixth at swordsmanship."

The Fifth's eyes widened. "You jest, my lord!"

"No, I certainly do not! On land he would be lower, of course, for he has no opportunity to practice footwork. But a civilian with that skill can be forgiven much."

That illogical reasoning impressed the swordsmen.

"I mention that as a warning, Master Polini. Now, tell me why you chose this ship."

At the return of his own problem, Polini stiffened. "It seemed well cared for, my lord."

Wallie nodded approvingly. "Would you consider a piece of advice?"

Of course he would, from a Seventh.

"Your trappings are of much value, master. There are no witnesses, in mid-River, and not all sailors are above a little piracy. Why not exchange your clothes and gear for something less tempting?"

Polini flushed. "I thank you for the advice, my lord!"

He was not going to take it, though. Wallie sighed. This was the sort of pigheaded attitude that he had been trying to domesticate in Nnanji. Polini could not stomach the thought of arriving back in Plo without his fancy kilt and harness and boots. It would lessen his infernal honor. Wallie had forgotten just how narrow swordsman thinking could be—which showed him how far he had brought Nnanji along.

"And you may well arrive at the tryst yet, master," he persisted. "Most of the swordsmen there will be frees. There will certainly be no First decked out like Novice Arganari."

He got a glare. The boy was frowning.

"I see now that this ship would be a poor choice for us, my

lord," Polini said, changing the subject. "Obviously She will require your valiant service in Her tryst. You sail to Casr."

Now it was Wallie's turn to become edgy. "Not so! I have been journeying these waters for two weeks since I heard of the tryst." The wind god had been cooperative since *Sapphire* left Ov, but the Goddess had not put out Her Hand to move the ship.

Polini looked astonished, as well he might. The Goddess not taking a Seventh?

"We are making good time, though," Wallie said. "Another week or so may get us to Casr."

"You know these waters, then, my lord," the boy said, and his tone made it a statement, while the words were a question. Now Wallie understood: Arganari was tone deaf. He would make himself a laughingstock if he attempted to chant, and even a royal priest would have to do that. So he had been sworn as a swordsman instead—no other craft had sufficient status for a king's son.

"I am getting to know them, novice. You see those mountains to the south? They are RegiVul, and the sorcerers' city of Vul lies somewhere within them." The swordsmen stared out over the bright waters. Above the low smudge of the far bank, the distant peaks shone faint and blue in the heat haze. The volcanic cloud above them was fainter still. "The River flows all around RegiVul. The left bank, the inside of the loop, has been taken by the sorcerers—all seven of its cities. Set no foot there, or you will certainly die."

"It is true, then?" Polini said. "There are legends of sorcerers in the mountains south of Plo, but I never believed in such men until we arrived here and heard the news of the tryst."

Holiyi, a very skinny sailor, came sauntering over to give Wallie another beer and a lopsided grin. Wallie thanked him and washed the foul taste from his mouth.

"It is true. This ship has called at all fourteen cities within the loop, but I freely admit that I hid within the deckhouse when we were in sorcerer ports."

Polini was shocked, but tried not to show it. "So they are as dangerous as the locals report?"

"Probably more so," Wallie assured him. "One slew a man on

this deck. A sorcerer can kill at a distance. Only speed will prevail against them, a throwing knife would be a better weapon than a sword." His hearers would have been horrified to hear that he had a knife hidden in his boot and that he practiced with it daily. He did not bother to point out the holes in the ship's rail that had been made by musket balls.

"But they are not invincible?" Arganari exclaimed, wiping beer froth from his lips. "The locals tell of one swordsman victory!"

"Do they now?" Wallie said. "Tell me that, then."

The boy beamed and began to chatter in a curious singsong, although Polini was already showing doubt on his craggy face.

"At Ov, my lord, two weeks ago. It is said that swordsmen from a ship attacked a band of sorcerers on the dock and survived the thunderbolts. They charged them in a wagon, my lord, and made great slaughter of the unholy ones. They were led by a Seventh and a very young, red-haired Fourth, my lord. We were told that they could have seized the evildoers' tower and taken back the city, except that . . . the Seventh. . . . chose . . . not to?" Horror spread over his youthful face.

Shouts and thumps drifted up from the dock; white birds soared by on the wind. A windlass on the next ship squeaked painfully.

Sevenths were rare. Sevenths who sailed these waters were as common as square eggs. Sevenths did not appreciate innuendoes of cowardice. Polini was rigid, obviously wondering what his protégé might have provoked.

"I am sure that he had excellent reason, my lord." the boy whispered.

"Probably," Wallie said bitterly. He had not expected the story to be up and down the River already. In this primitive World he expected no news to travel faster than the sorcerers' pigeons, and most to travel hardly at all. But now the Goddess was moving ships around like snowflakes. The news of the battle at Ov would be all along the River, and that meant all over the World—news of swordsmen battling sorcerers, a red-haired Fourth, and a black-haired Seventh who had called back his troops from the brink of victory. That was another problem, then, to add to his others—one he had not anticipated.

He discovered that he had been sitting in silence and scowling. So he smiled and said, "There may be more to that story than the dock gossip tells."

He got a chorus in reply.

"Of course, my lord!"

"Of course, my lord?"

At that moment Nnanji came up the plank, saw the meeting in progress, and strode over at once, homing in on visiting swordsmen like a bird dog. He was wearing his usual eager grin, and it seemed even wider than normal, perhaps because of what he had been doing ashore. He was tall, young, lanky, and very red-haired by the standards of the People. And he wore the orange kilt of a Fourth.

Polini and Arganari glanced at each other and then rose.

"May I have the honor, master. . ." Wallie presented Nnanji of the Fourth, protégé and oath brother; and after those formalities, he surprised Nnanji by presenting the First.

"Arganari?" Nnanji wrinkled his snub nose as he did when he was thinking. "There was a great hero once by that name."

"My ancestor, adept."

Nnanji thought it was a question and looked puzzled.

"The founder of his royal house," Wallie said to get his protégé pointing in the right direction.

The boy nodded proudly. "The Kingdom of Plo and Fex," he said. "My father has the honor to be the holy Arganari XIV, priest of the seventh rank."

So this Arganari was the oldest son. Polini's problem was even worse than Wallie had suspected.

"There are many great epics about him!" Nnanji declared solemnly. "My favorite is the one that begins . . ."

After about twenty lines, Wallie laid a hand on his arm to stop him and suggested that they all sit down again.

Nnanji squatted on his heels between Wallie and the visitors. "And of course, Arganari led the tryst of Xo," he said. Then he winked at Wallie and said, "With the topaz sword, the fourth sword of Chioxin!"

That was why the name had been familiar!

"My sword!" Arganari exclaimed proudly.

Nnanji looked at the boy's sword and frowned.

"He does not wear it," Polini said. "But it is the proudest possession of his house; and when he was inducted into the craft, Lord Kollorono, reeve of the palace guard, dedicated it to him. He is the first swordsman in the dynasty since the great Arganari, so it was fitting, and a most moving ceremony."

Wallie chuckled. "I am sure that you got it off him quickly afterward."

Polini smiled understandingly. "It would take a great swordsman to wear one of the seven for long, my lord."

"Describe the fourth to us," Nnanji said with a smile.

The boy's eyes shone with pride. "The guard is a golden basilisk, holding a topaz. The baslisk means 'Justice tempered with mercy,' so that is the motto of our house. And the blade is all inscribed with swordsmen fighting monsters on one side, and maidens playing with them on the other."

"It is a magnificent weapon," Polini said, probably glad of an impersonal topic in this awkward interview. "I tried it. The balance, the spring—magnificent! Chioxin's reputation was well deserved."

Nnanju turned his grin back to Wallie.

"Something like this?" Wallie asked. He drew his sword and held it out for them to see. The hilt had been behind his head all this time, and they would not have had a good look at it.

Polini and his protégé gasped loudly.

"The seventh!" Arganari shouted. "A sapphire and a griffon! And the pictures are much the same. Is it real? I mean, is it really the seventh sword of Chioxin?"

"Probably."

The legendary sword was having a bombshell effect on the swordsmen. Polini had gone perceptibly pale, and the boy quite pink with excitement.

"But, my lord . . ." Arganari was turning even pinker.

"Yes?"

"The six swords are famous . . . the saga has no stories of the seventh. It is said that Chioxin gave it to the Goddess."

"Perhaps the story is not finished yet?" Nnanji suggested, his enormous grin still firmly in place.

Polini and Arganari nodded solemnly, still fascinated by the sword.

"The griffon is the symbol of royalty. It means 'Power wisely used,'" the boy said, peering at the exquisitely fashioned guard.

"It is a very long blade." Polini would use a long sword, being tall.

"Want to try your luck?" Wallie asked.

Polini blanched. "Of course not, my lord!"

"It is in superb condition," the boy said, his strange way of speaking almost making it a question. "Mine is notched and worn. Just one flaw."

Nnanji nodded solemnly. "That mark was made by a sorcerer's thunderbolt."

Polini and his protégé again exchanged glances, then the boy went back to examining the sword. He pointed at the figures engraved in the blade. "You see the cross-hatching, mentor? It is said that Chioxin was left-handed. On all his swords, not just the seven, the cross-hatching goes from left to right."

"The devil you say?" Wallie murmured, peering. "Like Leonardo da Vinci? I thank you, novice. I did not know that. Then this isn't a forgery, after all!"

Nnanji snickered.

"My lord . . ." Arganari said and stopped. His mentor rumbled warningly at him.

"You want to know where I got it," Wallie said, replacing the priceless blade in his scabbard. He shrugged. "It is a reasonable question. I was given it by a god." He drank some beer.

The visitors were understandably astounded.

"He also gave me this sapphire hairclip and told me I had a task for the Goddess."

Now Polini understood and was impressed. "Then you are to be leader of the tryst, my lord!"

"Perhaps I am," Wallie said. "If so, then She is in no hurry to get me there, which may be where you come in." He looked to Nnanji, who nodded thoughtfully.

"Me? Us?"

"I am wondering if we were meant to meet, Master Polini. Stranger things can happen—indeed they happen to me all the time. It is curious that you chose this ship, and even more curious that you and your protégé should be familiar with one of the other seven swords of Chioxin. A tryst might be good training for a swordsman prince. After all, a novice will not be expected to do any fighting, so he will be in no great danger."

For the first time, the youngster showed some normal boyish excitement. He swung around to his mentor to see what he thought.

Polini rose disapprovingly. "You may well be right, my lord. I hope that you are. But I have already sworn my oath and I must attempt to return my protégé to Plo. If I am wrong, then I am sure that we shall meet again—in Casr."

The light died in the boy's eyes, and he stood up dutifully. Princes learned more than flowery speeches, and Firsts did not argue. Then he turned and looked up at Nnanji.

"Adept," he said, his voice now curiously flat, "was it truly you who led the wagon charge against the sorcerers in Ov?"

Nnanji grinned. "We skinned them! Fourteen dead sorcerers." He glanced regretfully at Wallie, who had spared an easy fifteenth.

The boy reached up and unfastened his ponytail. "I shall not likely be going to the tryst, adept," he said. "Lord Shonsu has a hairclip that was given him by a god, so he will not mind. This one belonged to my ancestor, and he wore it on the tryst of Xo. Will you take it for me and wear it against the evildoers?" He held out the silver clip.

"Novice!" Polini barked. "That clip has been in your family for centuries! Your father would not approve of your giving it away to a stranger. I forbid this!"

"Not a stranger, mentor, a hero."

"I think he is right, novice," Wallie said gently.

That settled the matter, of course, but Nnanji, immensely flattered at being called a hero, swallowed hard and said that he also agreed. Reluctantly Arganari replaced the clip, looking very juvenile between the three tall men.

"We thank you for your hospitality, my lord," Polini said formally. "I wish now to withdraw, with your permission, and seek a vessel. Probably a smaller would be more suitable. With no sailor-swordsmen Sixths!" he added, his smile openly skeptical.

Puzzled and vaguely worried, Wallie led the visitors back to the top of the gangplank, arriving just as Lae came aboard, closely followed by Jja. Jja had discarded the riverfolk bikini sashes she normally wore on the ship in favor of a conventional slave's black wrap. But the perfection of her figure could triumph over any costume, and her face was the stuff of legends. Wallie smiled her a welcome. He put an arm around her and unthinkingly proceeded to commit a major social blunder. Accustomed over many weeks now to the informality of ship life, he had forgotten the stilted formality of land-based culture in the World.

"Jja, my darling," he said, "here are visitors from your hometown, Master Polini and his Highness Novice Arganari."

The swordsmen stared aghast at the slavestripe on the woman's face. Jja was momentarily paralyzed, also. There was no ritual for presenting slaves, as Wallie should have remembered.

Then Jja fell to her knees and pressed her forehead to the deck. Wallie bit his lip in fury at his own stupidity. Polini was totally at a loss for words. It was young Arganari who reacted first. He stepped forward and raised her.

"Truly I see how Plo earned its reputation for beautiful women," he said in his singsong, childish voice. "If it did not have it before, then it would now."

That was a courtly speech.

†††

Master Polini headed down the plank with his protégé at his heels. He was probably relieved to escape from the insanity of *Sapphire*, with its incomprehensible Seventh and its rabid captain. If he breathed a prayer of thanks, then he breathed too soon, for another outrage was in store for him—on reaching the dock he came face-to-face with the returning Brota.

Female swordsmen were a heresy to landlubbers. Fat swordsmen were intolerable. Swordsmen who still bore their blades in middle age were contemptible. Brota was all of those, voluminous in her red robe, her ponytail streaked with gray, and a sword on her back. Wallie saw the encounter and chuckled. Apparently there was something in Polini's face that annoyed her, for she fixed him with her piggy eye and accosted him squarely. Then she drew and made the salute to an equal. With obvious reluctance, he responded. They exchanged a few words, then Polini set off along the road with furiously huge strides, his diminutive protégé almost trotting to keep up with him. Brota rolled up the plank wearing a satisfied smirk. As a water-rat swordsman she enjoyed baiting the landlubber variety almost as much as her sailor son did.

Polini had probably not even noticed Mata in the background, although she was still a fine-looking woman in her brown bra sash and breechclout. Wallie wondered what Polini would have said had he been told that she, a sailor of the third rank, a mother of four children, could probably give him a fair match with foil or sword.

Wallie had apologized to Jja, cursed himself several times for his stupidity, and then had to tell the beginning of the story to Nnanji, who had nodded in satisfaction and gone off with his head high, probably repeating "hero" to himself. A prince had said it—intoxicating stuff for the son of a rugmaker.

Brota rolled over to Wallie and scowled up at him under her curiously bushy white brows. "I suppose you are in haste to leave now, my lord?"

Wallie shrugged. "Not especially. If the Goddess is in a hurry, then She can speed our passage as She pleases. You found no trade?"

"Pah! Their prices are outrageous," she said.

Katanji had commented on the prices in the brothel. Katanji was a very astute young man in money matters. Now Wallie wondered if a tryst would create a local inflation. A few hundred active young men could certainly drive up the price of food—and women—in Casr, but he would not have thought that the effect would have reached so far as Tau.

That raised a whole new series of problems. Who was going to pay for this tryst? Probably most of the men arriving would be free swords. They would be penniless, and Casr would be in trouble. They would expect free shelter and board—and women. The economy of the World was a primitive, fragile thing. The demigod had given Wallie a fortune in sapphires and called it "expenses." Perhaps that had been another hint that he was expected to be leader of the tryst. Why, then, was he not being taken to it?

He looked across the dock road to the nearest warehouse. "The Goddess has guided you often in the past to the most profitable cargo, mistress," he suggested. "What do they offer over there?"

"Ox hides!" Brota snorted. "Nasty things! I don't want my ship full of smelly hides!"

"Hides?" Wallie repeated thoughtfully. Brota noticed at once. Brota and gold had a mutual attraction.

"Hides?" she echoed. The conversation was becoming monotonous.

"If we reach Casr . . . if I become leader of the tryst—and those are big 'ifs'—then I think hides might be of value."

"Scabbards? Boots?" She frowned in disbelief.

"Heavier grade than that, I should think."

"Saddle leather? You would fight sorcerers with leather, Shonsu?"

He smiled and nodded.

Brota studied him narrowly. "The sorcerers have driven all the tanners out of their cities. Any connection?"

"None whatsoever."

Brota pouted. Then she wheeled about, shouted for Mata, and rolled toward the plank.

Wallie glanced around. He was pleased to see that Katanji had reappeared on deck and had recovered most of his color. Wallie beckoned him over. "Feeling better now?" he inquired.

The lad gave him a pert and incredibly innocent smile. "Yes, thank you, my lord." Katanji could be angelically polite or diabolically vulgar, as circumstances required.

"I need a speck of additional wisdom from you, novice," said Wallie.

"I am always at your service and at that of the Goddess, my lord."

After the service of his own money pouch, of course.

"Good!" Wallie said with a conspiratorial smile. "Mistress

Brota is now bent on buying leather. I should like to know how much she spends on it."

Katanji grinned. "Is that all?" He nodded and walked away. He could probably discover details of the tanner's grandfather's sex life if Wallie needed them.

Wallie stayed by the rail, watching his spy trail after Brota. There were no swordsmen in sight. Then Nnanji reappeared at his side, suspicious of what his oath brother had wanted with his true brother. Nnanji's protégé was a constant trial to him, with his unswordsmanlike tendencies, and his mentor almost as bad. Wallie decided not to explain, out of pure perversity.

"Did you find Adept Kionijuiy?" he inquired.

Nnanji scowled. "Someone else got to him first, my lord brother."

On their previous visit to Tau, Kionijuiy had been de facto reeve. He had been absent from his post, leaving the town in the care of an inadequate garrison, and that lapse had offended Nnanji's ideals of swordsman honor. While the subject had not been discussed since, Wallie knew that Nnanji never forgot anything. He would certainly have sought to rectify the matter that morning.

"The new reeve is the Honorable Finderinoli," Nnanji added. "He and his band arrived at the lodge just before your message got there. So he came on to Tau and put things to rights at once. I did not meet him, but he seems to be doing a fine job." He nodded approvingly.

"What did he do to the old man?" Wallie asked. Kionijuiy's father had failed to resign when he grew too old to be reeve. Much worse, though, he had taught his civilian sons to fence. That was an abomination, a breach of the sutras, a violation of the swordsmen's closed-shop union rules.

"Drained him, too," Nnanji said simply, studying people on the dock road below.

Wallie shivered. "And the brothers?"

"Cut off their hands," Nnanji said. "Ah! Here she is!"

Thana was coming along the road—Brota's daughter, tall and slim and ravishing in a yellow wrap. Thana had a classic Grecian profile and dark curls. Whenever Wallie saw her with her sword on her back, as now, he thought of Diana the Huntress. When

Thana was in sight, Nnanji would not think readily of anything else.

Beside her was the tiny form of Honakura, ancient priest and one of Wallie's company—indeed, Honakura was the first person he had spoken to when he awoke in the World in Shonsu's body. Today the old man had gone to visit the temple in search of news. He was still wearing his anonymous black robe, hiding his craft-marks under a headband, and so being a Nameless One. Wallie had half expected Honakura to end this charade now, but apparently not. He had never explained its purpose; possibly he did not wish to admit that it had none.

Jja was comforting Vixini, who was fretting over another tooth. Katanji came strolling back from the warehouse. Honakura climbed wearily up the gangplank. Nnanji headed toward it to welcome Thana. Seven was the sacred number. When Wallie had left the temple at Hann to begin his mission for the gods, seven had been the number in his party. The seventh, Nnanji's moronic slave, had gone. If Nnanji had any say in the matter, Thana was destined to replace her. That would bring them back to seven again . . .

Sapphire had taken Wallie to all the cities of the RegiVul loop; its crew had provided his army for the battle of Ov. With *Sapphire* he had unmasked the sorcerers and discovered their secrets. Now someone—and he still did not know who—had called a tryst in Casr. To Casr he must go. Looking at Nnanji beaming idiotically as he held Thana's hands, he wondered if his party was about to be restored to the sacred number. Possibly *Sapphire*'s part in his mission was ended, and he was about to leave this easy, informal River life and complete his quest ashore.

Yet Apprentice Thana was showing few signs of cooperating, although Nnanji now proposed to her regularly—three times a day, after meals, Wallie suspected. She clearly had no illusions about that redheaded idealist who regarded honor as life's purpose, killing as his business, fencing and wenching as the only worthwhile recreations. Looking at the two of them, lost in their private conversation, Wallie would not have been surprised to learn that his lusty young protégé was describing his morning's exploits in the brothel. He was quite capable of doing so and then wondering how he had offended. Yet certainly Nnanji had some major part to play in the gods' mission, for Wallie had been directed to swear the fourth oath with him, the oath of brotherhood.

Oath of brotherhood or not, Nnanji would be reluctant to leave *Sapphire* without Thana. Suppose she would not go? What would the gods do then?

He must discuss that possibility with Honakura.

Two hours later, reeking like a tannery, *Sapphire* cast off. As she did so, another ship pulled into an empty berth ahead and two nimble young swordsman Seconds jumped ashore without even waiting for the plank. They were at once accosted by a Fourth and three Thirds, whom Wallie had already identified as followers of the head-hunting Sixth. By nightfall that Sixth would have collected all the loose swordsmen in town.

Wallie had gone up on the fo'c'sle to stay out of the sailors' way. He was leaning on the rail with Nnanji beside him. Thana was next to Nnanji.

"On to Casr!" Nnanji said in a satisfied tone.

"We may be back!" Wallie warned him, watching the two Seconds being marched off to meet the absent Sixth and swear their oaths.

"What! Why, brother?"

Wallie explained his theory that the Goddess might be wanting him to recruit a private army. Nnanji pouted mightily—he would be greatly outranked by a Sixth.

"I hope that is not the case," Wallie assured him. "But why else would she have brought all these swordsmen to Tau? It is a long way to Casr. I am sure that the Goddess is capable of better aim than that."

"Ah!" Nnanji looked relieved. "It is not only Tau! Swordsmen have been arriving at Dri and Wo, also. And Ki San, appparently. Even Quo."

The ways of gods were inscrutable. Perhaps, though, the docks at Casr could not handle the traffic, and the Goddess was using these outlying ports as way stations . . .

"Quo?" Wallie echoed.

Nnanji chuckled and glanced sideways at him. "It is on the

next loop of the River! There is a wagon trail over the hills from Casr to Quo, brother! One day by road and twenty weeks by water, so I'm told."

"Where did you hear this?"

"During intermission!" Nnanji leered. Then he remembered that Thana was present, and his face suddenly matched his hair; perhaps his social skills were improving, slightly.

There was also a trail from Ov to Aus, Wallie knew, although land travel was very rare in the World. There were no maps in the World, because there was no writing, and because the geography was subject to change without notice, at the whim of the Goddess. But Wallie had a mental picture of the usual form of the landscape, and he now sought to adjust it. What had Nnanji thought of, to put that grin on his face?

"Another loop?" Wallie said. "Then Casr is strategic!"

Nnanji looked vaguely disappointed that his mentor had worked that out so quickly. He would have had to consult the sutras.

"Right!" he said. "It has three neighbors, instead of two, like all the other cities."

"And therefore it may just be the sorcerers' next target?"

Nnanji nodded. The sorcerers had been seizing another city every two years or so. Now they had control of all the left bank, the inside of the loop. River travel was difficult or impossible through the Black Lands, so the RegiVul loop was closed. Their next move must to be to cross the River.

"Casr is very old," Nnanji added. "It's mentioned in some of the most ancient sagas. Been burned and sacked and rebuilt dozens of times, I expect."

"And it has a swordsman lodge," Wallie said.

Nnanji grinned and put his arm around Thana for a firm hug.

Wallie returned to watching the docks as they dwindled astern, masked now by a picket fence of masts and rigging. As the details became less visible, Tau seemed to become ever more like a scene from Tudor England.

Nnanji sniggered. "Still want to be reeve, brother?"

"Me?" Wallie said with astonishment, turning to stare at him.

Nnanji flashed his huge grin. "Forgotten? Last time we were here you said . . ." His eyes went slightly out of focus, and his voice deepened to mimic Shonsu's bass. "'Eventually, I suppose, I'll settle down in some quiet little town like this and be a reeve. And raise seven sons, like old Kioniarru. And seven daughters, also, if Jja wants them!' And I said, 'Reeve? Why not king?' And you said, 'Too much bloodshed to get it, and too much work when you do. But I like Tau, I think.'"

His eyes came back into focus and his grin returned. Neither commented on the feat of memory—they both knew it was child's play for Nnanji—but Thana was disgusted. "You weren't serious, my lord? Reeve? In a place like that?" She turned to stare at the thatched roofs of vanishing Tau.

"It's a nice little town," Wallie protested feebly.

"You can have it, brother," Nnanji said generously.

†† ††

The next day the wind god deserted them. A strange golden haze settled over the River, smelling faintly of burning stubble, while the water lay dead as white oil. Directly overhead the sky was a pallid, sickly blue, and all around there was only blank nothing. Tomiyano did not even hoist sail, and *Sapphire* drooped at anchor. Other becalmed vessels showed faintly at times in the distance, like flags planted to mark the edge of the World, but for most of the day *Sapphire* seemed to be abandoned by both men and gods.

This ominous change made the crew uneasy. Lord Shonsu was needed at Casr, they believed, to take command of Her tryst. Why was She not speeding him there? Had they offended Her in some way? Not putting their worry into words, the sailors performed the usual chores in nervous silence. They cleaned and polished and varnished; they made clothes for the coming winter; they instructed youngsters in the age-old ways of the River and the sutras of the sailors; they waited for wind.

Honakura was as distressed as any. He liked to think that he had been sent along on Shonsu's mission as pilot, a guide to interpret the will of the gods as it might be revealed from time to time, and he did not know what to make of this sudden change of pace. It was strange that She had not taken Shonsu directly to Her tryst from Ov after the battle with the sorcerers, but likely the swordsman was just being given time to think. There seemed to be many things worrying the big man, things he had trouble discussing, or preferred not to discuss, and he brooded relentlessly, quite unlike his normal self. And the wind god had buffeted them along in spanking fashion—until today.

This was not the first time *Sapphire*'s progress had been stayed, and each time there had been a reason for it. Either the gods had been waiting for something else to happen, or the mortals had overlooked something they were supposed to do. Honakura had no way of knowing which was the case now, but he suspected that the next move was up to the mortals—why else would the ship have been encased in mist? It was as if they had all been shut in a closet, as he himself had many times in the past locked up an errant protégé to meditate upon his shortcomings. By afternoon he was becoming seriously concerned.

He sat himself on his favorite fire bucket and surveyed the deck. Up on the fo'c'sle, the adolescents were clustered around Novice Katanji. From their antics, he guessed that the boy was telling dirty stories. The women had mostly gathered on the poop, knitting, mending, and chatting softly. A couple of men were fishing . . . without much success, he noted glumly.

For once there was no fencing lesson in progress. Adept Nnanji was sitting on the forward hatch cover with Novice Matarro and Apprentice Thana, grouped around three crossed swords. That was a stupid swordsman custom for reciting sutras. Priests taught sutras while pacing to and fro—much healthier and more sensible, letting exercise stimulate the brain.

Lord Shonsu sat alone on the other hatch. The crew understood that he needed to think and they left him alone when he wanted privacy, as now. He did have his slave beside him, so he probably would not think of himself as being alone. They were not talking, however, and that was unusual. Shonsu was probably the only swordsman in the World who talked with his night slave —except of course to say "Lie down."

Shonsu was whittling. He had taken up whittling after Ov, spending hours with scraps of wood and tools pilfered from the ship's chest. He refused to say what he was doing and he obviously did not enjoy doing it. His hands were too big for delicate work—they fit a sword hilt better than a knife handle. He scowled and chewed his tongue and nicked his fingers and spoiled what he was doing and started again. And he would not say why.

A sour sulfurous odor mingled with smells of woodsmoke and leather. They had met that before. Shonsu said it must come from RegiVul, where the Fire God danced on the peaks. A pale dust was settling on the planks.

Honakura sighed and sought a more comfortable position. The pains were getting worse. He remembered how his mother had baked bread when he was a child, and how she had run a knife around the inside of the pan to loosen the loaf so that it would come out cleanly. That was what the Goddess was doing to him—reminding him that death was not to be feared, that it was a beginning of something new and exciting, not an end. When he had left Hann with Shonsu, he had offered humble prayers that he might be spared long enough in this cycle to see the outcome of the Shonsu mission. Now he was not so presumptuous. He thought he might be happier not knowing.

If anyone had suggested to him half a year since that he could ever be friends with a swordsman, he would have laughed until his old bones fell apart in a heap. Yet it had happened so. He *liked* that huge slab of beef. He could even admire him and he had never admired a swordsman before. Of course Shonsu was not a swordsman at heart, but he tried very hard to obey the dictates of the gods, and struggled to reconcile his own gentle instincts with the killer requirements of his job. They were incompatible, of course. Shonsu knew that and was troubled within himself. But he tried, and he was a decent and honorable man.

Strange, therefore, that his divine master had not trusted him enough to explain exactly what his task was to be. That lapse had obviously bothered Shonsu, and still did. He thought he knew now what it was. He had been quite implacable toward the sorcerers once he met them—implacable for Shonsu, that is. Yet he had gathered wisdom at Ov, wisdom he could not or would not explain, and since then he had been more deeply troubled than ever.

Honakura was certain that he had a much better idea of what Shonsu's mission was than Shonsu did. He no longer wanted to see the end of it. The gods knew what they were doing and they knew why, even if mortals did not. And they could be cruel.

Sometimes they could even appear to be ungrateful.

A sudden ripple of change swept over the ship. Two of the women came chattering down from the poop and headed for the companionway in the fo'c'sle. The men abandoned their fishing at the same moment and went into the deckhouse, muttering about a game of dice. Apprentice Thana, tired of sutras, rose and stretched deliciously. Honakura sighed . . . If the Goddess sent him back at once, then in twenty years or less he would be after someone like Thana. Unless he came back as a woman, of course, in which case he would be looking for a Shonsu.

Adept Nnanji twisted his head round and shouted for his brother. Katanji pulled a face, left off his storytelling, and came down to join the sutra session. Nnanji could continue indefinitely. Despite his youth, he was the most single-minded person Honakura had ever met and he certainly possessed the finest memory.

That made him an incomparable learner. It had been entertaining to watch Shonsu struggle to make himself more of a swordsman—meaning in effect more like Nnanji, who was a swordsman born—while Nnanji strove to be more like his hero, Shonsu. There was no doubt which of the two had more thoroughly succeeded. Adept-and-soon-to-be-Master Nnanji was unrecognizable as the brash, wide-eyed juvenile who had trailed behind Shonsu that first day in the temple, after the death of Hardduju. Yet neither man could ever really succeed. They were as unlike as the lion and the eagle that made up the griffon on the seventh sword.

One lion plus one eagle did not make two griffons.

Then stillness inexplicably returned and motion ceased. The ship lay in its cocoon of golden haze, the silence broken only by a quiet drone of sutras.

Thana had wandered to the aft end of the deck and was sitting on the steps to the poop. There seemed to be something missing about Apprentice Thana. Honakura needed a moment to work it out—she was not wearing the pearls that Nnanji had given her. He decided, then, that he had not seen them for some days.

She was studying Shonsu and frowning, deep in thought.

Mm?

Of course Shonsu was worth studying from her point of view: huge, muscular—masculinity personified—and a swordsman of the seventh rank, a man of ultimate power among the People.

Brota and Tomiyano were incomparable pursuers of gold, but in Thana that family trait was subtly changed. She saw farther. Thana knew that gold was only a means, and the end was power. For most people gold was the surest means to that end, but power was largely a male attribute in the World, and there was a faster road to it for nubile young maidens.

Honakura rose and wandered across and joined her on the steps. She scowled.

Even at his age, it was pleasant to sit next to a Thana.

"When beautiful young ladies frown, they must have troubles," he said. "Troubles are my business."

"Beggars have no business."

He stared up at her until she averted her eyes.

"Pardon, holy one," she muttered.

They had all guessed that he was a priest, of course. His way of speaking would have told them that.

"Not a holy one at the moment," he said gently. "But I am on Her business. Now, what ails?"

"Just puzzled," she said. "Something Nnanji told me."

Honakura waited. He had a million times more patience than Apprentice Thana.

"He quoted something Lord Shonsu had said," she explained at last, "the first time he was in Tau. He talked of being reeve there. Well! A minnow town like that? This is after his mission is over, you understand? It just seemed odd. That's all."

"It doesn't seem odd to me, apprentice."

She glanced at him in surprise. "Why not? A Seventh? In a scruffy little hole like Tau?"

Honakura shook his head. "Shonsu never asked to be a Seventh. He did not even want to be a swordsman. The gods made him one for their own purposes. You are talking power, my lady, and power does not attract Shonsu."

"Power?" she repeated thoughtfully. "Yes, I suppose I am."

"Well, ambition. He has none! He is already a Seventh, so what is left? But Adept Nnanji . . . now there is ambition for you."

Thana frowned again. "He is a killer! Remember when the pirates came? Yes, it is good to kill pirates. But Shonsu wept afterward—I saw the tears on his cheeks. Nnanji laughed. He was soaked in blood, and loved it."

Honakura had known much worse killers than that amiable young man. "Killing is his job, apprentice. He welcomed a chance to do his job. He is honorable and kills only in the line of duty. A swordsman rarely gets a chance to use his skills. Adept Nnanji is very good at his job—better in some ways than Lord Shonsu is."

"You think Nnanji will be a Seventh one day?" she asked idly, but he sensed the steel in the question.

For a moment he hesitated, pondering the inexplicable lack of wind, the breathless pause in Shonsu's mission. Then he decided to gamble on this sudden hunch of his.

"I am certain."

"Certain, old man? Certain is a strong word." She sounded like her mother.

"This must be in confidence, Thana," he said.

She nodded, astonished.

"There is a prophecy," he told her. "When Shonsu spoke with the god, he was given a message for me. Shonsu did not understand it—it was a message that only a priest would hear. But it comes from a god. So, yes, I am certain."

She had very beautiful eyes, large and dark, set in very long lashes.

"This prophecy is about Nnanji?"

He nodded.

"I swear on my sword, holy one—on my honor as a swordsman. If you tell me, I will not reveal it."

"Then I shall trust you," he said. "The prophecy is the epigram from one of our sutras. We—the priests, I mean—have always regarded it as a great paradox, but perhaps to a swordsman it will not seem so. The epigram is this: *The pupil may be greater than the teacher.*"

Thana drew in her breath sharply. "That refers to Nnanji?"

"Yes, it does. He was destined to be Shonsu's protégé. He was only a Second, you know. Shonsu made him a Fourth in two weeks. And he is the equal of a Fifth now, Shonsu says."

"A Sixth!" she snapped, and fell silent, thinking.

He waited patiently and after a while she looked up. "It only says 'may' be greater. Not 'will' be."

Honakura shook his head. "Gods do not cheat like that, Thana. The god was saying that Nnanji *will* be greater. It is obvious! He is absurdly young for even his present rank, and Shonsu says he fences better every day, without exception. He forgets nothing. Yes, Nnanji will be a Seventh—and very soon, I think."

She frowned. "He thinks he is a Sixth now, but Shonsu will not tell him the sutras—the last few he needs to try for Sixth."

"I am sure," Honakura said, and then wondered if he was sure, "that Lord Shonsu has his protégé's best interests at heart. Nnanji had been very lucky to find a mentor like him—few do. Many mentors grow jealous of successful protégés and hold them back. Indeed, that is the thrust of that sutra I mentioned—that protégés must be encouraged and aided at all costs, not impeded." He chuckled, thinking of examples he had known. "Even priests can be guilty of that sin, and obviously there are special advantages to a swordsman in having a protégé who can fight above his rank. Whereas, when that protégé gains promotion, he may set off on his own. But I do not think that Lord Shonsu would ever do that to Nnanji. If he is holding him back from trying for Sixth, then it is only because he does not think that Nnanji is ready."

I think that, but Shonsu is no fool.

She nodded. "And when the tryst is over, then Nnanji will not be satisfied to be merely reeve of some polliwog village?"

"Nnanji wants to be a free sword. He would be happy just to lead a band of ragtag swordsmen around the countryside looking for sport, killing and wenching."

She nodded and sighed. Honakura carefully arranged a shy smile on his face.

He said, "I think he would be wasted doing that. The Goddess must have more important tasks for a man like Nnanji. He needs guidance!"

"You mean . . ."

He shook his head. "I don't think I need say more."

Thana blushed. She jumped up and strode away, the yellow tail of her breechclout swinging. She went by Shonsu without a glance, then by the three-man sutra session, which wailed into silence as the chanters were distracted. Then she vanished through the fo'c'sle door.

Honakura chuckled. The chanters went back to their droning. Shonsu continued his whittling—apparently he had not even noticed Thana go by him, although Jja had.

Honakura waited hopefully, but there was no sign of a wind rising, no diminution of the stabbing pain in his ribs. He sighed and told himself to be patient. However, perhaps he had earned one tiny reward—it would be satisfying to know just what that big swordsman was doing, littering Sailor Tomiyano's tidy deck with shavings.

The old man heaved stiffly off the steps, walked over to the hatch cover, and levered himself up beside Shonsu. He was accustomed to being small, but the big man made him feel like a tiny child. The swordsman turned his head in silence and regarded him. For just a moment Honakura could imagine that he was back on the temple steps that summer morning when he had so briefly met the original Shonsu—that steady glare, those vindictive black eyes with their promise of carnage. Startled, he reminded himself that this was a man from a dream world, not truly Shonsu, and it was not his fault that his gaze was as deadly as his sword.

"And how is Apprentice Thana?" the swordsman demanded in his distant-thunder rumble.

Another shock! Honakura could have sworn that Shonsu had not even seen Thana depart, let alone noticed the two of them talking together. "She is well," he said, carefully not showing reaction. Yet he knew that everything about Shonsu was of the seventh rank—his reflexes, his eyesight. Could his hearing be so acute that he had overheard the conversation? Impossible, surely?

The swordsman continued his inspection of Honakura for a moment and then turned his attention back to the peg he was shaping. After a minute or so he remarked, "Apprentice Thana has been surprising me."

"How so, my lord?" inquired Honakura, as expected.

"She has developed a sudden and passionate interest in sutras," Shonsu growled. "I assume that she plans to seek promotion when Nnanji does."

"Commendable! She is qualified, is she not?"

"In fencing, certainly," the swordsman said. "And she has been surprising me with her speed at picking up sutras. Not quite a Nnanji, perhaps, but remarkable."

Honakura waited, knowing there must be more.

There was. "Of course Nnanji is always available to coach her—he can gaze at her without interruption." Shonsu paused again. "Yet she has been pestering me, also, and even her mother. She sets it up with either Katanji or Matarro, keeping Nnanji out."

Honakura remembered now that the swordsmen had a limit of three to a sutra session, another foolish custom.

"Perhaps she is equally glad of a chance to gaze at your noble self, my lord."

The black eyes flashed dangerously at him. "No, she has some other reason. Apprentice Thana always has her impulses totally under control. She is a cold-blooded little golddigger!"

Honakura certainly was not about to say so, but he thought Lord Shonsu rather resented Thana's cold-bloodedness. With his rank and physical presence he could have any woman for a nod, with no questions asked. Not that he did, but he must be aware that he could. It was precisely because young Thana would have questions to ask—and would require the answers first—that he smarted over her immunity.

"Why are we becalmed?" Shonsu demanded suddenly, probably believing that he was changing the subject.

Honakura dared not say what he suspected. "I don't know, my lord."

"Is it because I was supposed to recruit an army in Tau, do you think?"

So he was still brooding over that? "I doubt it," the priest said. "As you suggested, we should be returned there if that were the case. We must just be patient."

Shonsu nodded and sighed.

"You are troubled, my lord?"

The swordsman nodded again. "I am perplexed by the encounter with Prince Arganari. That felt like the hand of the god, old man, but I don't understand what was required of me. How many swordsmen own one of the Chioxin seven? Not more than two or three in the whole World! The rest of the seven have been broken or lost. For us to meet by chance was utterly impossible . . . so why?"

He brooded in silence for a while. "I should have kept him on the ship, I think."

"But you said that Master Polini had sworn an oath?"

"Yes," Shonsu agreed miserably. "But I could have challenged him." He cut savagely at the peg and nicked his thumb. He swore and stuck it in his mouth. Jja reached up and pulled it out again to look at it.

"Tell me what you are making, my lord?" Honakura asked. "Is it some contrivance from your dream world, perhaps?"

"I am making a toy for Vixini," the swordsman said.

Which is what he always said.

Pain had made Honakura testy. "My lord! The god told you that you could trust me!"

Again Shonsu turned to regard the priest with that deadly killer gaze. "Yes, he did. Was he correct?"

Did that mean he had indeed overheard the conversation with Thana? It seemed impossible.

"Of course!" Honakura said, aware that dignity was hard to project in the garb of a Nameless One.

"Very well!" said the swordsman. "I will tell you what I am making if you tell me about Ikondorina's brothers."

Now it was the priest's turn to sigh. Why had he ever been such a fool as to mention those? It had been a serious indiscretion, even if it had happened very early in their relationship, before he had realized how much he himself was involved. When the god had sent word that Honakura was to tell Shonsu the story of Ikondorina, it had been an obvious chicanery. Even the swordsman had seen through that, but then Honakura had stupidly admitted that he knew of two other references to Ikondorina in the priestly sutras. Later, and even more stupidly, he had mentioned that they concerned Ikondorina's two brothers, his red-haired brother and his black-haired brother. He had been very tired that evening, he remembered.

"I fear I misled you, my lord," he said now. "Obviously there was a reference there to Nnanji and Katanji. But that was all—they joined your quest and the prophecy was fulfilled. There is nothing more to tell."

"I should like to be the judge of that!"

"I cannot reveal the sutras of my craft!"

"Then I cannot tell you what I am making."

Honakura turned his head away angrily. Swordsmen! It was so childish! Then he noticed that Apprentice Thana had reappeared on deck and was wearing the pearls again. Aha! And she had gone to lean on the rail where Nnanji would notice her. Sutra time would end soon, then.

He turned back to Shonsu, who was looking at Jja, and Honakura was just in time to catch the tail feathers of a vanishing grin on the slave's face. They were laughing at him!

"The stories are quite irrelevant!" he said angrily. "And trivial! The sutra that mentions the black-haired brother, for example—the epigram says merely *Water pipes are made of lead*."

That, he thought, would stop a whole army of swordsmen.

Shonsu nodded thoughtfully. "I approve, of course."

"Indeed? Perhaps you would be so kind as to expound further, my lord?"

The swordsman flashed Jja another glance that the priest could not see. He could not be winking, surely?

"Certainly!" he said. "A water pipe adds nothing and takes nothing away; it merely transmits a substance, water, from one place to another, just as Mistress Brota and her ship transmit goods from one port to another. But these are services vital to the well-being of the People. Water pipes are useful things, yet lead is the lowliest of metals. Conclusion: Humble folk, who may originate nothing themselves, may yet perform valuable duties, not to be despised. Correct, learned one?"

Angrily Honakura agreed that he was correct. After all these weeks, he should have remembered that this was no ordinary swordsman. Few priests, even, could have worked that out for themselves, and so quickly.

"The epitome, I would presume," Shonsu said, "would deal with the value of labor—no, commerce!"

Correct again, Honakura admitted grumpily.

"Then the episode, please?"

The priest was about to protest once more that he could not reveal arcane matters when he caught Shonsu's eye. A shy smile crept over the swordsman's face, making Honakura think of granite slabs being thrust aside by tree roots. But it was affectionate amusement—it invited him to share. Suddenly they both laughed. The knife twisted in Honakura's chest, but he felt better afterward.

"Very well, my lord! I suppose you have earned it. But I warn you that it is a foolish and banal doggerel."

"Which may yet transmit valuable thought?" Shonsu asked innocently.

Honakura laughed again in surrender and quietly chanted him the episode:

> Ikondorina's black-haired brother
> Late at night to village came,
> Weary from a long day's plodding,
> Very hungry, dry, and lame.
>
> Heard two peasants loud disputing,
> Also heard a farrow squeal.
> "There," proclaimed the black-haired swordsman,
> "I can hear my evening meal."
>
> "Villagers!" he then addressed them.
> "Notice, pray, my honest face.
> As a stranger come amongst you,
> Let me judge this sorry case."

The peasants laid the facts before him—
Each one claimed he owned the beast.
Swordsman, drawing his sword to slay it,
Bid the peasants share his feast.

The big man had a big laugh, and now Shonsu put his head back and uttered one enormous bellow of laughter, like a clap of thunder. Chanting stopped. From bowsprit to rudder, heads turned in astonishment. Smiles appeared, the sailors pleased that their hero was restored to his normal good humor.

"That's marvelous!" Shonsu said. "No artist could have drawn him better—Katanji to the life! *Honest face!* And you said it was irrelevant? Come now, holy one, share the other with me!"

"No, my lord."

The barbaric glare returned. "I am making a toy for Vixini."

"Not fair, my lord!" Honakura protested, although he no longer cared very much what Shonsu was doing. He must certainly not be told the other sutra.

"Half a truth deserves half a truth!" the swordsman persisted. "I figure that if Vixini can work this, then perhaps the swordsmen can . . . Why will you not tell me?"

"The god said you could trust me," Honakura replied. Nnanji and Thana were deep in a world of their own by the rail.

"But can I trust the god?" asked Shonsu.

"My lord!" Honakura displayed shock—but secretly he knew that he shared that doubt. It would depend how one defined trust, of course.

The swordsman was studying him closely. "Why would he not tell me exactly what is expected of me? How am I supposed to serve him under those conditions? What should I do, priest? You tell me, then, if you are so trustworthy."

"I am not a priest anymore," Honakura said. "I am a Nameless One."

"You're a priest when you want to be!" Shonsu roared. "All right, then, answer this one! After the battle on the holy island, the god put a swordsman fathermark on my right eyelid. Fair enough—my father in the dream world was a sort of swordsman. But after the battle of Ov, I was given a sorcerer's feather on my left eyelid. What does that mean? How can I ever expect the tryst to follow a man with a sorcerer for a mother?"

Honakura had no idea. He had worried about that since it happened.

Before he could reply, however, they were interrupted. Nnanji and Thana stood before them, hand in hand. Thana had her eyes demurely lowered, her pearl necklace shimmering with a virginal white glow like dawn over the River. Nnanji's face was as red as his hair, and his eyes bulged with excitement and joy.

"My lord mentor!" he shouted. "Your protégé humbly requests permission to get married."

†† † ††

The party began at once.

Of course Wallie gave his permission, choking down misgivings over the romantic, idealistic Nnanji being bound to that mercenary minx. Ignorant of the marriage customs of the People, he was carefully coached and then prompted by his sniggering protégé as he formally negotiated with Thana's mentor for the betrothal, tendering one copper as bride price. Brota accepted, but he suspected that she doubted the wisdom of the match as much as he did.

Even Wallie thought Thana worth more than one copper, but apparently it was that or serious bargaining—and then Brota would have taken everything both swordsmen possessed.

There was much hugging and kissing and laughter as the family acquiesced. The ship was at anchor, and the sun god would set in a couple of hours—of course the party must begin at once. Tomiyano produced some vials of the sorcerers' ensorceled wine, whose effects could be heard and seen almost immediately. Oligarro's mandolin and Holiyi's pan pipes and young Sinboro on his drums . . . there was dancing and singing. Children screamed with excitement as ancient Lina brought forth delicacies from some secret store—crystallized fruits and knots of preserved ginger and yet-stranger sweetmeats that Wallie could not identify.

He wondered how long engagements lasted in the World and what elaborate ritual the marriage itself would require. For him to say good morning to another Seventh required forty words and six gestures. On that scale a wedding service could take hours. And what gift would a highrank swordsman give his protégé? Not a microwave oven, certainly...

He danced with all the women and all the girls. He joined in some of the more raucous River shanties. He laughed at the bawdy bantering and Nnanji's boastful ripostes. He grew steadily more miserable.

The calm persisted, the sun god faded down into luminous mist, and the putrid sulfur stink from the volcanoes dissipated, leaving only the pungent aroma of the ox hides in the hold. The sky began to darken. Eventually Wallie slipped away and climbed alone to the fo'c'sle, where he could lean against the rail beyond the capstan and gaze out over still waters. He listened to the music and laughter and sometimes, when they momentarily waned, to the playful slap of wavelets against the bow. The mist grew cool and damp against his skin.

A free man could not marry a slave.

He brooded over this injustice and at last decided that a married protégé was just one more tiny worry to add to all his others. He began to list them again in his mind. The catalog never seemed to shrink, it only grew longer. Nnanji himself was becoming a pest, demanding that he be allowed to try for sixth rank, and Thana would add her nagging now, seeking to further her fiancé's career.

Honakura had instigated this stupid engagement! Wallie had overheard just enough of that whispered conversation to be sure. Certainly he had heard the word "prophecy" and he knew that must refer to the story of Ikondorina's red-haired brother. The old man's reticence on the subject was ominous, especially now that Wallie had wormed the other story out of him, and that other story had so obviously matched Katanji. What could have been prophesied about Nnanji that Wallie must not be told? He wished he had been able to hear more of what the old man had been telling Thana.

He wondered if those sutras had been changed by a miracle to fit the requirements of his mission. The demigod was quite capable of rearranging the memories of all the priests of the World. Indeed, he need change only Honakura's. Wallie decided he would search out a priest in Casr and ask him if he had ever heard of Ikondorina.

No, that would not work. A mortal could not outwit a god.

Yet Nnanji was hardly a worry to compare with his others. What might Wallie find in Casr when he met men and women who thought they knew him, who had known Shonsu? At least he need not worry about remembering names, because any conversation would begin with a formal salute. Those were as useful as the cutesy name tags of Earth: "Hi there, my name is . . ." Nor need he worry about being challenged. Only another Seventh would do that, and a brave one, for Shonsu's paramount skill must be known in Casr.

A greater danger was that he would be denounced, tried, convicted of cowardice, and executed. That was very likely, and his swordsmanship would not save him from that.

Explosions of laughter made him turn to look at the main deck. The center of amusement was a squirming heap of male adolescents. Even Holiyi was in there. Then it broke apart, revealing Nnanji underneath. Matarro had Nnanji's kilt and ran off waving it, with Nnanji leaping up to race in howling pursuit around the deck, while the spectators jeered and cheered.

Not so very long ago, such treatment from civilians would have provoked Nnanji to mayhem.

Wallie sighed. He ought to be down there, joining in the fun, not skulking up here being such a sourpuss.

Sorcerers!

They were the big problem, obviously. Mostly they were fakes and charlatans, their magic almost all sleight of hand, aided by the carefully prepared gowns, loaded with tricks.

Originally they must have been scribes, for their feather craftmarks represented quill pens. He had worked out a history for them. He had no evidence, but it all made so much sense that he was certain now that it must be the truth. Whether writing had been a gift of the gods or a mortal invention, it had been assigned to a separate craft, but reading and writing were such useful skills that the priests had coveted them. The scribes had resisted. Perhaps they had even initiated the violence. The swordsmen had sided with the priests—that was both obvious and inevitable—and driven the sorcerers away. They had taken refuge in mountain strongholds, like Vul, far from the River and the Goddess, claiming magical powers in self-defense. They had also roamed the World in disguise, preserving their monopoly by assassination. That explained both the present absence of writing and the swordsmen's implacable hostility.

Literacy made knowledge cumulative, and over the ages the sorcerers had accumulated knowledge, until now their fakery was assisted by primitive chemistry. Certainly they knew of gunpowder, phosphorus, some sort of bleach to remove facemarks, and the acid that had scarred Tomiyano. They might have other things, but nothing very terrible. Their guns were crude in the extreme, one-shot gadgets, slow to reload and not very accurate. The sorcerers themselves were only armed civilians. Faced with swordsmen in Ov, they had panicked. They would be little problem out in the open.

The towers were the danger. Wallie knew that the tower doors were booby-trapped and he could guess at cannons, shrapnel bombs, and other horrors. If the swordsmen tried to take a tower, they would be slaughtered. It could be done, of course, but not in the traditional ways of the craft, not going by the sutra.

There, it would seem, was where Wallie Smith came in. That was why the Goddess had put the soul of a chemist into the body of a swordsman—so he could take over the tryst, win the leadership by combat, and lead the swordsmen to victory. But why, oh why, had She chosen so fainthearted a mortal as Wallie Smith? There must be no lack of bloody-minded chemists in the universe. He hated bloodshed. He still had nightmares about the battles he had fought, about the jetty on the holy island, about the night the pirates came, about Ov. Why him?

The sky was almost dark, the Dream God gleaming hazily across the south. The ends of the rings were concealed in mist, only the crest of the arc showing. Down on the deck, the party was growing quieter. He must go back and join in.

This fog was bad—good pirate weather—and *Sapphire* was advertising her presence across half a hemisphere. Tomiyano would set double watch this night.

Sorcerers—fakes.

But were they? All the magic he had seen or heard of he could now explain—with one exception. When he had so stupidly gone ashore at Aus and met with sorcerers, they had told him what he had said to Jja before he left *Sapphire*'s deck. When a sorcerer had come on board at Wal, he had known Brota's name. In each case, that knowledge smelled like telepathy. Wallie could think of no other explanation. That was the only magic he could not rationalize away, and he had worried over that more than anything else since Ov.

Sorcery . . . science. They were incompatible, were they not? Surely he need not fight both at once?

But *no one* could have heard what he had said to Jja that day.

And Jja had not gone ashore in Aus. He had asked. That had shown him how worried he was—that he could even doubt Jja.

So that was his worst problem: he was not quite certain.

No. That was not the worst. There was another, hanging over him like the blade of a guillotine: *Whose side was he on?*

Then cool fingers slid around his ribs and linked up on his chest. A cheek was laid against his shoulder blade.

Jja was concerned about him. He had not tried to explain all his troubles to her, for she could never have understood them properly. She did not resent that, he was sure. She did what she could, offering wordless sympathy for unspoken pain, as now. He cherished it in silence for a moment.

"Thanji? Brotsu? Shota? Nnathansu?"

He twisted around and returned the embrace, pulling her tight and feeling her warmth against him through the thinness of cotton. "What are you babbling about, wench?" he asked gently.

"Naming their firstborn, of course!"

"Oh, my love," Wallie whispered. "How I wish that it were us!"

"Silly man!" she said, but in a tone no slave owner could have resented. "What does it matter? I am much more married than Thana will ever be."

And much more beautiful, he thought. Jja was no skinny wraith, no fashion model. She was tall and strong and deep-breasted and the most desirable woman in the World.

He told her so.

She purred.

"I was sent to fetch you, my lord Wallie," she whispered, "for they are waiting."

"For me?" he demanded. "Why?"

"For the wedding, of course."

"What? Now? Tonight? But . . . what do I have to do?"

"Just say yes," she said.

"Yes?"

"Yes!" Chuckling, she led him to the steps, and they picked their way down carefully in the dark.

No bridal gown, no bridesmaids, no orange blossoms? Nnanji and Thana were standing together, with Brota positioned behind Thana, and all of them facing Tomiyano. Obviously a ship's captain could perform a marriage, as a captain could on Earth. Wallie stepped into position behind Nnanji, who had retrieved his kilt and now turned to welcome his mentor with a broad leer. The rest of the crew, the family, had gathered around, vague faces smiling and silent in the night.

The ceremony was unbelievably short and even more revoltingly one-sided than Wallie had expected in this sexist World.

"Lord Shonsu, do you permit your protégé to marry this woman?

"Yes."

"Mistress Brota, do you permit your protégé to marry this man?"

"Yes."

"Adept Nnanji, swordsman of the fourth rank, do you take Thana, swordsman of the second rank, as your wife, promising to clothe and feed her, to feed her children, to teach them obedience to the gods and claim them as your own, to find them honorable crafts when they reach adulthood?"

"Yes."

"Apprentice Thana, swordsman of the second rank, do you

take this Nnanji, swordsman of the fourth rank, as your husband, offering your person for his pleasure and no other's, conceiving, bearing, and rearing his children, and obeying his commands?"

"Yes."

Along with one copper, Wallie thought, Brota was not obtaining much of a commitment from Nnanji, in return for exclusive enjoyment of Thana's person.

And now, obviously, all that was required to seal the marriage was a kiss. Eyes shining, Nnanji turned and put his arms around Thana. She raised her face.

He bent his head . . .

He raised it . . .

He looked wide-eyed at Wallie.

And then Wallie heard it also in the sudden silence, drifting across the water out of the darkness—the sound of clashing swords.

††† †††

Yes, there was something there, uncertainly visible through the dark and fog, something pale and glimmering, drifting slowly downstream toward *Sapphire*'s bow as she lay at anchor.

By the time Wallie had established that fact, Tomiyano had the tarpaulin off the starboard dinghy, and his orders were crackling through the night. The wine fumes had vanished and a well-trained crew was leaping to stations. Swords and boat hooks . . . the four adult male sailors would row, Tomiyano steer . . . the two swordsmen . . .

"No Thana!" the captain snapped.

"Yes, Thana!" Nnanji said firmly. There was a moment's pause. Then Tomiyano nodded and carried on; she was Nnanji's wife now, and he would decide. The boat went down with a rush to the water as Wallie vaguely registered Nnanji's thinking . . . Thana was as good a swordsman as any, and families were not divided on the River, for the Goddess could be fickle. Had Wallie not been there, *Sapphire*'s crew would probably not even have gone to investigate. They might have done so, for She would not penalize an act of mercy, but he wished he had Jja with him.

Then the four men were pulling the dinghy through the inky River with long, sure strokes, rowlocks squeaking, water hissing by in surges. Thana sat by her brother at the tiller. Wallie and Nnanji crouched in the bow—their amateurish efforts would only hinder if they tried to help with the rowing.

Stroke. Stroke. Silver flecks flew from the oars in the chill air. The Dream God was a road of shining mist through the dark sky, his light blurred and ineffective.

Stroke. Stroke. Metal clanged again in the darkness ahead, less faintly now. A cold cramp of fear knotted Wallie's gut—he thought he could guess who was out there. He took a deep breath and cupped his hands.

"What vessel?" he bellowed.

No reply. Stroke.

"In the name of the Goddess, lower your blades. I am a Seventh . . ."

Then, very faintly: "Help?"

A woman? A child's voice?

"What vessel?" Wallie yelled once more.

Stroke. Stroke. More clashing of blades, louder now.

"Sunflower!" came a male reply. "Stay clear!"

Stroke.

It was coming clearly into sight, the fog darkening and congealing into the shape of a small ship, barely more than a fishing boat, with fore-and-aft rigging. Her sails were raised, but there was something wrong with the foresail. She was listing slightly, drifting sideways.

Stroke.

"I am a swordsman of the Seventh! Put down your swords."

Stroke.

"Lord Shonsu." Again that high voice. Wallie was certain of it now, an adolescent voice made shrill by stress.

More strokes of the oars, more clattering of blades, and then a male voice, hard and breathless: "Polini, my lord!"

"Stay clear!" shouted another.

Stroke. Silver flew from the oars.

The fear had expanded. It filled Wallie with ice. He clenched his fists so hard that they hurt. He peered through the cold night air at that pale blur slowly growing. So slowly! He was going to be too late. The swords were ringing faster, and there was shouting and cursing. The victims would be murdered and dropped overboard before he could arrive. The piranha would dispose of the evidence.

"Polini! Hang on!" he roared. "We're coming!" He wanted to weep and scream with frustration. He drummed fists on the gunwale.

The fighting had stopped. *Oh, Goddess! Help them!*

Stroke. Stroke. Someone cried out—high, shrill, full of pain. Then the hull loomed suddenly close. Tomiyano swung the tiller and yelled to ship oars, barked a warning not to stand up yet. The dinghy veered and struck hard alongside; rocked. Swords glinted above them, faces showed as lighter blurs. Nnanji caught the rail with a boat hook. Holiyi stood and swung an oar. Wallie ducked under the stroke and caught the rail with his left hand as he drew the seventh sword with his right. Then he was up on the gunwale, parrying a blade. Nnanji was there, also. Metal rang in the night.

But they knew they were too late.

Swordsmen must not weep.

Polini was dead, killed in that last desperate attack. Young Arganari was going to die very soon. He had been run through, and there was nothing that all the healers in the World could do for him now. He lay on the black-stained deck, with Wallie kneeling at one side of him and Nnanji at the other. Fortunately the light was so poor that nothing was very distinct.

Amidships lay Polini's body, and two others. Three live men were penned at the stern, hemmed in by a line of dragons' teeth—swords held by *Sapphire*'s crew, angry and silent and waiting.

The anchor had been dropped and the sails lowered.

"Water . . . my lord," Arganari whispered again.

Wallie raised his head and Nnanji gave him another drink.

"Thank you," he said, his voice quavering. Then he turned his face and vomited a rush of blood, black in the night.

Swordsmen must not weep.

"What happened?" Wallie demanded, but he had already guessed. Of course the victims still wore their expensive boots and kilts and harnesses, their silver hairclips. Polini had not taken Wallie's advice, as Wallie had known he would not. The World was a place of poverty. Murder could be committed for much less than fancy clothes. Now the fancy clothes were all soaked with blood.

"They took our silver," the prince said. "We paid them." Even his whispering had a singsong strangeness to it. "They came for us last night." He gasped with sudden pain, and Nnanji took hold of his hand. "Master Polini held them off."

All night and all through the day? Stalemate—the big swordsman had made his stand in the bow, holding back five men, defending his ward. One against five. The boy would have been no use.

Polini had cut the forestay, causing the foresail to collapse. That would have made the boat unmanageable. Perhaps he had hoped, too, that it would attract attention and bring help. All night and all through the day until, when he had been weakened by exhaustion, by lack of food and water, they had come for him again.

And the Goddess had moved the boat.

But not soon enough!

Wallie's teeth ground like millstones. His fists trembled.

"I think I wounded one, adept." Arganari was ignoring Wallie now. Nnanji was his hero, the young Fourth who had killed sorcerers at Ov. Perhaps only three years lay between them, Wallie thought with sudden wonder, five at the most.

"You've done very well," Nnanji said. His voice was always soft, and now it was even softer, calm and level. "We'll get a healer to you shortly." He sounded totally under control. Wallie was beyond speech, his throat and eyes aching fiercely.

"Adept?"

"Yes, novice?" Nnanji said.

"You will take my hairclip."

"Yes, all right," Nnanji said. "I'll take it and wear it against the sorcerers. I'll wear it to Vul and when I get there, I'll tell them that you sent me. 'Novice Arganari sent me,' I'll say. 'I come in the name of Arganari.'"

There was no point in trying to move the boy. It would not be long. He gagged and then threw up more blood.

"Adept? Tell me about Ov."

So Nnanji related the battle of Ov, his tones quiet and matter-of-fact. The anchor chain creaked slightly and there was a low mutter of voices from the stern.

Then Arganari interrupted. Probably he had not been understanding very much. He was obviously in agony, trying not to whimper. "Nnanji. It hurts. I'm going to die?"

"Yes, I think so," Nnanji said. "Here, put your hand on your sword hilt. You promised to die holding it, remember?"

"I wish it was my other sword."

"I'll tell the minstrels at Casr," Nnanji said. "In the saga of the Tryst of Casr, your name and Master Polini's will be first among the glorious."

The boy seemed to smile. "I was trying to go home."

After a few minutes he said, "Nnanji. Return me?"

"If you wish," Nnanji replied calmly.

"I think . . . I do. It hurts."

"Should I use the seventh sword?" Nnanji asked.

There was no reply, but Nnanji rose and held out his hand to Wallie. Wallie stood also, passed over his sword, and turned away quickly. He could not do what Nnanji was now doing—not even if the boy was unconscious, not in a thousand centuries. Yet it would have been his swordsman obligation. Fervently he thanked the Goddess that it had been Nnanji who had been asked.

He stared into the dark and tried not to listen. He heard nothing. Swordsmen must not weep.

"No point in wiping it yet, is there?" Nnanji said.

Wallie turned round and accepted his sword back again, not looking down, not looking near his feet. "No. Not yet," he said, and the two of them headed aft, side by side along the obscurity of the deck, until they stood behind the line of sailors fencing the captives.

"Do it!" Wallie snapped at Nnanji.

Now even Nnanji's voice took on a harshness. "Lord Shonsu, I denounce these men for killing swordsmen."

"Have you any defense?" Wallie asked. He was the judge and a witness and he would be executioner.

A trio of voices began shouting indignantly. They all sounded quite young, but they all wore breechclouts and so were legally adults.

Then one voice drowned out the other two. "They took our ship at swordpoint, my lord! There were four of them. We got the others . . ."

Wallie let them rave on in the night for a while with their lies and slanders.

Then he shouted, "Quiet! I find you guilty."

Then there was silence, except that one of the three was sobbing.

Wallie was about to move, but Nnanji put a hand on his shoulder. "Let me do it, brother?"

"No! This will be my pleasure!"

Perhaps Nnanji thought Wallie did not want to do it, or was not capable, but he was shaking with rage, gripping his sword with every ounce of strength, his limbs quivering as if with eagerness. Shonsu's manic temper raged within him. Wallie Smith was just as insanely furious. He was brimming with hatred and contempt, and nausea also. He wanted to take these murderers by the throat, or tear them apart with his fingers.

No, Nnanji was begging. "Please, brother? As a wedding present?"

"Stand aside!" Wallie barked. He pushed between Tomiyano and Holiyi, stepped forward, and began to slash at three unarmed youths. They screamed a lot and tried to parry the seventh sword with bare hands. He could not see properly, so he hacked them to pieces to make sure. It was no pleasure, but he had no regrets.

He was senior. He spoke the words of farewell for Polini. At the end his voice cracked, and he asked Nnanji to perform the office for Arganari. As he listened his eyes began pouring tears, he trembled, he struggled desperately not to let the sounds of his sobbing escape into the night.

He watched the River boil and hiss as piranha consumed the bodies in instantaneous frenzy.

They said no words over the assassins, but the River boiled as hard for them as it had for honest men.

Then Wallie clawed back to self-control. "What will you do with the boat?" he asked Tomiyano.

"Leave it. Someone will find it."

That seemed out of character, but Wallie knew that a sailing ship could not tow another vessel, and to put a prize crew on her would divide the family. So *Sunflower* would be left for the Goddess.

Wallie climbed miserably into the dinghy for the return. A foggy spark of light showed where *Sapphire* waited.

The sailors rowed in silence, and slowly.

Wallie sat with his face in his hands and let the tears flow again.

It was all his fault.

He had not heard the message . . . No, he could not have stopped Polini leaving. He could not have kept the Fifth on board *Sapphire* without a challenge and almost certainly a fight. Polini would not have made obeisance. He would have accepted an impossible match against a Seventh, would perhaps have refused to yield even after Wallie had wounded him. Then Wallie would have had no choice but to kill him.

He could not have stopped Polini leaving.

But he could perhaps have changed the man's mulish, pigheaded mind about something else, had he insisted.

Then the deaths would not have been necessary.

He had not seen why that meeting had been ordained. He had failed. Six men and a boy had died, so that Nnanji could have a hairclip.

Why, O merciful Goddess—why?

A hairclip?

††† † †††

Brota was holding a lantern. Wallie had not known that there was such a thing on the ship. One by one the would-be rescuers stepped to the deck and were greeted by the ring of solemn faces, shining gold around the circle of light. The story was told, briefly and in hushed phrases. There was no comment. The World was a bleak place—sudden, senseless death was no stranger to *Sapphire*, but it would never be a familiar friend.

Wallie laid a hand on Nnanji's shoulder. "I'll take your watch tonight," he said. An hour ago that would have been cause for ribaldry. Now Nnanji merely nodded and put an arm around Thana to lead her away.

Some wedding night, Wallie thought bitterly.

His kilt was damp against his thighs. He was drenched in blood, a figure of horror. He was perversely proud of it, hating it and yet determined not to wash it off until morning. Childish, of course: *See what you have done, Goddess?*

He walked up to the poop, alone. Behind him, the lantern was extinguished.

How could he serve such gods? Where was faith now? Before him in the darkness the face of that solemn, dutiful boy hung like a blazon of shame. The tuneless adolescent voice echoed still in Wallie's ears.

Why? Why? How could I have known what You wanted of me?

Loyalty to the gods—loyalty to anything . . . The sorcerers were killers, also.

But were the swordsmen very much better?

Whose side was he on?

There was the big one, the greatest of his worries. If he could have leadership of the tryst for the asking, did he even want it?

The last part of the god's riddle:

> Finally return that sword,
> And to its destiny accord.

He would return the sword to the Goddess at Her temple in Casr, and its destiny could be to lead the tryst. Let some other butchering swordsman win the leadership and have it—Shonsu would stay with *Sapphire* and be a water rat.

Yet even as he made the resolve, he knew that he was deceiving himself. Bearing the seventh sword was like owning the Mona Lisa or the Taj Mahal. He would never be able to part with it, not if the Goddess Herself were to rise from Her River and demand it back. He could go to the temple, but he would still be carrying the sword when he left. When he had lain wounded on the ship, Nnanji had guarded it for him—and would have died to save it, had that been required of him. Given such an opportunity, almost any other swordsman in the World would have vanished at once, taking the sword with him. Nnanji, of course, would not even have been tempted.

So Wallie would die holding it, as he had promised. In a few years, when his speed began to fail, then the challenges would start. The ambitious and the greedy . . . they would come forward, and one day one of them would succeed.

Jja emerged from the darkness, holding a cape. He muttered thanks and slung it over his shoulders to keep out the dank chill of the fog. It was growing thicker. That made his watch easier, for even pirates could not find their way through such a murk.

"You will come below later?" Jja whispered.

"No," he said. "I'll bunk down in the deckhouse. You go to bed now."

"Yes, master." But she did not move.

He had told her never to call him that . . . but he had also vowed never to give her another order.

He kissed her forehead. "Please go to bed now."

He turned away. He did not realize she was still there until she spoke again.

"Jjonsu? Shona?"

He spun around and gripped her shoulders. "Are you sure?"

"I saw a midwife in Tau."

Then they were embracing and did not stop until he discovered that she was weeping.

"Why?" he said. "Aren't you happy?"

"Oh, yes!" She sniffed and wiped her face with the back of her hand. "Too happy! I so want to give you sons, my darling master, and nothing seemed to be happening. So happy . . . and they will be free?"

"How could you even ask?" he said. "And daughters will be welcomed, also."

So then he promised that he would come down to the cabin when his relief came and he persuaded her to go to bed.

And was alone with his thoughts once more.

A child? Biologically Shonsu's, of course, not Wallie Smith's. Yet that would not worry him. Vixini called him Daddy, and he loved the little tyke. Any child of Jja's would be dear to him. But what sort of world would these children inherit?

Technology—it would tear the World apart. The sorcerers were a thousand years ahead of the rest of the culture. So far they had done a good job of keeping their secrets, but it could not last—not now they had emerged from their remote refuges. Firearms and distillation, even writing itself . . . those would escape. Change would explode upon a world that did not know how to handle change. Chaos and upheaval, then war, then famine . . . Surely this was the danger that the Goddess foresaw, that She wanted Wallie Smith to prevent. The demigod, Her messenger, had said it was important. Wallie had not then dreamed how important.

And yet . . .

And yet the sorcerers were not so very far behind the Earth he had known, a few centuries at most. There was the temptation, for if they had such trivia as gunpowder, then they could not be far from anesthetics to relieve suffering, and antibiotics to succor sick babies, and steam power to supplant slavery. Even a simple written register of ship ownership could stamp out the piracy that plagued the River. Three hundred years, or four . . . The sorcerers held so much promise! They were even trying to foster trade in their cities—an idea that the swordsmen would treat with contempt, but one to appeal to a Wallie Smith, erstwhile citizen of a mercantile culture.

Whose side was he on?

His mission, obviously, was to drive the sorcerers back into the hills and restore the rule of swordsmen in the seven cities. Now that he knew what it was, he also knew why his divine master, the demigod, had been so chary of defining it. What would Wallie have replied, on that day when he received the sword, had he been told: "Go forth, Shonsu, and make the World safe for barbarism!"?

Whose side was he on?

A whisper: "My lord?" It was Honakura, frail as a dry leaf in the forest darkness.

"Go away!" Wallie said harshly. "I want none of your priestly dissertations tonight."

"But, my lord—"

"None!" Wallie shouted. "Yes, I know all the standard palliatives. You can soothe all hurts and calm all misgivings and have me laughing and giggling inside ten minutes. I must not judge the gods, you will tell me. I do not know all the story, you will say. The boy may have a brother who will make a better king than he, we may surmise. He may be rewarded in another life, very likely. Stock phrases, old man, threadbare promises! Just the old excuses that men make for gods."

He should have known that he could not scare Honakura away. The little priest merely stood there with his head bowed until Wallie ran dry like a water clock.

"It was my fault, my lord."

"Yours?" Wallie gaped. Then: "No! It was mine. Do you know why it happened, old man?" He dropped his voice to a hiss, remembering in time that there were portholes below him and there would be many folk not sleeping well this night on *Sapphire*. "It happened because your precious gods wanted Nnanji to have a hairclip!"

"I know."

"A silver hairclip, very old. It belonged to the great Arganari. Nnanji will love it! I can't think of anything in the World that would please him more. A generous wedding gift for a loyal . . . you knew?"

"Pardon, my lord," Honakura said, "I must sit . . ." He tottered over to the helmsman's bench. Wallie followed with suspicion, wondering if this was some ploy for sympathy. But the old man had been unusually subdued these last few days. Sparing a thought for something other than his own troubles, he now realized that Honakura had seemed very gray and shrunken lately, more so even than normal. He was incredibly old, of course, and this was not his former serene life of pampered luxury.

The priest settled on the bench, an indistinct hump in the darkness. Wallie stood before him, keeping a wary eye on the River beyond.

"My fault, my lord," he wheezed. "The god said that you

could trust me . . . but I did not trust you, you see."

Obviously! Wallie waited.

"I have known many swordsmen, my lord. So I did not trust you. You remember the curse?"

"What curse?"

Honakura coughed as if coughing hurt. "When you first met Adept Nnanji—Apprentice Nnanji, then. He could not fight his way across an empty courtyard, you said."

"Yes, I remember."

"Why, my lord? Did you ever wonder why the gods had laid a curse on him?"

Wallie believed that Nnanji had laid that curse on himself, a mental block caused by his ambivalent feelings toward the corrupt swordsmen of the temple guard—but this was no time to start discussing Freudian psychology. "Why?"

Another racking cough. "He would have been a threat, my lord."

Wallie tried to imagine the young Nnanji without that impediment. He would have shot up the ranks of the guard like a cat up a pole, even with the inferior instruction, a swan among the ducks. And Nnanji was incorruptible.

"Tarru?" he said.

"And Lord Hardduju," the old man agreed in a whisper. "They would have killed him. So the Goddess protected the only honest swordsman in Her guard, by hiding his talent. Seniors can impede good juniors. I have seen it happen, my lord, many times. In the case of swordsmen, the impediment may be permanent . . . I did not trust you."

"Nnanji?" Wallie scoffed. "Nnanji a threat to me? But we are oath brothers now! He would not hurt a hair on my head. He was willing to throw his life away to avenge me . . . You thought that I was frightened of Nnanji?"

The fog was moving in thicker around the ship and over the deck. Honakura rasped another half cough.

"Nnanji is no threat," Wallie said. "He fancies himself as a Sixth, but he isn't there yet. Another couple of years and he'll be a Seventh and a damned good one. But not yet—and I'm not worried about Nnanji anyway. Not my oath brother!"

"Not worried, my lord, no," the old man persisted. "But I thought you might become jealous. That was why I would not tell you the tale of Ikondorina's red-haired brother. I only thought you might be envious."

So he was going to tell it at last, was he?

"You saw the hairclip?" Honakura asked.

"Yes. I saw it."

Again the old man coughed. "I have not. But I had asked Adept Nnanji to recount the meeting in Tau, my lord, when Master Polini came aboard—like you, I thought it strange. Of course he gave me every word, and I heard of the hairclip."

"A silver griffon," Wallie said beginning to understand.

"The royal symbol," Honakura agreed hoarsely.

"Nnanji a king?"

Wallie's mind reeled. Of course, Nnanji was still so young. It was hard to imagine him five or ten years hence.

"I believe so, my lord. I don't think the prophecy has anything to do with your quest. I think it happens afterward. That was what I hinted to Apprentice Thana today—that Nnanji is too good to remain a free sword. The Goddess will have greater plans for him. The clip was a message to Thana, not to you."

Now Wallie understood the old man's machinations. But Nnanji as a king would take a lot of thought. He was conceivable as a revolutionary, perhaps, but not as a ruler. Like a dog chasing a car—good sport, but what did he do when he caught it? It was not hard to see Thana as Lady Macbeth, though, urging him on.

Wallie joined Honakura on the bench. The fog had thickened until the water around the ship was invisible and even the old man was hard to distinguish. All that guards could do in this weather was listen. There would be two of them on the main deck and another up on the fo'c'sle, standing in silence. Even to pace up and down would make noise—better to remain still and let possible marauders float by, unaware of a juicy prey lying in the gloom.

"So tell me the prophecy," Wallie said quietly.

"If you wish, my lord," the old man croaked. "But it is even more trivial than the other; it does not even rhyme."

Ikondorina's red-haired brother came to him and said, Brother you have wondrous skill with a sword; teach me, that like you I may wrest a kingdom. And he said, I will. So Ikondorina taught, and his brother learned, and then Ikondorina said, I can teach you no more, now go and find your kingdom; and his brother did so, and his realm was more vast and much greater.

Indeed?

"Had I told you sooner," Honakura whispered, "then you would have recognized the significance of the clip when it was first offered . . ."

Sutras could be long or short, complex or simple, banal or inscrutably devious. They could contain epitome, episode, and epigram, or any combination of those. But Wallie had never met one quite so puerile as that. A nasty worm of suspicion began wriggling around inside his mind.

"That is all?" he demanded.

"That is all," the old man wheezed.

"You swear that?"

After a pause, Honakura asked, "What oath will you have me swear, my lord?"

And Wallie's suspicions collapsed in a heap of guilt. Every craft had its oath, except the priesthood. A priest must never lie, not ever. For a priest even to compliment the chef was perjury, if the meal was bad. Honakura was as devious as a waltzing snake, but he would never tell an outright falsehood. Hastily Wallie begged forgiveness for his doubts.

King Nnanji? Obviously the old man had been correct. This was Nnanji's destiny, after the tryst, after the sorcerers. It had nothing to do with Wallie at all.

He discovered that he was relieved to know that—and so he had been worried! That was perhaps why he had been so relentlessly chewing at his other troubles: He had been keeping his mind off Nnanji and his griffon hairclip.

Then Honakura began to cough again, and Wallie's conscience sank its teeth into him. It was unkind and very foolish to keep the old man there in that cold dampness.

"Come, my reverend friend," he whispered when the attack had passed. "I shall guide you down the steps. This weather is not for you."

The fog was thicker now.

Wallie saw Honakura safely to his cabin and returned to his post. When Holiyi came to relieve him, he fulfilled his promise to Jja and went to her.

She was awake and waiting for him. They made love to celebrate her good news, and Jja, who had great skill in such matters, made sure that it was a long and very strenuous session of lovemaking, rousing her owner to innumerable peaks of passion and superhuman accomplishments of joy, finally wearing him out so thoroughly that he slept, when he had not expected to.

In the next cabin but two, Adept Nnanji had consummated his marriage with dispatch, expertise, encores, and vast satisfaction. He slept, also, while his young bride lay awake at his side, pondering their future.

Three cabins farther aft lay Novice Katanji, in Hana's bed, where he had no right to be, dreaming of Mei, whom he had visited earlier.

While in yet another cabin, Honakura, priest of the seventh rank, spent the rest of the night on his bony knees, weeping softly and begging his Goddess for forgiveness.

And in the morning the fog had lifted, and *Sapphire* was anchored about seven lengths offshore, at Casr.

BOOK TWO:

HOW THE SWORDSMAN MET HIS MATCH

†

The virtuous Huli, priestess of the third rank, came striding along the riverfront at Casr with the hem of her brown robe swirling around her ankles and dark thoughts churning over in her mind. The sun was warm, but the wind tugged and jostled at her, throwing dust in her eyes so that she hardly knew whether her tears came from the dust, or from anger and frustration.

The city had become a madhouse, an asylum for the criminally insane. There were no bars to restrain the inmates, and more of them were arriving every day. She passed a fruit seller's barrow on one side as two young swordsmen strutted by on the other, openly helping themselves to apples as they went. Not only did they not consider paying, they did not have the grace to thank the owner or even send him a nod of acknowledgment. So far as those two louts were concerned, the poor man did not exist—and he likely with eight or nine children at home to feed.

Swordsmen! She ground her teeth. She still had all her teeth.

Swordsmen in sixes. Swordsmen in dozens. They postured and they marched, they bullied and they lechered. She dodged angrily as a sword whistled—a Fifth leading ten men was saluting a Sixth with five. No one was safe anymore!

Daily the victims appealed to the temple—men mutilated or beaten, girls ravished, householders impoverished and driven out. The priests could give them little but solace. Daily, Priestess Huli gave thanks to the Holiest that, being a woman of the cloth, she was sacrosanct and safe from molestation. Of course those young debauchers normally preyed on less mature women than she, so that was another protection.

The tryst had turned the city sideways. Even her own humble existence . . . she had been giving very serious thought to accepting a proposal of marriage—from Jinjino of the Fourth, a most respected draper, a dignified and prosperous widower, father of three children who dearly needed a loving mother to teach them some manners. She had almost decided to accept. He had made most solemn promises that his demands on her person would be moderate and discreet. And now he had fled town, taking his children with him. That was something of a disappointment. The eldest was only twelve and even these sword-waving boors did not descend to *that*.

She scowled at the sight of three swordsmen encircling a young female, leering and bantering. Lewd humor, no doubt! She wondered if she could find the courage to intervene. They were only juvenile Seconds, but they were very large, rough-looking types. She paused in her progress, irresolute. Then she noticed with horror that the woman was obviously enjoying the attention—wanton! Huli continued on her way, frowning in disgust.

The wide plaza was always busy, but it was so vast that in ordinary times it could handle its traffic easily and still seem comparatively peaceful. On a normal day there might be a dozen ships tied up along the front, loading and unloading. Now there must be fifty, an almost continuous line of them, and the crowds swarmed everywhere. It was not only swordsmen who had invaded Casr, but their followers, also, from babes in arms to whores and cutthroats. Madhouse!

The problem was in knowing whom to blame. The most holy Lord Kadywinsi, high priest of Casr, was the obvious culprit, but she could hardly bring herself to pass judgment on a man so revered and venerable, even if he was, just perhaps, maybe, a tiny bit . . . senile? Be charitable, she told herself as she detoured around a wagon to avoid a group of pedestrian-baiting young swordsmen, the holy lord is not the man he was when you were a novice, but he is still worthy of your respect.

A blue ship, she had been told, by the double statue. There was a small blue ship visible in the distance now.

And if Kadywinsi of the Seventh was not at fault, it was certainly not Priestess Huli's place to criticize the Goddess.

She had been unsuspecting and excited that day two weeks back, when word had flashed around the temple that the castellan, the charming and handsome Lord Tivanixi, had ridden in with his men and had persuaded the high priest to join with him in calling a tryst. A tryst! It would be the first in centuries, if the Holiest heard their plea, and of course the risk involved was so terrifying! She had thought she might faint with horror as she had watched the ceremony. Forty-nine bullocks, poor things, the water scarlet and foaming, and the two valiant lords actually wading into the River behind them! She still perspired with horror at the thought.

Such faith! And so wonderfully blessed by the Most High! It had been less than an hour before the ships had begun arriving with swordsmen on board.

The blame, then, must be laid to Lord Tivanixi, for failing to control the swordsmen when they had come. But he was so handsome!

Suddenly she heard boots running. "Challenge!" shouted male voices. Swordsmen went running by her, and all the unattached swordsmen in the area took off after them, vanishing up a side street. Well! That certainly cleared this area for a while. She wondered if there would shortly be one less swordsman around to bully the innocent civilians, then reproved herself for an uncharitable thought. They were still arriving much faster than they were killing one another off.

Now she had reached the two bronze statues, so corroded that it was impossible to tell whether they represented men or women. There was the blue ship, as she had been told. She squared her shoulders and marched up the plank, then paused to look around the deck. She had never been on a ship before. It was not a large ship, but it was clean and smelled pleasantly of leather. Two or three sailors were sitting around and one of them rose and came over. He wore a knife, so he must be in charge. A Third, like herself . . . but she had been instructed to make the salute to a superior—a shameful concession from a priestess! His manner was not very respectful, but he responded smartly.

"I have a message for 'a swordsman of high rank,' Captain."

Rudely, the sailor jerked his head toward a door at the rear. With a sniff, Huli marched over to it and went in, finding a big, bright, almost bare room. A young slave woman was kneeling in the corner, entertaining three or four small children. A man rose from a large wooden chest where he had been sitting. A Seventh! And huge! His head and sword hilt almost touched the ceiling. Most of the swordsmen who had invaded Casr were slim, wiry men, but this one was a giant. A fine figure of a man, she admitted, and discovered to her astonishment that he was giving her a friendly smile, and that she was returning it. This was certainly the highrank she had been sent to find, so she saluted.

He responded.

Shonsu!

Of course! She had seen him many times in the distance—but he was supposed to have died! She staggered and then recovered herself with an effort. The infamous Shonsu come back! But . . .

He had noticed her reaction and his smile had gone. She did not like what had replaced it.

"In what way may I serve you, holy lady?"

Huli pulled her wits together. No wonder she had been warned not to discuss this. "I have a message for you, my lord, from a priest of the seventh rank." That was an odd way to describe Lord Kadywinsi, but it was what she had been told to say. There were no other priests of that rank in Casr, so who else could it be from?

"Come out of the closet at last, has he?"

"My lord?"

The swordsman laughed. "Forgive me, priestess. The message, if you please?"

Huli took a deep breath and repeated the words she had been given. "'The person of whom you inquired was born far off, arrived two years ago, and is unmarried, but has children. He held the office we understood and departed at the time we thought. He was believed dead, but there have recently been rumors. I shall remain at the temple until tomorrow.'"

It was demeaning for a priestess of her rank to be used as a common herald, and not to be told what it was all about, either, but she served the Goddess as her superiors decided. Now she had completed this trivial errand and could get back to . . . *thought to have died . . . came two years ago*? That message could apply to Shonsu himself!

"I thank you, priestess. There will be no reply, I think." The swordsman was studying her carefully, almost as if he could read her thoughts. "May we offer you refreshment before you depart?"

Huli stuttered a refusal. Shonsu! She wanted to get away by herself and think. What rumors? Shonsu was supposed to have been killed by sorcerers. Had not this terrible tryst been called to avenge him?

She made her formal farewell, hurried along the deck without a glance at the sailors, and almost ran down the plank. Shonsu come back? Casr had been well rid of Shonsu . . .

Angry and upset, Priestess Huli marched off across the sun-bright plaza, with the wind whipping and tugging at her brown robe. She barely noticed the lanky, red-haired swordsman of the Fourth who strode past her, wearing an expression of black despair.

††

Most cities presented a façade of warehouses to the River, but not Casr. Ships tied up alongside a wide plaza that ran off endlessly in both directions along the waterfront. Behind it loomed tall buildings and the entrances to wide streets, yet the general effect was one of improvisation. The buildings ranged through every architectural style imaginable—some old and some ancient, some smart and imposing, others crumbling and half in ruins. Arches and pillars and domes mingled at random among minarets and pilasters and arcades. Fragments of old walls jutted up in places, and the streets changed without warning from great avenues to narrow alleys like canyons, rolling up and down from one level to another as if the remains of a dozen cities had been shoveled out of a box. The only consistency was in color, for everything from the towers to the pavement was made of a shiny bronze stone like old gold, and even the scattered trees, those that had leaves remaining, glittered to match. Many of the windows sported bright-hued awnings, reds and blues and greens, like flashings of fire from a diamond.

Casr was old. Its statues had weathered to shapeless monoliths; the stone bollards along the waterfront were worn into mushrooms by the windings of centuries.

Wallie had sent his troops out to scout, while he spent the morning skulking in the deckhouse, almost as if Casr were a sorcerer city.

The usual wagons and heaps of trade goods were in evidence, and the gangs of dock slaves labored in Casr as in all ports. The traders and hawkers and busy citizens roamed as always, yet there was much less crowding and jostling than elsewhere, because of the sheer vastness of the plaza. In Casr business proceeded with more decorum and much less noise. The only thing hurrying was the wind, sweeping leaves along as if impatient to clean up before winter, flapping awnings like dust rags.

Everywhere were swordsmen. Not in one or twos, as at Tau, but in sixes or dozens, marching along with a senior in front, usually a green-kilted Sixth, rarely a red Fifth, and very rarely a blue Seventh. Browns were most common, of course, but there were absurd numbers of fresh-faced Firsts and Seconds, who would be more or less useless, mere errand boys and extra mouths to feed.

Even from the ship Wallie could detect tension in Casr. Gangs of small children ran along behind the troops sometimes, shouting rudenesses, and they would be taking that attitude from their elders. Swordsmen expected cheering, not jeering. He thought he saw some unobtrusive fist-waving from adults and certainly he saw petty pilfering, girls being accosted, men being roughly shouldered aside or insulted. If such things were going on in public, what was happening behind the shutters?

Free swords lived on charity, a primitive form of taxation. Such extortion was bearable for a night or two when a troop arrived in a town or village to clean up any crime that the garrison could not handle, to confirm that the resident swordsmen were themselves honest, to tumble the best-looking girls, and then to move on. A large city would hardly notice them, but even one as large as Casr would be reeling from this invasion. All these men must expect to eat regularly and sleep somewhere. And certainly not sleep alone, not swordsmen! Hundreds of active young men with nothing much to keep them occupied—who was in charge of this zoo? Who had been so brash as to call a tryst?

Wallie had kept his sword on his back, prepared to run down and intervene if he noticed any serious disturbances, but that had not been necessary. Yet obviously the tryst was chaos in spades. He wanted nothing to do with it.

Then came the message from Honakura, brought by a sour-faced priestess, and that was good news. To learn that Shonsu had no parents or other family in Casr gave Wallie a huge sense of relief. Lunch was almost due. He decided to celebrate with a tankard of beer and asked Jja to fetch it for him. Before he could drink, Nnanji's boots thumped on the deck, and he strode in, dusty and hot. His normal carefree cheerfulness had been replaced by an ominous angry scowl.

Wallie held out the beer: *"My goods are your goods,"* he said.

Nnanji shook his head. "No thank you, brother. I've been having that stuff thrust at me all morning."

A Fourth would be a good catch, a very tall and unusually young Fourth. The recruiting was blatant and ferocious. As soon as *Sapphire* had docked and the port officer had gone ashore again, no less than eight swordsmen had tried to come aboard, hunting for newcomers. Brota had donned her sword and stood at the top of the plank and glared, huge and red and ugly, a swordsman's nightmare. She had kept them away, but obviously Nnanji would have run into the problem in the town.

"How many times were you propositioned?" Wallie asked.

His protégé scowled and counted on his fingers. "Thirteen!" He shook his head, changed his mind, took the tankard, and drained it. Yet obviously it was not the recruiting that had been worrying him. There was something else.

"What did you say?" inquired Wallie, amused.

"Just that I had a mentor already. Then they wanted to know who and what rank; I quoted one seventy-five at them! Acch!"

Then Thana came in. Nnanji grabbed her to administer a long and doubtless beery kiss.

Jja tactfully shepherded the children out. Wallie seated himself on the chest by the window, where he had spent the morning. Nnanji and Thana settled on the other, arms around each other, and Wallie told them of Honakura's message.

Then Katanji strolled in, looking cheerful. He, also, had been scouting. His injured arm relieved him of the obligation to wear a sword, and probably that had been a big advantage for him, Wallie thought.

"Take a seat, novice," he said jovially, waving at the floor. "I don't suppose the press-gangs bothered you much?"

Katanji sank down cross-legged and grinned. "They did, my lord! Four times! Of course they could tell a good man when they saw one!"

Wallie was startled. If a crippled First was in demand, then the battle for numbers was being carried beyond all reason.

"Well, let's have the news," he said. "Novice?"

Katanji looked pleased with himself. He reported as if he had been rehearsing: "Lord Shonsu was previous castellan of the lodge. He came from somewhere far away, and I don't think he was married. He left about half a year ago and never came back. The new castellan is more popular."

"Where did you find this out?" Wallie asked.

He smirked. "At the stews, my lord. I asked some other people. All of them just laughed and said to go there and ask. So I did. The girls all knew Shonsu. I said he was my uncle and the Goddess had brought me to Casr, and I was trying to find him. He was a frequent customer, my lord, although he usually didn't pay. But the girls . . ." The smirk became a leer. "They shed no tears over his departure, I fancy."

Wallie knew of Shonsu's demonic sex drive and he had seen the petty pilfering going on at the hawkers' carts. Same principle.

"Nobody seems to know where Shonsu went or why. He just disappeared. I think that's all, my lord."

"Well done, novice," Wallie said. "Did you spend much on expenses?"

Katanji hesitated and then regretfully said, "No, my lord. The elders have declared the brothels free for swordsmen."

That was interesting. "Busy, are they?"

Katanji chuckled. "They were pleased to have the chance to just talk, my lord!"

He had probably done very well even to get the chance to talk to them, being only a First. "You just talked?" Wallie demanded disbelievingly.

Katanji opened his eyes very wide "My mentor has frequently impressed upon me, Lord Shonsu, the need to uphold the honor of the craft!" Nnanji snarled at the impudence.

Wallie laughed. "How about the other matter?"

"I did some checking, my lord." Katanji studied Wallie with mingled admiration and perplexity. "Yes, prices have fallen. How did you guess?"

"Prices of what?" Nnanji demanded.

"Gems," Wallie said. "And Lina is screaming that the cost of food has gone up. I'll give you all a lecture on it tonight, if you're interested. What did you discover, brother?"

Nnanji disengaged his arm from Thana and clasped his large hands on his knees. "Not much about Shonsu himself. The castellan before him was a Seventh named Narrinko. Shonsu came to town, fancied the job, and killed him."

"Nasty! What did the elders say?"

Nnanji rubbed his chin—and Wallie knew where he had picked up that gesture. "They don't seem to have any say, brother. This is a lodge city; it seems they're different. There is no garrison, no reeve. The castellan keeps order with whoever happens to be around."

Then it was the present castellan's fault that the city was such a madhouse now.

"The lodge is independent?" Thana said. "That's how the sorcerers' towers are, isn't it? At least I assume it is—the port officers always welcomed the ship on behalf of the elders and the wizard. In swordsmen towns they don't mention reeve. Curious!"

That was the first time Wallie had ever heard anyone on the ship express an interest in politics, and he was suddenly filled with admiration for Honakura's acumen. Lady Macbeth!

"Shonsu was a collector," Nnanji went on. He frowned in

disapproval—and that was a surprise from Nnanji.

"What's that, Nanj?" asked Katanji.

"A killer," Nnanji said, too intent on his reporting to notice the informality. "Collects dead men's swords. It seems he organized an expedition against the sorcerers. It wasn't a tryst, of course. Fifty men, I heard, and somehow he did it in secret. One day they just vanished. None of them ever returned."

Startled silence.

The demigod had said that Shonsu had failed disastrously. Wallie shivered at the thought of fifty young men running into armed sorcerers and being mowed down. "But what city? Why did we never hear of this on the other bank?"

Nnanji shrugged. "There are no swordsmen in town who knew Shonsu. He took them all. The guess is that he landed at some village jetty and set off to attack Vul itself."

"Gods!" Wallie exclaimed. "He went for a kill! I wonder if that's what the tryst is planning?"

Nnanji said he did not know. He was beginning to look very uneasy again, and Thana, sensing it, was studying him carefully.

"Tell me the bad news then," Wallie said.

Nnanji clenched his hands together once more and stared at them. "A few weeks later, early in summer, so I was told, the sorcerers in Aus paraded a swordsman through the streets." He stopped talking, but they all knew the rest—the swordsman had been crawling naked on his belly.

"And the name of the swordsman?"

"They think it was Shonsu."

Wallie nodded. "That's not quite how I recall it," he said. "I was captured and allowed to crawl back to the ship."

"But that's not what the rumors say!" Nnanji shouted angrily. "It sounds as if the sorcerers brought you out, showed you, and then put you back in a box somewhere."

There was Wallie's danger. The details did not matter. Trapped by the sorcerers, ashore and unarmed, he had felt that public humiliation was a small price to pay to save his life. He had not thought at the time what other swordsmen—real swordsmen—would think of his disgrace, or of what they would do to such a coward when they caught him.

"And the Ov story is worse, my lord brother! They say that a band of swordsmen attacked the docks—I got asked, because of this damned hair of mine." He looked totally miserable. "The massacre is all right, but then the story goes that you . . . that a Seventh, probably Shonsu because of his size . . . appeared and ordered us all back to our ships. *They make it sound like you were on their side!*"

Yes, that was bad. Misery filled the deckhouse. Wallie had been prepared to face an allegation of cowardice, but not treason. In the confusion of the fight at Ov, the facts could easily have become distorted. When the wagon charge had reached the sorcerers, he had been with them. Evidently his earlier run along the jetty and his capture had not been noticed.

Still, he could produce witnesses for Ov. The mess he had made at Aus was an insoluble disaster.

"I've loused it up," he said bitterly. "The Goddess gave me Her own sword, and I've thrown it all away. Now I'm going to be called a traitor." And his sorcerer mothermark would not help.

"A zombie," Nnanji growled. "That's what they say. That the sorcerers have Shonsu's body working for them."

"Do I look like a zombie?"

Nnanji managed to return the smile. "Not very."

Wallie scowled in silent misery and self-reproach. He had no regrets about his decision at Ov. Yet, ironically, at Ov he had gained a bullethole in his scabbard. No one else would know what it was, but to be wounded in the scabbard was swordsman slang for cowardice.

A clatter out on deck proclaimed that lunch was being laid out.

"What word on the tryst, then?" he asked.

Nnanji cheered up slightly. "Over a thousand swordsmen, not counting lowranks! The tryst was called by the castellan, of course, Lord Tivanixi, and the high priest, Lord Kadywinsi. More swordsmen still coming."

"And who is leader?"

"That is to be decided by combat. The popular favorite is someone called Boariyi, but there are bets on Tivanixi, too."

"Why not you, my lord?" asked Katanji, who was hugging his bony knees and listening intently.

Wallie sighed. "Nnanji, correct me if I'm wrong. The top

swordsmen, the Sevenths, decide by combat who is best, right? Then they all swear to be his vassals, swear the third oath to the leader. Then all the others swear the third oath to their mentors or a higher rack, in a pyramid. Am I right?"

Nnanji nodded.

"Do you know the third oath?" Wallie asked Katanji.

"No, my lord."

"It's a horror! The vassal is absolute slave to his liege. His own honor is of no account—he must obey any order whatsoever. That's why it may only be sworn before battle."

"But, my lord, if you're the best swordsman . . ."

Wallie shook his head and glanced at Nnanji, who did not look as if he was going to argue.

"I am a zombie or a traitor or a coward or all three, novice. It's a dead horse."

Silence fell, then Thana said, "Dead horses have their uses. They're better than live ones for skinning. And why is it a dead horse? You're the greatest swordsman in the world, Nnanji says."

"Perhaps!" said Wallie. "The god told me there were none better, but that one other might be as good. That's not the point. I once made Nnanji swear the third oath to me. I put my sword at his throat and said I was going to kill him." He did not need to tell her that a swordsman could never plead duress—Nnanji's oath had been as binding as it would have been if given freely. "But that won't work with a thousand men, Thana! I'd get the first one and a couple of the fat ones, but the other nine hundred and ninety-seven would be at Quo before I caught them. They would not swear to a traitor. They'd run."

It was hopeless—and suddenly Wallie felt a surge of relief. He need not worry about seeking the leadership, because he could not. That option did not exist, so he need not concern himself with it.

Yet he had promised Nnanji that he could try for promotion. As Nnanji's mentor, Wallie ought to accompany him. "Well, brother," he said. "What happens if I go to the lodge? Give me your judgment." Nnanji's predictions of swordsmen's behavior were usually better than his.

Nnanji looked startled. "Of course, you would be safe under

the ways of honor, brother. They know how Shonsu used metal —no one is going to challenge you. But . . ."

"But if they denounce me . . ." Wallie nodded. If they denounced him, the odds were a thousand to one. "Yet . . . Ov is all right. We have witnesses." Brota, Honakura, or even Thana— swordsmen preferred swordsman witnesses. "And they wouldn't have witnesses for what happened in Aus!"

Thana frowned. "They could get them, my lord—sailors, water rats . . ."

"But not this afternoon, they couldn't! Not right away! A quick visit, and then scamper? Let's do it!"

He grinned mischievously at Nnanji, expecting him to welcome the thought of such bravado. But Nnanji went pale and shook his head vigorously. Wallie had never seen him display fear when in personal danger—indeed, he seemed to enjoy danger, and Nnanji's acting skills were nonexistent. Apparently he just did not know what fear was. But he looked horrified at this risk to his oath brother. If even Nnanji thought it was too dangerous . . .

They all sat in silence for a while.

Then Katanji said, "Nanj? You said that all the great trysts were led by seven Sevenths? One Seventh called this tryst. Three Sevenths responded. Two Sixths have won promotion. I was told that they're still waiting for the Goddess to send a seventh Seventh!"

Superstition! The World ran on it.

Wallie laughed. "Well! That changes things! Then they won't throw me in the cesspool without a hearing, will they? Don't eat too much lunch, protégé; you have some fencing to do this afternoon."

Still Nnanji looked sick. "Brother! he warned. "If they denounce you as a traitor . . . or a coward . . ."

"No!" Wallie thumped his fist on the oak chest. "I'm tired of hiding on this ship! It's time to *do* something! They can't prove I'm a traitor . . . and I can certainly prove that I'm not a coward!"

Nnanji's eyes widened. "By going to the lodge?" He gulped, and then grinned admiringly. "Right!"

†††

Wearing a trim new ultramarine kilt that Jja had made for him, Wallie led his army down the gangplank. His sword hilt flashed in the sunlight, and his blood pumped eagerly at the prospect of action at last.

Next came Nnanji of the Fourth, his grin firmly anchored to his ears and his head in the stars. *Nnanji of the Fifth?* He was having trouble not marching straight up his mentor's back in his impatience to reach the lodge. He also wore his best, but his hairclip was the usual orange stone. Arganari's silver griffon had neither appeared nor been mentioned, which was unusual tact for Nnanji.

And after him was Thana, defiantly dressed in riverfolk breechclout and bra sash of buttercup yellow, her only concession to land life being a pair of shoes. Wallie had been hesitant when she had appeared with her sword on, announcing that she also was a candidate for promotion. The tryst would be quite antagonistic enough toward him without a female water rat at his side. True, she could handle the fencing for third rank with her eyes closed, and she had repeatedly astonished him in the sutra sessions, but he was sure that she had only just developed this feverish desire to learn sutras. There must be many that she had never even heard. Then Nnanji had put on his ill-treated-spaniel expression. Thinking that she would be company for Jja, Wallie had consented.

Behind Thana came Novice Katanji, attempting to maintain a man-of-the-World cynicism about this swordsman childishness, but not succeeding very well in hiding his excitement at the prospect of seeing the lodge and of being brother to a Fifth. Tucked under his cast, steadied by his good hand, he carried two sheathed swords.

Finally came Jja, bearing a bundle—a swordsman might carry nothing except a foil or a spare sword, because that would diminish his honor. She wore sandals and the usual slave's black wrap, but it had been skillfully tailored by herself from the finest linen her owner had been able to purchase and have appropriately dyed.

They had barely started across the wind-whipped, eye-watering plaza, the sailors' good wishes had scarcely died away behind them, when they were spotted by some juniors, whose reaction was obvious. Here was the expected seventh Seventh! The juniors turned and headed for the lodge. Other swordsmen, including the press-gangs, saw the activity and gave chase.

Nnanji was calling directions, but soon Wallie did not need them, for an increasing crowd of swordsmen was preceding him, gathering newcomers like a snowball, and all he had to do was follow. The citizens noticed the excitement, also, pausing in their business to stare. Several times Wallie thought he saw recognition, or heard his name being spoken. Shonsu was returning from the dead.

Their way led toward the center of town, then through a narrow alley and out into an open space too irregular ever to be called a square. Most of the flanking buildings seemed to be deserted ruins. At the far side was a huge block, set at an odd angle, and the mob of swordsmen was pouring into it through a single arched doorway.

All that showed from the outside was a blank stone wall like the side of a cube, with the archway and a single balcony high above it. A bronze sword hung on the wall above that. There were no windows. As Wallie and his followers approached, the tail end of his unofficial vanguard was streaming in to be present when he arrived.

By the time he had crossed the court, the crowd had vanished inside. Two guards of the third rank flashed their swords in salute and a solitary figure came marching out to greet him. He was a Seventh, but no swordsman. He was built like a blue bullfrog, a bald head perching on the shoulders of his robe without intervention of neck. Wallie eyed the unfamiliar facemarks doubtfully—they looked like mouths—and waited for the salute.

He was a herald, and he reacted to Wallie's name with obvious shock.

"Lord Shonsu!" he repeated, and then recovered himself. "By what titles does your lordship wish to be proclaimed?" He had a voice like falling rocks.

"My name will suffice, my lord herald."

The herald bowed and led the way through a dark tunnel that emerged into a courtyard. The lodge, it seemed, was a shoe box, a hollow rectangle whose outside walls were bare and whose interior was lined with balconies, layer upon layer of them overlooking the open space in the center. Wallie found himself at the top of a short flight of steps, surveying what in normal times was probably a charming and peaceful place. But these were not normal times, and now it was not charming and certainly not peaceful.

The courtyard was huge. At each end stood venerable and gnarled oak trees, bare now of leaves, symbols of strength and endurance. Between these a central rectangle was marked off by stone benches and plinths bearing statues of marble or bronze, weathered and corroded by age to travesties of the warriors they had once represented. Probably this smaller central area was intended for fencing. It was larger than all of *Sapphire*.

Far from peaceful! The court seethed with noisy swordsmen, busy as a fairground. The center space had been divided into four sections by wooden hurdles, and each of these smaller spaces contained a fencing match. Around the outside, and in many of the lower balconies, crowds of spectators heckled and cheered as their favorites performed. Seniors with entourages were pushing through, around, and over the tops of cross-legged sutra sessions. Discussions and arguments were being shouted everywhere in total disregard for everything else. At least two minstrels were trying to sing above the noise of hawkers shouting their wares. Swordsmen were sharpening swords on treadle grindstones, eating, arguing, playing dice, cooking food on braziers, and even wrestling. A line of colored flags hung like washing across the center of the court, dropping almost to head height in the middle. Real washing or bedding being aired hung from half the balconies.

Nor were there only swordsmen. Wallie saw slaves and cooks and dozens of other civilians he could not identify at a distance. Many of them were women. Fairground! He disapproved, and he thought Shonsu's instincts did, also.

The herald was not the only one to have been alerted, for a Seventh and some Sixths were waiting at the base of the steps, and as Wallie came through the archway a blaring fanfare exploded from a balcony directly above his head. It raised a cloud of pigeons from the roof, reverberated off the walls, drowned the racket completely, and then was itself swallowed by a roll of drums that left his ears ringing. The dueling stopped. A last chanted sutra faded into a respectful and merciful silence. At least a thousand eyes turned to examine the long-awaited seventh Seventh and his companions.

The Seventh at the bottom of the steps had to be the castellan, Tivanixi. He was little older than Shonsu—probably about thirty—slim and poised and handsome. His ponytail was longer than most, wavy, and the same golden-brown shade as his skin. His kilt and harness were an unusual cobalt blue, his boots the same, and everything he wore looked expensive and elegant—except his sword hilt, which was starkly plain. That was obviously a calculated effect and quite impressive—in fact he was an impressive sight altogether.

Even before the herald spoke, while the trumpets were still screaming, the smile of welcome faded from his face. Speed was more valuable than strength to swordsmen. Big men were rare. Giant, black-haired Sevenths were . . . unique. This could only be his predecessor, and Tivanixi would not be human were he not then wondering whether Shonsu had returned to reclaim his job. Shonsu, who collected dead men's swords? Shonsu, rumored to be a tool of the sorcerers? Then his eyes switched to Nnanji, stepping into place on Wallie's left, and surprise showed, also. A red-haired Fourth? That mysterious hero from the battle of Ov must have been the subject of much discussion, and here was such a man at the side of Shonsu. The Sixths behind him were still smiling. Tivanixi, Wallie concluded, was a fast thinker.

The human bullfrog took a leisurely breath and then raised the birds again, outdoing the trumpets in volume. "My lords . . . in the name of the Goddess . . . and in the ways and traditions of your honorable and ancient craft . . . give welcome to the valiant Lord . . . *SHONSU* . . . swordsman of the seventh rank."

Shock!

Disgust!

Incredulity!

Superstitious creepy feelings?

For a moment Wallie stood and enjoyed the drama, then he drew his sword and made the salute to a company. A buzz of conversation like a plague of bees began and grew steadily louder. All smiles had vanished except one—Tivanixi's was now back in place.

Wallie walked down the steps and silence fell once more, as if the onlookers had not believed their ears and wanted to hear that name spoken again. And again Wallie drew, to make the salute to an equal.

The castellan responded, confirming his identity, maintaining a wary smile of greeting and displaying a confident and easy grace in his sword movements. To an experienced eye like Shonsu's, even those were revealing. "I am Tivanixi, swordsman of the seventh rank, castellan of the lodge in Casr; I am honored by your courtesy and do most humbly extend the same felicitations to your noble self-and-welcome-to-the-lodge-and-to-the-tryst-my-lord."

That very fast addition had perhaps made him host, therefore immune to challenge. It was debatable, for the visitor had not requested hospitality.

The Sixths were edging gently backward. They did not wish to be presented. The crowd was silent, intent, frowning.

"I did not come to join the tryst."

More shock from the onlookers, increased wariness from the castellan. "It is a holy cause to which the Goddess has summoned Her swordsman, my lord."

Wallie bowed his head slightly. "Certainly! I stop here only in passing, though. I have two items of business to attend to."

That might be a threat? "What other business is more important than a tryst?" Tivanixi demanded. The onlookers at the limit of hearing were shushing those farther away, but most of the swordsmen present were listening intently.

"An oath."

For a moment Wallie thought that Tivanixi was going to point out that a quick visit to the temple could dispose of an inconvenient oath . . . but discretion prevailed.

"In what way may we be of assistance, then?"

Wallie raised his voice until the echoes rolled. "A sad duty and a pleasant one. Sadly I bring news of two honorable and valorous swordsmen slain by pirates on their way here. I performed justice upon the guilty."

The news was digested in silence.

"The happier task is to seek promotion for two swordsmen. Lord castellan, may I have the honor..." Wallie presented Nnanji of the Fourth, protégé and oath brother. Thana he omitted for the time being.

Tivanixi, sheathing his sword after the response, could not restrain his curiosity. "We have heard of a red-haired Fourth who led a battle against the ungodly in Ov, adept."

Nnanji looked boyish and ungainly compared to the suave Tivanixi, but he smiled triumphantly and said, almost shouting, "That battle was led by Lord Shonsu, my lord. I helped, but the honor is his."

More surprise and whispers. Tivanixi beamed. "That is good news, my lord! We must summon minstrels and have that noble encounter recorded. The facts may have not been correctly reported here."

Wallie released a trace of a smile to show that he knew what had been reported.

"Before that, let us honor the fallen, my lord," he said. "I believe that there are swordsmen here from the Kingdom of Plo and Fex?"

"Let us honor the greater dead first," replied the castellan with a curious expression on his face now. "Newcomers are shown our memorial, the cause that led to the calling of this tryst." He half turned, pointed to the row of limp flags hanging across the center of the court, and then studied Lord Shonsu's expression.

Flags? Curious flags! Brown at the ends, then orange, red, a couple of greens, and a solitary blue in the middle? Not flags. Kilts! Some were torn, some burned, and the stains could only be blood. Wallie was sure his face had turned pale, which must be providing the onlookers with satisfaction.

"Explain?" he stuttered.

"They were returned to Casr by a sailor, acting on a request from a certain Lord Rotanxi, who calls himself wizard of Sen." Tivanixi's voice was grim. "The next day I called this tryst—which the Holiest has blessed."

So these were the remains of Shonsu's ill-fated attack on Vul?

To return the clothes and trappings of the fallen was a swordsmen courtesy. To send the kilts alone had probably been intended as an insult. Tivanixi had cleverly turned the insult into a challenge, shame into glory. Wallie had hardly taken in that thought, when he was struck by another—the sorcerers had deliberately provoked the tryst, or something like it. Did Tivanixi realize that he might be swallowing dangerous bait?

And the blue kilt must have belonged to Shonsu. It did look marginally larger than those hanging nearby. Wallie would cheerfully have given his hairclip to be certain, but he would have to assume that there had been no other Sevenths on that ill-fated venture. Surely it would have been out of character for Shonsu to share command?

The swordsmen were waiting for him. The ritual was clear: He was expected to go forward and make the salute to the dead—to his own kilt? He nodded to Nnanji, who had turned vaguely green, and then he started to march, the crowd parting for him. He passed between two stone benches, then through a gap in the first row of hurdles. He could hear Nnanji's boots behind him and he signed to him to stop.

The line of kilts hung over the second row of hurdles. The blue kilt was the lowest, in the middle. Without breaking stride, Wallie jumped up on the bar, drew his sword, swung it overhead, leaped backward before he lost his balance, and had the blade sheathed as he reached the ground again. Not a bad feat of swordsman gymnastics at all! The blue kilt flopped down to the ground. He turned and retraced his steps to a proper distance, where Nnanji was waiting for him, wide-eyed but approving.

They made the salute together, then headed back to Tivanixi and the silent circle of onlookers.

"That one was a forgery, my lord," Wallie said. "The rest need be avenged, but not that." He had no idea what had happened to Shonsu—he might even have escaped without his kilt, for he had been a Nameless One when he had arrived at Hann. No one else seemed to know either, perhaps not even the sorcerers.

Tivanixi's suspicion had not decreased—what sort of a leader is the only survivor?

"I have minstrels here, Lord Shonsu. Will you list for us the names of the fallen, so that they may be revered?"

How to handle that one? This was like fencing in the dark. Worse! Yet forty-nine names after half a year—even in this preliterate culture, that would be asking much.

"No, my lord. Neither names nor ranks. Let them be equal in glory."

"Then recount to us their heroism and the abomination of sorcery that slew them."

Wallie was sweating now, and hoping it did not show too much. He had been so worried over his own blunders that he had forgotten he would be blamed for Shonsu's also. "Nor that, either."

Hostility burned in silence around him. A general loses an army and then refuses to discuss the matter?

No one argued with a swordsman of the Seventh, except possibly another. Tivanixi seemed to be on the point of doing so, but he was bound by the ways of honor—he could not call on assistance from the troops standing beside him. He could accept this refusal, or he could challenge.

Or he could call for a denunciation.

The castellan's face was granite hard. "And you will not join the tryst and seek vengeance, my lord?"

Wallie shook his head. "I have an oath to fulfill, my lord."

"But the Goddess brought you here?" Perhaps Tivanixi and the others were wondering to which god that oath had been sworn.

"She did," Wallie said, and saw the suspicion relax a trifle, the bewilderment increase. "But about Plo?" he insisted. "Call up your heralds, Lord Tivanixi."

A voice said, "I am from Plo, my lords." A nervous-looking Third pushed his way to the front. He saluted the castellan and then Wallie. His harness was studded with topazes.

Wallie turned to Tivanixi. "The minstrels?"

The castellan waved a hand at a group of civilians jostling for access. The swordsmen reluctantly opened to let a dozen or so press through, then closed to shut out the rest. Minstrels came in all shapes and sexes. Wallie noted a fat, elderly woman of the Fourth, and two bony men in yellow loincloths, and a very tall youth at the back, peering over everyone. Minstrels wore their hair long and they all carried lutes on their backs. Lutes were their facemarks, also.

Taking the bundle of kilts and harnesses from Jja, and the two swords from Katanji, Wallie began the story. He did not mention his advice to Polini, but he stressed the man's lonely day-long stand and he thought he told it rather well. Then he asked Nnanji if he had anything to add, and Nnanji gave the final, pathetic conversation, word for word.

The swordsmen had forgotten any other business they might have had. This Shonsu was the day's event, and they had all clustered around to listen. As Nnanji was speaking, Wallie noticed more of them streaming in the gate. None were leaving. At the end of the tale the minstrels asked a couple of questions, then bowed and withdrew to compose the official version. Minstrels necessarily had Nnanji-type memories, of course, as well as good voices. They took with them—for background information, Wallie supposed—the Third from Plo, who was clutching the bundle and the swords, and not even trying to hold back his sobs.

Tivanixi looked angry and puzzled. Lord Shonsu could apparently behave in a proper swordsman fashion when he chose to, but why honor two and not forty-nine?

"Now your promotions, my lord," he said, "and then we shall call more minstrels to hear of the events at Ov."

Wallie nodded.

Tivanixi glanced at Thana's sailor costume and smiled knowingly. "Adept Nnanji, we have a wide selection of opponents to offer you, but space has become a problem. Promotions have been going through here like sheep pellets. We have been forced to limit fencing to these small areas, but if you wish to go outside in the plaza, we could arrange that."

Nnanji grinned and said that he would try to do his best in the cramped conditions. Apparently this routine affair was going to receive the castellan's personal attention, which suited Wallie. He was aware of the murderous suspicion and resentment around him. He felt like a mouse in a snakepit and he knew that only the ways of honor were protecting him. Tivanixi doubtless wanted to keep an eye on Shonsu. Shonsu was happy to stay close to Tivanixi.

There had to be more formalities, of course. A reluctant Sixth was selected as the second judge and presented. Wallie made sure that Jja was safely positioned between Thana and Katanji, behind one of the stone benches. Then he followed Nnanji and the judges into the fencing area. The crowd spread along the hurdles that formed one side, and along the roped benches and statues that made the other three.

Tivanixi glanced over the spectators and carefully selected a Fifth, who was naturally several years older than Nnanji, and who made a joke about infanticide, which raised a laugh. Nnanji smiled tolerantly and said nothing. There was no need to review the rules—promotions required two matches, best of three. Tivanixi called for the fencing to begin.

Lunge!

"One!" Nnanji called.

"Agreed!" said the judges, somewhat startled. "Continue!"

Lunge! Parry! Riposte!

"Two!" Nnanji said. "Next one please."

The Fifth departed in shocked humiliation. The crowd was stunned to silence, but it seemed to ripple, and suddenly Fifths were as rare as dinosaurs in the courtyard. Tivanixi sent Wallie a broad and quite genuine-looking smile. It suited him. For the moment, suspicions could be forgotten in the pleasure of good swordsmanship and the shared superiority of high rank.

"Strange!" he said. "There were some here a moment ago." He sprang lightly up on a bench, glanced over the heads, and called a name. The crowd parted to admit a heavyset, swarthy Fifth, younger than the first, but obviously reluctant and angry at not having escaped in time.

The second match lasted no longer. The courtyard erupted in cheers. When Nnanji's grin emerged from the mask, Wallie matched it and shook his hand.

Now came the sutra test, which was dull, and the crowd indulged itself in discussion and muttering. The lodge standards were high. The judges called for sutra after sutra. Nnanji spouted them all at top speed, without a moment's hesitation. They shifted to tricky ones, and he never broke stride.

Tivanixi threw up his hands and rose. "I had heard that Lord Shonsu was a great teacher," he said. "Master Nnanji, I congratulate you on the most impressive promotion I have ever seen."

Nnanji beamed. "Thank you, my lord."

The castellan glanced at Wallie and then back to the new Fifth. "You would not care to try for Sixth?"

Nnanji gave his mentor a reproachful look. "Unfortunately I do not know all the sutras required for that rank, my lord."

Tivanixi looked surprised, but he nodded sympathetically. "Many good swordsmen find them the hard part."

"Very true," Wallie said sadly—and Nnanji glared at him furiously.

"And now my wife?" Nnanji demanded.

Tivanixi pulled a face and studied Wallie thoughtfully, perhaps wondering if this was some sort of trap to justify a challenge. He evidently decided it was not, and smiled once more. "I never heard of a female swordsman having the audacity even to approach a lodge, let alone seek promotion there. However, Master Nnanji, in your case I will allow an exception. Present her."

The onlookers muttered, but Thana was presented and Tivanixi found himself being charmed against his will.

"Two Thirds, I assume, apprentice?" he said, smiling.

"Fourths!" Thana said.

Wallie choked back an objection. Certainly Thana could make a good try at the fencing, for this confined space would suit her water-rat style admirably and confound her opponents, but he was almost certain that she did not know enough sutras even for Third. . . . He turned to question Nnanji and got a big grin. Nnanji must have been giving her more lessons than they had revealed. Wallie shrugged and the chance to intervene had passed. Then he decided that there had been something very strange about that grin of Nnanji's . . .

Tivanixi rolled his eyes at some of the watching Sixths. He started a hunt for opponents. The first two Fourths he asked turned him down at once. He gave Wallie a what-do-you-expect look, but on the third attempt he found one. Word that the good-looking female was going to fence provoked much grumbling and talk of heresy. Nevertheless the crowd congealed once more around the site, and some juniors clambered into trees for a better view.

Thana started with a big advantage: her opponent had surely never fought a woman before. He also badly underestimated her, then got rattled when he lost the first pass. She won the second point, also. By now bets were being placed at the back of the crowd and the old arguments about the legality of female swordsmen were being rehashed.

It should have been hard to find another Fourth willing to risk his reputation, but Thana was accustomed to having her own way. She picked out a tall young man and smiled at him bewitchingly. He was about to refuse, but his companions pushed him forward, laughing. Wallie guessed at once, and his guess was very soon confirmed. Thana had stumbled on a sleeper—he was at least a good Fifth, and would likely have given even a Sixth a fair match. He was as good as Nnanji! Certainly he could have wiped Thana off the court as easily as Nnanji had disposed of his opponents, but he chose instead to toy with her. The crowd understood, and the laughter began. Thana leaped and lunged and cut, and the Fourth hardly shifted his feet, as if he could do this all day. He never let her foil come close to him . . . a wildcat fighting a rainbow.

Nnanji turned blood-red with fury, growling about sleepers. Even the judges were grinning. Thana was young and fit, but she began to flag at last.

By then calls for a draw had begun at the back of the crowd. They grew louder and more numerous. The candidate had demonstrated her swordsmanship, and an outright win was not required. The judges at last agreed. The mood had changed. Prejudice had been overcome by professional admiration—and some sympathy. Male enjoyment of watching a nubile female body in motion was probably not without influence, either.

After a pause for the candidate to recover her breath—and for Wallie to persuade Nnanji that he need not challenge the smirking Fourth—it was time for the sutra test. The two judges sat opposite Thana, three swords crossed on the ground between them. The crowd lost interest and some wandered away. Tivanixi began six thirty-five, "On the Design of a Fortress," and Wallie groaned, for it was long, dull, hard, and not one he had ever heard her try. Thana smiled back at Wallie and chanted the words slowly and carefully. She stumbled twice, recovered, and reached the end safely. The Sixth began another, and she got that right, too. Wallie was bewildered—how did she do that? He turned to

Nnanji beside him and received a triumphant super-grin. Yet there was something wrong with that grin, also. It did not seem to be conveying quite the right message.

Nnanji went back to studying the examination—six thirteen, "On Long-distance Marching," smiling encouragingly. Wallie stared at him, then looked around, then back at Thana.

Sudden understanding hit him like an earthquake.

Thana was using sorcery.

†† ††

When Wallie had gone ashore at Aus, the sorcerers had known what he had said to Jja before he had left *Sapphire*'s deck. The sorcerer who had come aboard in Wal had known Brota's name. The port officials were being kept honest in all the sorcerer cities except Ov—and at Ov there were no warehouses overlooking the moorings.

When Katanji had infiltrated the tower at Sen he had seen a female sorcerer rubbing a plate on something—casting a spell, he had thought. Grinding a lens?

Now Wallie looked again along the line of spectators beside him. At least half of them were moving their lips. Nnanji was—he always did. Wallie looked back at Thana, and her eyes were flickering to and fro along that gallery of faces. Then she glanced at him and in silence he mouthed the words: "You are cheating, Thana."

The candidate stuttered and stopped her chanting.

"I cannot keep a secret from Nnanji," Wallie said, still silent. "He is my oath brother."

She started up again and stumbled once more. The watchers held their breath, like an audience when an actor gets stage fright. The lip-moving became more obvious, but there was no sound.

"He will kill you, Thana." That might be an exaggeration, but perhaps not much of one. Honakura and Wallie had worked very hard on Nnanji to soften his rigid, implacable standards. From them he had learned mercy and tolerance, until he had even been able to forgive the killing of swordsmen by civilians—under very exceptional circumstances. But there were no exceptional circumstances here. Thana was blatantly cheating. Nnanji's fury and shame would have no limit.

"Start again," Tivanixi suggested helpfully.

Thana flushed scarlet. "No, I think not, my lord."

Nnanji ran forward to help her rise and give her a hug of condolence. The judges politely wished her better luck next time and congratulated her on her swordsmanship.

Wallie was exultant. The last mystery solved! The final veil had been torn off the sorcerers for him and he owed it to Thana's ambition!

Wallie brought his attention back to Tivanixi with a start. "I beg pardon, my lord?"

The castellan had his hand on the shoulder of a young First, who held a rack of foils. "I asked if you would care for a pass or two yourself, Lord Shonsu? We both know how hard it is for Sevenths to find good practice."

Wallie was about to refuse until he saw that Tivanixi was studying him very intently and with obvious suspicion. Perhaps the castellan was not quite at the point of suspecting a zombie, but he now wanted to check this mysterious stranger's credentials. Nnanji had proved that he was a genuine swordsman—was his companion also one, or was he an imposter?

Wallie, for his part, was curious about this graceful and gracious Seventh. And he dared not refuse, anyway. "Why not?" he said. "Best of five?" He selected a foil, the longest he could find.

Tivanixi, wanting no burdens, removed his sword and handed it to a nearby Sixth. Wallie copied him, giving his to Nnanji. Then he slipped between the benches once more, onto the fencing ground.

If the leadership was to be decided by combat, then the Sevenths would have been testing one another out with foils under the guise of practice. The final battle with real blades would likely be a pure formality, which the minstrels would adorn with blood and drama for the general public and future generations; swordsmen admired courage, but they were not utterly brainless.

The word had gone out and the crowd reassembled yet again.

The balconies filled up by some sort of telepathy, and the noise dwindled.

The opponents faced off, took each other's foils cautiously, and feinted a few times. The castellan had the grace of a ballet dancer, smooth as a sunbeam. He was very good, indeed, and very fast, and he proceeded to give Wallie his first real test since the god had made him a swordsman. They leaped and bounded in landlubber style, very unlike the deadly, close-in fencing of the water rats. Tivanixi, of course, had several other Sevenths to play with now, whereas Shonsu had not had practice on this level since before Wallie took him over.

The crowd muttered or cheered from time to time, but mostly just watched. Feint—thrust—parry—riposte—back and forth they clattered.

"One!"

Wallie learned a few things and taught a few more, but if there was another swordsman equal to Shonsu, this was not he.

"Two!"

They paused for a moment's panting, then went to guard again. Clatter . . . clatter . . . Then some loud voices, some disturbance among the spectators; Wallie's attention flickered momentarily from that shimmering silver haze that the castellan brandished.

"One!" Tivanixi exulted.

Damn! Shonsu should be winning this on straight points. Wallie growled angrily and drove in hard, forcing Tivanixi back against the barricade, where footwork would count for less.

"Three!" Wallie said; best of five.

They removed the masks and breathlessly thanked each other. The crowd applauded loudly for a fine match and began to discuss the form sheet, doubtless with many comments that this Shonsu might have lost an army, but was certainly a good man with metal.

Wallie yielded mask and foil back to the First and accepted a towel. Wiping and panting, he headed toward his companions, expecting smiles. Instead he saw warning looks and glances to his rear. He spun around. Two Sevenths stood behind the far hurdles.

Damnation!

He almost lost Shonsu's diabolical temper on the spot.

True, he had revealed his style and his abilities to Tivanixi, but that had been a fair exchange. He had not planned on giving a free demonstration to these two. They were quite within their rights in being there, but he felt as if he had been spied upon. A surge of fury came burning up his throat and red fringes flickered inside his eyelids. He made a huge effort to force that berserker madness back down again, balling his fist to keep it from making the sign of challenge.

One of the Sevenths could be dismissed at a glance, but the other . . .

The popular favorite was somebody called Boariyi, Nnanji had said. The other Seventh was taller than Shonsu, and that was unfair; Wallie had met almost no one taller than himself in the World. He was also younger. Unfair again; Shonsu was a very young Seventh, and Wallie was proud of that.

This must be a Boariyi. He was a human mantis, a basketball player, obviously built from a sutra on giraffes. His kilt was a thin blue tube around gibbon hips and thighs like baseball bats. He had a jaw too big for his head and a mouth too wide for his jaw and a single dark slash of eyebrow across the top of his ugly face, and he was standing with one leg vertical and the other sloped, with golf club arms crossed over a birdcage chest, head slightly tilted to one side, gazing at Wallie with a supercilious smirk on oversize rubbery lips.

In that moment of fury the decision was made.

You sneaky, arrogant young lout! Wallie thought—and it was all he could do not to shout the thought aloud. *Think you can take me, do you? Well, Mister Boariyi, if that's your name, I'll tell you this: You'll be leader of this tryst only over my dead body!*

For a moment longer Wallie stood alone in the middle of the fencing area, aware that his fury must be blazing in his face and obvious to the crowd. Then the tableau was broken by the older of the two newcomers. He drew his sword and made the salute to an equal . . . Zoariyi, swordsman of the Seventh.

He was a slight, short, and wiry man, gray haired, well into middle age. However great his skill, his speed would be deserting him now, which was why Shonsu's instincts had rejected him as a threat. He wore the unadorned garb of a free and he was conspicuously scarred. He had the same continuous eyebrow as his younger companion and his name was very similar—father and son?

Wallie grabbed a foil from the startled First and made his response with it. It was intended as an insult, and Zoariyi frowned.

Then the beanpole beside him drew his sword—a very long sword, of course—and perfunctorily saluted without shifting from his slouched, hip-tilted stance. His smirk did not change. He was indeed Boariyi, the popular favorite. With those arms the reason was obvious.

Wallie used the foil again. The kid's contemptuous amusement increased. One of his facemarks was not quite healed.

He might be little older than Nnanji, and that was ridiculous for a Seventh. Thirty was normal. Indeed the system was designed to prevent youngsters from advancing too quickly. Systems always are. By the time a man had mastered eleven hundred and forty-four sutras, fought his way up through the six lower ranks, found a Seventh as mentor, and then could manage to find two Sevenths together as examiners—which must be extremely rare—he had to be at least thirty. How Shonsu had managed it sooner, Wallie could not guess. Nnanji was going to do better, because of his memory, and because he had found a mentor who really cared, and who could teach well.

All of which suggested that Zoariyi was the power behind Boariyi.

Wallie took another look at the older man and decided that, yes, he might be a great deal shrewder than that smirking pituitary malfunction beside him. Then he swung around and strolled over to the bench behind which Nnanji was standing. "My sword now, please," he said loudly.

Nnanji was staring in doubt at his mentor, but he was about to hand over the seventh sword . . .

"Let me see that!" Tivanixi demanded sharply. Nnanji reacted instinctively to the tone of authority and handed the seventh sword to the castellan.

He studied the griffon on the hilt, the sapphire in its beak, and then the blade; especially the blade. Wallie passed his foil back to the First, returned a grin from Katanji and a smile from Jja, and continued to wipe at himself with the towel. The crowd waited.

"Shonsu!" Thana whispered urgently, and he looked at her in surprise. She was staring past him, toward Boariyi. "Don't challenge!" she hissed.

Wallie resisted the temptation to turn around.

"No matter what!" she added in the same whisper.

"This is a remarkable sword, Lord Shonsu!" The castellan had a strange expression on his face.

Wallie smiled and nodded.

"May I ask where you got this?"

"It was given me," Wallie said.

Tivanixi directed a calculating stare at him. "It looks as if it came fresh from the forge yesterday."

Wallie smiled blandly. "Not quite—one previous owner."

Tivanixi paled. "Do you mean what I think you mean?"

"Yes."

The castellan gazed at him hard and long. "Yet you will not join the tryst?"

Wallie shook his head. "I'm still considering."

Tivanixi's eyes shifted toward Boariyi and Zoariyi, then back to Wallie. "I would not wear this," he said quietly.

Wallie thought of young Arganari and the Chioxin topaz. The boy would have borne that priceless heirloom for only a few minutes after it was formally given to him. Then he would have been quickly given another to wear.

"We all must bear our burdens," Wallie said. He took the seventh sword back from Tivanixi, who continued to stare at him in bewilderment.

A voice said: "The name of Shonsu is well known in this lodge."

Wallie turned around to face Boariyi and unobtrusively sheathed his sword.

"The name of Boariyi, however, is not."

The kid's eyes narrowed. "Not all reputations are good."

"But nothing is still nothing."

Boariyi's hand twitched and the older man growled something quietly. There was a forest of green Sixths behind those two Sevenths, and a desert of red-kilted Fifths behind them—and they were not pressing in to the barricades as the rest of the audience was. They were standing in proper military form, behind their superiors. Boariyi, as popular favorite, had collected a large following—and disciplined it.

Wallie turned back to face his own entourage. Nnanji was frowning and moving his lips as if reviewing sutras. Katanji had lost his grin. Thana flashed another warning glance at Wallie and went back to studying the opponents.

"His uncle," Tivanixi remarked quietly, to no one special.

With a warm rush of relief, Wallie realized that the castellan was now on his side.

Boariyi called across the fencing ground once more. "You have come to join the tryst, I suppose, Lord Shonsu?"

Wallie turned again.

"No."

That was a surprise, and Boariyi glanced down at the man who must be his uncle, if Tivanixi's remark meant anything.

"It is an honorable cause, for honorable men."

"I am sure it is," Wallie replied calmly.

"Afraid of the sorcerers?"

The audience gasped in unison. That was grounds for opening arteries.

Wallie's hand had started to rise before he remembered Thana's warning and lowered it again. Was this to be the combat for leadership—no formalities, just a vulgar squabble escalating to challenge? Then he understood. He was going to be baited into making the challenge—and Boariyi would refuse it, claiming that Shonsu was not a man of honor. In the absence of witnesses and a prepared case, a denunciation would be dangerous, for if an accuser failed to prove his charges, then he must pay the penalty. This way was safer because Tivanixi, as host and interim leader of the tryst, would have to judge. All Boariyi would be risking, at worst, was having to accept the challenge, while in the meantime he would have been able to drag out all the unsubstantiated rumors in support of his position. It was a sneaky plan, obviously the brainchild of the older, more experienced Zoariyi. If Wallie refused to rise to the bait, he would be exposed as a coward. His only defense was to try to force a challenge out of Boariyi, for that would be an admission that Wallie was a man of honor. Not that it would work, but it was all he could do.

He walked slowly across to the middle of the fencing area, letting the tension build, frantically trying to think up some ammunition, and unhappily aware that a fight was almost inevitable now . . . and that Boariyi thought he was the better man.

"Let me ask you a question, sonny, before I answer that. Have you ever seen a sorcerer?"

Boariyi scowled angrily. "Not yet. But—"

"Well, I have!" Wallie shouted. "And I will answer your question. Yes, I am afraid of sorcerers. Have you seen that?" He pointed up at the line of kilts hanging over the court behind Boariyi's head. "Any man who knows what that means and yet is not afraid of sorcerers is too dumb to be allowed out of the womb. But being afraid doesn't mean that you can't fight them! We killed fourteen at Ov, my young friend, so I haven't quite paid off the score yet. But I'm fourteen ahead of you."

"No, Shonsu! You're thirty-five behind."

Ouch! The kid was not as dumb as he looked.

"You plan to be leader of the tryst, do you, sonny?"

"If that is the will of the Goddess." Boariyi was obviously confident that it was.

Almost the whole tryst must be present now, standing in silent fascination at this confrontation between Sevenths.

"You'd better learn to count better than that, then," Wallie roared, hearing his voice booming back from the walls. "Eleven years ago in Aus: eighteen swordsmen killed by twenty sorcerers wielding thunderbolts, and at least another dozen killed there since. Four years before that, in Wal: thirty-two swordsmen killed by twenty-eight sorcerers. And about two years ago a party of four swordsmen came ashore . . ."

He had learned how to do without notebooks—he used Nnanji, and the two of them had been over these numbers a hundred times. One by one he went around the cities of the loop, calling out the ghastly toll . . . Aus and Wal and Sen and Cha and Gor . . . the whole garrison with one thunderbolt at Gor. Perhaps this was all recorded somewhere in the libraries of Vul, but he was certain that no swordsman had ever worked it out before. He had gathered this information—Katanji and Honakura and the sailors had gathered it, quietly asking questions and listening in the sorcerer towns. Fifteen years of sorcerer infiltration and fifteen years of rank stupidity by swordsmen. None of them had learned a thing in fifteen years. And Amb and Ov . . . forty men ripped to pieces in Ov. . .

"So add it all up, sonny," he concluded. "Add in the forty-nine and you'll come up with three hundred and thirty dead swordsmen. That's the best estimate I can make. How many did you make it? Will you try for *thirteen* hundred and thirty?"

The echoes died away into stunned silence. Boariyi and his uncle looked as shocked as anyone. Everyone was shocked. Lord Shonsu had scared the kilts off the entire tryst of Casr with his litany of death. It was Zoariyi who recovered first.

"You were castellan here, Lord Shonsu! Why did you not act sooner? Why did you not call this holy tryst?"

For a moment Wallie considered challenging him instead of his nephew, but the same problem arose: He would refuse.

"Thank the Goddess I did not, Lord Zoariyi!" Again he pointed to the pathetic line of kilts hanging over the court. "It would have been a thousand kilts there, not fifty. I did not know how to fight sorcerers! But now I do. I proved that at Ov!"

He turned and stalked away. Hopefully they would let it rest now, while they thought about it. Tavanixi's face was pale—Shonsu was imperiling his tryst.

He had barely moved when Boariyi spoke again: "But you wouldn't attack the tower in Ov? What sort of leader calls off his men when he has victory within his grasp?"

Ov was safer ground. Wallie beckoned to Katanji, who jumped in shock and clattered his cast against a rack of foils, then reluctantly came forward. Wallie faced him toward Boariyi and stood behind him with his hands on his shoulders, looking over his head.

"This, my lords, is Novice Katanji, my oath brother's protégé, and therefore mine, also. I shan't present him, because he can't salute with an injured arm." *And you might not respond, which would force me to challenge*. "It was broken by a sorcerer's thunderbolt." He raised his voice even higher, over the sudden clamor. "All of you, take note! This boy is the bravest man in this courtyard. He has been ashore in every one of the sorcerer towns, risking a terrible death every time. He was captured at Ov, and we rescued him. He has been inside one of the towers and has seen what is in there—probably he is the only swordsman in the history of the World who has done that and lived."

He had to wait for the sensation to die down.

"How large is a tower, Lord Boariyi? How thick are the walls, Lord Boariyi? How many doors, Lord Boariyi? How high are the first windows, Lord Boariyi? You don't know, Lord Boariyi? But Novice Katanji does! He's forgotten more about sorcerers than you'll ever know, Lord Boariyi. And I say he's better fitted to lead this tryst than you'll ever be!"

"Stop!" Tivanixi came marching forward and stood between the two factions. "This is not a proper discussion to be held in public. Lord Zoariyi, Lord Boariyi, you will excuse us. Lord Shonsu, I wish a word with you in private!"

Whew! Saved!

Tivanixi herded Wallie and Katanji back to the others. "Master Nnanji, you need to see our facemarker. We have a tailor here who can provide you with the kilt you have so richly earned. Lord Shonsu, perhaps we could visit the museum together?"

Wallie nodded. "You will see that my friends are not harassed?"

Tivanixi frowned and snapped his fingers to bring a Sixth. He gave orders, then looked expectantly at Wallie. "Lead the way, Lord Shonsu."

"After you Lord Tivanixi," Wallie said politely.

†† † ††

Tivanixi headed toward the southwest corner, and a quick glance showed Wallie that there was a doorway in each corner of the great rectangle. From the shapes of the windows, he could guess that each opened into a stairwell. A nice, simple architectural plan, he mused cynically—not so complicated that swordsmen might get confused.

The stairs wound up and up, the treads of the lower flights dished by generations of swordsman boots. The lower floors of the lodge were noisy and smelled of bodies, but as the two Sevenths climbed higher, the sounds died away, and the steps were less worn. The air grew cool and musty until finally the men reached the top, sneaking glances at each other to see which was puffing harder.

"Think we can manage the bar?" the castellan asked.

There was only one door, and the gigantic iron bar across it was fit with six handles, not four.

"I always did it one-handed," Wallie said modestly, but it was a struggle for two men to lift the monster and set it down without crushing feet, or wrenching things necessary for swordwork. The floor there was scored and gouged and had been patched a few times, he noticed. It took three men or two strong ones to rob the museum. There were no locks in the World.

The massive door opened with a groan of pain. The swordsmen walked into a long gallery, smelling of mice and rot and sheer antiquity. Along one side were windows fogged over with dust; the opposite wall was paneled and hung with hundreds of rust-spotted swords. The floor was filthy with litter and crumbling rubbish, cluttered by a line of wormy tables bearing miscellaneous heaps of anonymous relics. Overhead, remnants of banners trailed down from the ceiling, webbed, shredded by insects, and faded to a uniform gray in the dim, cold light. Even the air felt old. One of the windows rattled continuously in the wind.

Wallie shivered as he followed Tivanixi's footsteps along that mournful room. The castellan stopped and lifted a fragment of a sword blade from the wall.

"The ruby," he said. "The fifth. Or so it is said." He swept the fragment across the top of the nearest table, showering garbage to the floor, raising a cloud of rancid dust. Then he laid it down, and Wallie placed the seventh sword beside it.

Tivanixi bent to compare them. Wallie took a walk down to the end of the room and back. He had never seen a place that depressed him more; designed to honor the valor of young men whose names were forgotten, whose very descendants must have forgotten them . . . those who had survived to have descendants. The honored kilts in the courtyard would be brought here one day, with ceremony and pomp perhaps, and empty words. The mice would rejoice, and within a generation the kilts would be a nameless heap of filth like the rest of this junk.

He turned to inspect the myraid blades on the wall, of every possible design and quality. Most were very long swords, he noticed. Perhaps the men of the People were getting smaller, but more likely the usable weapons had been quietly pilfered away.

He rejoined Tivanixi, who was cleaning off a spot on the fragment with his whetstone so that he could study the damask. There was no hilt. It was just as Wallie had remembered it—long ago, it seemed now—in the only glimpse he had ever been given of Shonsu's personal memories: half a sword, with no hilt and no point. No point at all . . . just like this whole depressing junk room.

The chasing on the two blades was similar. Swordsmen battled mythical monsters on one side, maidens played with the same monsters on the other. The order was different and no pose was repeated exactly, but the superlative artistry was unmistakably the same.

"I am convinced," Tivanixi said, still studying.

Then he lifted the seventh and tested its balance and flexibility before handing it back to Wallie with a penetrating stare.

"It is too long for me," he said.

"But not for our skinny friend."

Tivanixi shook his head, leaned back against the table, and folded his arms across his cobalt harness.

"You did not know the way to this room, my lord."

"No, I didn't."

"You did not know Doa."

"Who?"

The castellan shrugged. "A minstrel . . . Shonsu should know Doa."

Wallie made his decision—but perhaps he had made it earlier. "I am Shonsu—and I am not Shonsu," he said. "I shall tell you, but you will have to decide for yourself whether I am sent by the Goddess, or by the sorcerers."

Tivanixi nodded. He was a brave man to come alone to this place with someone who might be a sorcerer, and the strain was showing in his eyes.

Wallie began, and he told the whole story of Wallie Smith and

Shonsu, and it took a long, long time. The castellan listened in silence, watching his face. Wallie, in turn, studied his reaction. Yes, this was an unusually intelligent swordsman—not a blustering bully, a cold-blooded killer as Shonsu must have been, not an impractical idealist like Nnanji had been once, not even a pig-headed showboat like Polini. With this man there might be hope of rational response . . . but could he believe?

When he finished, Tivanixi said, "And the only evidence is that sword?"

"There is a priest," Wallie said. "A Seventh from Hann."

Even in a World where few people knew the name of the next city—and that might change anyway—everyone had heard of Hann. Hann was Rome, Mecca, Jerusalem.

"And my parentmarks. I don't know what Shonsu's were, but not these, I am sure."

The castellan reached up, removed his hairclip, and looked expectantly at Wallie, who puzzled down into Shonsu's swordsman memories, for obviously this was a ritual. Then he reeled between two mental worlds. *He was letting his hair down!* The expression translated word for word and the absurdity of that equivalence collided with the paradox of Tivanixi's appearance in terrestrial terms: a handsome man in a skirt and leather harness, with wavy gold-brown hair streaming down around his shoulders. Yet this was the epitome of macho in the World, the role model for every red-blooded boy, the ultimate male sex symbol. If Wallie had allowed his lips to twitch he would have exploded into giggles. Letting his hair down! It did not mean quite the same, though. Here it meant: "I shall speak frankly," but it also meant "I shall not challenge; I waive the dictates of honor."

Keeping his face rigid, Wallie unclipped his sapphire and released his own black mane.

"As it happens I do know Shonsu's parentmarks," Tivanixi said. "You . . . he . . . left a few juniors here, Firsts and a couple of Seconds. One of them offered you foils today and you did not know him, either." He hesitated. "But there was a joke—both Shonsu's parentmarks were swords. It was said that both his parents were men."

Wallie guffawed. "Said behind his back?"

The castellan smiled. "A long way behind, I fancy."

It had been a test—this was not Shonsu.

"I accept that your sword is the seventh sword of Chioxin, my lord, but it does not show the wear of seven hundred years. No one knows where it has been. No royal family could have kept it secret this long . . . but a temple could. He gave it to the Goddess . . ."

"Say it!"

"You could have stolen it from the temple at Hann."

"I didn't. Talk to the priest."

Tivanixi began to pace, his boots echoing and sending up puffs of dust, scattering the mouse droppings.

Still pacing, he said, "I was about to denounce you. Your fencing made me hesitate, for if the sorcerers can create a swordsman like you, then we are all dead men. The sword confused me completely. Your tales of the sorcerers have made it worse, and yet if you have truly been scouting on the left bank, I am ashamed, for I called the tryst without knowing what I was calling it against. We need your counsel!"

"Leave the question open, then," Wallie said, "for the moment. You have another problem. Even assuming that I was sent by the gods, am I a man of honor? I have screwed things up mightily a couple of times. Especially at Aus. I went ashore—idiocy! Without my sword—more idiocy! I was captured and given the choice of dying on the spot or crawling back to my ship. I was on the docks. I could have jumped. Instead I crawled. Perhaps it was the wrong decision."

An odd expression came over Tivanixi's face. He went to stand at one of the windows, as if he could see out through the golden glare of the grime. "Very few swordsmen have not eaten dirt at one time or another," he said, very quietly.

That was news to Wallie. Shonsu's history was a blank to him; the only swordsman he knew well was Nnanji. He could not imagine Nnanji performing the ritual of abasement—but Nnanji was not cut from ordinary cloth.

"When I was a Second," Tivanixi said. "I was challenged. I had talked my way into the wrong bed." He had tried to make that sound humorous, but every muscle in his back had gone taut and his voice was barely audible. "He was two ranks above me and his eyes were red. He made the sign. I rolled over. He demanded the abasement. He even made me go and bring my friends to watch—and *I did it!* All the time I was telling myself that afterward I would go and wash my sword."

Wallie was fascinated . . . and stayed silent.

"I went down to the River," the castellan whispered to the window. "I stood on the edge of the water for an hour and my feet would not move. Then I went home and grew my hair back . . .

"I have never told anyone that before, my lord."

"I shall not repeat it," Wallie promised. "But you waded into the River when you called the tryst." Which was why Tivanixi could tell the story now, he thought.

The castellan laughed and turned around. "Oh—that was different. I had not just told myself I was going to do it, I had told everyone. There was a crowd! It was a ceremony. We had the remains of forty-nine bullocks still dying in front of us." He shivered. "But a very strange feeling!

"What I mean is," he continued, "that most of us have made obeisance at some time to swordsmen. You did it to sorcerers, that is all. If I had that on my conscience, I would not expect to have it thrown back in my face, except by someone who wanted to start a fight, and there are always ways of starting fights. But I don't know that I would try to become leader of a tryst, my lord."

Quite! "Ov was different. I make no apologies for Ov. I made the right decision."

Tivanixi nodded approvingly. "I think you did. You had no army, only an ad hoc rabble of swordsmen, no plan, no chain of command—you could not have even given orders, for you did not know their names. You were right—but only highranks know the sutras on strategy. The cubs will howl."

"Tell me what happens now," Wallie said.

The castellan shrugged and leaned back against the table again. "The ancient stories are not quite clear, but it seems that we must wait for seven Sevenths. When the last appears, then I proclaim the tryst and call for challenge."

He stared glumly down at his boots. "I hope he is not too rough."

A heavier than normal gust of wind played a tattoo with the

loose window. Wallie said, "I see that calling trysts is no task for small men, my lord. What if two challenge?"

"I fight the first and the surviv—the winner calls for challenges and then fights the next. When no one responds, that is the leader."

"Then tell me what happens if I challenge and win. Supposing I can beat Boariyi? Will they swear to me?"

He had to wait a long time for a reply, while Tivanixi studied his expensive boots and fingered his hair. At last he said, "I don't think so. Not to Shonsu. I think they would flee, or riot. But it will never come to that. Boariyi will denounce you. Zoariyi was improvising today—now he will have time to prepare a case, with witnesses who saw you in Aus. He may have men down at the docks already; they have plenty of men."

Wallie nodded glumly. "And Shonsu lost an army, or sold it. Now he has come back to sell another. . .The god gave me a hard task, Lord Tivanixi, even without my own follies."

The castellan nodded. "Tell me again of his riddle."

"Seven lines . . ." Wallie said. "First chain my brother, and I did that when Nnanji and I swore the fourth oath. The mighty spurned was my stupidity in Aus, so the god foresaw that. Turning the circle was my reconnaissance of the sorcerer cities, and I earned an army by saving *Sapphire* from pirates. Next to gain wisdom and I have done that—that was Katanji showing me the truth about the sorcerers. The last instruction is to return the sword, and that I do not understand yet."

Tivanixi smiled. "You have done that, too. According to local tradition, Chioxin was a Casr man."

Wallie swore quietly.

"That sword was made in this lodge."

Wallie nodded, thinking he could hear the shrill laughter of the little god. *You amuse me!* The gods had tricked him before and now they had tricked him again. He hoped it made them very happy.

"And you did not know that!" Tivanixi was studying Wallie thoughtfully. He seemed to approve of his surprise.

"So now I must accord to the destiny of the sword," Wallie said glumly. "To lead the tryst, obviously. Whoever bears it. At least three of the seven led trysts." Suddenly, chillingly, he saw why—a tryst was led by the best swordsman in the World. Any lesser man who wore one of the Chioxin masterpieces soon died. The epics did not mention that. Heroes were heroes.

"How much time is there?" he asked. "You cannot promote another Sixth?"

"Not very likely now," the castellan said, pacing again. He was speaking absently, his mind still wrestling with the bigger problem. "Of course the next boat may always bring someone . . . You would think that you could get more than two Sevenths out of three dozen Sixths, wouldn't you? But many are past their primes. A few are not there yet. Others never expected the opportunity and have not learned the sutras—why bother, when they were doing well as Sixths? Many are working on it, but it takes time. Some tried and failed and must wait until next year." He chuckled. "Honorable Fiendori and I have been together since we were Thirds. On a good day he can beat me like a drum . . . but sutras? Zoariyi asked him for nine twenty. He started in ten thirteen, detoured through eight seventy-two, and finished up in nine eighteen!"

He gave Wallie a long, long stare. Then he sighed. He had made his decision. Wallie had become too familiar with the seventh sword to appreciate the impact it had on a swordsman—its quality, its beauty, and its legend. In a world where only the sorcerers could read, the Goddess could hardly have given him a letter of introduction. *To whom it may concern: The bearer of this missive, our trusty and well-beloved Shonsu . . .* She had given him the next best thing, the greatest sword ever made, and Tivanixi had heard the message.

"I shall accept you, Lord Shonsu, as being sent by the Goddess, with Her sword. Obviously She wants us to have the benefit of your wisdom as well as your sword. But I warn you—if you are a traitor, I shall kill you myself, at any cost."

"I shall not betray your trust, my lord," Wallie said, astonished and delighted, shaking his hand warmly. Here was an invaluable ally—and potentially a good friend, he thought. Then he remembered his doubts in the night . . . whose side was he on? He strangled the memory quickly. He, also, had made a decision.

"One thing I have not heard, though," he said. "For what exact purpose did you call this tryst? If you are planning to wreak vengeance on the civilians of the left bank for harboring sorcerers, then I want no part of it."

The castellan picked up the fragment of the fifth sword and wandered over to replace it on its pegs. "I wanted to call it to avenge Shonsu." He chuckled. "That would have been a problem when you came back, wouldn't it? But there were rumors that you had been seen, and also the priests started spinning their webs of words, as usual, wanting to know how I could call sorcerers as witnesses, and so on. And none of us knew at that time how many cities had been taken! So we finally decided to keep it simple. We called the tryst of Casr 'To restore the honor of the swordsmen's craft.' Helpfully vague, yes?"

"Very good indeed!" Wallie said. That committed no one to anything and every swordsman must support it, but he wondered how the citizens of Casr felt about swordsmen's honor at the moment.

"And by nightfall the swordsmen were arriving," Tivanixi said proudly. He must have hoped to be leader, but he had earned his immortality as the man who called the tryst, the one whose prayer had been answered. "And now She has sent Her own sword!"

"But who will bear it?" Wallie asked. Now it was his turn to start pacing.

"He is the better swordsman, my lord. In eight or ten bouts, I have never touched him. Of course his reach is . . ." The castellan smiled. "Well, it's unfair! He is incredibly fast—and completely ambidextrous. Zoariyi has taught him every trick in the craft. You might do better if you had more practice. You are rusty as the ruby, Shonsu. I could tell."

"What sort of a leader would he make?" Wallie asked sadly. "His uncle is the brains?"

"Of course. But you know the blood oath—absolute power. He can tell his uncle to disembowel himself if he wants to, once he has sworn that oath. He might, too! If I cannot be leader, then I had rather you than he, my lord. You may yet be traitor, but Boariyi is sure disaster."

Wallie reached the far wall and started back. "How is he at leadership?"

Tivanixi snorted. "At his age?"

Wallie was surprised. He did not think that leadership depended very much on age—Nnanji certainly had it, and had proved so more than once. But a moment's thought showed him that this was a language problem, and perhaps a cultural one. To the swordsmen, leadership implied a certain public dignity, eminence, nobility . . . the word did not quite translate exactly.

"I believe that I am supposed to be leader. But I can't beat Boariyi, you say, and the tryst would not accept me anyway."

"You know how to fight these thunderbolts?"

Wallie shrugged. "They have at least three types of thunderbolt. Apart from that they are mostly fakes. Speed is the key, but it will not work against the towers. I have some ideas, though. If Boariyi were leader, would he take my advice?"

"I doubt it," Tivanixi said. "Just being a Seventh has gone to his head, and being liege lord will boil his brains." Obviously he bitterly resented this upstart Boariyi. "And you will have to give him the sword! He either did not notice it, or he has not heard of Chioxin, but one of his men will have told him by now. In fact," he said, with a worried frown, "it is surprising that he has not come looking for you already. He will certainly not let it escape from the lodge."

He went to the window and started wiping a pane, speaking over his shoulder. "Choose another, my lord! Take any one off the wall. I will say the words to give it to you, and you can put it in your scabbard."

Wallie discovered that he was a man of more honor than that. To walk out with a rusty old relic on his back and the seventh sword under his arm would be a public admission that he no longer felt worthy to wear it, and at the moment he needed all the prestige and self-esteem he could find.

"Yes, he is still down there," said Tivanixi.

"Is there a back door?" Wallie asked. "If I can reach my ship, I am safe. On *Sapphire*'s deck I can beat any man."

The castellan swung around. He frowned and then shrugged. "Yes, there is. Let's go, then."

They clipped their hair up and went out, pushing the wailing door closed, shutting the ghosts back in their cold gray solitude.

"Leave the bar," the castellan said as Wallie reached for it. "I'll send some juniors to get the hernias." They started down the stairs. "I can return Master Nnanji and the others with an escort. Have you a password he will know?"

Wallie thought and then chuckled. "'Killer earthworm.' It was how he fenced when I first met him."

"He is more of a cobra now, Lord Shonsu! A pity he cannot manage the sutras; he would have a good chance to make Sixth."

They clattered down a second flight. There were two doors on this floor, one on either side of the stairwell. "Through here." The door led into another long room—smelly, grimy, and littered with bedding rolls and the small packs of belongings that free swords might carry on their gypsy life. All the rooms in the lodge must be this shape, long and narrow, with windows on one side out to a balcony.

"If no other Seventh appears, how much time do I have?" Wallie asked as they paced through.

"Very little, I fear! You announced that you would not join the tryst, so they can't count you. But if no other appears, then I don't think we can wait much longer." They went out through the far door and down more stairs. "The town can't take much more of this."

So Tivanixi did care about what was happening in the city?

"You can't impose discipline?"

He got an angry and resentful glare. "I have tried! It risks gang warfare, my men versus your men. It is the unattached Sixths, and a couple of Fifths; slack disciplinarians have less trouble recruiting, of course. The Sevenths are all keeping their protégés under control, I think, but the others are troublemakers. It is hard on the citizens. And taxes are another problem—I had no idea how much this was going to cost, and the elders scream when I ask for more money."

He opened another door, leading into another long room, rank and unbelievably cluttered. Half the windowpanes were missing, panels had warped away from the walls. There was mold on the heaps of old furniture and high-piled bedding, harnesses, clothes, and boxes that almost filled it. The floor had sagged in places and the air stank of rot and decay.

"Tell the elders," Wallie said as they edged their way through the piled furniture, along a narrow, crooked path, "that feeding a tryst costs less than building a sorcerer's tower."

Tivanixi stopped and stared back at him. "I hadn't thought of that!"

"It is their logical next move."

"Sorcerers cannot cross the River!"

"Oh yes, they can! I assure you, Lord Tivanixi, that there is at least one sorcerer down there in that courtyard at this moment. Most likely he is a slave, or a hawker, or someone else inconspicuous. News of my arrival will be on its way to Vul already."

††† †††

Wallie had been quite prepared to return to the ship alone, but with a glance at his hairclip Tivanixi had tactfully insisted on providing an escort and he had put his longtime friend Fiendori of the Sixth in charge of it. Thus Wallie marched through the narrow alleys and across the wide squares with Fiendori and half a dozen swordsmen at his back.

He glowed with a new exuberance, his doubts withered away. Thanks to the ambitious Thana, he now understood the sorcerers' apparent telepathy. Minx! She had sought sutra lessons from him, and from Nnanji, and from her mother, so that no one could know what she had been taught. Obviously Nnanji had been assuming that it was Wallie who had instructed her in Fourth-rank sutras, as a surprise for him. He wondered how many sutras Brota knew—the water rats were little impressed by ritual.

Lip reading was probably well known to the riverfolk, useful up in the shrouds in a strong wind, when neither voices nor gestures could be used. The sorcerers had adopted it and combined it with the telescope. That was typical of their methods, a fragment of technology plus a bushel of showmanship, combined to give an impression of magic powers. Obviously they could know of the telescope—it ought to have been invented on Earth long before it had been.

Also, Wallie had completed the god's riddle. He had returned the sword to the lodge where it had been made. And he had accorded to its destiny, accepting that he must lead the tryst.

The need was obvious. Boariyi was a brash kid. Tivanixi

seemed intelligent enough, yet even he had already blundered conspicuously. He had been tricked into calling the tryst at the wrong time of year, with winter coming. He had charged ahead without finding out anything about the enemy. He had obviously given no thought at all to finance. Faith in the Goddess was fine, but the gods helped those who knew what they were doing. The tryst needed not only Wallie's superior knowledge of the enemies' powers, but also some good management techniques—aim identification, cost-benefit studies, critical path analysis, command structure definitions, budgetary forecasts . . .

The tiny battle of Ov had shown Wallie that the sorcerers were poor fighters, merely armed civilians who lost their heads, while the swordsmen were trained tacticians. Yet Tivanixi's impetuous response to the sorcerers' defiance suggested that, on the higher level of strategy, the sorcerers might be better than the swordsmen. There were sutras on strategy, but who ever got to use them? War was rare in the World. Few swordsmen would ever command a force of more than a dozen or so, while the sorcerers had obviously been working to a careful plan for fifteen years. Now they had run out of cities on the left bank. They must either rest with the conquests they had, or cross the River. They could write; they had records; they had communications and organization; they could see the bigger picture. Wallie Smith still thought that way, although he was now illiterate. He had the additional advantage of knowing a little history from another world, a much more warlike planet than this. His feel for strategy and planning was better than that of the other swordsmen. They were iron-age barbarians; he was a cultivated, educated, and reasonably well-informed twentieth-century technologist . . . who just happened to be an iron-age barbarian on the outside. The tryst needed his way of thinking as much as it needed his knowledge of the sorcerers' technology. He must somehow put himself at its head.

How?

He needed to do something dramatic and he could not demand a miracle from the gods. But heroes were allowed to be lucky. Already he had an idea of what was going to be needed, and luck would certainly be a vital ingredient.

The swordsmen of the tryst and their natural distrust of him were one problem. Boariyi himself was another. The god had hinted that there was one other swordsman who might be as good as Shonsu—who else but Boariyi? That had been an obvious warning, for if equals meet, and one is out of practice while the other is not, who will win?

Right first time.

That meant practice, and practice meant a partner. Nnanji was not good enough. But—Wallie now realized—marching right behind him was a Sixth who could sometimes beat Tivanixi himself. The castellan had left Wallie waiting a bladder-testing long time beside the rear door while he went off to fetch Fiendori. That might mean that friend Fiendori had been well briefed, might it not?

By the time Wallie had got this far in his thoughts, he had come to the wide and windy plaza where the River shone through a haze of masts and rigging that curved away into the distance in both directions. *Sapphire* was visible a short way downstream. He gestured for Fiendori to move up beside him.

He was a pleasant-seeming fellow, not tall, but thick and broad, and he had a big, friendly grin. He moved and walked with the same athletic grace as his mentor.

Wallie opened the conversation by asking how he had come to Casr, and when. He was told that Lord Tivanixi's band of frees, arriving at Quo, had heard that there was a lodge at Casr and had decided to go there in the hope of picking up a promising junior or two. They had ridden in about three days after Shonsu had left, to find four Firsts and two Seconds attempting to maintain order, with a conspicuous lack of success.

"They were looting house to house by that time, my lord," Fiendori said with disgust, but without explaining who "they" were. "We rolled a few heads across this avenue, here, my lord, and soon stopped that!"

Clearly, in Fiendori's eyes Lord Tivanixi was the perfect swordsman, a hero in the great tradition, a man who could do no wrong. Tivanixi had cleaned up the town and then stayed on, waiting for Shonsu to return. The weeks had rolled by, and the rumors of disaster had sifted back, and—without any specific announcement or decision, more or less by default—Tivanixi had become castellan in Shonsu's place. His men had no complaint.

Whatever duty the gods sent and the boss accepted was fine by them.

"I don't know if the castellan told you, your honor," Wallie said, "but I need some practice. I have been ship-bound for many weeks."

The big, loose grin flashed. "He told me to put myself at your disposal, if I could be of any help to your lordship. Subject to an emergency arising where he might need me, that is."

Good for Tivanixi! He had been 'way out ahead. Wallie expressed his gratitude. "Then we shall need to find somewhere with space," he said, "and privacy! He spoke highly of your skills. Did he mention my sword to you?"

"Yes, my lord." Fiendori glanced up at the hilt. "A great honor, but also a great burden, if I may say so."

Wallie suspected that this Sixth was a born follower and probably not in the Nobel league for original thinking, but that remark sounded like a tactful reference to the need for keeping out of Boariyi's way, so Wallie did not labor the point. He was about to ask if his companion knew of any convenient courtyard that might be rented, preferably close to the docks, when conversation was ended by the sight of a disturbance in progress.

Two slaves were in trouble on the *Sapphire*'s gangplank. Between them was a sedan chair. The slave at the rear was taking most of the weight, because of the tilt of the plank, and was starting to buckle. The slave at the front was in greater difficulty, because he was facing Tomiyano, and there was no power in the World that was going to get that sedan chair on that deck. The slave, however, had his orders and a mere Third was seemingly not enough to change them. An irresistible enforcement had met an immovable objector.

A swordsman of the Seventh, however, was different. Wallie ordered the rear slave to start backing, and the man at the front had no choice but to follow. The chair returned to the dock and the slaves set it down. Wallie waved cheerfully at Tomiyano's glare. Then he stepped forward and pulled aside the curtain.

As he had expected, Honakura was sitting inside, grinning toothlessly.

"I thought that earthquake voice must be yours, my lord." He chuckled. "You have been to the lodge." That was not a question;

Honakura could pull information out of cobblestones. "How is Lord Boariyi?"

"Better, I'm afraid," said Wallie. "How is the holy Lord Kadywinsi?"

"Senile!" whispered the old man. "But I shall help him." Then he accepted a helping hand to disembark.

The black garb of a Nameless One had gone. He stepped out, still tiny and bald and toothless, but with the seven wavy lines now uncovered on his forehead, wearing a gown of sky-blue satin shimmering with that same holy pattern. His face was a dangerous gray shade and he looked very weary, but all his old authority had returned, the presence that could face down swordsmen of any rank. Wallie backed up and flashed the seventh sword in the greeting to an equal, and the old man responded in his slurred voice. Then Wallie presented the Honorable Fiendori of the Sixth, who was impressed.

Wallie had stopped distrusting coincidences a long time ago. He edged Honakura and Fiendori slightly away from the troop of swordsmen, while passing pedestrians made a wide and wary circuit around them. "Holy one," he explained, "his honor and I were just debating where we might find a convenient and private place to do some fencing. Roomy, you understand, and not subject to unexpected intruders."

Honakura looked up at him with amusement. "I was asked to inform you that the priests of Casr will be more than grateful for an opportunity to help Her champion in any way they can be of service."

Look out, Boariyi!

"There we are, then," Wallie told Fiendori. "Today is almost gone—meet us at the temple in the morning. I assume that we can move *Sapphire* there?" he asked the old man.

"I gather that the water is shallow, my lord, but you can anchor offshore and come in by dinghy. Mistress Brota will be fretting about dock fees soon."

Wallie laughed and agreed. He dismissed his escort and conducted the priest up the gangplank.

The transformation had been noted, and the rail was lined with startled faces. Tomiyano was so overcome that he volunteered the salute to a superior and babbled that his ship would be honored to receive such a visitor. The rest of the sailors were staring with open mouths, as if an egg in the ship's larder had suddenly hatched a dragon. *This* was the old man who had cleaned pots in their galley? They had all guessed that he was a priest, but not a Seventh. A Seventh's prestige was so great in their culture that none of them found it strange when Wallie solemnly presented everyone old enough to salute. Each saluted reverently and received the response. That done, there was a bewildered pause. Honakura looked around at their faces, tottered across to sit on his favorite fire bucket, and started to laugh. Then they all laughed.

The riverfront plaza was beginning to empty as evening approached, the sky blushing in the west and even the wind seeming inclined to stop work for the day. Wallie now could attend to that stein of ale he had promised himself earlier. He took some beer down to the two slaves waiting on the dock—to their stunned amazement—and then settled himself on a hatch cover, while *Sapphire*'s crew gathered around. Then he recounted the events at the lodge.

"What happens now, great leader?" Tomiyano demanded from the other hatch cover.

"Possibly we get boarded," Wallie said. "If a very tall Seventh appears, *don't* try your tongue on him—he'll cut it out. Leave him to me, and the rest of you scamper." There was, after all, just a chance that Boariyi, once he learned the significance of the seventh sword, would come foaming down to the dock. Wallie could handle him easily on the ship. Zoariyi might not know that there were two kinds of swordsmanship in the World. Even if he did, his nephew might not heed his warnings.

"And apart from that?" the captain persisted.

Wallie was wondering where Nnanji and the others had got to—they should have arrived by now—but he started to explain between mouthfuls of beer and peanuts.

"Two problems. The popular favorite to win the leadership is this human giraffe called Boariyi. I'm told he is better than me."

"Bilge!" Brota muttered loyally.

"Maybe not! He has an arm like your bowsprit. So I have to get in some practice. Soon! The other problem is that the swordsmen don't trust me. The other Shonsu lost an army. They think I might lose another. They know about my screw-up at Aus, too. So I can't just win the leadership by simple combat, as Boariyi or the castellan could. But I'd be the only leader with a hope of averting disaster. The sorcerers are evil and the swordsmen are stupid! You and I—if you're still with me—are going to prevent a massacre."

Tomiyano looked skeptical. "How?"

"Good question. We must do something dramatic, I think. Anyone got any ideas?"

"Yes," the captain said. "You do. Tell us."

Wallie smiled at their faith—or was it that these shrewd traders could read his face? "No more voyages to the left bank for *Sapphire*," he said. "But there will be danger—this is war. Are you still with me?"

They were still with him, every one of them, from ancient old Lina, who was possibly as old as Honakura, down to the wide-eyed children. He thanked them sincerely, more moved than he wanted to show. Then he eyed the old man. "How much help can we have from the priests, holy one?"

"Whatever you want," Honakura said complacently.

If Honakura could deliver the temple, then Boariyi had hit the iceberg and was listing already. Wallie pondered in silence for a while, but then decided his harebrained plan was the only one he was going to come up with. He took a deep breath and began. "I think I have jobs for all of you, then. You, Cap'n, buy me a ship."

Tomiyano was surprised. "Big or small? What rig?"

Wallie shrugged. "Something that will carry eight or ten, I suppose. As fast as possible. Large enough to stand up in below-decks."

Sailors anywhere enjoy evaluating boats. Tomiyano rose and peered along the front, then at the scattering of vessels anchored out in the River. "Like that? How about that?"

"Whatever you can get," Wallie said. "How much must I pay?"

"Two or three thousand."

Wallie looked at Brota beside him and was almost turned to ice by the look in her eye. She was afraid that he was going to ask for Donations to a Good Cause. She probably had several times that much hidden away somewhere in *Sapphire*, the profits of thirty years' trading.

He smiled innocently. "That's all right, then."

She frowned even more and shot a glance at her son.

Tomiyano grunted. "So you do have more of them!"

Wallie reached in his money pouch and brought out a handful of blue fire. "I do. Would it have mattered, had you known?"

The captain showed his teeth in a fierce grin. "Possibly! I was ready to do it for your hairclip alone; I couldn't think what we'd do with the sword. She wouldn't let me . . . but she would have done, if she'd known about those."

He was joking, but he might not be lying—his mother was glaring at him.

Wallie laughed and put the gems back. "Then I am grateful to you, mistress! Perhaps you and Katanji could sell some of these for me, when we know how much we'll need?"

"One moment, my lord," said Honakura. "I assume that the god gave you those jewels?"

Wallie nodded.

"Then they are rather special. The temple might well be interested in purchasing them."

"Thank you, holy one." Wallie spoke solemnly, but he was grinning inside. The old rascal was saying that he would raid the temple treasury for him. "Brota, we shall need silk. I suppose we can buy some silk in this city? Good-quality silk?"

"Very good silk," Brota agreed cautiously.

"Orange would be best, of course. What could we use to waterproof it, do you think? Some sort of wax? Beeswax?"

"Shoemakers' wax, perhaps," she replied.

"Lina?" Wallie said. "Is that copper pot still in the galley? The one with the coil on it, which I used when I showed you how the sorcerers ensorcel wine?"

The low sun was in Lina's eyes; she shaded them with a hand that was almost transparent as she peered across the deck at him. "It was getting in my way, nasty thing. It's down in the bilge somewhere."

Tomiyano was turning pink and trying not to explode. Honakura was showing his gums and trying not to laugh.

"Right! Captain, have we any ensorceled wine left?"

Tomiyano thought there might be a bottle or two around somewhere.

"No matter," Wallie said. "We'll get five or six bottles and then ensorcel them again and get double-ensorceled wine."

"Love a squid!" said Tomiyano. "Is it that much stronger again if you do that?"

"No, about the same. But I need it very pure. We'd better do that ashore somewhere—it's too much of a fire hazard. Mata, would you do that for me? I'll show you how."

The sailors were now clearly divided into those who were annoyed at being teased and those who were enjoying the annoyance of the first group.

"Lae?" Wallie said. "Could you make me a gown?"

The ship's honorary grandmother frowned. "Jja's a better seamstress than me, my lord."

"But she'll be sewing the silk bags," Wallie said as if that were obvious. Where was Jja? What was keeping them all? "What I want from you is a blue gown, with a hood and those big, droopy sleeves."

"You're going to pretend to be a sorcerer?" Tomiyano shouted. "You're going ashore as a sorcerer?"

Wallie feigned surprise. "You think I'm crazy?"

"The thought had drifted across my mind, perhaps."

"Nonsense!" Wallie said. "Holiyi, you're the best carpenter on board. You'll cut some holes in the ship for me, won't you?"

Holiyi was as skinny as Boariyi, although not especially tall. He probably had not spoken for hours—Holiyi seemed to get through the day on a handful of words like the legendary Arab on a handful of dates—but now he not only nodded, he exclaimed, "Of course!" as if he had expected the request. The grins grew wider.

Wallie rose and walked over to the rail to stare across the plaza. "Well, I think that's about everything, then. The holy lord suggests that you anchor by the temple and save dock fees."

"Where are you going in this ship of yours?" Tomiyano demanded. "This ship with the holes in it, and the silk bags full of ensorceled wine, and you in your sorcerer's robe?"

Wallie pointed east, toward Vul. The volcanoes were dormant again, hardly smoking at all.

"And who's going to sail it for you?"

This was the tricky part, and all the mystifying had been mostly to get the man intrigued enough that he might agree. "I hoped that you would, Captain."

"Me? Leave *Sapphire*? You're crazy even to ask!" Tomiyano was taking the suggestion as an insult.

"It is important," Wallie said seriously. "I've been making a game of it, but it is important! If the swordsmen walk into the sorcerers' trap, then they'll all die, hundreds of them."

The sailor's face grew red. "No! I've cooperated with the Goddess. We've risked our ship and our lives, and I'll help still, but I'm not leaving *Sapphire*. And that's final."

"Fool!" Honakura squirmed down from the fire bucket. "You, a sailor, would defy Her? The Goddess is the River and the River is the Goddess! They are Her swordsmen!" The captain paled as the tiny old man marched across to him, shrill with anger. "You will never find fair wind again! Never reach the port you want! Never know a night without pirates! Is that what you want, Captain Tomiyano? How long will you survive on the River if you anger the Goddess?"

"Oh, *hell!*" Tomiyano scowled at the deck. "I guess I'll come, then."

"Thanks, Captain," Wallie said quietly.

"Just a moment, my lord!" Brota was suspicious. "You said that you had work for all of us. Haven't you kept a few things back?" She hunched her head down in her pillowed shoulders and frowned at him.

"Well, yes," Wallie admitted. "When I'm off playing in my new ship, there will be a small job—at least for you, mistress."

"Such as?"

"I'll handle the sorcerers. You have to stop the tryst."

Even Brota could be startled sometimes. Some of the children giggled.

Then Tomiyano began to laugh—and that was rare as summer snow. "Shonsu," he said, "you're not the only one who's going to need some fencing practice."

††† † †††

Nnanji of the Fifth bounded up the gangplank and landed with both feet firmly on the deck, arms wide to receive plaudits and bouquets, timed to an inaudible fanfare from an invisible band—*Ta-RAH*! His new red kilt was absurdly short and a horrible raspberry shade that clashed with his hair, but his facemarks were symmetrical for the first time since Wallie had known him, and he was somehow contriving to laugh and grin at the same time.

There, Wallie thought, was one swordsman who would never again have problems handling sailors, unlike the late Polini. And had the younger Nnanji of the temple guard been required to leave a lodge full of swordsmen to go and mix with riverfolk, he would have sulked for hours.

Thana appeared at his side, sliding an arm around him to share in his triumph as the crew rushed forward with congratulations. She noticed Wallie, smiled, and then stuck out her tongue. He mouthed "Cheat!" at her silently, and she smirked, unrepentant. Katanji came on board, also grinning.

Then Jja—she noted where Vixini was even as she ran over to Wallie. Vixi had been contentedly sitting beside Fala, but now he dropped the bone on which he had been sharpening his latest tooth and levered himself upright, bottom first. There was his favorite mother . . .

Wallie grabbed her in a fierce hug. She was laughing under his kiss as Vixini cannoned into her.

"What kept you all?" Wallie demanded. "I was ready to declare war!"

She scooped up Vixini. "Minstrels!" She was excited and happy. "Just after you left, a minstrel started singing an epic—about you! You and Nnanji and the fight against the Honorable Tarru and his men. You horrible dirty River monster!" The last remark was directed at Vixini.

Great gods! The battle with Tarru, the escape from the holy island—how long ago that seemed! But of course Yoningu had promised Nnanji that he would tell the tale to the first minstrel who came by the barracks. So that minstrel was now here in Casr, or one who had heard the story from him.

He laughed. "Was it a good epic?"

She smiled mischievously. "Very good! So Master Nnanji says."

"He's biased! Well, he'll be happy." Ecstatic, more like! And an epic would be excellent public relations.

Then Nnanji himself came pushing forward through the throng, disentangling himself from the more youthful admirers. "I met four Sevenths today, my lord brother," he said solemnly. "That makes seven all together in my whole life!"

"Who was the fourth, then?" Wallie asked.

"Lord Chinarama. He'll be no problem for you, though—he's old!"

For Nnanji, senescence began at thirty. "How old?"

Nnanji pondered. "At least seventy . . . but a nice old relic. Says he's always dreamed of a tryst, so when he heard about this one, he retrieved his sword from the woodshed and came along in the hope of giving counsel." Then he added, "I don't suppose he'll hurt."

"What did you think of Boariyi?" Wallie asked.

"He is a man of honor," Nnanji said cautiously. "He is very troubled about the lack of discipline, thinks it is a disgrace to the craft. And he says I am younger than he was when he reached Fifth!"

Boariyi had found the keys to Nnanji's heart.

"And I have an epic for you!" Nnanji beamed and turned to address everyone. "Who wants to hear an epic?"

"Not now!" Wallie said. "We have a war to fight."

Casr had become a dangerous place for him. By now Zoariyi and his nephew must have learned the importance of the seventh sword and would be anxious to prevent it leaving town. If they could locate a water rat, or even a sailor, who had witnessed Wallie's disgrace in Aus, then a denunciation would follow at once—the posse would arrive at the gangplank. He must vanish into the mists of the River, and the sooner the better.

He was shouted down. The World was a leisurely place. *Sapphire* was having a vacation. His war could wait. He almost lost his temper, but Honakura said firmly that he wanted to hear an epic, and that was that. Wagons and horses and chattering people were winding their way home, the wind was still listlessly flapping awnings and sails, but such details would not keep Nnanji from his epic. So Wallie reluctantly sat down and leaned back against the bulwark, out of the wind, his arm around Jja.

Nnanji jumped up on the aft hatch cover. "Right!" he said. "Gather round! Ready? *How Nnanji of the Fourth and Shonsu of the Seventh Fought Ten Renegade Swordsmen!*" He glanced at Wallie.

"What! You get star billing?" Wallie protested—it translated as "place of honor."

Nnanji smirked. "That was what you told Yoningu, brother!"

So it was—Wallie had joked that Nnanji's name should be first. He had not then cared for the dubious honor of being hero of a barbarian romance . . . but at that time he had not been running for office.

With a title like that, he thought sourly, it would never make the best-seller list. As soon as Nnanji started, though, he saw that it well might—it was a very good epic. No, it was excellent, far superior to the ephemeral jingles in which the minstrels normally reported current events, the doggerel that he had once dismissed as swordsman sports news. At times he had wondered if one day he would find a Homer to record whatever feat he might achieve for the Goddess. If the author of this work was present in Casr, then perhaps he had. True, it used all the stock phrases and conventions—long dramatic speeches between sword strokes, vile villains and heroic heroes—but the meter was certain and the imagery vivid. Moreover, the bard had taken wide liberties with the story line to make it more dramatic. As the tale unfolded, Wallie began to feel very uneasy.

Nnanji of the Second had sought promotion in the temple guard—*true*—and challenged two Fourths, killing one—*true*—and had then denounced the guard as venal—*false and improbable: How did he gain a promotion after that?* Then the new "blood-headed" Nnanji of the Fourth, facemarks still dramatically bleeding, had set off with his brother . . .

Wallie choked down an interruption as he saw Katanji grinning expectantly at him. How had he gotten into this? He had been present, but only a very minor character. Now Wallie was astounded to realize that the minstrel had been extemporizing, creating the epic as he went along. Having the basic story in some form or other, he had adapted it to the earlier events of the afternoon, downplaying the unsavory Shonsu, emphasizing the "blood-headed" hero of Ov and the brother who had been so dramatically presented as the bravest man in the courtyard—giving his audience what it wanted to hear. In all this ridiculous farrago, Shonsu had not even been mentioned yet.

The scene changed to the jetty, where the impossibly vile Tarru of the Sixth swore terrible vows and pledged evil minions by the blood oath. Nnanji and Katanji came on stage. Tarru mocked them—and David promptly challenged Goliath in iambic pentameters.

Leaving the battle in suspense, the bard then switched to the holy cave behind the sacred waterfall, where the Goddess expounded on the honor of her swordsmen, the sins of Tarru, the virtue and future greatness of Nnanji, and finally summoned a demigod, commanding him to save Her hero.

Wallie looked in exasperation at Honakura and saw that he was turning purple with suppressed laughter.

The demigod found Shonsu—*where? at the relief office?*—gave him the seventh sword—described in lines stolen from the saga of Chioxin—and then transported him by a miracle to the battle.

Copious blood spurted. With a little help on the side from Shonsu, the magnificent Nnanji was victorious. Virtue triumphed. The two heroes swore the oath of brotherhood and sailed away to continue the battle against evil. End of epic, applause.

The seventh sword was understandable—Imperkanni's men back at the jetty at Hann had known of that—but no one except the crew of *Sapphire* had been aware of the fourth oath until Wallie had mentioned it in the lodge. Very few of those present would ever have heard of the oath before.

Certainly Homer had been present in the courtyard!

So now the seventh sword was public knowledge! And Wallie felt like Agamemnon hearing the *Iliad*; it was good public relations, but for the wrong man. He hoped he was managing to hide his pique as he applauded with the others. The youngsters wanted to hear it all again, but Nnanji refused. Perhaps Wallie's face was not so waterproof as he hoped.

"Not exactly the way I recall the way it went," Wallie said, squeezing out a toothpaste smile, "but superb poetry! Who was the minstrel?"

Nnanji shrugged. "Don't know. Not bad, though, was it?" He looked a little disillusioned. "I suppose one shouldn't believe everything one hears in epics."

The crew rose, ready to take on the war now. "Where to, great leader?" Tomiyano asked.

"Vanish!" Wallie said. "The mysterious Shonsu disappears as mysteriously as he mysteriously appeared."

Nnanji stared at him in horror and dismay.

"Then we creep back and go to the temple."

"Ah! And what do we do there, brother?"

"Fence," Wallie said.

"Oh!" Nnanji looked surprised, but fencing was always acceptable behavior.

Honakura descended from his bucket. "I shall see you there. I was told to suggest the up end of the grounds. Dinghies," he added, "look even worse than mules, whereas I find sedan chair riding to be excellent exercise, not tiring at all."

Wallie escorted the priest to the gangplank, while *Sapphire*'s crew prepared to cast off. Somewhere out on that wide plaza there would be watchers, waiting to see what this Shonsu did.

He wandered back to where Nnanji stood with a firm grip on Thana. He had been out of bed for hours and was obviously feeling deprived.

"That's a hideous kilt," Wallie said.

"It was all they had," Nnanji protested, looking smug. "Fifths are supposed to be short or fat."

Wallie explained that Jja had made him one—very smart, with a griffon embroidered on the hem. Pleased, Nnanji said he would go and change. Thana remarked that new kilts were tricky, perhaps she should come and help. They fell agiggling again.

"Thank you, Thana," Wallie said, "for the warning about Boariyi—you saved the day."

"What warning?" Nnanji demanded.

"Never mind," Thana retorted quickly. "Let's get that ghastly kilt off you first." There was an offer that he would not refuse, and the two of them ran off.

The gangplank was being hauled in—time to start detailed planning. Wallie returned to Jja's side near the deckhouse, meaning to explain about silk and sewing. There was no sign of swordsmen heading for the ship.

"Did you like the epic, darling?" she inquired, and there was something lurking in those dark, unreadable eyes.

"It was great poetry, even if it wasn't very accurate. Why?"

"There will be others!" she said. "Nnanji told the minstrels about Ov."

Wallie had promised Tivanixi he would do that, then had forgotten. No matter—Nnanji would have done it better. "How many minstrels are there, anyway?"

"Dozens, love," she said, frowning.

So many? A thousand swordsmen, plus juniors—three or four hundred juniors. Minstrels, of course, would flock to a tryst. Heralds? Armorers? Camp followers? Wives? Children? Musicians? Night slaves? He wondered how many thousands had invaded Casr. Small wonder that the elders were unhappy.

"And Thana told them how you and Nnanji fought the pirates."

He brought his mind back to Jja. She was concerned about something.

"What's worrying you, love? The pirate story is all right." Of course the pirates had been only dispossessed sailors, half of them women. In the minstrels' version they would be Morgan and Blackbeard and Long John Silver, but it would be a harmless piece of swashbuckling. Free swords hated pirates because they could do nothing about them, so the story would be appreciated.

She dropped her eyes shyly, not wanting to prompt a master who was usually so quick. "Who started the fighting?"

Nnanji had. Wallie had lifted him out of the window. Now he understood! The pattern had been set. Nnanji was the hero of the fight against Tarru, he would be the hero of the battle of Ov and of the pirate fight, also. With Thana telling the pirate story, Wallie would be lucky to get into a footnote.

"They were asked about Gi, too," Jja said. "If it was you who arrived with the shipload of tools after the fire and who organized the town again."

Wallie smiled. "Well, at least Nnanji can't steal that one."

"The tools came from Amb, darling."

Amb—a sorcerer city! The suspicion would be there . . . He was not usually so dumb, but then Jja had had more time to think about it.

"And Katanji was asked about the sorcerers' tower," she said.

Damn! Wallie just stared, too shocked to speak. Of course Katanji would have been asked—it was Wallie's own fault for mentioning the subject. Katanji was sharp beyond his years, but he would not have been able to resist an audience like that . . . dozens of minstrels?

Damn! Damn! What would the swordsmen think of a Seventh who hid in safety on a ship and sent a First into danger—and disguised him as a slave, too? They would react as Nnanji had reacted, saying that changing facemarks was an abomination. They could never approve of a plainclothes swordsman. The pirate story might do no harm, but the Katanji tale would be pure disaster for Shonsu's image.

Damn! Damn! Damn! Minstrels! Wallie had forgotten the position that minstrels held in the World. While he had been babbling smugly to himself about modern management techniques, his subordinates had been blowing their heads off at a press conference.

BOOK THREE:

HOW THE BEST SWORD WON

†

As a man may have an off day, so Casr was having an off century, and nothing showed that more clearly than the temple. A smaller version of the great archetype at Hann, it faced its seven arches toward the River whose Goddess it honored, although here the arches had been glassed in, as a concession to a colder climate. Two of the seven spires had fallen and much of the gold leaf had peeled from the others. Many of the glass panes were missing, also, and even some of the stone filigree that had held them. As the sun god rose over RegiVul, his glory was mirrored in this façade with black gaps spotting the reflection like mildew.

Adjoining the temple and its complex of buildings, on the upstream side, lay a wilderness of unkempt trees, shrubbery, and ruins, with a deserted, ramshackle pier. This had to be the jetty that Honakura had recommended, and when Wallie was rowed ashore, shivering slightly in the cool dawn air, he was met by a delegation of priests. After much ritual handwaving and bowing, he was led through wet and tangled undergrowth to an abandoned refectory, a huge room, half underground, with a high, barrel-vault ceiling and stone-slabbed floor. It was dank and musty, but it would have been perfect for his purpose had the lighting been stronger. As it was, it would do very well. The windows were few and located high in the walls, partly obscured by moss and ferns. The sound of foils would barely be heard outside. And of course the refectory had an adjoining kitchen, filthy and littered, but ideal for the distillery he needed and convenient for him to supervise. The priests waited anxiously for his verdict, and he said yes, it would serve.

Brota and Pora would go shopping for silk and waxes and oils, Lae for some heavy blue material. Tomiyano and Oligarro would hunt for ships. Thana and Jja and Katanji had been warned to stay on board *Sapphire*. With all those details under control, Wallie could start on his fencing right away. He dismissed the priests, asking that Honorable Fiendori be brought to him as soon as he arrived.

Now that his eyes had adjusted to the dimness, the great stone room looked like an excellent gym.

"Right, Master Nnanji," he said. "As I have no one else here to butcher . . . you're first!"

Nnanji grinned cheerfully. "*My secrets are your secrets*, brother?" he asked.

"Of course," Wallie said. "Don't think I don't trust the sailors, Nnanji, it's just that any false word could kill us. I'm sure that the sorcerers have spies in Casr." He wandered over to a scabrous wooden bench, but decided it needed cleaning before it could be used. "What I have in mind is this. Shonsu lost, and lost badly. At Aus, I lost. That's two losses, right? At Ov, we won. We need another win! And I want a thunderbolt!" Had he not been knocked senseless at Ov, he would have gathered up the dead sorcerers' weapons. Nnanji had not thought to do so, but could not be blamed for that lapse.

Nnanji's eyes widened. "You're going to capture a sorcerer?"

"I hope so," Wallie said. "Alive, if possible. But mostly I want his thunderbolt—I'll use it to kill an ox or something for the tryst and show them what they're up against. Maybe then they'll listen to me!"

His young friend did not look as excited and pleased as Wallie had hoped. He looked worried. "When, though? It'll take us a week, at least, to go to Sen and back; longer to Wal. How long until the swordsmen are sworn?"

As long as Tivanixi could hold them off, Wallie said.

Nnanji chewed his lip. "Once the tryst is sworn, brother, it'll be too late. There will be nothing you can do then!"

Perhaps that was true, but Wallie did not see that there was anything he could do before the tryst was sworn, either—not if the swordsmen would not accept Shonsu as leader. He was flying blind.

At that moment Fiendori was ushered in, accompanied by another Sixth, Forarfi. He, as Wallie soon learned, had been a free sword, one of the first to be delivered to Casr by the Goddess. He had summed up Tivanixi as a good man and sworn to him within the first couple of days.

Any Sixth relished a chance to practice against a Seventh, so the masks went on and the work began. Fiendori was erratic, but at his best a fair Seventh with a foil. Forarfi was consistent, a high Sixth—and left-handed. Wallie enjoyed the challenge, the exercise, and the joy of doing something that he was good at, offering advice sometimes, trying new things, dredging up unusual routines from Shonsu's skills, finding a half-forgotten sharpness creeping back as he faced these experts. Fiendori and Forarfi were enthusiasts—like Nnanji they would cheerfully fence all day. Nnanji certainly could not see why two keen fencers should stand around idle, so usually there were two matches going on in the high, echoing refectory, two clouds of dust rising, eight feet pounding.

Not even Shonsu's physique could keep it up without a break, of course, and common sense dictated that Wallie not work himself to exhaustion, lest a certain tall Seventh should appear with a smirk and a challenge. In any case there were constant interruptions. Honakura appeared, bringing the high priest, Kadywinsi of the Seventh, to meet the honored guest. Kadywinsi was almost as tiny and ancient as Honakura, but he had a few teeth left and a halo of silver curls floated like evening mist upon his scalp. He was pleasant and gracious and did not seem especially senile, except in contrast to the chisel mind of Honakura. Later Honakura brought other priests to discuss Wallie's sapphires, then took them off to consult the temple bursar.

Lae returned with blue flannel, the closest material she could find to the weighty stuff the sorcerers used for their gowns. She also brought a very large brown robe for Wallie to try. It was a fair fit, except across the shoulders, and she took it away to use as a pattern.

More fencing . . .

Mata set up the copper still on a range in the kitchen area with Sinboro and Matarro as stokers. Soon a heady odor of alcohol and woodsmoke came drifting through the hall.

The next morning the fencers went at it again, all four of them stiff and aching and determined not to admit it. Later that day Tomiyano and Oligarro arrived to announce that they had found a ship that met Lord Shonsu's specifications. They described it in detail, most of which Wallie could not follow, but what he understood seemed to be satisfactory.

"How much, then?" he asked.

"Oh, he wants twenty-eight hundred," Tomiyano said. "But he'll come down in a day or two."

"Time we have not got. Buy it!"

Tomiyano pouted.

More fencing . . .

Jja came from *Sapphire* to display samples of her work with the silk and Wallie was delighted. The seams were incredibly fine.

But waterproofing was a problem. Brota and Fala tried their best, but they produced sticky silk, oily silk, stiff silk, not what he needed. Experimentation was not in their culture—they required a sutra, and Lord Shonsu could not produce one, for he only knew what he wanted, not how to do it. Then he remembered Katanji, sulking under ship arrest because his cast was so conspicuous. Katanji was an original thinker and too young to have been frozen into the conventional thought patterns of the People. At lunchtime that day Wallie returned to *Sapphire* and explained the difficulty. By nightfall Katanji had solved it for him with a mixture of oil, two waxes, and some of the double-ensorceled wine.

That lunchtime, also, Wallie inspected his new ship. Compared to *Sapphire* she was only a pointed box with a mast. She was filthy, stank nauseatingly, and had not seen paint since Casr was a hamlet, but her fore-and-aft rigging would give her a fair speed and require only a small crew, or so the sailors said. Belowdecks she had a single, grubby hold, with one tiny cabin aft. Wallie explained to Holiyi the alterations he needed. Holiyi smiled and went to fetch his tools. Her sails were new and satisfactory, Tomiyano said.

"What shall we call her?" he asked.

"*Vomit*," said Nnanji, holding his nose.

Wallie said, "*Griffon*."

Then they went back to fencing.

The days fled. *Sapphire* was moved frequently. It would have taken a suspicious mind and a sailor's eye to pick her out each day in the ever-changing flotilla anchored offshore, to note that this ship was a resident. Brota and a few of the older crew members spent their days among traders and sailors on the waterfront, working on preparations of their own.

Wallie could feel improvement in his fencing, which Fiendori confirmed, but while Wallie was recovering lost ground, Nnanji was exploring new territory, climbing through fifth rank and undeniably now approaching Sixth.

Honakura bustled around, amusing himself by bullying the priests to provide whatever Wallie needed, making excuses when they wanted to hold formal dinner parties for him, bringing gossip and news. Physically he was failing, Wallie was sure, but he would hear no talk of taking life easy. His mind was as sparkling as ever, and he was obviously enjoying himself hugely, subverting the local priesthood to his own use.

Near the evening of the third day, while the fencers were taking a break, drooping in the dim refectory on the two rickety wooden benches, the old priest came shuffling in and sat down to make conversation.

After a while he looked at Fiendori and remarked, "I understand that the minstrels have been singing new songs?"

"True, holy one," the Sixth muttered with a worried glance at Wallie. "I heard some last night."

"*Ten Renegade Swordsmen?*" Wallie asked, and got a nod. "What else about 'blood-headed' Nnanji?"

"*How Adept Nnanji Fought the Pirates*, my lord, and *How Relief Came to Gi*. There's two or three versions of *The Battle of Ov*."

It sounded, then, as if Nnanji was getting most of the publicity, as Wallie had feared.

"*Nnanji's Farewell to the Prince*," Forarfi said "Now there's a sad one!"

"I should like to hear those," Nnanji said eagerly. "Are they as well done as the *Renegades*?"

No, Fiendori said, he didn't think so.

"What about the Katanji thing?" Honakura inquired with great innocence. The two Sixths both scowled.

"What Katanji thing?" Wallie asked.

It seemed there was a song going round the town: *Novice Katanji to the Dark Tower Came*, a catchy jingle with a good tune and comic words. Juniors sang it when the seniors were not listening. The townsfolk had picked it up, and the street urchins chanted it behind marching swordsmen. Wallie demanded a sample and got one verse and the chorus from Fiendori, embarrassed and unsure of his key. A swordsman disguised as a slave was not funny in his eyes, and sorcerers were not figures of fun, either. Wallie made no excuses, for he knew of no way to fight ridicule, but obviously his popularity with the highrank swordsmen would be lower than ever.

Honakura chuckled and went wandering off, humming the tune. Nnanji scowled hideously and deliberately changed the subject.

"Brother," he said. "Explain: *A tiger that looks like a mouse is as dangerous as a tiger; a mouse that looks like a tiger is more so.*"

Wallie turned to the two Sixths. They did not meet his eye.

"It is a mentor's obligation and privilege to teach his protégé the sutras, your honors, is it not?" Wallie said.

They nodded in guilty silence.

"Then pray do not meddle!"

More fencing . . .

††

On the fourth afternoon, while Wallie was fencing with Fiendori and Nnanji with Forarfi, two figures appeared in the doorway, dark against sunlight. Wallie noted through the grid of his mask that one was a swordsman and thought that Boariyi had found him. Then he saw the visitors were the high priest and the castellan. He removed the mask, gathered his sword from a bench, and advanced to make his salutes, still breathing hard. He felt grubby and scruffy in comparison with their cool elegance.

"Pray continue your match, my lord," Tivanixi said. "I was enjoying it."

Wallie declined and led them over to the benches. The newcomers sat on one bench and he on the other. Nnanji and the two Sixths tactfully departed.

"From the little I saw," the castellan remarked, "you have made good use of your time."

"Care to judge form, then?" Wallie asked, smiling.

Tivanixi was not in a smiling mood. "I could not. I have never seen Boariyi fence against Fiendori. He is too uneven to use as a standard, anyway."

"My time is up?" Wallie asked.

"I fear so. No swordsmen have arrived for two days now. The other Sevenths are unanimous in interpreting this as a sign—the Goddess wishes the tryst to proceed. Lord Kadywinsi concurs."

Wallie sighed. The ship would be ready by evening, alterations complete, stores loaded. The sewing and waterproofing and distilling were done. Now he must decide whether to use them—to go ahead with the insane gamble he had planned, or to scrap it all and play by the swordsmen's rules.

"Can you hold off a little longer?"

"How long?" the castellan asked reluctantly.

"Six days, maybe seven?"

"Impossible! The town is ready to riot. We had eight challenges yesterday, and today already three. There will be no one left to swear if this goes on. I fear a duel may wax into pitched battle. No, my lord, we must proceed with the invocation of the tryst and selection of a leader."

Wallie leaned his elbows on his knees and stared glumly at the floor. "Your judgment, then, please, my lord. Have the minstrels helped? If I can beat Boariyi, will the tryst accept me?"

Tivanixi hesitated, looked to the priest for aid, and got a useless bland smile. "Some will, some won't. If you get enough, of course, you can force the rest at swordpoint."

That would not do, and they both knew it. A reluctant tryst would obey orders, but grudgingly and sloppily, and any leader would need much more than that. Wallie stared at Tivanixi thoughtfully.

"Would you?"

The castellan frowned. "Would I what?"

"Given a free choice between me and Boariyi, would you still choose me?"

For a long moment there was no answer. Then Wallie reached up and unclipped his hair.

Tivanixi said, "No."

Perhaps the impact of the seventh sword had worn off. Perhaps Boariyi had been charming Tivanixi as he had charmed Nnanji. But Wallie had a hunch that it was the ridicule of *Novice Katanji to the Dark Tower Came* that had tipped the scales. He would never know.

"Thank you," he said, and replaced his hairclip. "I can only ask that you hold off the contest as long as you can, my lord. I am leaving town."

Tivanixi's face burned with sudden anger. He jumped to his feet.

"Then I do not know what you are doing, my lord, or what you have been doing these last four days. There is a very good Sixth who will be eligible to try again for promotion tomorrow. Perhaps he is destined to be our seventh Seventh. Perhaps you should be counted although you have spurned Her summons." He bowed slightly. "May the Goddess be with you . . . and you with She."

That ending could be grounds for challenge, but Wallie ignored it. The visitors left. He stayed slouched on the bench, staring morosely at the floor, pondering his best course of action. If he remained in Casr and tried to win the leadership, he would probably be denounced before he got the chance. If he succeeded in fighting Boariyi then he might be killed. If he won, then the swordsmen likely would not swear allegiance to him anyway.

The alternative was a madcap venture, risking both his life and the lives of his friends. Even if it worked, he might not persuade the swordsmen to listen, or he might be too late. Of course, the Goddess could move his ship to Sen and back in a twinkling, but he did not expect that sort of help. Great deeds done by mortals were what the gods wanted, not their own miracles. The People did not regard the geographical mutations as miracles—they were too frequent, like rainbows or lightning—but Wallie certainly did.

Goddess! There *was* no best course of action!

Tivanixi would have removed his Sixths, of course, so when a solitary shadow appeared in the puddle of light from the doorway he assumed it was Nnanji—a tall figure with a sword hilt beside the right ear.

Then he saw it was not Nnanji and jumped to his feet.

It was not Boariyi, either. It was a woman. She walked slowly forward, and he saw her clearly as she passed through the first shaft of dust-twinkling sunlight falling from one of the high windows. She was extraordinarily tall, almost as tall as he was—the tallest woman he had seen in the World. Her hair was long and hung loose. What had seemed to be a sword hilt was the peg-box of a lute on her back. She floated over the flagstones toward him, swathed in a long wrap reaching almost to the floor . . . a sapphire-blue wrap. She was a minstrel of the seventh rank.

Then she reached him and stopped. The etiquette was clear: He was male and a swordsman, she was the newcomer. She must make the salute and he respond; but she merely stood and regarded him.

He had seen her in the lodge, peering over the heads of the other minstrels. He had assumed then that she was a young man, because of her height.

She was not conventionally beautiful. Her mouth was too large and her nose was high-prowed and bony, but cascades of shining brown hair flowed over bare shoulders, and the wrap was supported by firm breasts. Not overly conspicuous breasts, he thought, but she was so big overall that they were quite adequate. The face was plain, but her figure could not be faulted. A goddess! Her sheath was of gleaming silk, almost sheer . . . clinging. She had stature. She had aplomb. Suddenly Wallie was very conscious that this astonishing visitor was a maddeningly desirable woman. And she knew it.

The silence continued.

Tivanixi had mentioned some minstrel whom Shonsu should have known. Wallie could not recall the name. Had the castellan brought her, or had she followed him?

"Did anyone else come with you?" he demanded.

She shook her head.

He wondered if he ought to kiss her. That might inform him of the relationship she expected. She might run or . . . or he might become even more disconcerted than he was already. He wished she would speak. Her arrogant poise was somehow inflammatory.

"Sing for me, if you do not wish to talk," he said.

She raised an eyebrow skeptically. "Since when have you cared for music?"

He knew the voice, a rich contralto. Nnanji had mimicked it when he sang the *Ten Renegade Swordsmen*.

"I appreciate a lot of things that I used not to," he said, wondering what she would make of that.

"What are you going to do?" she demanded.

"Do about what?"

Impatiently she said, "About the tryst. Will you be leader?"

The lack of formal greeting proved that this woman had been intimate with Shonsu. How intimate? The idea of Shonsu having a platonic relationship lacked all conviction—which meant that his hands had stroked those splendid limbs, those breasts had crushed against his body, those lips . . .

Maybe not, though. This woman could have great resistance.

"The *Ten Renegade Swordsmen*?" he asked. "That was yours?"

"Yes."

"Then you have been to Hann?"

She shook her head. "We went over to Quo and down from there. I met a minstrel, who told me the story. Then I knew that you were still alive, so I came back. What about the tryst?"

We?

"I don't think the swordsmen would accept me."

She smiled. He was shocked to see satisfaction in that smile. "Wise of them."

"So what are you going to do?" he asked, his mind whirling.

She was regarding him strangely now, her suspicions aroused. "What I always said I would do—sing at your funeral."

That cleared the board a little.

Yet there was still provocation in her posture. Could the remark have been some sort of humor? Which should he believe—her words or her eyes?

"I am reluctant to give you the opportunity, my lady," he said. "I think I shall leave town again."

"Going where?"

"I am not at liberty to say."

She shook her head, frowning narrowly. "You don't give up like that."

He sat down on the bench and waved at the other. She remained standing. She was certainly wearing nothing under that filmy wrap. He was sweating.

"I told you," he said. "I have changed. Whatever was between us is over." That was comfortingly vague. "I would appreciate it if you did not mention to anyone that you saw me here." He hoped that she would accept his words as dismissal.

"On the contrary." She unslung her lute. "I feel a ballad coming on. *Shonsu the Priest*, perhaps, or *In the Ruins of the Temple?*"

She touched the strings and a ripple of music flowed through the bare stone hall.

"*Katanji to the Dark Tower* . . . was that yours, also?"

She laughed harshly and sat down, facing him. "Not bad, is it? But I think *Shonsu the Priest* will be better."

"What I need," he said, with sudden inspiration, "is *Shonsu the Hero*. If you would do for me what the minstrels have done for my protégé, then I could be leader of the tryst!"

A smile of catlike pleasure crossed her face. She bent her head over the lute and strummed a chord. "Yes? Yes, I could do that. Why should I?" she demanded, looking up at him.

"For the sake of the Goddess, my lady," he said. "I know much more about sorcerers than Lord Boariyi does, or any of the others. If I cannot somehow become leader, then the tryst is doomed."

Her imperious stare was unnerving. "What subject would you recommend? Your visit to Aus? *Shonsu the Snake? Shonsu the Worm?*"

He sighed. She was an electrifying woman, and the battle of wits was a challenge, but he was wasting time, dreaming dreams, and her overpowering presence was making him fall apart.

"Try *Shonsu the Sailor*, my lady," he said and rose to his feet. "I must go and be about Her service. But I do beg of you not to speak of this meeting."

He was halfway to the door when the lute rang out and her voice rose in song:

Shonsu . . . Shonsu . . .

He stopped. It was a lament, echoing eerily across the barren chamber.

Where have you taken our boys?
Where have you taken our joys?
Shonsu . . . Shonsu . . .
The hilts of their swords were bright in the sun,
They held up their heads and submitted to none,
Lovers and brothers and fathers and sons . . .

He walked back slowly. She stopped and began again, this time with a slightly changed melody, the pathos and heartrending emotion even stronger, and she added two more lines. It was a dirge for the forty-nine dead—and she was composing it on the spot.

It would destroy Shonsu utterly.

She stopped and looked up at him mockingly.

He said, "Tell me if you plan to complete that, lady. For if you do, then my cause is lost."

She rose and slung the lute on her back once more. "I shall come with you!"

"Impossible! There will be great danger."

She shrugged. "I am coming."

Minstrels were the news media of the World. She wanted to see the next Shonsu battle at firsthand, as a war correspondent. He hesitated, Wallie Smith's mind suddenly aware of Shonsu's rampaging glands.

"I-I may fail!" he stammered.

She smiled. "I hope so! I shall enjoy watching you die."

Indeed?

"I may disappoint you, of course. I may triumph. You had better stay home with the children."

No reaction to that, thank the gods!

She pouted and seemed to bargain. "If you do succeed, I shall compose an epic for you, Shonsu the hero. It will make you leader."

He wondered if she were mad, or if he were.

Of course! Honakura!

The old man was meddling again . . . but surely this was the hand of the Goddess? Nnanji, Katanji, Honakura himself—they were all extraordinary people, sent by the gods to help in his mission. Certainly this superlative minstrel was another. She was a genius. Honakura had seen that and had recruited her. Typical of the old rascal not to give warning!

"There will be great danger," he said again.

She shrugged. "I have met sorcerers before. They appreciate music more than swordsmen do."

A spy? There was another possibility!

She started toward the door. He stared after her, thinking of the tiny ship and a week's voyage. What had she been to Shonsu? Then she reached the bright archway. Sunlight struck through the gauzy wrap as she mounted the steps, and she was a naked woman bearing a lute and walking in blue fire. He had lost his wits to Shonsu's rage before—now suddenly he blazed with irresistible lust. Shonsu's mistress! He must have her!

He ran in pursuit.

Nnanji and Thana were sitting outside on a crumbled stump of a wall, hand in hand, lost to everything except each other. They sprang up as the tall woman reached them. Evidently Nnanji had not met her before and probably not known she was there, for he looked startled. He drew his sword and saluted.

Wallie was just in time to catch her response: "I am Doa, minstrel of the seventh rank . . ."

It was good to know her name, he thought cynically—in case he wanted to speak to her in the dark.

In sunshine and a rollicking wind, *Sapphire*'s dinghy romped over the water. Thana held the tiller with Nnanji sitting close, both of them staring in mingled astonishment and amusement at the unexpected recruit. Doa leaned back in complacent contemplation of the scenery, her long brown tresses streaming like a flag. Wallie could not take his eyes off her. His hands trembled.

He had never promised Jja that he would be faithful to her only. He had tried to; she had stopped him from saying the words. Having now heard the People's version of a marriage contract, he could understand why. He had scoffed at Nnanji's infatuation over Thana, yet he was behaving like a witless swain himself. He tried to find excuses—this woman had been Shonsu's mistress and so his reaction was a conditioned reflex.

His conscience did not believe an atom of that.

He told his conscience to shut up.

She might well be a sorcerer spy. He would go and talk with Honakura as soon as he had seen her safely confined aboard *Sapphire*. Then he saw that *Sapphire* was not their destination. *Griffon* had completed her shakedown cruise and was now anchored near the temple. They were almost there.

Thana ran the dinghy alongside and willing hands made her fast. Familiar faces grinned down—most of the males from *Sapphire* had come along for the ride.

Griffon's deck was much higher than the dinghy. Wallie wondered how Doa would manage the climb in her impractical silk sheath. He offered a hand. She ignored it, reached for her hem, flashed a brief glimpse of long and shapely legs, and then she was up on the deck, glancing back down at him with a flicker of mockery.

She swung around and made her salute to Tomiyano, who was staring up at her like an astonished boy. Then he recovered his wits and began introducing the others.

Wallie scrambled aboard. "How is she?" he demanded, when the captain was available for business.

"The ship you mean?"

"Of course the ship!"

"Not bad at all," Tomiyano conceded. There was, of course, only one vessel that could ever be described as good. "Nimble! We could make her faster if we had a couple more days."

"That we don't." Wallie glanced at the sun; two or three hours of daylight left. "We could leave at dawn?"

Tomiyano shrugged. "We could leave now."

Wallie looked to Nnanji and got an excited nod. Why not? Speed was a priceless skill in warfare.

"Then let's do so!"

"Who?" the captain asked.

Very good question! "You and me and Nnanji and Thana . . ." They nodded in turn as he looked their way. "And Lady Doa. We need another sailor." He turned to the eager group of faces. The youngsters would give their teeth to come, of course: Sinboro and Matarro, for instance. No, he would not fight with children. The obvious choice was the skinny and taciturn Holiyi, who was leaning against the mast with a sardonic smile on his face. He was a bachelor. He had obviously worked it out already.

"Holiyi? Would you?"

Holiyi nodded. Why waste two words when none will do?

"That should be enough," Wallie said.

Nnanji frowned. "That's only six!"

Wallie sighed. By the rules of the World it would have to be seven. Jja? But she was not present. He had counted Vixini before, so would have to count him this time, making eight, and to separate Jja from her baby would be . . . would be as bad as having Jja along with Doa. Not Jja.

Then he saw hope gleaming in impish dark eyes . . . That seemed ridiculous. With a smashed arm he would be of no practical use. Yet somehow it felt right. He had been ashore in Sen, which was the closest city of the left bank, and must therefore be their destination. An aura of good fortune hung around him . . . and Wallie would much prefer to keep Katanji under his eye than running wild in Casr when he was away.

Nnanji chuckled and said, "I think so, brother! He brings wisdom."

Katanji it must be, then. The others would return to *Sapphire* in the dinghy, and the *Griffon* expedition could sail at once. If Doa were a spy, she would have no chance to report.

And Wallie would not have to face Jja.

Nnanji began calling out the list of requirements: silk bags, ensorceled wine, food . . . Each item was acknowledged by whoever had stowed it aboard.

Wallie went over to Doa, who was leaning on the rail, studying the temple. She turned to give him a sultry glance, and it was all he could do to keep his hands off her. "How much did the old man tell you?" he asked.

"Which old man?"

"Lord Honakura."

Doa frowned. "Who?"

†††

The World was a simple place. Possessions were few and paperwork nonexistent. Little time was needed to organize the departure. Wallie himself hauled in the anchor as the sailors raised the sails. The stay-at-homes cheered from the dinghy; *Griffon* leaned her shoulder to the wind and leaped forward.

She was more than nimble. She was speedy, with a sprightliness that belied her obvious great age. Her deck was much closer to the water than *Sapphire*'s and it heeled over at an angle that Wallie at first found alarming. She rocked in the tiny waves of the River. Very soon, though, he began to relax. A madcap venture this might be, but for the next two or three days he could enjoy a cruise.

Griffon was a simple ship—one mast and a single flat deck, walled around, of course, because anyone who fell off a ship on the River did not live long enough to call for a life preserver. Her planks were scuffed and shabby and bespangled with fish scales. She had two hatches, a small one aft for people and a larger forward for cargo, both presently uncovered. There was also a small dinghy, upturned on the deck, close behind the mast and almost opposite the gate where the plank went out. Clean her up and paint her to kill the stench, Wallie thought, and *Griffon* would be a very pleasant little vessel.

Yet *Griffon* was also now a custom-built sorcerer trap, thanks to Holiyi's carpentry. Even that innocent-seeming upturned dinghy was part of it.

Bright sun and a boisterous wind . . . and a broad grin on Tomiyano's face as he sought the feel of the tiller, squeezing speed from this new toy like juice from a fruit. A cargo ship larger than

Sapphire was lumbering along ahead, and Wallie was astonished to see how fast *Griffon* was overtaking her. Already the first great bend was coming up. He faced aft again and saw that Casr had dwindled into the distance. There was much less shipping there now than there had been—the Goddess had closed down Her swordsman delivery service.

The favorable wind was an encouraging omen, he decided. Of course, if he had made a wrong decision, that next bend might bring him back to Casr. The others were making themselves comfortable on the windward side of the deck, leaning back against the bulwarks . . . only four? Where was the minstrel?

Then Doa came scrambling up the ladder. She had ripped her silk wrap into strips and fashioned herself a sailor bikini, as daringly skimpy as Thana's. She stalked over to the rail to study the scenery.

She *was* the scenery. Shonsu's glands went into thundering overdrive again. Barefoot, with waist-length hair surging in the wind, with her unprepossessing face averted and that bare minimum of garment concealing almost nothing, her astounding figure was a fanfare of trumpets to Wallie. Jja was a tall woman, but she was not built on Shonsu's scale, as this Amazonian minstrel was. He decided it was time to try a little wooing. He had unwittingly offended by ignoring her at the lodge. Wishing he could think of some plausible explanation for that, he walked over to her side and put an arm around her bare flank.

She was fast. Only his own lightning reflexes saved his eyes. He reeled back, fingering a bleeding scrape on his cheek.

"Don't touch me!"

As he stared open-mouthed, she marched away to join the others.

The others were tying themselves in knots to suppress laughter, waiting to see what Great Lover would do next.

The sun had set. The sky was darkening; remains of the evening meal were being tidied away by Thana. *Griffon*'s crew were stretched out at the aft end of the deck.

"Almost time to anchor, Cap'n?" Wallie inquired, pulling a blanket over his shoulders.

"Why?" Tomiyano had at last, reluctantly, given Holiyi a chance to try the helm. "Clear sky, good breeze."

"Fine!" Wallie had not experienced night sailing on the River since he left the holy island, but evidently *Griffon* could take risks that *Sapphire* must not. Heroes were allowed to be lucky. He went back to considering Doa.

The others had been deferential to her rank. Her attitude to them had been haughty and aloof, yet she had replied graciously to their questions and comments, been tolerant or even friendly. Toward Wallie her behavior was the exact opposite—seductive glances under lowered eyelashes, deep breathing, signals imploring intimacy, but the few words she had spared him had been waspish or openly scurrilous. The combination made no sense at all, a welcome sign hung on a locked door, and he was at a loss to know what reaction was expected of him.

Now she was talking with Katanji, a remarkable concession from a Seventh to a First, even a First with his great social skills. Of course it had been Katanji who had supplied the subject matter for her satirical ballad, and now she discovered that he had not yet heard it. She picked up her lute, struck a chord, and launched into *Novice Katanji to the Dark Tower Came*. Thana and the two sailors hooted with laughter as the tale unfolded; Katanji was soon almost choking. Nnanji's initial smiles turned rapidly to glares. Wallie tried hard to bury his own resentment under admiration for her troubadour skill, but the satire bit like adders: Shonsu cowering in a ship, sending forth his one-boy army disguised as a slave. The sorcerers were savaged, also, but the swordsmen came off worse.

When she had finished, Nnanji said coldly, "And one for me, my lady? The *Farewell*, perhaps?"

Pouting, Doa began to strum in a minor key. The conversation between Nnanji and the dying Arganari came drifting across the darkening deck to Wallie. His eyes prickled as memory clenched his heart.

Suddenly Doa stopped. "Junk!" she snarled. "Give me a minute." She stroked the strings, and Wallie recognized wisps of the lament she had begun in the refectory. In a few minutes she had it ready and began to sing once more: "Nnanji . . . Nnanji . . ."

The first song had not been junk, but now she made it seem

so—genius outshining mere competence. Her lyric was vastly better, and the new melody as haunting and soul-rending as *Shenandoah* or *The Londonderry Air*. Soon Wallie found that his cheeks were wet. In silence he wept for a tone-deaf stripling who could not have appreciated one note of the supreme creation his death had inspired. It died away at last, and he saw that the others were as moved as he.

He was awestruck. He felt that he had been present at the unveiling of something that ought to be immortal—and yet it had been an impromptu creation. She was Mozart or Shakespeare, or both. He had found his Homer—if she would deign to help.

That night *Griffon* danced with the wind god over waters of ebony inlaid with platinum. A red beacon burned for her on the peaks of RegiVul. Tomiyano and Holiyi steered and kept watch, while the others lay in the putrid, damp hold.

Wallie offered Doa the single cabin. She inquired if the door could be bolted, but Holiyi had moved the fastening to the outside, turning the tiny room into a jail. She declined the offer.

Wallie slept there himself, still hoping wistfully that later, under the secretive blindfold of darkness, he might be granted company. But no one came. He slept poorly, unaccustomed to the motion of the ship, harkening to the creaks and water noises, conscious of the foul and fetid stink. And conscious, also, of a savage unrequited desire.

She had been Shonsu's mistress. Shonsu's expedition had met disaster. Whose side was Doa on?

Near to sunset of the second day, *Griffon* dropped anchor off Sen, less than a mile from shore. The wind god had been an enthusiastic helper, and they had made excellent time. Only one thing had been denied them—a short period of calm for Wallie to test his sorcerer bait. His equipment would not work in a strong breeze, but perhaps gods did not appreciate a need for rehearsal. The wind was dropping now, as if made to order. The former Wallie Smith would have been concerned by that, for a dead calm would leave him hopelessly trapped within the sorcerers' reach. Now he would indulge in superstitious faith and trust the gods.

Heroes were allowed to be lucky.

Or put it another way: Without luck, a man did not survive to be a hero.

No, the first way was better.

He was making other wild assumptions, also. He was guessing that the sorcerers were keeping careful watch on the River and its traffic. He was presuming that they used telescopes, and that those were of no great capacity. About a ten power, he thought, would be their limit. Most of all, he was counting on the swordsmen's reputation. The last thing the sorcerers should be expecting from swordsmen was trickery.

Still, it would be great folly to underestimate the opposition. The swordsmen had never learned by their mistakes, but he was sure that sorcerers would, and they had been grievously mauled at Ov. Shonsu's arrival at Casr and his subsequent disappearance would be known. They would be especially cautious of a large Seventh or a red-haired Fourth, and he would even give the enemy's intelligence network credit for reporting that the Fourth was now a Fifth.

Nnanji, therefore, had been banished belowdecks before Sen even came in sight—red hair was rare among the People. Katanji, also, had been sent below, because of his cast. Doa's great height made her conspicuous and her association with the original Shonsu might be known. She might be a sorcerer agent—Doa was down in the hold, too.

Wallie wore the blue gown that Lae had make for him. He had the cowl raised and he was keeping his face averted from the city. Tomiyano had smeared a cosmetic brown paste over his sorcerer brand. That left only Thana's facemarks as a danger signal, and Wallie did not think that those would show at this distance. If the watchers were male, they would be studying other things when they looked at Thana, anyway.

The anchor was down, the sails were lowered. He had his equipment spread out on the deck—lying in the shadow of the bulwarks, for the sun was low. There were no other ships near. The wind had faded to a gentle breeze. Wallie had gone over the plan with his helpers a thousand times during the last two days. Conscious of a dry mouth and a thumping heart, he reviewed everything again in his mind, wondering what he might have overlooked and worrying over the million risks he had not.

Had he stayed too far out? Perhaps even ten power was beyond the sorcerers' skills. He must not look to the city itself, but he could see the bank just downstream from it, and the houses seemed very tiny. What if his bait were not even noticed? What if it did not work at all? What if . . .

"Well, great leader?" Tomiyano asked impatiently.

"What if the wind dies on us?"

"Bah!" The captain walked across to the innocent-seeming scrap of rug that was yet another part of the plan. He adjusted it with one horny foot. "The winds have been singing to your lute, Shonsu! Every time we rounded a bend, the wind backed for us. Where's your faith, Champion-of-the-Goddess?"

He was nervous, also, and trying not to show it.

"Then let's go!"

Wallie knelt and tipped alcohol into a copper pan. Playing the part she had been given, Thana lit tinder with a flint—a skill that he had not yet mastered. He slid the tinder into the pan as she steadied it. The flame was invisible, but Wallie could feel heat. He straightened, lifting the apex of the orange silk bag high, mentally crossing fingers. The cup might be too heavy, or not large enough, or the catgut holding it might burn through, or he might set the ship on fire, or nothing might work at all . . .

The bag began to swell. Thana looked up in alarm and Tomiyano made the sign of the Goddess. The bag filled more rapidly. The wind breathed on it and Wallie held it firm with two hands. Then he decided that it was full enough. He stooped and took the copper pan from Thana to raise it, steadying the bag with his other hand as it wallowed free. He felt lift, so he let go.

The World's first hot-air balloon soared away in the breeze, spinning slowly . . . rising higher . . . floating over the River. He vaguely heard exclamations from his companions, but he was too intent to listen. Surely the sorcerers would never have seen anything like that before? They would think he was one of them, coming to call with a new magic. In a few minutes the balloon would fall from the sky, but by then they would have lost it in the haze and the sun's glare.

It had gone. He looked around and saw that he was being regarded with superstitious awe. Thana was quaking and Holiyi pale.

There was another bag, the one he had planned to use for rehearsal. "Let's do that again!" He chuckled, and they launched a second balloon. It climbed faster. Now his magic could not be dismissed as a freak illusion.

"Take her in, Captain!" he said hoarsely, resisting the natural impulse to turn and look at the town. Keeping his face hidden in his cowl, he headed for the hatch.

Would the wind serve, or would it die and leave them stranded? Holiyi and Tomiyano remained on deck, while the others fretted and chewed fingernails in the hold. Even with both hatch covers off, the hold stank. At each tack bilge swirled under the gratings, stirring unidentified nasty things as it did so. There was a ladder below the smaller hatch and a door to the little cabin, but otherwise it was a barren wooden box . . . a communal coffin, perhaps. The bedrolls and foodstuffs formed a small heap in the bow. Ropes for tying prisoners had been laid out, in a show of optimism.

Nnanji and Thana fidgeted, holding drawn swords already. Doa seemed quite relaxed, sitting on a bedroll and sending seductive little smiles toward Wallie. He was tense enough himself now that he found them easy to ignore, and evidently he need not worry about his passenger having hysterics. Katanji sat in a corner with his arms around his knees, making himself very tiny.

How many tacks? There were no portholes and Wallie dared not go near a hatch to peer out. Then he heard a shot from the deck and, in the distance, a clatter of horses.

"Almost there!" he said. "I think we have to add one thing that was not in the drill. Lady Doa will be bound and gagged. Thana, please?"

"You would not dare!" roared the minstrel.

"I certainly would," Wallie said. "If necessary I'll knock you out, or tie you up myself, but I'm not having any warning shouts! Now, which is to be?"

Glaring murderously, Doa allowed herself to be trussed.

Then *Griffon* thumped softly against fenders. Pulleys squealed as the sails were taken in. A moment later Tomiyano skidded down the ladder and scuttled over to the others, who were all staying well away from the hatches.

"Lots of room, anyway!" the captain said with a cheerfulness that rang false.

Wallie wondered what that meant, but he was too intent to spare time for conversation. Holiyi had cut two ports in the ship's side directly below the hawsers. Nnanji and Thana now fumbled to remove their makeshift shutters. Being below quay level, these unorthodox gaps would be invisible to viewers on the dock.

Wallie stepped up on a balk of timber and thrust his head through yet another hole, this one cut in the deck. That put his eyes inside the upturned dinghy, so he could peer out the peephole in its side and watch the top of the gangplank. Unfortunately he did not have as good a view as he would have liked, for he could see only the gateway and not down the length of the plank. His reaction would have to be very swift.

Tomiyano's scar was obvious at close quarters, so Holiyi must wear the dagger and be captain. Everything now depended on the skinny sailor.

Minutes crawled by. The strain of waiting seemed to grow without limit. Holiyi's bare feet and bony legs went past the peephole and later returned.

Normally a port official came first, then went ashore. Afterward, if the bait had worked, a sorcerer or two should embark to greet the visitor. But at Ov sorcerers had accompanied the port official—was that a new procedure since the calling of the tryst, or just the way things were done at Ov? Would Holiyi be able to satisfy the port official?

"What if they ignore us?" Thana asked with a giggle that was just wrong enough to reveal nervousness.

No one spoke. The answer would have been that they would have to make an assault ashore and try to overpower a patrolling sorcerer. Sorcerers patrolled in groups and they carried guns.

Wallie was streaming sweat. His neck hurt. The stink was nauseating. He was just making a solemn vow that he would never eat fish again, when Holiyi was convulsed by coughing. That was the signal. A gown came into Wallie's field of view—a long gown, reaching to the ground. That was no port official . . .

"Now!" As the sorcerer's shoe landed on the scrap of rug at

the top of the plank, Wallie triggered the trapdoor below it. Thana and Nnanji reached out with their swords to cut the hawsers. It was only then, as the victim came crashing down into the hold, that Wallie's mind registered the overwhelming impossibility. The gown had been blue. He had captured a sorcerer of the seventh rank.

†† ††

Then many things happened all at once. Tomiyano and one-armed Katanji guided the ends of oars through the ports as Wallie stepped down and struck the sorcerer on the head with a bar of wood. Voices yelled on the dock. Nnanji grabbed Katanji's oar and heaved, while Tomiyano heaved on his. Holiyi took a running jump through the cargo hatch and his feet hit the gratings with a crash. *Griffon* surged and began to move, propelled by the oars pushing against the dock. Wallie went to help Nnanji; Holiyi to Tomiyano. The clatter of the falling gangplank mingled with a scream and a splash—possibly a sorcerer had gone to the Goddess—then the oars fell uselessly through the ports and the ship was adrift . . . and no one else had boarded.

"Down!" Wallie yelled, but the others were already dropping to the smelly gratings. A fusillade of shots made three small holes in the planking and a shower of splinters spattered. Then the sound of chaos, familiar from Ov—horses screaming, people yelling, wagons overturning . . .

Griffon rocked gently and calmly. The sunlight below the hatches moved as the ship turned in the current and the wind. How long to reload the pistols? Would the wind hold for their escape? Would *Griffon* foul another vessel and be invaded by a troop of outraged sorcerers? The prisoner was unconscious. Awkwardly, and without rising, Wallie reached over and tied the man's hands behind his back.

The noise from the dock was fading. The sorcerers should have been able to reload by now. What were they doing instead? Wallie rose to his feet and dashed for the ladder. Two rungs up he saw rigging over the gunwale, but far away. Then the tower came into view, and the tops of warehouses, all black against the darkening sky. He decided he was out of reasonable musket range and finished his climb to the deck.

At once he saw what Tomiyano had meant about plenty of room. There were many ships at both ends of the harbor, leaving the center strangely empty. The slimy masonry of the dock itself was visible, and the road and the warehouses beyond it. The captain had moored in that long gap—any captain would.

It was a trap!

Wallie bellowed for the sailors and began to fumble inexpertly with ropes. Crowds had been running for shelter, horses bolting and rearing at the noise, but the road was clearing rapidly.

Tomiyano and Holiyi appeared and began to hoist sail. There was wind, but not very much. *Griffon* acknowledged it sluggishly, swinging her bow toward open River with reluctance. As nasty crawling feelings ran over his skin, Wallie studied the dock and waited. He was out of range for pistols, but not for cannon. The two closest ships were flying red flags, so the orders had been to stay out of the flagged area . . .

Nnanji and Thana came scrambling up the ladder, and Wallie yelled to them to take cover again, but Doa was coming up behind them, free of her bonds.

Almost simultaneously, three columns of black smoke jetted skyward beside the warehouses. Two more followed at once. The roar of cannons thumped at his ears and he saw the horses panic once more. Vertical? He raised his eyes and thought he saw one black speck in motion.

"Those were very big thunderbolts, brother," Nnanji said judiciously. Then waterspouts reared all around and *Griffon* staggered. A spray of mist blew over the deck. Close!

Mortars would not take long to reload. Wallie was about to order everyone below again, then decided that a cannonball could kill all of them just as easily there as here. They all began coughing as the cloud of gray smoke overtook the ship. Black powder made an astonishing amount of smoke.

"Tack!" he shouted. Tomiyano started to argue and Wallie yelled at him. *Griffon* changed course slightly as two—four—five more explosions mushroomed from the roadway. This time he certainly saw a couple of the balls in flight and pointed them out. They seemed to take a long time falling. Mortars would have less chance of hitting a ship than cannons, but they would do far more damage, knocking a hole in the keel. Traveling horizontally, a cannonball would merely go straight through the hull, unless it was lucky enough to hit a mast.

Waterspouts again—and one just off the bow. A torrent of water fell against the sails and over the deck, making the ship shudder and heel. Katanji and Thana were hurled down and everyone was soaked. Tomiyano swore angrily and changed course slightly again. Now he could see the need to dodge. Wallie peered into the hatch, but there was surprisingly little water in the hold. He hoped that piranha could not survive being carried aboard in that rough fashion, or the prisoner would be nibbled to tatters.

Much too close for comfort! Their escape was agonizingly slow. The sorcerers would be able to get in at least one more good shot before *Griffon* was out of effective range. Why was it taking them so long?

His friends were battle-tested veterans. They were tense and most of them were clutching the rail very firmly, but there was no panic. He looked to see how Doa was reacting and saw at once that he need not worry. She was soaked, her hair bedraggled, but her face glowed with excitement. Her eyes were shining. She noticed his attention, smiled happily, and said, "Wonderful!" She was an astonishing woman!

Obviously *Griffon* had arrived while the sorcerers were rehearsing their reception for the arrival of the tryst. A wide empty space would attract the unsuspecting ships and allow a clear field of fire. That might even explain why a Seventh had been down at the docks.

"Nnanji?" Wallie said in the calmest voice he could muster. "We never heard of a sorcerer city having more than one Seventh, did we?"

"No, brother."

"Then you realize who that is in the hold?"

"Rotanxi!" Nnanji shouted. "The wizard! The man who sent the kilts to the lodge?"

Before Wallie could answer, smoke gushed once more from the warehouse doors where the cannons were; but this time the jets were horizontal, and there were no waterspouts. As the noise arrived, so the River boiled—astern of *Griffon* and off to each side. White clouds of mist rose and then faded again. Grapeshot! Wallie shivered convulsively.

The gods might have ruled out miracles, but they were not withholding good luck. The sorcerers had been prepared to repulse an approaching attack, not to destroy a departing fugitive, so initially the cannons had been set in mortar position and armed with balls, for distance. Probably it took time to reset them for their close-range use as cannons, firing grapeshot. Against ships full of swordsmen the grape would be a hundred times more deadly—it would sweep the decks clean. Had the grape come first, while *Griffon* was nearer, then she would have been blasted to sawdust.

Slowly, so slowly, they were retreating from the dock.

"Get below!" he roared. "All of you!"

He tried to take the tiller from Tomiyano while the others obeyed orders; there was an argument. Before the matter was settled, the sorcerers tried again. This time the shots fell short. Wallie relaxed and wiped his brow. They were out of range of the grape and only a very lucky shot with a ball could hit them now. Today the luck was with the swordsmen.

Conscious and wearing his cowled gown, the sorcerer would be an imposing figure. He was tall and ruddy-faced, with eyebrows like snowbanks and stark, craggy features. Wallie guessed that he was a well-preserved seventy.

He was beginning to stir and groan. Wallie untied his hands and stripped off the heavy robe. As Katanji had noted long ago, a sorcerer's gown was lumpy. It held innumerable pockets, bulging with mysterious clunky objects. Wallie thrilled with satisfaction at the thought of unmasking the sorcerers' craft with this evidence.

His victim was not imposing now. He was a pathetic figure in a short cotton shirt that failed to hide a potbelly and spindly old-man's legs, blotched with varicose veins. His white hair was thin and matted in two places with dried blood, but his injuries seemed to be confined to those. Wallie dressed him in the fake gown that Lae had made, slung him over his shoulder, and carried him up to the deck.

Pulse, pupils . . . the old man was apparently in fair shape and now he was starting to come around, blinking, groaning, and drooling. Wallie leaned him against the upturned dinghy and turned to Nnanji, whose face bore enough satisfaction to embellish a victorious army.

"Watch him, master!" Wallie said. "He'll be over the rail in a flash if we let him—and we want him alive!"

Then he went below to fetch the mysterious robe and a flask of wine.

The wind was rising again. The sun balanced still on the horizon, bloodied by volcanic dust, so obviously the whole escapade had taken much less time than it had seemed to. Triumph! Heroes were certainly allowed to be lucky. Remembering how close to *Griffon* the grapeshot had foamed, Wallie dampened his self-congratulation with a silent prayer of thanksgiving. The gunnery had been impressive—but so had the good fortune.

He sat on the deck close to Tomiyano, facing the sorcerer. The others gathered around, chattering and grinning in victory and relief. Nnanji and Thana were cuddling each other, release of tension rousing other instincts. Doa, strangely solemn, was studying the sorcerer and absentmindedly tugging a comb through her wet hair, while Wallie ran his eye longingly over the wondrous length of her shapely legs, conscious of his own instincts in action. She noticed his attention and sent him a coquettishly inviting smile. It was probably no more genuine than its predecessors, but it still raised his heartbeat for a moment.

He passed the wine bottle around and studied the gown spread out before him. It was soaked and smelly with bilge. One of the lumps had seemed to twitch when he touched it, so he started with that. After a cautious peek in the pocket, he reached in, fumbled, and pulled out a bird. Tomiyano said he would be a barnacle's grandmother.

"Not just a bird," Wallie crowed. "It's a pigeon and it has a band on its leg." The others exchanged impressed glances. He put the bird back in the pocket and tried the next.

"And what's this?" He set his discovery upon his nose and the audience howled with laughter. Eyeglasses were the first step toward the telescope, of course. Everything had to be explained, and they all tried the glasses.

"And here's a . . ." He tried to say "quill pen" and stuttered into silence. "Quill . . . brush?" That came out. "Must be ink in this bottle? Right!" He knew the word for ink, although it meant only what came out of an octopus.

The same pocket also held tiny fragments of vellum, so fine that it might have been bird skin. Wallie chuckled, suddenly remembering his childhood and the Christmas parties when his father had hidden favors in a bran tub for the youngsters to find. This was more fun.

"Will you all promise not to tell anyone else about this?" he asked, and got a ballet of nodding heads. With the quill and the small ink bottle, he drew seven swords on one of the scraps of vellum and held it out for them to look at it.

"What does that mean?" he asked.

Chorus: "A swordsman of the Seventh."

Then he attempted to draw a griffon. It looked like a pregnant camel. "And what does that all mean?"

A puzzled, frowning silence was broken by Katanji. "The seventh sword?"

"Right you are!" There was still enough light for flying; Wallie waved the vellum to dry it, then retrieved the pigeon and slid the message into its band. "Let's send the sign back to the tower." He tossed the bird into the air. They watched it circle and climb and vanish in the direction of Sen.

"That is how they send messages," Wallie explained. "The ink comes from the squid. You tend to get it on your fingers, of course," he added ruefully as he recorked the bottle—he was not experienced with a quill. He studied faces. They looked impressed and happy. Nnanji and Thana were paying more attention to each other, sniggering again already. The sailors were grinning. Only Doa seemed worried and puzzled. Katanji was staring at the pen and the vellum, thinking.

"You are becoming a nuisance," the sorcerer said in a deep voice, glaring. "Lord Shonsu!" He looked around. "Master Nnanji, the wagon driver? And Novice Katanji, who understandably prefers being a slave to being a swordsman. The mendacious

Captain Tomiyano, of course. Lady Doa, you keep strange company!"

The audience hissed at this sorcery. Wallie laughed and pointed at Holiyi. "What's his name?"

The sorcerer shrugged. "It is upon you that I shall set my curses," he said. "I have summoned demons—"

"Pigeon droppings!" Wallie said. "You have spies in Casr, so you know who we are. I don't scare with demons and curses, Lord Rotanxi."

The man was groggy still, or else too proud, for he did not deny the name.

Doa said quietly, "It is you who are in strange company, my lord."

"He probably has a sore head," Wallie said. "Would you like a drink of water? No? Just speak up if you want a blanket or something. Now, let's carry on." Carefully he reached into another pocket. "Any guesses on this treasure? Little sticks with something on the ends!" Matches? He struck one and his audience gasped. That meant phosphorus, so his guess had been correct. "Sorcerer, what's your name for the stuff you make these with? It's soft and yellow, and you have to keep it under water or it goes on fire. Come on, man, I know all about it! I just want to know what you call it."

Furious silence.

"Do you know how to make it safer by heating it?" Wallie asked. "It turns red."

Obviously the answer was yes. "How do you know these things?" the prisoner demanded, shocked.

"That's a long story. I'm a better sorcerer than you are. I know that you can see a long way from your tower with a thing made of glass. And I know how to make messages with your quill and the ink, although I can't do it in your words."

The sorcerer seemed to shrink.

Wallie went back to the gown. "Now what's in this pocket? Ah, here we have the thunderbolt." He showed the others the pistol. It was a single-barrel muzzle-loader. He had anticipated a flintlock, but the mechanism used a phosphorus-based friction cap—very ingenious. The workmanship was exquisite, the butt scrolled with silver and mother-of-pearl. More rummaging uncovered lead balls, but also measured packets of gunpowder like cartridges, and fortunately these had stayed dry, in a separate leather bag. He had expected a powder horn.

"This, I suppose, you would call thunderpowder. It's made from sulfur and charcoal and saltpeter." Wallie examined the balls and explained how the pistol shot them out. Nnanji scowled and the others were disgusted.

Rotanxi was pale. This display of knowledge must be more of a shock to him than the rough treatment had been. "Who are you?" he demanded.

"My name is Shonsu, as you said. I am on the side of the Goddess and the swordsmen and I am going to take you to Casr and show the tryst this weapon. That was what I came for, and you yourself are only a bonus. I hope that I can become leader, so that the tryst will not do stupid things like making frontal attacks on Sen."

The sorcerer straightened his back against the dinghy and attempted a triumphant sneer. He had an arrogant, aristocrat's face —deep-set eyes below those snowy eyebrows, high aquiline nose, long upper lip—a good face for sneering, a Roman fallen among Goths. "You are too late, Shonsu. Yesterday the swordsmen held their absurd ceremony of trying to kill each other to see who is the biggest butcher. The juvenile Boariyi won. How curious to choose a leader by the length of his arms!"

Nnanji muttered an oath and looked at Wallie to see if he ought to believe this.

"So they are on their way?" Wallie inquired.

The sorcerer hesitated, and then said, "They embark tomorrow at dawn."

"That's very quick work!" Wallie said as innocently as he could manage. "All that food and stuff . . ."

Rotanxi sneered. "They have no choice, because they have no money left."

"Well, then we shall intercept them and warn them about your big thunderbolts."

"Ha! You can't! They are going to Wal, not coming here. It is possible that they will change their minds, but Sen is ready if they do."

"Wal is much farther," Wallie said, frowning. "It seems foolish, especially since it was you who sent the kilts. Why Wal?"

"They think to outsmart sorcerers!" Rotanxi retorted with an ocean of contempt.

"Seems to me that Lord Shonsu outsmarted you easily enough!" Nnanji snarled. That broke the spell. The old man's lips tightened. He had said too much.

"But I had not thought Lord Boariyi capable of such subtlety!" Wallie thought for a moment that Rotanxi would say more, but he did not. Probably Wal had been the brainchild of Uncle Zoariyi, and the sorcerer's hesitation suggested that he might even be aware of that. He was extremely well informed about the tryst, even to its finances.

"So you have failed, Shonsu!" Doa said with satisfaction.

"I hope not, my lady." Wallie tried to convey a confidence he did not quite feel. "I took steps to prevent the tryst from departing."

She frowned doubtfully.

"My lord?" asked Katanji. "How does he know about Lord Boariyi being leader?"

"Pigeons!" Wallie said. "His spies release pigeons, which return to their mates in Sen. Of course birds fly three or four times as fast as even *Griffon* can sail, and they don't have to go around all the bends in the River."

"Pigeons can't talk, my lord," Katanji protested. His face was growing vague in the fading light, but the doubt showed.

"You saw the little piece of vellum I sent with the bird we released," Wallie explained, his eyes on the sorcerer. "Well, they could have had a code arranged—a triangle for Boariyi, a circle for Tivanixi . . ."

He was not fooling the sorcerer, of course, but he did not want to explain writing to the others. That knowledge could be fatal if the sorcerers ever discovered that they had it. It would destroy the sorcerers' craft if it ever became widely known; it might disrupt the whole culture of the World. That was a threat he might find useful, and must keep in reserve. But he did not think he had convinced Katanji.

The wind was growing chill. He turned his attention back to the gown. "Let's see what else we can find," he muttered. But the next thing he found was a wicked little knife. It looked sharp as a razor, and he thought that it was coated with something, probably a poison.

"On second thought, we'll leave the rest until tomorrow, when the light is better. Lord Rotanxi, you will be confined in the cabin. Probably you will be more comfortable in there than the rest of us will be in the hold. You will be allowed on deck by day, under supervision. You will be fed and well treated."

"Kept in good shape for the interrogation, of course!" The old man sneered.

"You will not be tortured, if that is what you fear."

Rotanxi snorted disbelievingly. "Indeed? The great Shonsu is well known for castrating men in brothel quarrels. Did you not once burn down a house because a child threw a tomato at you from the window? Your idea of good treatment may not agree with mine, my lord."

Wallie winced and could find no reply. It was Nnanji who spoke next.

"Those days are over, sorcerer. You can trust his word. If it were me, I should start at your toenails and work upward, but Lord Shonsu will treat you well. Much too well, I expect."

Even in the blurred conflict of light from the fading sunset and the brightening Dream God, Nnanji's young face radiated sincerity. The sorcerer seemed surprised and was silent.

"Take him below," Wallie said. "Give him food and water and blankets. Let's eat; I'm hungry!"

He bundled up the sorcerer's gown and rose to his feet. Red flame flickered over RegiVul and the air stank again of sulfur. The Fire God was angry—as he should be, Wallie thought. With the evidence he had now, he could rip the mystery from the sorcerers' craft and destroy their mystique . . . if the swordsmen would listen.

The River was bright. Tomiyano would keep sailing, eager to return to his beloved *Sapphire*.

"I wanted to see you die."

Wallie turned and found Doa, standing very close.

"My apologies for disappointing you, my lady."

"Now, I suppose, you expect me to create an epic for you?"

Her tone was sweet and she was smiling. With any other woman he would have taken her in his arms and tried to kiss her. The invitation was that obvious, and totally at variance with her words. Genius was next to madness—he was convinced now that she was mad. He wondered what Shonsu had done to her to produce this poisonous hatred and the uncanny fascination that seemed to accompany it. Probably any song she composed about the day's events would be murder to Shonsu's reputation—a verbal assassination set to some immortal melody. Even if she played fair, an epic about the day's events could help him little, for all he had done was use trickery. That would not disgust the swordsmen as much as the Katanji story, perhaps, but it would certainly not impress them, either.

Yet she was a lot of woman. Her extraordinary height excited him still. Having trouble keeping his voice calm, he said, "I should be honored to be mentioned in any of your works, my lady."

Her eyes seemed to flash in the night. "You think I can't? You think an epic without blood is impossible?"

"I think the gods have sent me a great victory today. I am very glad that there was no blood spilled."

"Bah!" she said, unconvinced. She stepped over to the rail to stare out at the last red glow over the western horizon. His feet moved to follow her, although he was not conscious of having told them to do so.

"Tell me about the first time," she said softly. "What happened to the forty-nine?"

"I don't know."

Startled, she turned to look at him. She edged closer—oh, so close! "You expect me to believe that?"

"It is true, Doa. I got a bang on the head. I remember nothing before Hann. I did meet with a god, as you were told. He did give me this sword. But I do not remember living in Casr, or leading the forty-nine . . . I do not even remember knowing you. That was why I did not acknowledge you in the lodge that day. I thought you were a boy."

Her tone stayed delicate as gossamer. "You are a contemptible bastard, Shonsu. You treat me as if I were filth, but you need not think I am stupid."

"That was another Shonsu, my lady."

"Swine."

Wallie threw ropes around his temper. "It is the truth—I swear by my sword."

"But I will show you. I will create the greatest epic the World has ever heard—even without blood."

"I shall be honored."

She paused, irresolute. "I must know about the forty-nine!"

"I can't help you."

"You are a bastard. Then I shall ask the sorcerer tomorrow." Doa spun on her heel and stalked away.

On the longest, loveliest legs in the World.

†† † ††

"Oh, am I glad to see you!" Brota roared, advancing like a red galleon under full sail, her robe rippling in the wind, flabby arms outstretched. *Griffon* had just nudged against *Sapphire*'s fenders and was not even tied up yet. Wallie had newly clambered aboard. Brota enveloped him like a runaway tent, and he hugged her in return, having no option. Then she backed away a pace, and he saw the strain in her face, the tension under the joviality.

Then Jja. He was foul and fishy and not fit for intimacy, but she threw her arms around him and kissed him, and he returned the embrace and the kiss with fervor and joy. It was good to be back. It was good to hold a woman who knew her own emotions, a woman who was beautiful and loving and—above all—supremely sane.

The blustery wind that had swept him in from Sen was pitching and rocking *Sapphire* as she lay at anchor off Casr in cool morning sunshine. There was mention of rain in the air.

The rest of the crew were gathering around. Their faces, also, were stressed and wan, although *Griffon*'s crew were in much worse shape after four days on a tossing, putrid tub. There were hugs and slappings of backs.

Two other ships were anchored in the distance downstream, and two more tied up at the waterfront, but the great plaza was almost deserted, given over to the lonely wind, stark as a vacant tomb. The golden streets were empty as old-fashioned Sunday mornings.

"You've been to Sen?" Brota demanded. "There and back in four days? How did you manage that?"

"With our eyes closed!" Tomiyano snapped, joining the group. "In the dark. What's been happening?"

Brota scowled at Wallie. "You have a town full of mad, mad swordsmen and mad, mad citizens. The tryst chose its leader the day after you left."

"So the sorcerers told us," Wallie said and smiled as her eyes widened. "They tried to seize ships, then?"

Brota pulled a face. "They had no chance! We'd passed the word, as you said; and as soon as the leader was proclaimed, the sailors started to panic. The nervous ones left, and then nobody wanted to be the last—the whole waterfront cleared in about half an hour."

"And the swordsmen?"

She smiled grimly. "By the time they saw what was happening, it was too late. They came out in boats, of course, and we just sailed up and down, but there was nothing they could do."

Nnanji and Thana had come on board and were helping Katanji up.

"What about nighttime?" Wallie asked.

"We moved upriver." Brota pointed a baggy arm at the vessels in the distance. Like *Sapphire*, they were flying quarantine flags. "Those two agreed to show the sign at the down end, and that helped." Then she pointed at the two ships moored in lonely splendor at the quay. "A couple slipped by—didn't see or didn't believe. The swordsmen grabbed them."

She wiped a tear that might have been caused by the wind. "We couldn't have held out much longer, though. They've been sending a fleet out after us every day. Little boats. Now they have those two ships, and I expected them to come after us in those today."

It showed in the restless eyes, the quickness of speech, the tone and cadence—testing endured, adversity surmounted.

"You stood your post, swordsman!" Wallie assured her, giving her another hug. The riverfolk—sailors and traders—were a hardheaded clique. Only a supreme negotiator like Brota could have made them see the danger of being requisitioned by the tryst and could have persuaded them to forgo their trading. But the strain of being hunted by a thousand swordsmen was not something to overlook, either. "I know why the gods chose this ship for me, mistress, and you were the main reason."

She simpered mockingly, but she was flattered, perhaps for the first time in years. "Well, I'm glad you're back. I didn't expect you for days yet." *Or never?*

"Whose is the dinghy?" asked Tomiyano, ever suspicious. The strange boat tethered to *Sapphire* had made them all fearful as *Griffon* approached.

Brota looked around in surprise and then pointed. Cousins, aunts, and uncles cleared out of the way so that Wallie could see Honakura, sitting on a fire bucket at the far side of the deck, smiling. Two priests of the Third stood beside him. Wallie went over and made his salute. He was disturbed by the old man's appearance. Four days had done nothing to reduce his ominous pallor. He seemed even more shrunken than before. His smile was forced.

"You are welcome back, my lord," he said softly.

"They brought us food," Brota said. "We were running low."

Wallie knelt down to put his eyes level with Honakura's.

"I fear that I failed to deliver what I promised," the old man sighed, "and what I owed the Goddess. The tryst has chosen its leader."

"Boariyi! A sorcerer told us."

"How could . . . ? Well, it is true. Lord Kadywinsi had agreed and I talked him out of it. The swordsmen came calling again and talked him into it. I talked him out of it again." He managed one of his old chuckles. "Then the swordsmen went ahead anyway. But they only have six Sevenths."

"It is a complication," Wallie agreed. "What happens now?"

Honakura compressed his wrinkles in a scowl. "Kadywinsi is back on the wrong side of the loom again. The service of dedication is to be held this morning."

Wallie frowned. "I thought the tryst was planning to depart two days ago?"

"Yes. The liege is an impetuous young man and he wouldn't allow the absence of a blessing stop him. But you and Mistress Brota stopped him—I suppose it is a sort of face-saving to have a service now and pretend that that was what they planned all along."

Wallie smiled at the woebegone old eyes. "You've done very

well, holy one! You didn't stop them, but you delayed them—and I'm sure most of them weigh three times what you do. A whole temple plus a thousand swordsmen is not a fair match against half a priest!"

Honakura sighed. "It used to be. I feel as old as all of them put together." Then he snarled. "And dinghies are just as bad as I feared."

"How is the town?" Wallie asked, aware that Nnanji and Thana had come to stand in the crowd around him, waiting for orders—and he did not know what orders he could give.

"Very peaceful!" Honakura conceded. "Lord Boariyi imposed discipline right away. There hasn't been as much as a cookie stolen since. Not a lewd glance!" He chuckled. "Well, I suppose I exaggerate there, but the virtuous maidens are emerging from the cellars. It is the evildoers who are leaving town, they say."

Wallie glanced up to see the satisfaction that he knew would be showing on Nnanji's face. Some of what Boariyi had said to him had been sincere, evidently, and Nnanji's lecherous tendencies in personal matters never interfered with his puritanical professional standards.

How to assess this new idea? The sorcerer's information about Boariyi had been correct, but Wallie's scheme to delay the tryst had succeeded. Now what? He had argued this case with Nnanji for hours, without reaching any decision. He felt limp and battered, filthy and foul both inside and out, after four days of sailing—and two of those confined with both an arrogant, bitter old captive and a lunatic minstrel.

"This service, holy one," Wallie asked. "I don't suppose we can have the call for challengers included again?"

Honakura shook his hairless old head. "It is a blessing on the tryst, that is all."

"They will all be sworn," Nnanji agreed. "It is too late for that."

"You will not swear this terrible oath of yours to Lord Boariyi and accept him as leader?" the priest asked.

"No!" Wallie barked. "The first thing he would do would be to demand my sword. He would probably even make me give it to him!" Seeing the priest's puzzled look, he explained: "Dedicate it—kneel to him and say the words. No one gets the seventh sword, except off my dead body! I'd rather challenge him."

Nnanji snorted. "Challenge a thousand men? He would send them up in threes and save the last place for himself."

Boariyi was paramount. The ways of honor would not apply now unless he wished them to. "Then I need counsel," Wallie said. "We did catch a sorcerer, the wizard of Sen himself, the man who provoked the tryst."

Honakura gasped and beamed. "That is a great triumph! Another miracle? No, a Great Deed! Wonderful, Lord Shonsu! How can we use him, do you suppose?" He screwed up his wrinkles in thought.

The wind blew, the sun shone, the ship rocked, and after a while he shook his head. Everyone looked blankly at everyone else.

No ideas.

"You could call another tryst, my lord," Nnanji suggested.

"The Goddess has blessed this one," the priest said. "Surely She sent Her sword for the leader to use? Otherwise, I just don't understand."

Wallie rose stiffly to his feet. "If you don't, holy one, then none of us do. It is a long sword. It needs a tall swordsman. Boariyi is taller than I am. I suppose I must give him his chance at it."

"But you need a fair match!" Nnanji shouted. "You can't fight the whole tryst!"

"If the swordsmen are gathered," a rich contralto voice said, "then I shall sing them my new epic."

Doa had come aboard and was standing behind the listening sailors, peering over their heads. She looked worse than anyone, her eyes sunk into her head, her face drawn and bonier than ever, her hair a tangled bush. She had probably not slept at all since Sen. She had done what she had said, spending two hours locked up with Rotanxi—interrogating him, Wallie supposed, although perhaps merely reporting to him, if she were indeed a sorcerer spy. Then she had retreated to a corner of the hold to strum aimlessly on her lute at all hours of day and night. She had refused food and conversation. Any attempts to reason with her had been met with screams that she was to be left alone, that she was composing an epic without blood. He had been expecting her to lapse into complete autism.

Now, astonishingly, she seemed to have recovered her former arrogance and poise, despite her haggard appearance. Her eyes were dark with exhaustion, but the wildness had gone. So the epic was complete? Wallie had commissioned an epic and he was going to get one, but he had no intention at all of letting her loose with it until he had had a chance to hear it himself—and probably not then.

The sailors moved aside hurriedly to let her in, immensely tall and barely decent in her two twists of filthy blue silk. Honakura gaped toothlessly at her, and then at Wallie. He rose to his feet and she saluted calmly.

"What is this epic about, then?" he asked, cautiously.

"It is about Lord Shonsu. It is very good."

Swordsman and priest exchanged glances again. Wallie rolled his eyes to convey disapproval.

"I never heard of a minstrel performing in a temple," Honakura said. "I should have to discuss it with Lord Kadywinsi."

"My lady," Wallie said, "you are tired and need refreshment. Thana, would you show Lady Doa the showers, find her some food and perhaps a place she could rest?"

Thana gave him a knowing glance and agreed. She led the minstrel away, and she went quietly. Wallie breathed more easily. Now back to the real problem . . .

"An epic?" Honakura mused.

"*No!*" Wallie sighed and avoided Jja's eye. "I was a fool to take her in the first place—I was thinking with the wrong end of my spine. Perhaps she has composed something, but what good could it do? Another song about Lord Shonsu hiding in a ship and being devious? Forget Doa!"

The old man nodded doubtfully.

"If I go to the temple, am I safe there?" Wallie asked.

Honakura said, "Certainly!" as Nnanji said, "No!"

There was another silence.

Wallie felt angry and baffled. "This blessing? Who is blessed? The men? The leaders? The tryst itself?"

Honakura stared up at him, and then a wicked little smile

settled in around his shriveled lips. "Why not the sword?" he asked.

The tiny cabin was dim and rank. Its port had been boarded over before *Griffon* departed, and it had held a captive for two days and three nights. He was sitting in a corner, wrapped in his blankets, when Wallie and Nnanji went in.

Confinement had taken toll of a man accustomed to authority and respect. His face was skull-like, with dark caves around his eyes, and the lines near his mouth had deepened to slashes. His thin white hair was disheveled. Yet this prisoner had been well treated by the standards of the World—Wallie knew that from experience.

"We are at Casr," Wallie said. "The tryst did not sail."

"So you won?"

"So far. If you will accompany us on board *Sapphire* now, my lord, we shall allow you to bathe and we shall provide clean clothes, although not your own. Sorcerers' gowns are what give them their power, you understand. That's how we made you harmless."

Rotanxi frowned and then nodded admiringly. "And what happens then?" The arrogance had softened, and he was almost pathetic, instinctively huddling back against the wall.

Wallie held up a rope. "I'm damned if I know! I shall have to keep you tethered, of course. I never imagined that we would capture a Seventh." He chuckled. "You see, my Lord Rotanxi, the position is rather complicated at the moment. On one bank there are sorcerers and on the other swordsmen. The infamous Shonsu and his nefarious gang have been running up and down between the two camps, playing havoc with both. If you were to auction me off at the moment, I think the swordsmen might even outbid the sorcerers to get their hands on me."

The sorcerer stared at him curiously for a moment and then reached for his shoes. "I doubt that," he said. "Are you open to bribes?"

Wallie thought of the power of the demigod and smiled. "Not if you offered me the World! I shall display you as my captive, of course, but I swear you my oath that there will be no torture, and as little degradation as is possible under the circumstances. And as you are likely to be of more value alive than dead, you will not be harmed."

"So I am to behave myself? You take me for a fool, Shonsu." Rotanxi was not too humbled to sneer. He rose stiffly.

Wallie shrugged. "I cannot make any real promises, because my own life is at risk this day, but if Master Nnanji succeeds me as your captor, he will respect my wishes."

He led the way to the ladder. He and Nnanji were clean now. Thana and Katanji were dressing. Honakura and the priests had departed already.

"Where are you taking me in such a hurry? Are your coals cooling off?"

"The tryst is assembling in the temple," Wallie explained. "I shall produce you before the swordsmen and claim the leadership."

The sorcerer regarded him warily. "And then what happens?"

"Then," Nnanji snarled, "the swordsmen will denounce him as a traitor, and he will not be protected by the ways of honor, and they will kill him."

"I see!" Rotanxi glanced from one to the other thoughtfully. "I detect a disagreement on strategy. And when Shonsu is dead, whose prisoner am I?"

"You're mine," Nnanji said savagely. "But I die right after. Then you will belong to the tryst. Have a nice day, my lord."

Their dinghy was met at the familiar ruined jetty by a nervous-looking priest of the Sixth, pudgy and elderly. Wallie knelt on the slimy planks and held out a hand to Tomiyano, still down in the boat.

"Captain," he said, "if neither Nnanji or I . . . well, look after Jja and Vixini? And thanks for everything."

Tomiyano's eyebrows rose, pushing his shipmarks into his hair. He shook hands. "What do you fancy for dinner, my lord? I'll tell Lina."

Wallie smiled and rose to follow the impatient priest.

The way led past the well-remembered refectory, then between the disused buildings, along paths choked with weeds, through canted fences with fallen gates . . . past old icehouses and deserted chapels, abandoned stables, dormitories, and erstwhile lawns now converted to impenetrable bush. The tide was out in Casr, but in some other century prosperity would return, and all this would again be needed by a waxing temple bureaucracy.

The way led also toward the towering bulk of the temple itself, and soon it dominated half the sky. Then . . . an unobtrusive side door and endless dark corridors and hallways smelling of mold and rot. A distant sound of chanting ahead, and the guiding priest turned and put his finger to his lips. He opened a door, very slowly, and the chanting became loud.

It was more a large alcove than a small room, for one side was a bead curtain, beyond which lay the nave of the temple. The watchers could see out and not be seen; the half dozen could spy on the thousand. So Wallie stopped to watch and his followers crowded around to peer by him.

His first impression was how much smaller this temple was than the great edifice at Hann. Yet to his left stood the swordsmen of the tryst—five Sevenths in blue; behind them, at a respectful distance, a row of thirty or forty Sixths; and behind them, in turn, ranks of red-kilted Fifths. A thousand men and more—the Fifths hid the middlerank colors, so that only their heads and sword hilts showed—but the nave was not crowded, so smallness was relative. This was still as large as any cathedral Wallie had ever seen. Not all were swordsmen. Behind the narrow-shouldered Firsts at the back was a collection without swords—heralds, bandsmen, armorers, healers, minstrels, and perhaps notables from the town.

To his right stood the choir, endlessly warbling up and down their dissonant scale. They faced toward the Goddess, an idol of carved stone that copied the great, naturally weathered figure at Hann—a seated and robed woman, hair streaming down, featureless face staring along the nave to the seven arches and the River beyond. Yet the sculptor had failed to catch the same air of majesty. The blue paint was flaking from the stone, giving it a scabby appearance, a Goddess with eczema. The dais bore treasures, but nothing to compare to the unmeasurable hoard at Hann. Perhaps this temple had been looted a few times.

Wallie discovered that his Shonsu instincts were busily checking for escape routes. Some hope! The main doors would be in the arches at the front, of course, below the glass screens. From the interior the missing panes showed as bright spots, unsoiled by the grime that blurred most of the vista of the River and far-off RegiVul under its guardian smoke plume. Between him and those doors stood the swordsmen. There was another bead curtain opposite him and there was probably a door behind that. There would be others behind the idol, also.

Then he saw Boariyi, standing by himself and looking very lonely. By rights, surely, he should have been directly in front of the Sevenths, at the head of his army. Instead, he had been placed well toward the far side. That seemed a strange location, but he was opposite Wallie. If Wallie emerged through this bead curtain, the two of them would be facing each other across the nave like equals. That was a welcome sign that the priests were indeed under Honakura's control. Obviously Kadywinsi was an uncertain and unreliable ally, given to supporting whoever had spoken to him most recently. Hopefully, while this interminable chanting went on, Honakura was busy somewhere else, keeping the high priest's vertebrae fused.

Boariyi was too far off for his expression to be discerned. Probably he had been granted no more time for sword practice these last few days than Wallie, but he had not been bouncing around in *Griffon*'s madhouse, either, and that thought made Wallie realize how incredibly weary he felt.

Tivanixi, standing with the other Sevenths, had a bandaged arm.

Wallie glanced around at his own party. The sorcerer stood with hands bound, unkempt in an ill-fitting blue gown, fixed sneer on haggard face. Nnanji held the other end of his tether, trying to look cheerful—Nnanji said this was not going to work and Nnanji was usually correct when it came to judging swordsmen. Thana had insisted on coming, and Katanji was there, also, looking tiny and absurdly young and grinning widely, black eyes sparkling in the gloom.

Katanji had a small leather bag dangling at his waist and suddenly Wallie guessed that it must be his ill-gotten loot from Gi, a fortune in jewels. If Nnanji had returned that tainted hoard to his brother, then Nnanji did not think he was going to survive this day.

The congregation was starting to fidget and twitch. The unseen juniors at the back would be into spitballs soon.

At Hann the sides of the nave had been lined by stained glass. Here they were walls of mosaic, much of which seemed to be crumbling off. Wallie glanced up to check the roof, wondering how safe that was.

He decided that he might be the only person present who was not anxious for the interminable chanting to end. He had the sorcerer's pistol stuck in his belt, and some spare powder and shot in his pouch, but he would never have time to reload. There was a climax coming. The odds against him were probably about a hundred to one, yet he felt more resigned than nervous. The gods had forced this, snapping at his heels and driving him like a sheep into this pen. Perhaps this was the last line of the riddle. *And to its destiny accord*—give it to Boariyi. How old was Alexander the Great when he took his father's army and set off to conquer the Earth? Twenty? Boariyi was probably older than that. He just did not look like an Alexander, somehow.

The sun vanished behind a cloud; shadow flooded the high, cold place.

At welcome last the chant was over, dying away into a quiet sigh of collective relief from the audience. The choir genuflected and trooped back in two lines to stand on either side of the idol, out of Wallie's view. A tiny figure in blue shuffled forward, eased down on ancient knees to make obeisance, rose even more slowly, and turned to face the congregation. The high priest, Kadywinsi, his snowy hair shining in the gloom, raised his arms and began a long ritual of blessing. Boariyi and his Sevenths relaxed —evidently the ceremony was nearing its end. The old man wailed away to silence. Then he swung around and faced the idol.

"Holiest!" he bleated. "Your castellan and I had the honor of calling this tryst and the honor of seeing You bless it. We thank You for hearing our prayers, for sending us the novices, the apprentices, the swordsmen, the adepts, the masters, their honors, and their lordships . . . but most of all for sending us Your chosen champion, a noble and courageous swordsman, a man who has met the sorcerers before and has shown he can defeat them, a worthy leader, sent by You, *bearing Your own sword*."

A gasp of surprise from the congregation grew to an angry, animal roar. Hints of riot filled the temple. Boariyi straightened up and put his hands on his hips, thrusting his head forward. The other five Sevenths registered shock, most of them turning a furious red at the suggestion that they had sworn to the wrong man.

Wallie reached for the curtain and a command came from behind: "Not yet!" He turned to frown at the priest—surely this was the dramatic moment?

In a sudden silence the sun reappeared, flooding the nave with brilliance, gleaming on Kadywinsi's silver hair and on a tall woman in blue strolling forward, carrying a lute.

††† †††

Wallie wheeled to stare at the others. "I thought she was still on board!" he snapped, loud enough to make them jump.

Nnanji nodded, but Thana shook her head. "She went with the priests."

Wallie had been in the shower. Furious, he turned back to watch. Doa was clean and groomed. She was calm, now, and dignified. Her streaming brown hair shone again, no longer tangled like tumbleweed. Her dress was a priest's cotton gown, a cheap thing, baggy and not long enough, yet she wore it regally, as if it had been tailored for her by a master couturier. The audience was rustling. Wallie could only hope that Honakura knew what he was doing. Perhaps he had interrogated her in the dinghy. It was equally possible that he was flying this whole thing on blind faith.

Doa made no salute, announced no title for her epic. She showed neither nervousness nor excitement, only an air of intense concentration as she stood and plucked the lute quietly, adjusting the tuning. Then she raised her head, struck a chord, and filled the temple with a voice dark and shining as zircon.

The swordsmen in the morning come with glory on their brows,
With justice on their shoulders borne,
And honor in their vows.
Evil they will overcome and righteousness espouse.
Her swords go marching on!

Again Wallie glanced back at Nnanji, and his astonished expression showed that he had never heard of a marching song in an epic, either.

It was a rousing tune, though, and . . . No! Could it be? He listened carefully to the chorus, and the second verse . . .

No, even allowing for the seven-tone scale, it was not the same. Close . . . but even better, more rousing, than what he had just for a moment suspected. He could guess that it would be adopted at once by the tryst. Feet were beginning to tap. Or perhaps not—it was about Shonsu, leading his army through the mountains to Vul. Now he was about to hear what had happened in that disaster—if Rotanxi had told the truth to Doa, and if Doa had not changed it for her own purposes.

The music slipped to classic epic style while the villainous sorcerers plotted their defense. The chief of the evildoers was, of course, Lord Rotanxi, swearing hatred against all swordsmen, summoning a fire demon. Wallie looked around, and the sorcerer's face was a kaleidoscope of emotions: anger, amusement, and surprise.

Another change, to a restless, anguished theme, and the singer's voice changed, also. The swordsmen had reached a bridge over a chasm, could see Vul itself in the distance. They began to cross. The sorcerer's fire demon struck in dissonance, in thunder and flame. Bridge and swordsmen all plunged into the abyss.

A mined bridge? Of course! What would have been easier for the sorcerers than that, or more unexpected to the swordsmen? Without thinking, Wallie turned to Rotanxi and whispered, "Is that what happened?"

He received a look of astonishment, but no answer.

Only Shonsu had escaped, marching in front of his army. Struck to the ground by the fire demon's passing, he had lost his sword and been seized by the triumphant sorcerers. Then the music changed again, to a dirge, and Wallie began to appreciate that what he was hearing was the birth of a whole new art form, the heroic oratorio. Nnanji's jaw was hanging open. Epics were the news and entertainment of the World. Swordsmen hankered after them as Italians craved opera. This was superb, the audience transfixed.

The names and ranks of the dead . . . of course Doa had known those all the time. She had been Shonsu's mistress. Had Tivanixi never thought to ask her, or had she refused to talk?

Then the dirge ended. A wild, galloping theme accompanied the story of Shonsu's escape. Tied to a tree, about to be tortured, he snapped his bonds and plunged naked and unarmed into the forest . . .

A haunting lament told how the Goddess' demons drove him to Hann. Doa had made a masterly selection of the facts. Shonsu demanded an exorcism. It failed. He hurled himself into the sacred falls in penance—no mention that his only alternative was to be thrown.

Now the Goddess sang an aria, refusing the offer of his soul, lamenting the deaths of the forty-nine and the injured honor of Her swordsmen. The melody was the theme that Wallie had heard Doa try twice before, but now she had brought it to perfection; it soared, it tore at the heart, it filled the temple with sorrow and anguish. He saw the entranced swordsmen blinking back tears and felt his own eyes prickle. But subtly the theme changed from plaint to resolve, as the Goddess commanded Shonsu to go back and try again, taking Her sword . . . Tears dried and blood surged with righteous fury.

Back in traditional epic style, Rotanxi plotted again. He sent the kilts to Casr, the tryst was called, the swordsmen assembled, and Shonsu appeared, bearing the seventh sword—and a jigging, mocking theme described how the swordsmen spurned him and drove him from the lodge. It had not happened that way, but everyone knew, even Nnanji, that one did not believe everything one heard in epics.

Drama returned. The sorcerers plotted once more, in an echo of the earlier scene, but this time in an unnamed port on the River, foreseeing the arrival of the swordsmen, summoning their demons to destroy the tryst—the temple had never held a more attentive congregation than it did right then. The fiendish Lord Rotanxi stalked the dock, proclaiming the horrors he would release.

Then, with music that started creepily and mysteriously and mounted steadily in excitement until it peaked in triumph, a ship arrived. Shonsu appeared on its deck and mockingly explained that he had blocked the tryst's departure and balked the sorcerers' evil scheme. Dramatic speeches flew to and fro until Rotanxi announced that he would deal with this arrogant young swordsman himself. He marched on board—and his magic failed before the holy sword.

Griffon cast off, and Shonsu claimed Rotanxi as his prisoner, to be taken back to Casr to die. Just for a moment the audience could be heard muttering in disbelief, then it fell silent once more, hanging on the minstrel's words.

Molto vivace! Now the demons were released—fire demons, water demons, sky demons, demons of lightning and storm. They roared and blazed and boiled around the ship, but in godlike defiance Shonsu brandished the sword of the Goddess and turned aside the evil. The spirits slunk away, defeated . . .

And the finale, a repeat of the rousing opening theme, a victory march now, the words slightly altered as the swordsmen tramped on to certain glory.

Silence—utter, total silence.

Wallie blinked and looked around. Nnanji's mouth had closed, but his eyes were glazed and he had dropped the prisoner's tether. Rotanxi could have slipped away unnoticed, except that he, also, was entranced. So was Thana. Katanji caught Wallie's eye and grinned. Wallie grabbed the rope and handed it back to Nnanji with a scowl that broke the spell.

And the audience in the temple had also been spellbound until that same moment. Usually swordsmen applauded by stamping their boots, sometimes by clapping, and rarely by cheering. Now they did all three, and every man in the vast throng seemed to be making as much noise as he could. A hurricane of sound crashed back toward the singer. Even the Sevenths were applauding, even Boariyi. And Doa herself seemed to snap out of a trance. She smiled slightly, bowed, and then turned to genuflect before the idol. Old Kadywinsi was still standing there. He gave her a blessing, and she walked out of view, while the tumult of applause went on and on. Wallie was sure that he had been present at something as significant as the opening night of *Hamlet* . . . Mr. Homer will recite from his new poem about Odysseus . . . The epics of the World would never be the same.

She had done what she had promised. Could a vote now be called, he would be elected leader by acclamation after that performance. But the tryst was sworn. Autocracy ruled, not democracy.

"My lord," he said to the sorcerer, almost having to shout, "even if we die this day, we two, we have achieved immortality."

He did not get the usual sneer. The old man studied him for a moment and then said, "I believe you are right, Lord Shonsu. It is, perhaps, a small comfort."

"Now, my lord!" the priest said.

"In a moment." The din was continuing unabated. "What's next on the program?"

"Nothing, my lord."

Obviously that must be changed. Wallie looked out into the nave again, just in time to see Boariyi raise a hand for silence—and get it, instantly. Impressive as hell! So Wallie pushed through the curtain and walked out to meet the tryst.

He very nearly wrecked his chances totally by tripping over a step and falling flat on his face; he had not noticed that the speakers' area was slightly raised. That obstacle surmounted, he walked forward until he was almost at the center line, but not quite. He faced the idol and made the salute to the Goddess, then wheeled to salute the company. The echoes of his sepulchral voice came rumbling back from the glassed arches.

Facing him, just below the step, were the five Sevenths. Zoariyi, the shortest, was expressionless except for a wariness in his eyes. Tivanixi looking confused and unhappy. One quite elderly man must be the Lord Chin-something whom Nnanji had mentioned. There was a chubby man with a scar, and a younger, nondescript man. Beyond them the line of green-kilted Sixths, some frowning, some puzzled, one or two grinning at the drama

. . . and behind them, halfway to the arches, rows and rows of sword hilts and male faces.

Then Wallie half turned to address the beanpole Boariyi, who had his arms folded, his chin high, and a very red, furious expression on his rubbery face.

"My Lord Boariyi, I come to claim the leadership of the tryst, as I am commanded of the Goddess."

The temple was silent. Had he closed his eyes, Wallie could have believed that it was empty. He had no idea what to expect. There were about fifteen hundred swordsmen there, but only one will. However impressive Doa's epic, why should Boariyi yield the leadership voluntarily?

"Indeed? You are too late, Lord Shonsu. The tryst is sworn." His voice lacked the depth of Shonsu's, but it carried well.

"I apologize. I had business in Sen, as you heard."

"Oooo!" said the juniors at the back of the crowd.

Boariyi's eyes narrowed. "You seriously expect us to believe that? Your longtime relationship with Lady Doa is well known, Lord Shonsu, and while we all enjoyed that performance, you will need more evidence than that." He swung round to face his army, ready to dismiss it; smart move!

"I have a prisoner as evidence," Wallie boomed. Excitement surged through the audience like wind in corn.

Boariyi turned back to him with sudden doubt in his face.

"My prisoner is Lord Rotanxi, sorcerer of the seventh rank, wizard of Sen, a man who sends kilts—" He was drowned out.

Again Boariyi gestured for silence and got it. His face had turned even redder. "Produce this prisoner!"

Wallie pretended to hesitate. "I could send for him . . . You will stipulate that he is *my* prisoner, according to the sutras?"

"I will not take your prisoner while you live," Boariyi roared, "but I give no guarantees of your own safety."

"I am fully protected by the ways of honor and my sword," Wallie said, wishing he believed that. Then he turned and beckoned.

Rotanxi stumbled through the curtain with a large hand at the scruff of his neck. All the splendor of the Dream God could not have contained Nnanji's grin as he thrust the old man ahead of him across the width of the temple toward Boariyi. With right arm straight and tether held in his left, he propelled the sorcerer at great speed over to the liege lord, who recoiled in astonishment at the facemarks thus revealed. Then Nnanji swung his victim around and jostled him along the front of the congregation, past the Sixths and the Sevenths so that they could see, also, and finally looped around to end beside Wallie, directing his grin at the whole tryst. The silence shattered again in a rising rumble like shingle stirred by surf, mounting like the surf itself, exploding with the crash of breakers.

Thana and Katanji had emerged and lined up beside their leader, and Wallie could almost chuckle through the tension and fatigue at the ridiculous contrast. The swordsmen must see it, also: Boariyi with his horde; Shonsu with an injured First, a female Second, and a copper-haired youth dressed as Fifth. But Shonsu had the prisoner . . . and what a prisoner!

Now Boariyi had very few options for extricating himself with dignity. The old priest stood between them, facing the tryst. He turned to look at the leader and so did everyone else.

Boariyi's voice was harsh with anger. "I came here expecting a blessing," he said. "Not a mummery. Do you challenge, Lord Shonsu?"

Tricky—Wallie would be damned if he said yes and dismissed if he said no.

"I do not wish to fight you, my lord, but I am not afraid to do so, for I am a better swordsman and I have the Goddess on my side." He hoped. "But I will not fight the whole tryst. Will you meet me man to man, or do you hide behind the protection of the blood oath?"

Boariyi's eyes flickered toward his uncle, the short and graying Zoariyi, standing with the other Sevenths. "Such events in a temple service are new to me. I will consult my council." The Sevenths obediently walked over to him. It was a good move for Boariyi, giving him an imposing backing, so that he no longer stood alone.

There was a brief huddle, while the congregation held its breath, hushed and tense. Zoariyi obviously did the talking, his nephew standing with his head bent to hear. Then he stepped forward so that the others were behind him.

"My council advises me that this is not an affair of honor! Was it not you, Shonsu, who led the force of fifty swordsmen destroyed by the sorcerers?"

"It was," Wallie said and was interrupted before he could say more.

"Was it not you who crawled naked in the dirt before sorcerers at Aus?"

"It was—"

"Was it not you who stopped the triumphant swordsmen at Ov, when they would have followed up their success by attacking the tower?"

"Yes, but—"

"Was it not you who betrayed the plans of the tryst to the sailors, drove away the ships, falsely posted a quarantine flag upon the harbor, and frustrated our attack?"

"Yes, but only because—"

Boariyi raised a very long arm and pointed. "Then I declare you to be a false swordsman, an abomination, and an agent of the sorcerers. I condemn you to death as an enemy of the tryst. Sevenths—kill that man!"

Wallie was preparing his reply in his mind. He glanced round at his friends. Nnanji looked ill. The sorcerer gave him a look of mockery, although his welfare depended on Wallie's.

He turned back toward Boariyi and the council, and saw that there was not going to be a reply. They had drawn their swords and were advancing in line abreast. They were coming slowly, perhaps hoping that he might somehow escape, but coming. Nnanji had been correct.

Wallie pulled the pistol from his belt and rejected the temptation to shoot down Boariyi. He needed a target that would not cause a ricochet, so he aimed over the heads of the tryst at the distant arches and the faraway vista of mountains.

He pulled the trigger.

The explosion roared much louder than he expected. The gun kicked in his hand, and a vast cloud of acrid smoke billowed out at the ranks of Sixths. No one there except the sorcerer and members of the Shonsu expedition had ever heard a noise like that before. Plaster sprinkled from the roof; tiles tinkled down from the walls. He scored a direct hit on the windows of the central arch, evidently on a vulnerable spot in the rotting stone trelliswork. While the echo of the shot was still reverberating back, it was joined by a thunderous clamor of smashing glass as the entire central window structure collapsed, row after row, glass and stone together, panes and framework avalanching in chain reaction, a repeating cascade of corruscating crystal to the floor, emptying the whole arch.

The tryst panicked. From Firsts to Sevenths they turned and ran. Wallie put the pistol back in his belt without bothering to reload. He glanced round at his companions. Even the sorcerer looked astonished at the effect. Nnanji swallowed hard, then grinned, and said: "Wow!"

Behind them a mob of priests in various shades was fighting to get through a door beside the idol. Only tiny Honakura was standing still; he smiled and raised a hand in congratulation. The Sevenths recovered first, forming up in a tight bunch about where they had been before, starting a fierce argument with many shamefaced glances toward Wallie. Many of the civilians continued their flight, but the rest of the swordsmen recovered themselves before they reached the snowbank of glass by the main door. They started ashamedly dribbling back to their places. It was clear to all that only Wallie's party had stood its ground.

He did not wait for them to finish lining up.

"Yes," he proclaimed, "I led the doomed expedition to Vul. For that I must make amends." He had everyone's attention now. The priests had fallen silent behind him and the Sevenths had stopped talking to listen. "Yes, I went ashore at Aus. I went unarmed, which was folly, and I paid a great price for that folly.

"Yes, I stopped the attack at Ov and for the same reason that I stopped the tryst: You do not know how to fight sorcerers! I do—now I do. I captured Lord Rotanxi and I rendered him harmless. That thunderbolt was one of the spells he was carrying —a little thing that he had in his pocket. Call it a thunderbolt of the first rank, if you like. They have greater horrors, thunderbolts of the seventh rank. They had those lined up on the docks at Sen and hurled them at our ship. The minstrel described the effects very well, but there were no demons. I have no magic, my lords. The sword—" He drew it. "—is not magic. But it is sacred. It belongs to the Most High, and it was She who saved us."

"She sent me to lead the tryst, for courage alone is not

enough. I do not question your courage, swordsmen, but only I can teach you how to fight sorcerers. The Goddess gave me Her sword and She has also given me wisdom. I can lead you all to victory—but you, Lord Boariyi, cannot. Dare you resist Her divine will?"

The Sevenths were arguing fiercely. The priest Kadywinsi stepped forward, but Wallie held up a hand to silence him. The decision had to be Boariyi's, and Wallie felt sorry for him. He must have been sure of gaining immortality as the leader of a tryst and he was being cheated of it by a combination of sorcery and priestly subterfuge. Yet his decision was almost inevitable now, for Wallie had been able to state his case and so reduce it to a personal challenge. Boariyi could no longer refuse and still hope to hold the loyalty of the tryst.

He had reached the same conclusion. He silenced the councilors around him and looked over their heads at Wallie with that same insolent, contemptuous sneer that he had worn when they first met—and Wallie's temper flared at the sight of it.

Then the human mantis stepped forward, putting his hands on his skinny hips. "You say you are from the Goddess? I repeat that you were sent by the sorcerers. The priest blessed the leader who wears that sword. Very well! I will kill you and take it. Make your challenge, my Lord Shonsu."

††† † †††

The weather had turned for the worse, spitting raindrops from low, ugly clouds, whirling leaves and dust along the ground. Wallie stood alone outside the temple, scowling at the damage his lucky shot had caused. Three arches on each side now reflected the storm over RegiVul, while the center was a dark blank. He was uneasily reminded of the little jewel god with his missing tooth, and he did not know if he was being irreverent, or if the god was truly playing jokes.

The whole tryst had been assembled into a wide arc around the temple forecourt, facing the water. Wallie stood at one end, alone, Boariyi at the other, surrounded by the council. Of course the Sevenths were Boariyi's vassals and must attend him, but that did not lessen Wallie's feeling of being abandoned. In the center of the arc were the heralds and the bandsmen. A discussion was in progress between the heralds and the two seconds, Nnanji and Zoariyi. It was taking forever.

To entrust such negotiations to Nnanji seemed crazy. Surely that wily Zoariyi would knot him like a pretzel? Yet the rules for dueling left no choice, and Nnanji had already successfully contrived to have Thana take the prisoner back to *Sapphire*, much against the swordsmen's will. Wallie had not expected him to win that point and had watched with pleased surprise as the transfer took place. Then there had been some sort of ceremony involving Nnanji being presented to all the Sevenths, probably to dispose of the vengeance problem.

It was oddly reassuring that the juvenile Katanji was also involved in the discussions. Twice he and Nnanji had stepped aside to confer, Nnanji bending over to talk or listen. Each time Wallie has assumed that he was going to be sent a message, but each time the two brothers had returned to the group together. Katanji knew nothing of the technicalities or legalities, but he knew people—what was surprising was that Nnanji would now take him seriously enough to pay heed.

Boariyi towered over his companions. He had the advantage of reach, certainly, and he was defending his own ground. He had also seen Wallie go against Tivanixi. But he was fighting either a sorcerer or a hero sent by the gods—neither an encouraging prospect. He might even be faster. Wallie was stronger and had the Goddess on his side. Or did he? He had been told to expect no miracles.

Cursing himself for thinking such thoughts, Wallie turned to look at the wind-whipped, gun-metal River and the rocking ships. *Sapphire* was moored just offshore, her crew lined up along the rail. He saw the massive Brota, then Jja, and waved. The quarantine flag had gone and already a few vessels were venturing into port.

The arc of onlookers was swelling as priests and citizens arrived to see the sport, crowding in behind the swordsmen. A serious contest between Sevenths must be a very rare event. Wallie wondered if even Shonsu had ever had to fight another Seventh in earnest. He himself had fought Hardduju, of course, but that had been an execution.

At last the conference broke up, the seconds stalking over to their respective principals. Katanji gave Wallie an appraising, sympathetic glance. Nnanji merely looked cheerful.

Nnanji was flying with the angels. This was the meat and bone of romantic swordsmanship for him, a mere Fifth negotiating with Sevenths, arranging a trial by combat—which was almost as rare in the World as it would have been on Earth, the stuff of epics, not sutras—playing a part in the gods' mission. Nnanji could never be happier than he was right there.

"I think I got all you need, brother," he said. "Zoariyi wouldn't accept that your sword belonged to the Goddess, but he agreed to put 'coward' in, although he claims that his principal never used the word."

"Great! How about child abuse and nose-picking?" Wallie snapped. "Let's not leave any stone unthrown."

Nnanji smiled courteously and glanced around as if wanting to sit down and cross his legs. Then he straightened and proceeded to recite the draft proclamation, word for word, in a voice that shadowed the booming tones of the chief herald.

"*Hear ye*, my lords, your honors, masters, adepts, swordsmen, apprentices, novices, and all this good company assembled —*whereas* the valiant Lord Shonsu, swordsman of the seventh rank, has appeared before the council of the noble tryst of Casr, and *whereas* the said valiant lord has represented to the said council that the legendary seventh sword of Chioxin has been given into his hand by a god in order that he may drive the abomination of sorcery from the cities of Aus, Wal, Sen, Cha, Gor, Amb, and Ov, and *whereas* the said valiant lord represents that he is the best swordsman here present and ought therefore by right of prowess be liege lord of this exalted tryst, and *whereas* the valorous Lord Boariyi, swordsman of the seventh rank, liege lord of the noble tryst of Casr, has responded that the said valiant lord has previously failed in battle against the sorcerers, and *whereas* the said valorous lord has further represented that the said valiant lord was disgraced by sorcerers in Aus, thereby showing himself to be without honor and a coward, and *whereas* the said valorous lord has further represented that the said valiant lord frustrated and impeded a victorious group of swordsmen in battle at Ov, and *whereas* the said valorous lord has further represented that the said valiant lord is an imposter, being an agent of the sorcerers and enemy of the tryst, and *whereas* the said valorous lord represents that he is by prowess in combat by due form established rightful leader of this noble tryst, and *whereas* these two intrepid lords have agreed that the matter between them shall be settled by honorable passage of arms, according to the ancient rubrics and sutras of their craft, the said valorous lord having waived and negated onus of vengeance by his vassals, and the two audacious lords having agreed upon this time and place for their meeting, *now therefore* you are bid approach and witness this illustrious encounter, and may the Goddess judge between them and grant victory to the right!"

Wallie had him repeat it.

"I don't like that 'driving the abomination of sorcery' bit," he said. "The tryst was called to restore the honor of the craft; let's stick with that."

"Right!" Nnanji said. "Good point."

It was easy enough for him to treat all this lunacy as an exercise in heraldic pomp, Wallie thought.

"Another thing—I thought this was a naked match and I heard something in there about Boariyi waiving the onus of vengeance. How about you, brother?"

Nnanji smiled at him as if sharing a joke. "None of them seem to have thought of that! The fourth oath is pretty obscure, remember."

"So what happens if I lose?"

Nnanji laughed. "You soften him up, and I'll finish him off."

"Think you can take him, do you?"

Then Nnanji guessed what he was thinking and recoiled. "Of course not! I'm no Seventh. He'd spit me in a flicker, brother. You don't think I'd . . . that I want . . ."

"Then put it in the proclamation!" Wallie barked, feeling guilty for doubting him. "I also waive the onus of vengeance."

"You can't!" Nnanji said, recovering his good humor and chuckling. "Remember the words of the sutra: *paramount, absolute, and irrevocable*? You can't release me and I can't escape it. If he does you, then I'm up right after. Don't make me mention it, please, because then they might wriggle out of this somehow!"

So it was not hypothetical to Nnanji! It was a matter of life and death to him, also. It just happened to be fun, as well. Katanji was standing in silence, his eyes going from one face to the other, and it was not fun to Katanji.

But Nnanji was right. The fourth oath was irrevocable, so Wallie could not release him. He was going to be fighting for two lives. He grunted that the proclamation was fine. Nnanji nodded, gave him a worried sort of look, and then went striding off back to the heralds, his ponytail wagging happily.

Was it possible? If Wallie died and Nnanji challenged Boariyi, and by some miracle won, would the tryst accept him as leader? This was not the formal combat for leadership. The onus of vengeance had not been waived for anyone, only for this match. Wallie puzzled it out and concluded with a curious relief that it would not work; the other Sevenths would counterchallenge one after the other, then the Sixths. Of course Nnanji could not beat Boariyi . . . except by a miracle. Nnanji was trustworthy, but the gods were not.

"Will you kill him, my lord?" Katanji had stayed behind.

Wallie snapped out of his gloomy thoughts to reply. "Not if I can help it. Why?"

"Nanj is worried. He says you'll try for a flesh wound, but Lord Boariyi will be going for a kill, to win the sword. He says it will be like the time you fought the captain with foil against blade."

"I don't need your advice on swordsmanship, novice."

Katanji dropped his eyes and was silent.

This time the conference was brief. The heralds and seconds all seemed to be nodding. The rain had stopped. The meeting broke up and Nnanji came striding over the windy court again.

"The Goddess be with you, my lord," Katanji whispered. He turned and headed for the perimeter.

"All agreed!" Nnanji announced. He fixed Wallie with a stern look. "You realize that he's got to kill you, don't you?"

"I don't need your advice on swordsmanship!"

Nnanji looked repentant. "I'm sorry, brother!" He studied Wallie carefully and put on an encouraging grin. "You're not seriously worried, are you? You have the seventh sword!"

"And he has the arms of a gorrilla!" Wallie said softly. "Nnanji, I've never fought anyone taller than me. Perhaps Shonsu never did, either!"

"He must have been smaller when he was little, mustn't he?"

"Yes, of course." Wallie managed a chuckle. "You're right. Thank you, Nnanji." He hesitated. "You did very well in the negotiations, brother!"

Nnanji grinned. "I smothered him in sagas! Precedents, you know? The epic of Xo, and the epic . . . " He reeled off a dozen, counting on his fingers.

Wallie laughed aloud, but before he could comment, the proceedings began. A roll of drums echoed off the temple and the bullfrog herald made his proclamation in a voice that the thunder god might have envied.

There was another roll of drums. "Good!" Wallie said. "Now maybe they'll let us get on with it."

No. The herald, having spoken in the direction of the River, now wheeled about and made the same proclamation, complete with drums, toward the temple; and when he had done that, he had to repeat it again both upstream and downstream. The final version was applauded by a peal of thunder. Even if the gods had forsworn miracles, Wallie thought, they were not giving up on dramatic effects. The rain started again.

The herald beckoned, and the two parties approached him to take up their stations. Wallie eyed his gangly opponent carefully. Boariyi was similarly eyeing him, his big jaw set tight in concentration, his continuous bar of eyebrow pulled down in a frown, no trace of a sneer. What was he—cautious or rash? Serious fights between unfamiliar adversaries usually began with a little careful testing. Wallie decided to try for a quick decision.

"You may proceed, my lords."

Wallie lunged recklessly. He was parried instantly and jumped back with blood streaming from his upper arm.

The crowd roared.

In any normal match Zoariyi would have called "Yield?" at that point. He said nothing. Shonsu was not to be given that option.

It was a shallow cut, but a terrible beginning, and it must give the tall man more confidence, showing that the possible sorcerer or possible hero could bleed. It also hurt. Boariyi lunged. Parry, riposte, recover. Wallie felt a faint beginning of the bloodlust and suppressed it at once. Berserkers would not feel pain, would fight until chopped into cutlets. He had no wish to win and then discover that he had been mortally wounded in the process.

Lunge. Riposte. He was being driven steadily back. His opponent was grinning at him. How *did* one fight a human gorilla? He remembered Hardduju and tried dropping his guard a fraction, waiting for the outside cut to the wrist. It came instantly. He parried and tried a riposte, but Boariyi covered just as fast and it was Wallie who barely escaped.

Tivanixi had been correct. Shonsu had met his match.

Forward and back they danced, but it was more back than forward for Wallie. How far was he from the River?

Dimly he could hear a continuous roar from the spectators. His right arm was streaming blood. He must rest it to stop the flow. Lunge. Recover. Taking a dreadful risk, he whipped his feet around and transferred the sword to his left hand. Boariyi flashed an instant attack, countering his left-hand riposte as easily as before, then mockingly performed the same tactic, so they were southpaw to southpaw. The crowd noise exploded—that was one for the legends.

Lunge. Parry. Riposte.

Wallie tried every trick in his book, even some he had not thought to teach Nnanji. Boariyi countered them all and responded with some that were new to Wallie. They were evenly matched.

The swords rang like a smithy. It was an endurance test. The spindly Boariyi had the build of a marathon runner. The man's reach was incredible. Wallie could not get near him. His sword must be a fingerlength longer than even the seventh sword. Parry. Parry. Parry. . .

Long swords could be weak. The seventh sword? If Shonsu could not win this, then perhaps Wallie Smith could? Perhaps Chioxin could? Riposte. He had the better blade. Dare he try something so unorthodox against such a supreme opponent?

How long could flesh keep this up? He was tiring. Lunge. Slowing down. Parry. Boariyi had noticed. He switched on his sneer—and again Wallie's temper flared up at the sight of it.

He changed tactics, turned his attack from the man to the sword, hacking as hard as he could at Boariyi's blade. Just maybe Wallie could treat it as Tomiyano had treated Wallie's foil, so very long ago. Parry. Cut. Parry. Cut . . .

The tall man was surprised at the unorthodox assault and yielded a little before the brute force. Then he began to react and Wallie found he was being led off balance. Again and again that deadly blade whipped within a hairsbreadth of his skin. He persisted. Clash, clash, clash. Boariyi had guessed his purpose. He was parrying more carefully, turning Wallie's blade at an angle. Parry. Wallie saw with despair that he had been driven back almost to the water's edge. The crowd was screaming continuously at this spectacular display of swordsmanship.

Clash. Clash.

Snap.

The seventh sword sliced through the other blade and swept on past Boariyi's face. For a moment it seemed to have missed him, but the razor tip had slit along the line of swordmarks on his forehead, and a curtain of blood fell over his eyes. He dropped his sword hilt—beaten!

"Yield?" Nnanji screamed, his voice cracking with excitement.

"Yield!" Zoariyi agreed. His nephew fell to his knees, gasping and panting, blinded by the blood pouring over his face.

Wallie himself was in little better shape; his chest heaving with its fight for air, breath rasping, heart hammering like a woodpecker inside his skull. For a moment he was incapable of thinking, wrapped in drapes of nauseous black fog. He had come very close to his limit. The heralds came running forward, followed by healers and minstrels, and the council of Sevenths. Then the ranks broke, and the whole assembly flooded in to form a tight circle around the combatants, cheering, jostling, and finally falling silent once more in some sort of order.

Slowly Wallie's head began to quieten. He wondered why no one was assisting the wounded Boariyi, then remembered that the fight was still incomplete—the victor must state his terms and sheath his sword before anyone else could intervene. Now he could demand the third oath: *Blood needs be shed; declare your allegiance*.

He hesitated, puzzled by something, fuzzily studying Boariyi. The kid was on his knees, his bony rib cage pumping like bellows, soaked with mingled blood and rain and sweat, eyes shut against the sheen of blood covering his face and streaming down his chest to soak into his kilt. Yet . . . there was something wrong. Nnanji? Something like Nnanji? Wallie looked helplessly around for his second, but he had disappeared. Boariyi's expression was unreadable through that red mask, but the corners of his jaw were knotted, his arms were locked into vertical rods above clenched fists—his head was back, blind face upturned, every sinew in his neck tensed. Normally a panting man held his head down.

Boariyi was waiting for the victor's demand. Then he was going to refuse. And when he did that, Wallie would have no choice at all except to execute him.

That rigidity he had seen before: Nnanji, facing death before dishonor. Well, give him a minute to brood on it, take a moment more to recover. Still gasping, Wallie glanced at Zoariyi. His evident dismay as he stared at his nephew was all the confirmation anyone could need. The three of them, one kneeling, two standing, were walled in by a silent circle of onlookers. Fearfully the sun uncovered its face, and the blood shone more brilliant red.

"Healer!" Wallie croaked. "Give me a cloth."

It was scruffy but he took it in his free hand, wadded it, and tossed it to the blinded Boariyi, who flinched when it hit his chest and fell on his knees. He made no move to pick it up—more confirmation.

Where the hell had Nnanji gone?

Now the silence was too old. He had to speak, and he was almost capable of it.

"Lord Boariyi . . ." Louder: "Lord Boariyi, you did not lose. My sword won, yours lost. I have not met a swordsman like you before. In a best of ten, I should be proud to get five on you."

The tall man's face twitched, but he did not speak.

Wallie continued. "Now you will order the council to swear the third oath to me. But not you. From you I require only the first."

There was a pause while the words sank in. Then Boariyi fumbled to find the cloth, raise it to wipe his face and then press it one-handed over his forehead. He opened his eyes—startling eyes in a bloody mask—and stared up unbelievingly at Wallie.

"The first oath?" he mumbled.

"I need you to fight sorcerers," Wallie whispered.

"But I ordered them to kill you."

"I need you," Wallie repeated. "The tryst needs you!"

The loser took a deep breath. Life won over honor. "So be it!"

Wallie sheathed his sword and held out a hand to help him rise, then lifted their joined hands high. The spectators roared.

"Bravely fought, my lords!" That was Tivanixi, beaming. "A legendary feat of arms! Never have I seen such a match!"

"And you won't again—not from me, anyway," Wallie said with feeling. He thumped Boariyi on the back. "You?"

"Never, my lord!"

The healers were flocking to his wound like blowflies, but Wallie pushed them away. His arm had almost stopped bleeding and another bout of blood poisoning, he did not desire.

"My lords . . ." The bullfrog herald was trumpeting the outcome of the match. Big raindrops began to fall in the sunshine. Wallie began to shiver as the inevitable reaction rushed in on him.

Boariyi had been fitted with a bandage and now he, too, waved the healers away. "My lord vassals, you will swear the blood oath to Lord Shonsu. Lord Shonsu, may I have the honor . . ."

He presented Tivanixi, and Wallie responded, feeling about a thousand years old and afraid he might be swaying on his feet. "Where the hell is Nnanji?" he demanded, looking around.

Tivanixi smiled and said softly, "Eleven forty-four."

There were puzzled frowns as the Sevenths worked it out, and annoyed glares from most of the Sixths who formed the front rank of spectators—although a few of them nodded wisely to show that they knew all the sutras, even the last. A couple of the Sevenths remained puzzled, not understanding.

But Wallie understood and felt shock. *Your oaths are my oaths!* Nnanji was going to be liege lord, too! Wallie had not thought of that implication of the fourth oath, but Nnanji had. If he was present, then the Sevenths would have to kiss his boot, also, but he was only a Fifth. Nnanji would find that as outrageous as they would, so he had tactfully migrated elsewhere.

The five Sevenths were presented, prostrating themselves to swear the terrible blood oath and kiss Wallie's foot. The sun died away, and the rain grew serious. Then Boariyi borrowed a sword and swore the trivial first, promising to obey Lord Shonsu's commands—but reserving his honor, which could mean anything at all.

"You will address the company, my lord?" the chief herald inquired.

The rain was excuse enough. Wallie shook his head wearily. "Tomorrow I shall meet with the council and the Sixths to explain how to fight sorcerers. Lord Zoariyi, your nephew proclaimed certain rules of discipline regarding behavior toward civilians. Pray have those reissued in my name. Lord Tivanixi? Two ships were seized?"

The castellan nodded uneasily.

"Release them and compensate the crew. Five golds apiece." For a moment Wallie thought he was going to get an argument, which probably meant that the treasury was almost empty. "Proclaim to the sailors and traders that the tryst will not commandeer any vessels in future and will charter any shipping required at negotiated rates. I swear this on my sword."

What else? His head was spinning. He was nauseated. "Who is the best horseman on the council?"

They exchanged glances of astonishment and—after a suitable pause for modesty—Tivanixi said that he had done some riding in his youth.

"Then pray attend me an hour before sunset. Bring a saddler and a blacksmith."

"But no minstrels," Nnanji said, appearing magically at Wallie's side with an extra-large grin.

Gratefully Wallie draped an arm on his shoulder and almost fell. "Take me home," he whispered. He was dead on his feet.

Nnanji staggered under the weight and then looked him over, appraising his condition.

"Right!" He pointed inpudently at two large Sixths. "You! And you! Up!" Then—even worse—he turned to the cluster of Sevenths. "You will follow, my lords!" Wallie found himself being hoisted, protesting, on the Sixths' shoulders, but Nnanji was not done yet. "Bandsmen? Minstrels? *The Swordsmen in the Morning!*"

Tomiyano had been lingering offshore in one of *Sapphire*'s dinghies lest anyone need make a fast escape. Nnanji had the choice of two jetties, so he chose the farther. The band started a march beat, a trumpeter began the tune, the minstrels picked up the words, and off went the tryst, the two brawny Sixths bearing the new liege shoulder-high to his boat, with the Sevenths following behind and then everyone else; all joyfully singing the song that was evermore to be not merely the march of the tryst of Casr, but the instilled marching song of the whole craft: *The Swordsmen in the Morning*. While out in front, leading the whole parade with drawn sword, singing as loudly as anyone and somehow grinning as well, stalked Nnanji of the Fifth.

BOOK FOUR:

HOW THE SWORDSMAN TOOK COMMAND

†

"What do I do now?"

The question rang out so clearly that for a moment he thought it had been spoken aloud. It startled him. His eyes flicked open and stared unseeing at the bare planks above. If the words had been spoken, though, then his had been the voice saying them.

He was in his cabin on *Sapphire*, his wounded arm throbbing dimly in its bandage. His skin had the all-over softness, the woolly feel that sleep can bring, but Jja had washed away the blood with hot water, an unthinkable luxury on a wooden ship. His fatigue had gone, also—which meant that his body had already replaced that lost blood. He felt good. Now his danger was over and his task began.

Bare plank ceiling, bare plank walls—yet it felt like home. If Brota agreed, he would continue to live on board. A general should stay with his army, but he would never make a conventional leader. Probably Brota would keep her ship at Casr for a while, rather than lose Thana.

Daylight still shone through the port, so he had not slept long. Life was simple in the World—no television sets or air conditioners or furnaces, no books or magazines. All they had in the cabin was a bedroll, covers, and a small chest to hold a few spare garments. Vixi's small bedding was tucked in a corner . . . few possessions.

Then he saw another possession. She was sitting cross-legged, watching him. She might have been there all the time he was asleep, like a statue, a buddha, waiting for him with the timeless stoicism of a slave—smooth brown skin and two black sashes, dark eyes inscrutable, dark hair grown to a decent length at last. Her smile told peacefully of things that could not be adequately confined to words.

"What do I do now?" he asked.

In one graceful movement like the swoop of a bird, she moved from her position by the wall to lie alongside him. She laid a cool hand on his face and gazed into his eyes—amused, content.

"Whatever you want. Are you hungry? Thirsty?" She paused. "Lonely?"

He smiled and tried to reach for her, but her weight and warmth were against his good arm, and he abandoned an attempt to move the other. "None of those, my love. No . . . I have an army now. I am liege lord. I have more than a thousand men sworn to obey me, to die for me. What do I do now?"

Jja slid fingers into his hair and steadied his head while her lips met his in a chaste, sisterly kiss. But her other hand slid down to stroke his chest. When the kiss ended she held her face only a few inches away from his and waited, expectant.

"In a minute," he said. "What do I do then?"

"I don't think a liege lord should ask his slave such things."

He had taken the tryst away from Boariyi to stop him doing whatever it was he was going to do with it. But he had made no decisions on what he would do with it himself, once he had it.

"But I do ask."

She studied him gravely. "Do what feels right!"

He was very conscious of her warm silk smoothness against him. That felt right.

The other problem did not feel right. "The thought of a war horrifies me, my love—death and maiming, bereavement and suffering, cities burned . . . Yet the Goddess wants the sorcerers driven out, thrown back into their mountains—doesn't she? Isn't that my mission? It is Her army, Her tryst, Her swordsmen. She has put me in charge. What do I do now?"

Jja laid her lips on his again and this time the kiss was less sisterly. Her hand continued its caressing, exploring. Inexplicably her bra sash had come loose.

"I said 'in a minute'!" he insisted, when she let him speak. "Talk about this first—I can't think straight afterward. The gods are cruel, Jja! That little prince . . . A few thousand deaths don't worry them. They live forever. So what if a mortal dies—it must seem so unimportant."

She shook her head gently, her hair sweeping his brow.

Forestalling another kiss, he turned his head away and spoke to the wall. "I can do it . . . if I can ever make the swordsmen listen."

"Do what seems right," she said again.

"But if what I do is not what they want the gods will stop me."

"No."

He looked at her. "How can you tell?"

"You really ask your slave this?"

"Yes. You are saner than anyone else in the World, my darling. Tell me. Explain."

She frowned. Jja did not communicate with speech unless she must. "The Goddess would not have given you Her tryst if She did not think you were the best man to have it." Her lips came closer again. "So you must do . . . what . . . feels . . . right."

The kissing was growing more frequent, more insistent, more exploratory; and her hand continued its travels, also.

He tried to resist and winced at a complaint from his other arm. "Yes! All right! We'll do that soon. But what do I do after?"

"The same again," she whispered urgently from somewhere.

"And after that?" His good arm was free now and his hand slid to the knot on her other sash.

"More!"

"Glutton!"

She chuckled very quietly. "I must serve my master."

Then her actions achieved her purpose. Suddenly it felt right.

It felt very good indeed.

The deck was silvery with rain, RegiVul and the far bank hidden by misty nothing. Gray tendrils of cloud traveled the deserted streets of Casr. Few ships lay alongside the wide plaza since the Goddess had ceased Her sendings.

Tomiyano was handing round wine in the deckhouse, and the whole family had gathered to honor Lord Shonsu, liege lord of the tryst. There had been toasts and congratulations, and now there was merriment and loud conversation. Wallie was more touched than he liked to show, but the difficult parts were over. With only the two wood chests to sit on in the big room, people usually sat on the floor. Today, because this was a special occasion, they were all standing, as if at a cocktail party. Then an unexpected gap in the talk brought silence, broken by the pattering of rain.

"Who's missing?" he demanded, looking around.

"The priest," Nnanji suggested. He was pink. It was unknown for Nnanji to drink too much; the pinkness had other causes. Thana was certainly merry and was continually whispering things in his ear. He would probably consent very soon.

"Katanji?"

Nnanji nodded glumly. "He stayed in town. I wonder what he'll get up to this time?"

Katanji had his fortune with him.

Wallie chuckled. "I expect he'll buy the lodge and raise the rent. I know who's missing—our sorcerer! What did you do with him?"

"Bolted him in a cabin," Nnanji said.

"Bring him, brother, if you please."

Nnanji freed himself from Thana and stalked off, pouting. In a few minutes he returned with drawn sword, driving Rotanxi. The old man's hands were tied and his feet bare. He wore the ill-fitting blue gown he had been given for his appearance in the temple. It had no cowl and his white hair was disheveled. Probably he had been asleep. After *Griffon*, *Sapphire* was restful.

The conversation died as the sailors studied this awesome yet pathetic captive.

"Untie him, please, Nnanji," Wallie said. "We are having a celebration, my lord. Do sorcerers drink wine, or does it muddle their spells?"

The sorcerer straightened, striving for dignity. "I have nothing to celebrate."

"But you do! Lord Boariyi is probably a fast man with pincers. You should celebrate the fact that I won."

Rotanxi would never have been handsome, but he had probably always had presence, and in latter days power, even nobility of a sort. Now these were blurred, overlain by age, by defeat, and by bitterness. "For the sake of my craft, I wish that you had lost, Shonsu."

Wallie nodded thoughtfully. To have captured a Seventh was outside rational expectations. He had been sent this devious old villain for some purpose. "Will you swear an oath with me?"

"What oath?" Rotanxi demanded, surprised and suspicious.

"Your parole, my lord. I promised you no torture and I repeat that. Common sense says that I should lock you up in a dungeon —I suppose the lodge has dungeons. I should prefer to keep you here. Your friends may well seek to silence you, and *Sapphire* will be safer than a dungeon. Mistress, will you allow Lord Rotanxi to remain as my guest, if he behaves?"

Brota scowled, but she nodded.

Nnanji growled: "Urgh!"

"The quarters are plain, but the food is superb," Wallie said. "You will be well treated." He offered a goblet of wine to the sorcerer, whose hands were now free. It was refused with a gesture. "But I need your oath. Swear that you will not leave this ship until I bid you leave, that you will not harm it or anyone aboard, and that you will not communicate with anyone ashore or in any other vessel."

"For how long?" The tone was sharp, but the sorcerer was tempted.

"Sixty days should do it," Wallie said. "At the end of that time, I shall return you unharmed to the left bank. Oh—and you must agree to wear a gown without a cowl."

There was a pause while the sorcerer studied him and then glanced around the circle of sailors—men, women, children, all in turn studying him.

"What commitments afterward? What other conditions?"

"None," Wallie said. "The war will be won or lost by then."

The old man waved his hands helplessly. "I have no choice. I so swear, my lord."

"Good! I shall swear by my sword, of course. You will not object to coming with me now to the galley, so that you may swear over fire?"

A flicker of hesitation, then Rotanxi said, "Of course not."

He had not expected that, though.

"Excellent!" Wallie said cheerfully. "Then you are our guest, my lord! I shall present your hosts to you as soon as we return, but perhaps you would give Captain Tomiyano back his dagger now?"

In the ensuing chorus of oaths and exclamations, Tomiyano's were the loudest and most lurid. The sorcerer sent Wallie a thin smile that might easily have congealed blood, but he stretched out a hand, and the dagger appeared in it.

"It was up his sleeve," Wallie said resignedly, but he thought that no one believed him, not even Nnanji.

††

". . . teak strakes but rarely in these parts," Tivanixi was saying as Tomiyano ushered into the deckhouse, "but the masts are fir, are they not?"

Wallie suppressed a grin at the expression on the captain's face—he abhorred swordsmen, but the personable castellan had already won him over. Then Tivanixi saw the sorcerer and froze.

"Good evening, vassal," Wallie said quickly. He received a startled glance and a courtesy, fist-on-heart salute—they had been through the full formalities earlier that day. "Lord Rotanxi has given me his parole, so he is being treated as our guest. Allow me to present you."

Grim-faced, the two Sevenths exchanged ritual greetings, mouthing the words as if they were acid. Nnanji began edging toward the door and Wallie stopped him with a headshake.

"And Mistress Brota, the swordsperson who held off the entire tryst of Casr."

Tivanixi returned to charming. "Now I know where the beautiful Apprentice Thana gained her skill . . ." He melted Brota as rapidly as he had her son, but he had been disturbed by the presence of the sorcerer, his old suspicions twitching once more.

Then Nnanji—fist on heart again.

"I may swear the oath to you, now, my liege?" he inquired.

Red and unhappy, Nnanji looked a plea toward Wallie.

"Vassal," Wallie said, "the oath of brotherhood that Master Nnanji and I have sworn has produced a strange complication. It would indeed appear that he, also, is your liege. As we all know that you are thus pledged to him automatically, we do not feel that a formal public affirmation is required."

Wallie had expected relief, but Tivanixi squared his shoulders and frowned. "With all respect, my liege, as I am bound, I should prefer to make open acknowledgment."

"Very well. Shall we withdraw to a more private place?"

Not that, either, apparently. "It is a matter of honor, my liege, not of shame."

So the unhappy Nnanji had to stand for a Seventh prostrating himself on the floor, swearing unquestioning obedience to the death, and kissing his boot. The sailors watched open-mouthed. The sorcerer sneered. Wallie decided he would never understand swordsmen. The demigod had warned him that they were addicted to fearsome oaths, but why this unnecessary humiliation?

He could well remember a day in early summer when Apprentice Nnanji of the Second had sworn that oath to him on the shingle by the temple. How very much younger he had seemed then! And who could have foreseen that before winter Nnanji himself would accept that oath from a Seventh? Miracle!

He looked up in time to see a tigerish joy in Thana's eye.

Eventually all the formalities were cleared away, and then the castellan produced the blacksmith and saddler whom Wallie had ordered. Both Fourths, stolid artisans, they stood in the doorway, biting lips and shuffling feet at being in the presence of three Sevenths.

"How many complete sets of tack could we locate in the lodge, do you suppose?" Wallie inquired of the castellan.

Tivanixi had foreseen the question. "I located a dozen, my liege. There are undoubtedly more somewhere, but most will be as old as the sutras and probably rife with rats."

"Twelve will do to start with." Wallie produced a piece of wood, one of those he had spent so many hours whittling—a loop, flattened on one side. He began to explain to the smith.

"My liege!" Tivanixi was shocked. "There are civilians—"

"You mean there is a sorcerer present?" Wallie smiled. "What I am about to show you, lord vassal, is a World-shaking device, one of those inventions that are absurdly hard to make and yet seem ridiculously simple and obvious afterward. But it will be absolutely impossible to keep it a secret. So let him listen! Adept, can you make me twenty-four of these by morning?"

He explained it. He described the leathers he would need, and how they must be attached to the saddles. The two men nodded, although they had probably never in their lives made anything without a guiding sutra. Then he promised them a gold apiece and sent them off to the waiting boat. He must just hope for the best. He must also hope that the gods would permit this innovation. The stirrup would turn the World on its ear. If the Roman Empire had known of the stirrup, and used it, it need never have fallen to the barbarians.

The sailors were starting to sit down, which was a signal that the evening meal was on its way. Wallie invited Tivanixi to join them and offered him some wine. An air of puzzled frustration remained in the deckhouse—Nnanji put it into words.

"That *thing* will help fight sorcerers, brother?"

Wallie nodded, amused. He turned to Tivanixi. "A horse is a good way to get to a battle, of course. But did you ever try to wield your sword while on horseback, vassal?"

"Only once! When I was a First." He chuckled.

"What happened?"

"I fell off and almost ruined my evenings ever after."

"With those you would not have fallen off," Wallie assured him. "We are going to create a cavalry, and I hereby put you in charge. You will need practice, of course, but with stirrups a man can strike at an enemy, wheel his horse, shoot a bow—all those things and more without falling off. Man and horse together become a six-limbed fighting animal."

Tivanixi pondered for a moment, and then his eyes began to gleam. Rotanxi frowned; he was not stupid, either. Nnanji wrinkled his nose in disgust—not a proper swordsman way to fight.

Now the food was being brought in by some of the youngsters—sturgeon in batter, steaming haunch of auroch that filled the room with its savory scent, foamy fresh bread, and bright-hued, high-piled vegetables. How old Lina produced such daily marvels from her tiny galley was a miracle to baffle the gods.

Wallie was annoyed to notice Rotanxi and Tivanixi drifting away in opposite directions. One was a prisoner of war and the other sworn to unlimited obedience. He decided to impose his authority, set them against each other, and see what resulted. It might be entertaining, even informative. Thus he carefully summoned the sorcerer to his left and the swordsman to his right, placing himself in a corner so that their backs were against different walls and they could not ignore each other completely. Rotanxi seated himself with the calculated movements of age. The graceful castellan settled like a snowflake, although he had to make the additional maneuver of drawing his sword, no easy task under the low ceiling. Jja, interpreting her master's wink correctly, became waitress for the evening.

While the rest of the company gathered around the food there was tense silence in the corner. Wallie pointed at Tivanixi's bandage, matching his own. "Lord Boariyi favors shoulder cuts, I see."

The swordsman looked abashed. "This rag is not really necessary, I confess! The combat for leadership, round one—but he was very gentle, hardly enough blood for the crowd to see. Yet I thought we had put on a good show, my liege, until I saw round two! I shall tell my grandsons about that!"

Rotanxi snorted. The castellan scowled. "You will instruct us tomorrow how to kill off the sorcerer vermin, my liege?"

"I will," Wallie said. "Sorcerers themselves are no great problem, as we showed at Ov, but their towers will be harder."

"Much harder!" the sorcerer commented.

Jja appeared with two platters, one in each hand. She tactfully offered them simultaneously, giving precedence to neither guest. Wallie smiled his approval.

"Still, we have odds of fifty to one."

"That would be about a fair match, I should think," Rotanxi said.

He had the advantage, for Tivanixi was fighting in the dark, so Wallie decided to throw his weight in. He could feel the antipathy around him like static. Earth had its ancient enmities—Christian versus Jew, Catholic versus Protestant—but none was a fraction as old as this hatred between sorcerer and swordsman.

"It might be fair under the old rules, my lord sorcerer. Of course I intend to instruct the swordsmen in some new techniques."

By tradition, *Sapphire*'s crew sat around the walls when eating in the deckhouse, with the food on one chest and Brota on the other. Nnanji, however, now chose to sit directly in front of Wallie and be part of the discussion. His plate was piled obscenely high, as always. In a moment Thana came to sit at his side.

"What techniques are those, my lord?" Rotanxi inquired.

"The horses, of course," Wallie said, ignoring a warning grunt from his vassal. "Bows and arrows—which are probably deadlier than your thunderbolts. And catapults, to knock down the walls."

Tivanixi grinned so widely that he could hardly bite on his next mouthful.

The sorcerer raised a snowy eyebrow. "Indeed? It will take some time to train cavalry and build catapults, will it not?"

"It will," Wallie agreed.

Silence fell for a moment. Then Wallie kicked the ball the other way. "Lord Rotanxi informed me that the tryst's funds are low, my lord vassal."

Tivanixi scowled. "His information is correct, my liege."

"How bad?"

With great reluctance the castellan said, "We have about twenty golds left. Of course we had laid in a good supply of food for . . . we have a good supply of food."

"For your canceled voyage," Rotanxi agreed drily. "A week's supply, I should guess? You will train cavalry in a week? And you must buy horses and lumber, not to mention bows and hay and saddles . . ."

"Leather?" Nnanji whispered, and Thana smiled and glanced over at her mother. Everyone was eating now, but everyone was also listening.

"Leather for saddles and also for the catapults," Wallie agreed. "And pitch."

"Pitch?" Nnanji asked, disapproving on principle although he could have no idea what the pitch would be for.

"We shall hurl flaming pitch at the towers. The results may be spectacular, may they not, Lord Rotanxi? Especially if we can put a shot through the third window up, extreme south on the east side?"

That was the room where Katanji had seen sacks being stored in the Sen tower. Katanji insisted that all towers were identical. Wallie had assumed that the sacks included the gunpowder supply, and Rotanxi's sudden pallor confirmed his guess. Point to Wallie.

Tivanixi would not understand that, but he noted the reaction and continued his meal in smiling silence. In a moment the sorcerer riposted.

"That is still assuming that you can finance this assault?"

Wallie passed that one to Tivanixi with an inquiring glance.

Angrily he said, "We have twice asked the elders for money. Each time they imposed a special tax that raised four hundred golds—but we spend fifty golds a day! We boarded as many as we could in the lodge, but that meant that we had to buy bedding —and slaves, of course. The rest are billeted on citizens and we must pay an allowance—"

"Is that money passed on?" demanded Nnanji.

The castellan flushed angrily, but this impudent Fifth was his liege. "I believe it is, now. Much of it was not, before Lord Boariyi imposed discipline. And there has been compensation for damage and injuries. There are not only swordsmen, my liege, there are wives and night slaves and children and minstrels and heralds. Profiteers are driving up prices outrageously. If you are planning a delay in departure, we shall have to think of winter clothing. Catapults and horses will certainly be expensive; stabling, saddles—and you promised to compensate the sailors for transportation . . ." His voice tailed off in a note of despair.

It sounded terrible. Wallie had been thinking that he could sell *Griffon* and recover his expense money. Obviously he, also, had underestimated what a tryst cost. Two or three thousand golds would not be near enough if he was looking at a delay of several weeks—and he would need *Griffon,* anyway. Rotanxi reached for the wine bottle and poured himself another goblet in private celebration. Brota and Tomiyano exchanged glances. Money was a subject they enjoyed more than swordsman talk.

"What sort of tax?" Wallie asked.

"A hearth tax," the castellan replied, showing surprise. "Normally it is collected annually."

In a world without writing the taxation system would be primitive in the extreme. Even a poll tax might be impossible to collect. A hearth tax? Wallie tried to remember the skyline of Casr; he recalled many chimneys—which meant cold winters.

"How much per hearth?"

"Two silvers."

Hearth tax and dock tax? Probably the elders were a mixture of traders and landowners. Wallie was still thinking about that when Thana intervened. "Four hundred golds would be only a part of what was collected. Who got the rest?"

Tivanixi frowned at her presumption, but Rotanxi saw a chance to score. "The tax collectors, of course."

"Like the corrupt port officers?" she said. "Relatives of the elders? And the elders get a kickback?"

The sorcerer nodded, smiling grimly. "And so do the swordsmen who accompany the collectors to enforce payment. There were people selling furniture to pay the last impost, my lord. What will you take from them now, their clothes?" His spies had reported well.

The swordsmen were silent, but Thana was obviously nurturing an interest in politics. "Who appoints elders?"

"Elders do," Rotanxi said, beaming at her like a grandfather. "They appoint the garrison, also, of course, and the swordsmen keep the elders in power. Parasites!"

Thana looked at Nnanji, who was frowning, hopelessly lost in this discussion of politics and finance. "Let's be elders, darling," she said.

Wallie wished Honakura were present to hear that remark.

The swordsmen seemed to have lost the last few points, and Nnanji could be counted on to make it worse.

"Brother?" he said. "You let Lord Boariyi off with the first oath. He must have vassals? Does that mean we have two trysts now?"

Wallie had not thought of that problem. He looked to Tivanixi, who scowled.

"Yes, I suppose it does, my liege Nnanji. He has a great many of the Sixths sworn to him—almost half, I should say."

Rotanxi took another sip of wine.

Nnanji rose and went to refill his plate.

"What do the elders do with all that money?" Thana inquired, still pondering the intricacies of government.

Wallie looked at Tivanixi, who shrugged blankly. Swordsmen did not worry about such things—but apparently wizards did.

"Oh, they perform a few services," Rotanxi said. "Clean the streets once in a while, gather nightsoil—which they sell at a profit to the farmers—maintain the docks and the wells. The garrison is always the largest expense, of course. Mostly, though, they give banquets for visiting swordsmen!"

Tivanixi flushed and then saw that his liege expected an explanation. "There are always balls and other social events! As visitors in town, the highranks were invited. There is one planned for tomorrow night. Now that the tryst is not departing, you will be invited, of course."

"And Nnanji?" Thana demanded.

"Er . . . yes, I expect so."

Thana clapped her hands in delight. "I shall need a gown! Jja, would you—"

She stopped with a gulp. Jja dropped her eyes to her plate. Discomfort reigned, while all Thana's relatives glared at her.

Wallie ought to attend any civic function, to reassure the elders and mend some fences. He could certainly not take Jja. To go without an escort might look very odd. Damn! As if he did not have enough problems! Nnanji would certainly be invited . . . Worse than the thought of not going was the thought of Nnanji running loose, playing junior-half-of-liege-lord.

And Nnanji had returned and heard the news from Thana. "Fine!" he said cheerfully. "I hope I'm not too exhausted to dance! How many Sixths are there, vassal?"

"Thirty-nine," Tivanixi said.

Nnanji rolled his eyes blissfully, without stopping chewing. "And I'm their liege! I can order them out to fence! Let's see, at six a day . . ." He lapsed into a long, frowning calculation.

So Nnanji thought a tryst was one big fencing practice, did he?

"They'll butcher you!" Wallie said. "And I may have a few things for you to do."

Nnanji grinned with his mouth full. "Anything, of course! But I can't ride and I don't know archery. I could collect taxes, maybe?"

"But you could find out who does ride! There must be a thousand useful skills in the tryst. Remember Kandoru? He was a fine horse doctor, Quili said. Thana is a great sailor. We shall need smiths and archers and horsemen and carpenters—"

"Carpenters?" Nnanji exploded. "That's a craft! So's smithing!"

Wallie glared at him. This was typical of the straight-line thinking that he would have to overcome, and he had hoped Nnanji knew better. "Will you take carpenters into battle with you to repair the catapults?"

Nnanji chewed thoughtfully for a while, then swallowed and said, "No, of course not. And saddlery's a craft, but we have sutras on leather, horses . . . and cooking! Lots of things! Thank you, brother! So you parade the swordsmen past me and have each one say his name and what he can do, apart from swordsmaning . . . It'll take a while, but I can do that for you." He smiled happily and stuffed a whole beetroot into the smile.

Wallie was relieved. He had been afraid that Nnanji might take offense at being asked to be the tryst's filing system.

"My liege Nnanji," Tivanixi said quietly, "how many sutras are you short for Sixth rank?"

Damn!

Nnanji beamed disgustingly. "I'm at ten eighty-two. I need to be at eleven fourteen." Both he and Tivanixi began counting on their fingers.

"Thirty-two," Wallie said glumly. If Tivanixi must have a liege of lower rank—the absurdity created by that infernal fourth oath—then he would much rather that liege be a Sixth than a Fifth. "I don't think he's quite ready yet, my lord vassal."

Tivanixi would not argue with his liege.

"He could beat Forarfi by the third day!" Thana protested sharply.

"That's only because it *was* the third day," Wallie snapped. "He's very good at learning his opponents. Two unknown Sixths would be another matter."

"What do you think?" Nnanji demanded of Tivanixi.

So Tivanixi had his chance. "I thought you were good enough that first time we met, my liege. You humiliated those two Fifths, and I hadn't chosen easy marks for you. Honorable Forarfi is an exceptional Sixth, a very high Sixth. Fiendori says—"

He stopped. They all looked at Wallie. "I disagree!" he said heavily. "He's a good Fifth, but he's not near Sixth yet."

The matter was closed. Nnanji continued to chew noisily. Everyone else had finished main course. Apple pie was being passed around. The deckhouse was growing dim.

"After all," Tivanixi said in a quiet, reflective voice, seemingly to no one in particular, "it isn't as if he could go on and try for Seventh."

"It isn't?" Wallie said, irritated. Did they think he was jealous of Nnanji?

"It would not be possible, my liege. All the Sevenths in town are his direct vassals and hence ineligible as examiners—all except Lord Boariyi, and I doubt if anyone would ask him! There is just no way Master Nnanji can become a Seventh until after the tryst is disbanded."

"I hadn't thought of that!" Wallie said, wondering why the news was welcome. Nnanji was looking wistful. "All right! Tomorrow at dawn—let's get it over with."

Nnanji threw an arm around Thana and hugged her, grinning like a maniac.

Tivanixi gasped. "Tomorrow? Thirty-two sutras?"

Wallie smiled with the best grace he could raise. "Nnanji is reputed to remember what his mother wore on the day he was born, my lord. I have just lost an hour's sleep, that's all."

"Pity about seventh rank, though," Nnanji remarked. "I was planning to ask Lord Chinarama!"

The swordsmen all laughed, then explained to the sailors.

"What do you do about that?" Wallie inquired, suddenly curious. "You must have some real duffers in a thousand men. The Goddess brought them by the shipload. She had to take whoever was on board."

Tivanixi nodded. "The easy ones get known. We simply gave them orders that they were not to accept any further requests. A few have been sent home."

"How about challenges?" Nnanji asked, passing small pie

along, keeping large pie. How did he stay so skinny?

"Promotion is not normally done by challenge."

"But it can be," Nnanji persisted. "I've done it."

The castellan nodded. "True. With most ranks we have plenty of choice, of course. Challenge was hinted at by one brave Sixth, and the other Sevenths quietly passed the word that a challenge to Lord Chinarama would result in severe anemia afterward."

"Tomorrow, then," said Wallie as the pies stopped traveling and he saw that he was holding what must be his piece. Nnanji had three. "Will you pick out a couple of Sixths? Real horrors, strong as bulls, swift as stooping falcons, terrible as the she-bear defending her young?"

"I know just the two," Tivanixi said. "True butchers! Vicious sadists! We call them Collarbone and Testicle." The listening sailors guffawed.

"Hey!" Nnanji yelped. "You're my vassal, too. You pick a couple of elderly cripples! Arthritic and preferably almost blind."

"I can see this divided allegiance may become a problem." Tivanixi sighed. "I shall choose one of each." He was clearly very pleased.

"There's no honor in being an easy mark!" Wallie snapped. "And we don't want the tryst to think that Nnanji is being favored. You pick good ones!" If the gods wanted Nnanji as a Sixth, then they could throw in a dash of miracle. Failure would do his ego no harm. He would not be eligible to try again for a year, so it would also stop his whining.

The castellan flushed and said of course he had been joking. He would choose highly respected Sixths. Thana and Nnanji pulled faces.

The meal was ended, night drawing in. Wallie's mind was churning with all the plans he had for the next day. Everyone else was relaxed and good-humored, congratulating Lina on the meal. Even Rotanxi made a joke about the quality of the prisoners' fare in Casr. The women began pressing Nnanji to sing more of Doa's epic, some of which he had apparently passed on earlier. He said maybe later, but he was going to finish that pie if no one else . . .

"Nearer eight!" Rotanxi said.

Wallie jerked back into the conversation. Talk of the epic had brought mention of the seventh sword.

"I beg pardon, my lord?"

"I said that your sword is nearer eight hundred years old, Lord Shonsu, even if Chioxin made it in the last year of his life."

Now Wallie was alert. "How so?"

"He died seven hundred and seventy-seven years ago!" The sorcerer grimaced in satisfaction at his superior knowledge.

Nnanji made skeptical noises, but Wallie was thinking hard. The sorcerers' spy network was astonishingly efficient. That sword had only become news on the day he had arrived at the lodge. Rotanxi had received word of it, but surely the written records of such trivia would only be kept in Vul itself; there was no hint that the sorcerers had invented printing yet, so all books would be handwritten, and copying a tedious process. Rotanxi had sent an inquiry to the main library in Vul and received a reply before Wallie had captured him. Very fast work!

"What else do you know of Chioxin, my lord? Apart from his being left-handed, that is?"

Rotanxi shrugged vaguely in the gloom. "He was short and fat."

"Bah! Sorcerers' flimflam!" Nnanji was now a complete skeptic, knowing nothing of written records.

"You think so, master? Then I suggest you go to Quo and look at his statue!"

"Oh!" Nnanji fell silent.

Wallie shivered in sudden apprehension. "Quo? Why Quo?"

"Because that's where he lived."

"Chioxin was armorer for the lodge!" Tivanixi said angrily.

Smugly the sorcerer agreed. "Yes he was. But in those days, my lord, the lodge was located in Quo. It only moved to Casr a couple of centuries later."

Wallie did not doubt him—Rotanxi had no reason to lie about this. But the news was shattering. That line of the riddle had never felt right. *First your brother*... when he had seen what that meant—Nnanji and the fourth oath—then he had known at once that it fit. *From another wisdom again*... he had never really doubted that the second line referred to Katanji. The rest had all become clear in its own time...

But when Tivanixi had told him that he had already fulfilled the ending by bringing the sword back to Casr, he had felt no instant surge of satisfaction. It had felt wrong. And Tivanixi had been mistaken.

The riddle yet remained unsolved.

Finally return that sword.

Finally?

Lord Shonsu had not yet returned the sword. The puzzle remained. Return to where? To whom? To Quo? To the Goddess?

And to its destiny accord.

But what could be its destiny, if not to lead the tryst?

†††

"Hit!" called the Sixth, lowering his foil.

"Was not?" Nnanji cried.

"I did not see it," the first judge said.

The second judge hesitated and then agreed: "No hit! Continue."

The great courtyard of the lodge was blue with predawn shadow and clammy with dew. There were no sounds in it except the clatter of the two foils and the panting of the fencers sending out puffs of steam in the early-morning air; no one around except those called for this match. Bare branches shone darkly against a silver sky.

This was the third time Wallie had watched his protégé go up for promotion. The first two had been easy for him, but now he was having a struggle. Tivanixi had followed orders and chosen good Sixths to be Nnanji's examiners.

But Wallie had said nothing about judges. Being the candidate's direct vassal, Tivanixi was himself ineligible, and he had selected two judges with care. Probably he had done nothing so crude as to drop hints to them. He had merely selected men who could pick up their own hints. He had met Wallie at the door, suave and elegant despite the early hour, presenting his four Sixths, two to fence and two to judge. But a facemarker and a tailor had been routed out of bed to attend, and that was hardly routine. He had given Nnanji the salute to a superior. He had suggested that the light was still poor for fencing—would the judges consider doing the sutra test first, he had asked, knowing that Nnanji was good at that. The judges had shown their understanding by throwing easy ones. If the fencing examiners had not gotten the message from that, then they should have understood when the hurdles were left in place, cramping the work although the whole courtyard was available.

The first examiner was certainly a good Sixth, but much older than Nnanji, so Nnanji had naturally played for time, winding him—yet it was the Sixth who had been reprimanded for not making a fight of it. Disheartened by that obvious injustice, he had lost the bout shortly thereafter.

The second opponent had resented these sleazy tactics and had fought hard. Then, with the score tied at one all, had come this disputed point. Such things happened all the time—that was why there were judges—but Wallie would have made the award against Nnanji, had he been judging.

Yet that was hardly fair, either, for he was barely paying attention. He had so many things whirling in his mind that he could hardly stand still beside the hurdles, wanting to pace up and down among the statues and benches. Sleepy spectators were appearing on the balconies, roused by the clatter.

"Hit!" Nnanji shouted.

The judges agreed.

Nnanji of the Sixth! Wallie stepped forward to congratulate him, half angry at the manipulation, half amused that even his righteous oath brother could bend his standards enough to ignore it. Yet it was a valuable lesson in the difference between obedience and cooperation—Tivanixi was looking very smug.

The tailor bowed and held out a green kilt. Nnanji tried it against himself and said in surprise that it seemed like a perfect fit. The tailor bowed once more and smiled. "Lord Tivanixi brought around a Second who was the same size as your honor."

So it had been specially made during the night? Wallie frowned reproachfully at Tivanixi, who avoided his eye. Nnanji threw off his red and put on the green, grinned in delight at nowhere in particular, then sat down on one of the benches while the facemarker pulled up his stool. Wallie could not express his feelings without creating a scandal, so he merely thanked all four Sixths and dismissed them.

"Your orders for the day, my liege?" Tivanixi inquired blandly.

Where to start?

"I wish to meet with the council as soon as possible," Wallie said. "Then with the Sixths. The town is being patrolled as usual, I suppose?" He pondered. "There must be many retired swordsmen in this city."

The castellan nodded, puzzled. "They hang around the lodge all the time."

"Pick one that looks as much like our sorcerer as possible. Swear him to the tryst, then smuggle him down to *Sapphire*—"

Tivanixi laughed. "And parade him back in chains? Bands playing? Crowds booing?"

Wallie nodded approvingly. This man was quick.

"Should we also arrange for other imposters to scream in relays from the dungeons, do you think?" Tivanixi asked.

Wallie chuckled and said he thought that might be going too far. "Are any of these ex-swordsmen elders?" he inquired. "Or city employees of any sort?"

"One is a port officer, my liege."

"Great!" Just what Wallie had hoped for. "Swear him, also! At swordpoint if necessary."

The castellan frowned, trying to work out this one.

"We need to know the official scale of dock fees," Wallie explained. "A ship of *Sapphire*'s size pays two golds in a sorcerer town, but five in a swordsman town. The difference is supposedly graft."

"My liege?" Tivanixi was still puzzled.

"The sorcerers have made their port officers honest. They are trying to increase trade, because some ships shirk their ports. We, however, are merely going to take over collection of dock fees in Casr. We need to know the official scale and the real charges. Then—in the example I quoted—we shall remit two golds to the town, as required by law, and three to the tryst for providing the service. That solves the money problem."

Tivanixi gasped and very nearly slapped his liege lord on the shoulder. He slapped his own thigh instead. "Brilliant, my liege! I shall see to it! Honorable Fiendori is the man for that job!"

He went off, almost skipping. Wallie sighed. It could not possibly be as easy as he had just made it seem, but perhaps he had gained some time to work on more secure finances. Nnanji came sauntering over, grinning and rubbing his forehead with the back of his hand.

"Congratulations once more, Honorable Nnanji," Wallie said. "You look about half the right age for the job, but I am sure you can handle it."

"Thank you, brother!" Then he blurted out, "I'm not an easy mark now?"

"No, I don't think so," Wallie replied carefully. "You were an exceptional Fifth. You're an average Sixth, I should say. A pity about that disputed hit," he added, "but I do not dispute the call."

Nnanji's eyes glittered coldly. "Thank you, brother," he said again. "I assure you that I did not feel a hit."

Wallie winced. Of course Nnanji would not have lied about that. And the reason he had not rejected Tivanixi's underhanded assistance was that he had not even noticed it. "You ought to try a longer foil, brother," he said hastily.

Nnanji shook his head. "It was the same length as my sword." He pulled out his sword and measured it in the traditional fashion by holding it above his head and seeing where the point came on his chest. Then he just stared at Wallie, bewildered.

And Wallie stared back in shock. "When we bought that sword for you, back in the temple armory, your eyes were not level with mine." He had not noticed the change in height. It had been gradual. And now he could see that it had also been masked by the broadening shoulders, the thickening layers of muscle. All that day-long fencing was starting to show results. "Tell me, Nnanji, is it usual in this World for a man of your age to be still growing like that?"

Again Nnanji shook his head. His eyes were not only level with Wallie's now, they were suddenly shining in the dawn light. "No! Of course not! This must be a miracle for me, brother!"

"It's Lina's cooking!" Wallie was trying not to show how uneasy this discovery made him, but he was also still feeling guilty for having doubted Nnanji's honesty. "Come on," he said, "I'll find you a new one."

Then he jumped as a bugler shattered the peace of the lodge with the opening bars of *The Swordsmen in the Morning*.

Wallie led the way to the museum, pausing halfway up to recruit a trio of burly, eye-rubbing juniors from one of the dormitories. He had them lift the great bar from the door, then sent them away, awed by his rank and looking puzzled. The door creaked in agony and Wallie led Nnanji inside.

The long room was even colder than before, dark and dusty and depressing. Nnanji's eyes went wide as he saw what it was.

"There's the Chioxin," Wallie said. "Thought to be the ruby. But I doubt if much of the rest of this stuff is known at all. Pick a sword. Help yourself."

Nnanji stared at the long wall covered with swords. "That would be stealing, brother!"

"No it wouldn't! Who owns this?"

"The lodge? The craft? The Goddess?"

"Well?" Wallie demanded. "You are liege lord of Her tryst. I'm sure that She wants you to have a good sword. Help yourself."

"Oh!" Nnanji said, his teeth shining in the gloom as he grinned. "Well, I shall leave my old one, the sword that won the battle of Ov—very historical. Now, let's see."

They measured a few against him and chose a length, then both wandered up and down the room, checking swords of that size. As Wallie had noticed before, long swords were surprisingly common. Some were rusted, but the best steels had fought back and were still good. Quite soon Nnanji said, "This one!"

Wallie took it to a window and bent it and swung it and said yes, that was a fine blade, better than his old one, even.

"Now you need someone to give it to you," he said. "I'm sure that anyone would be proud. Tivanixi, Boariyi . . . even Katanji, if you like. Thana, maybe?"

"You haven't shown me the Sixths' signs yet, mentor," Nnanji said coyly.

"True! There are six of them." Wallie proceeded to do so: the challenge, the obeisance, the warning, the appeal for assistance, the acknowledgment, and the reversal of meaning. Of course he needed to demonstrate each of them only once.

"And that's all!" he finished. "There are no secret signs for seventh rank. If a Seventh wants to signal to a Seventh, he uses those."

"Why not?" Nnanji demanded, sounding cheated.

"I suppose because Sevenths are so rare that they don't meet very often."

Nnanji chuckled. "Well, that's done! Now I'm a Sixth and you're not my mentor anymore." The second oath lapsed when a protégé achieved promotion. "You will allow me to swear to you again?"

"Of course. My honor! And I'm sure that you'll make Seventh, probably right after we disband the tryst."

"Thank you!" Nnanji had no doubts at all. "But right now you're not my mentor, so it would be all right for you to give me this sword . . . if you would? I should like that, oath brother."

"If you wish," Wallie said, although he thought it was bending the tradition slightly—he was only temporarily not Nnanji's mentor. He knelt on one knee and held out the sword in the ancient ritual. "Live by this. Wield it in Her service. Die holding it."

He thought of young Arganari being given the Chioxin topaz.

"It shall be my honor and my pride." The traditional words, although Nnanji probably meant them more than most. He took the sword and put it in his scabbard, then hung his old one on the wall. "Now I may swear the second oath, Lord Shonsu?"

"For the last time, Honorable Nnanji," said Wallie. "And we should both see about getting some more protégés. And bodyguards. The sorcerers are sure to start reacting soon."

When they reached the courtyard, it was starting to bustle. Slaves were working two pumps, filling a long trough at which naked swordsmen were washing themselves. Other slaves were tending fires in makeshift iron ranges, starting to cook breakfast. Nnanji headed for a grindstone to sharpen his new sword, enlisting a First to tread for him. More men were trickling out of doorways and a large party came marching in from the street, led by Boariyi and his uncle and about a dozen Sixths.

Tivanixi appeared at Wallie's elbow. "I have spoken to Fiendori, my liege. Port officers will be escorted in future." He laughed. "I think the elders may have some comments to make on the subject."

"Why?" Wallie asked innocently. "We are performing a service for them."

The castellan chuckled, then nodded at the procession approaching. "Money is your stroke at the other tryst, my liege. Lord Boariyi cannot afford to feed his men. Perhaps you should invite him to have breakfast?"

"Too obvious. We'll give him a few days. Say nothing." But it was a pleasing thought. He could coerce Boariyi with money.

Boariyi came to a halt and made the salute to an equal, his face expressionless below a blue bandage on which he had marked seven swords with charcoal. Wallie responded to him, then to a salute from Zoariyi, who looked resentful and suspicious. Nnanji was still busy with his sword on the grindstone. Tivanixi saw Wallie's glance toward him.

"We can proceed with the council meeting at once, my liege, as you wished," he said. "The others are waiting." For propriety's sake, Nnanji should not meet the other Sevenths in public until they had sworn to him.

Wallie agreed. Tivanixi led the way. They entered the building by the door closest to the street exit and walked into another of the long rooms. One side was all windows, looking out at a litter of kitchen equipment. The other was paneled, much of the wood scuffed and split with age. The ceiling lurked above a mist of cobwebs.

The room was already full of swordsmen, standing or sitting on stools and benches, muttering and laughing. As the seniors entered, they sprang to their feet in a rattle of furniture and boots. Among these middleranks, to Wallie's surprise, was Katanji.

His white kilt was soiled and rumpled, half his ponytail had escaped from his hairclip, and his eyes were red-rimmed, but he smiled when he saw Willie, seeming quite relaxed. Still the boy hero, he had apparently been entertaining the company with his stories, yet he looked as if he had not slept all night. What had the little devil been up to this time? He showed no signs of wishing to talk. Reluctant to ask, Wallie merely nodded and smiled as he passed by.

This was an antechamber. A door at the far end led into a smaller, square room, although it was large also. At the far side was a huge stone fireplace, its hearth strewn with old ashes.

Three walls were paneled, the fourth all grimy windows. A filthy gray rug only partly covered a floor of splintered planks; in its center was a circle of seven stools. Along the wall opposite the windows stood a large chest, a single brocade chair—shabby and leaking feathers—and, surprisingly, a bed covered with a greasy fur. A foggy bronze mirror hung beside the door. Evidently this grubby, stale-smelling chamber had several uses.

Three Sevenths rose and made their salutes. Most conspicuous was the elderly Chinarama, shriveled and slightly ridiculous compared to his much younger and more muscular companions. His ponytail was a white wisp and his harness fitted badly, but his eyes were quick and clear. An older man might be a valuable counselor. As Nnanji had said, he wouldn't hurt. His movements were awkward, hinting perhaps at arthritis, and his face none too friendly. A Boariyi supporter, then.

Then there was Jansilui, who was around thirty, square-jawed and stocky, with one facemark not properly healed. He seemed less hostile, probably caring little who was leader if it could not be himself.

Linumino was older, about fifty, and running to fat. One side of his face was hideously scarred where a sword cut had removed half the eyebrow and cheek and, seemingly, part of the underlying bone as well. The skin there was sunken and a puckered white, like weathered leather. It was a miracle that his eye had survived. He would not have been a contender for the leadership. His salute was perfunctory, so he was another Boariyi supporter at heart. Wallie wondered briefly which of the six he would ask if he were Nnanji trying for promotion; with old Chinarama out of bounds, certainly this portly Linumino, and probably Zoariyi, who was similarly nearing retirement.

Wallie invited them all to be seated. Suspicion hung in the air like a bad smell. In trial by combat the Goddess had declared him innocent, yet that fight had been as near as possible a draw, and trial by combat was not a normal procedure anyway. They did not completely trust him; they would obey him, but they might obey willingly or—as Tivanixi had done over Nnanji's promotion—reluctantly, honoring his words while thwarting his purpose.

He mentioned that Nnanji had gained promotion and would be there shortly to receive their homage, but, as a Sixth, would not be a member of the council. Wallie had some special duties in mind for Nnanji. Then he went on to the subject of money, explaining how the tryst was going to divert the unofficial portion of the harbor dues. They all smiled at that.

"So you have solved the finance problem at one stroke, my liege?" Chinarama asked.

"For the moment," Wallie said. He turned to more difficult matters. "Lord Boariyi, you have sworn the first oath only. I propose to treat you as a full member of this council, and your vassals as members of the tryst. In return, I ask—"

Nnanji never knocked on doors. He marched in and slammed this one behind him. He was scowling. The Sevenths rose to their feet again, most of them returning his scowl.

He wiped a hand on his new green kilt. He reached for his sword. He gave Lord Boariyi the salute to a superior in impeccable fashion, then glanced cryptically at Wallie and waited.

Who saluted whom? The damnable fourth oath was fouling up all the rituals. Hesitantly Wallie presented Nnanji to Chinarama, and the two exchanged salute and response.

"Now I swear the third oath to you, Honorable Nnanji?" the old man inquired petulantly.

"It distresses me, my lord," Nnanji said in his soft voice, "to have to accept such an oath from a respected senior such as yourself, but that seems to be what Lord Shonsu's position . . ."

Wallie saw a look of horror come over Boariyi's face, then Tivanixi's. He followed their gaze. Nnanji was tugging his left earlobe, he had his right thumb in his belt, his right knee was slightly bent.

Nnanji was making the sign of secret challenge to Chinarama.

What! Had he gone insane? Promotion? Of course not—he would need to secure judges first, and courtesy would demand that he ask before he challenged, and it was illegal anyway. . .

Nnanji was still babbling on about oaths. Chinarama was paying no attention to the signal. Then he became aware of the tension about him, and his eyes flickered warily around the group.

Wallie flashed out his sword left-handed and laid the point at the old man's throat. "Put your hands straight up in the air!" he bellowed, pushing Nnanji aside with his injured arm, which hurt. "Say it, Nnanji!"

"I denounce this man as an imposter."

Chinarama curled his lip in a sneer. "So there are some swordsmen with brains, are there?" Then he burst into a diatribe of obscenities and vituperation, a lifelong hatred of swordsmen spilling out like pus as he ranted about rapists and murderers and thieves, perverts and bullies . . . It was rank and nauseating, but Wallie let it run on until it died away of itself; he kept the sword-point steady. There would be no need to try this case. The man had confessed.

"Lord Zoariyi," he said. "Go behind him. The rest of you stand back. Now, remove his harness, if you please. And his kilt."

"Is this necessary?" Boariyi objected.

"Yes." Wallie did not move his eyes from the hate-filled eyes of the old man. "His hairclip, too! Let me see your hands!"

The imposter showed them. "Fancy all you husky young swordsmen being scared of one old man," he sneered.

Wallie ignored the remark. "You may sit to remove your boots," he said.

It was only when the pathetic figure was stark naked and all his gear was safely out of reach that Wallie relaxed and sheathed his sword. He looked around at the faces filled with horror, fear, shame, and anger. "Later I will show you some of the sorcerer tricks," he explained, finding that his voice was defensive. It did seem ludicrous to take such precautions against such a weakling. "How did you know, Nnanji?"

Nnanji was staring at Chinarama with disgust and contempt. "Katanji told me, brother."

"Katanji? But how. . ."

"You remember on *Griffon* you showed us some of the sorcerer magic, brother? You got your fingers dirty. Yesterday Katanji was with me when I was presented to this . . . man. He had the same marks on his fingers. I didn't notice and Katanji didn't say anything. But he followed him afterward. He went to the house of a merchant and spent a long time there. They have a cage of pigeons in the yard—"

"Pigeons?" Boariyi spluttered.

"We don't understand, but we are grateful, my liege Nnanji," Tivanixi said, "to you and your brother. And to you, my liege

Shonsu. We are very much in your debt." His face was basaltic with rage and humiliation. The others looked much the same.

"What do we do with him?" Zoariyi inquired.

"Let's get him safely locked up first," Wallie said, turning and heading for the door. He was staggered by the thought of a spy within the council itself—yet why not? All Chinarama had needed to know had been the salutes and oaths, which were public. He had not been required to fight. He could always plead an old man's failing memory when queried on anything. Obviously the younger men had secretly admired him as a tough old boy. They had protected him. He had told Rotanxi of the tryst's plans and finances, and of the importance of the seventh sword. It was all so infuriatingly obvious now that it was pointed out—and by Katanji, of course! That was why he had been the right one to take along on the *Griffon* expedition; he brought wisdom. And his eyes missed nothing, not even inkstains on fingers.

Wallie reached for the door handle, heard a board creak behind him, and whirled around, sword in hand. Chinarama crashed to the floor, slammed down by Nnanji like a swatted bug in a splash of blood, his head almost severed from his shoulders. A knife clattered at Wallie's feet.

They were all too stunned even to swear. For a moment the only sound was the death rattle, the only movement the twitching of the corpse. Boariyi had his sword out, Tivanixi's hand was on the hilt of his. The other three had their hands raised.

Wallie said, "Thank you, Nnanji," and his voice quavered.

Nnanji lifted his eyes from the body. He looked at Wallie and then grinned. His new sword was still dripping blood.

Wallie bent to pick up the knife. It was small and looked deadly sharp, but he did not test it with his thumb because the blade had been coated with something, like the knives he had found in Rotanxi's gown. Standard sorcerer issue?

This grubby room with its dirt-smeared windows, cobwebs on the panels, old ashes in the fireplace—it suddenly all became horribly sharp and clear, made more real by the awareness of death. He had so very nearly died here. They would have laid him on that filthy bed. Probably this had been Shonsu's room, so perhaps that was where Doa had lain, waiting for her lover to return from the brothel. He hoped his trembling was not showing, but it probably was. He had just had a very narrow escape. Only Nnanji's incredible reflexes had saved him.

"Lord Shonsu!" Boariyi had turned red. "I was wrong, very wrong! I wish now to swear the third oath."

Nnanji was wiping his sword with Chinarama's kilt. The others were smiling, their suspicions forgotten. Honorable Nnanji had unmasked a spy, and the spy had tried to kill Lord Shonsu—there were no doubts about loyalties now.

"Honorable Nnanji," Boariyi continued, "I have never seen a more masterful piece of swordsmanship. I was a year behind you." He stepped over the body and held out a hand in admiration. Nnanji sheathed his sword and shook hands, grinning shyly up at the giant.

"I agree with that," Tivanixi said. "I had hardly started. Magnificent! The knife—was that sorcery?"

"In his boot, I expect," Nnanji said airily. He had one in his own boot because his mentor had told him to bring it.

"I may swear the third oath now, Lord Shonsu?" Boariyi asked.

"Wait! My lords!" Zoariyi was beaming. "Is this not a clear case for eleven thirty-nine?"

There was a pause as five minds searched the sutras. Then four faces broke into smiles and there was a chorus of agreement.

Nnanji, puzzled and irritated, looked at the smiles and then at Wallie. Wallie did not feel like smiling at all. The Sevenths had found a way out of their stupid status problem at the cost of turning Nnanji into a laughingstock. He struggled to maintain what he hoped was a poker face, but they were all waiting hopefully for him to speak. There was no way that he could deny them, none at all. Once again Nnanji had saved his life.

He must agree.

He turned toward Nnanji, therefore, and raised his sword. Nnanji blinked in surprise.

Wallie paused, then said it: "I am Shonsu, swordsman of the seventh rank, liege lord of the tryst of Casr, and I give thanks to the Most High . . ."

He was drowned out by Nnanji's astonished whoop and the others' laughter.

It was the salute to an equal.

†† ††

Thana stepped through the arch and paused at the top of the steps to survey the busy, noisy courtyard in its shadowing box of balconied walls. Swordsmen fencing, chanting sutras, arguing, singing, gambling . . . very nice! Men from bank to bank.

She glanced then at Jja, who was carrying a bundle and trying not to seem apprehensive. "Don't worry! You're Shonsu's. Just mention that and you'll have no trouble here."

Jja smiled and nodded without much confidence. Thana herself was aware of uneasy shiverings deep down inside. Ever since Yok she had been unable to see landlubber swordsmen in groups without those shiverings. Yet she had been assured that these swordsmen were well behaved now, bound by the blood oath and by strict rules of behavior toward civilians. But did those rules mention swordswomen? Still, Jja was Shonsu's and she was Nnanji's and he was liege lord, too. How many knew that, though?

Some juniors passing by at the bottom of the steps had seen them and stopped to admire. They were grinning, thumbs in belts, balancing on one foot and stamping the other, which was a humorous sign of approval, reminiscent of bulls pawing the ground. They did not look dangerous. Rather fun. "Come on," Thana said, and led the way down.

Wait by the steps, they had been told, and they would have had trouble doing otherwise, for soon the juniors were all around them, grinning, kidding, making slyly obscene suggestions about lunging lessons and how about a trip on your ship. Virile young men, fit and smart—most of them—and supremely confident and pleased with themselves, for the Goddess had called them to Her tryst. Firsts and Seconds to start with, then Thirds edged them out. No, there was no harm, and much flattery. A couple of them were knockouts, quite scrumptious. It was harder for Jja, of course, who could not banter back, but Thana was aware that she herself was enjoying this, giving as good as she was getting. It made her realize again how very young Nnanji was for his rank.

She wondered how he'd made out. If he had failed, the one-year wait would kill him. He'd been unbearable.

Fanfare! Now what? The courtyard fell silent, faces turning toward the balcony where the trumpet was bellowing. The council was coming out—Shonsu, huge and looking very bleak, and right behind him was Nnanji. In a green kilt! He had made it! Jja grabbed Thana's arm in excitement and whispered congratulations. They began to edge closer. Nnanji of the Sixth! Party tonight!

Then the others. No, not all—the old one was missing. *And Katanji?* How did he get in there?

"Your honors, masters . . ." The squat chief herald had joined the notables and started to thunder his proclamation.

"Landlubbers!" Thana snarled in Jja's ear. "They do love this bilgey pomp, don't they?"

Then the herald described the unmasking of Chinarama as a sorcerer. Thana jumped as an explosion of male booing burst out all around, but she and Jja joined in, grinning at each other and adding a treble note to the chorus.

They almost missed the next bit, but it was about Nnanji killing the spy; it sounded as if Shonsu had just had a narrow escape. Thana put an arm round Jja, who had turned pale.

"Sutra eleven thirty-nine . . . outstanding courage or swordsmanship in the presence of an enemy shall be just and sufficient cause for promotion . . ." She had been studying Nnanji's grin, and everyone around her was talking—was that what she had heard? *Seventh?* Now Jja was hugging her, so it must be. She had done it! She'd always said she would.

Of course! Why had she ever doubted? Now it had actually happened, it felt quite inevitable.

"I've got one, too, Jja!" she said, and the slave woman nodded and laughed with her.

Much muttering around her.

"Never heard of that . . ."

"You mean he doesn't have to prove it . . ."

"What about the sutras . . ."

"That's a strip of rust . . ."

She studied the faces. The juniors were grinning and laughing, but the older men were scowling. Well, what would you expect?

Lord Nnanji? It sounded good! And now they were on about his brother—it was hard to hear and even harder to see, now, for the crowd was filling in, packing closer around them. *Third?* Well, trust Katanji!

A few voices started the chorus from the song about him and were glared into silence by the seniors. Now there was cheering. The councilors were going back inside.

Lord Nnanji!

She wanted to dance a hornpipe. Wait till Tom'o hears about this!

"Aw, come on! Just a quick look!" said a voice behind her, but she wasn't paying attention. A tall Fourth with very well developed pectorals was asking her about Nnanji, and she was saying proudly that yes she was, and then Jja half squealed and half screamed, and Thana swung around and couldn't find her in the crowd of bare male shoulders and sword hilts and ponytails. Then she saw that a couple of Seconds had pulled Jja's wrap off and were tugging at the bundle she was holding in front of her. There was much laughter and some angry shouting, and Thana grabbed the Fourth and screamed that that was Shonsu's slave and there would be hell—

Then there was hell.

Where Shonsu had come from, she didn't know, but he came through the crowd as if it were long grass. There seemed to be bodies flying in all directions, and she was knocked down and rolled into a forest of legs and boots and a canopy of kilts. After a few kicks and stampings she was dragged to her feet and she began panicking her way toward the exit, fighting in a tumult of kilted men until she was carried backward by the current—and then Nnanji was there and he hugged her, and she clung to him.

His face was murderous. He began pulling her roughly back through the throng. He could see over the heads, but she could not; she hadn't realized quite how tall he was. She caught glimpses of Shonsu looming over the others as she and her husband pushed through the crowd, moving toward him slowly, for Nnanji might have top rank now, but what was needed here was beef and weight—although he was doing all right. And then they arrived at the edge of a clearing.

The two Seconds were kneeling there and Shonsu was blazing

in the middle. Blazing! It was the only word she could think of. She had never seen a fury like that—he was a giant, rampant. He glanced at someone in her direction, and *his eyes were red*. Impossible! He was roaring and he had his sword out, the Chioxin sword, and all around him there was emptiness surrounded by an army of cowering men. The other Sevenths were there, but they weren't speaking except when Shonsu spoke to them. He turned again in her direction and no, his eyes were not red, but . . . Then the two kneeling Seconds bent their heads forward, and the seventh sword arced and flashed with an audible hiss, and she screamed, thinking that the boys were going to be beheaded, but it was their ponytails that fell to the ground.

"Take them away!" That was Shonsu, to a chalk-faced Fourth.

"Nnanji!" she said. "What's happening?"

He looked almost as grim as Shonsu. "Slavery. He's ordered them sold."

Oh, no!

Jja, dressed again, rushed forward, clutching at her owner's shoulder, saying something. He hurled her away without a word. She sprawled at Lord Tivanixi's feet, and he bent to help her up.

"Nnanji!" Thana shouted. "They were only playing! They weren't going to do anything more. Stripping a pretty slave is—it happens all the time!"

He hardly looked at her. "Shonsu is liege. Whatever he says, happens."

The whole tryst was cringing, she could see, and now Shonsu had opened his fury wide. He was speaking to Tivanixi, but he could have been heard down by the docks.

"How many sleep in the lodge?" She couldn't hear the answer, but the castellan was pale, too. "How many are billeted?" It looked as if Tivanixi didn't know. "Very well! You take that side. Zoariyi, that one. Jansilui, Boariyi—I want to know how many dormitories on each wall, how many men they could hold, and how many other rooms can be cleared of junk. *Move!*"

The four Sevenths plowed into the crowd and, as it opened for them, ran. Then that human thunder roared again: "Linumino? Take a party of Sixths and inspect all the nearby buildings. Are there any that would make dormitories—halls or empty warehouses? *Move!*" Another Seventh ran.

"Everyone! Those of you who sleep here, go back to your rooms and *clean them up!* They're pigsties! Clean floors, clean windows, bedding neatly rolled, packs tidy! There's going to be an inspection, and may the gods help those who don't pass! The rest of you stand by for work details to tidy out the other rooms. You! Go and do the council room! You! Start on the stairwells."

"Come on!" Nnanji whispered to Thana and led her over to Jja, who was weeping. "Look after her." Then he vanished, following Shonsu.

The two women found a stone bench and sat down. The courtyard was clearing, but the turmoil of men running in all directions made it seem just as full as before. Nobody seemed to know what was happening.

A little later Katanji appeared, grinning rather jumpily.

"Congratulations!" Thana said calmly. She had her arm around Jja, who was sobbing on her shoulder and didn't seem to want to do anything else, ever again.

"Thank you," Katanji said smugly. He sat down on the bench.

"Third? How the devils did you manage that?"

"I'm not sure!" He looked bewildered and was trying not to. There were red rims round his eyes; his face was drawn. He yawned suddenly, and she guessed that he had not been to bed. "I think it was Nanj," he said. "They were going to make him a Seventh, and he refused unless they promoted me; I think that must be what happened. I had to promise to learn the sutras, and they made me a Third." He smirked.

Thana found this part of the events rather amusing—Nnanji, who was so prickly about rituals? "What about the swordsmanship? What happens if you get challenged?"

A strange expression came over Katanji's normally cheeky face, one she had never seen on it before. He gazed down at his cast for a minute. "I can't move my fingers, Thana. I don't know they're there unless I look. I'll never hold a sword again. I promised that, too."

She said she was sorry, she hadn't known.

"It's all right. I'd never have been any good, anyway. Nanj didn't know that sutra until now, see? Nobody does except Sevenths. But you know Nanj and sutras—he said if courage counted . . . and you heard what Shonsu said about me last time we were here? So *he* had to agree, and the others wanted Nanj a Seventh." He sniggered. "Unanimous! A First can't own things —but a Third can!"

That hadn't stopped him before. She fingered the pearls round her neck. He noticed and scowled as he always did. Then he laughed, and the old mischief twinkled in his eyes again.

"That was small stuff!" he said mysteriously. "Look, I've got to go. Business!" He jumped up and vanished into the confusion. She caught a glimpse of him running out the gate.

Two hundred golds' worth of pearls—small stuff?

The courtyard was much emptier and quieter. Then someone shouted warning. A stool came off a balcony and exploded in splinters on the paving. A broken bedstead followed it. Other balconies started raining old furniture and bundles and boxes and timbers. Clouds of dust came whirling around. Suddenly the courtyard was full of falling debris. Jja recovered enough to sit up, sniffing and red-eyed, and watch the display.

Nnanji appeared out of the fog, grinning. He had his seventh swordmark, but he still wore the green kilt.

"What the gods is going on?" Thana demanded.

He sat down beside her and hugged her negligently. Sex was rarely far from Nnanji's mind, but for once his excitement was coming from other things. "Housecleaning!" he said. "There's lots of room here to hold the tryst, but Tivanixi never organized it. A couple of the floors are unsafe, but mostly the place is one big junk heap. Shonsu is organizing. Clean out and clean up! He's threatened to flog the next man he sees with a dirty kilt, so half of them have stripped completely—you want to leave, or stay and enjoy that?"

Thana glanced at Jja. "We can dump the bundle and go?"

He nodded. He was grinning hugely. "I'll look after it. But you're going to miss a lot of fun. Now he's talking water supply and hygiene and latrines and cooking! He's going to sell all the slaves Tivanixi bought and buy more bedding and stuff with the money. He'll make the juniors do the cooking and cleaning. Only swordsmen are to be allowed in at all. Even the heralds will need escorts!" He laughed. "Glad you're not his vassal?"

She studied him in surprise. "You don't think that those things are beneath a swordsman's honor?"

He shook his head. "Not in battle! Not once the third oath has been sworn! There are sutras on all of them. He'd have us in tents if the money was available, I think. They haven't had enough to do. Thanks, Jja."

Jja's face was a desolation, her face swollen, her eyes raw with weeping, but she stared up at him in astonishment, and he grinned again. "He lost his temper! He needs to do that more often. Now they know they have a liege lord!"

"But, Hon—Lord Nnanji? He sold those two swordsmen into slavery? He hates slavery!"

Nnanji frowned angrily. "By rights he should have killed them! It was good for the tryst, Jja. They disobeyed orders from their liege. He should have killed them, really; I would have done. But I suppose the others are more shocked by slavery; and their mentors have each had one rankmark blotted and are in charge of nightsoil removal until further notice." He snickered. "I'd never have thought of that!" Then he turned to watch the torrents of filth pouring off the balconies and the hills of refuse rising below. "Some were pretty scruffy. Almost as bad as the temple guard, some of them, anyway. Not many."

Thana stood up. After this madhouse, *Sapphire* would be a nice, calm place. She would take Jja back there, then go and see about a gown for the ball. Jja was weeping again.

But . . . Lord Nnanji!

Her husband had won his seventh sword.

†† † ††

The long antechamber was now clean, at least in theory. The fireplace was empty, the dust more evenly distributed. The paneling had been carefully smeared as high as a man on a stool could reach with a rag, although above that a cornice of dust and cobwebs remained, its base scalloped in graceful arcs. The window-panes had been rubbed to a greasy sheen.

Racket drifted in from an anthill of activity outside in the courtyard. One row of ants was carrying garbage out to a bonfire in the middle of the plaza; another row of ants was returning, and that included those who had been billeted on citizens and were now bringing in their belongings. On almost every balcony a man was cleaning windows. Down in the yard itself a work gang hammered and sawed, building extra latrines and washhouses. Two streets away, an unused temple was being converted to women's quarters.

Wallie had ordered a table placed in the middle of the room, six stools in front of the windows, and two rows of stools along the other side, thirty-nine of them for thirty-nine Sixths. The Firsts who had moved the furniture had thought that a very strange arrangement, but to Wallie it was a long, narrow lecture room. *Next slide, please*. He had recovered his temper and did not feel very guilty over losing it . . . not *very*. Nnanji had approved, which was reassuring.

That young man was already sitting on one of the six stools, legs crossed, eyes staring dreamily into space. He had been carefully instructed and could probably be relied upon to pick up his cue. Nothing could spoil this day for Nnanji, Lord Nnanji, swordsman of the seventh rank, member of the council. For the tryst, Nnanji was the true seventh Seventh. He had achieved his ambition, the dream of every young boy in the World. He was perhaps the youngest Seventh in the history of the People. What was he going to do with the rest of his life?

Now the Sixths were dribbling in, cowed and dusty and possibly resentful, but certainly obedient. They filled up the two rows opposite the windows—starting at the ends, so that the last arrivals would be in the center, closest to the dread liege as he leaned against the table. Then the last Sixths and the last of the council, and the door was closed, and everyone waited apprehensively.

Wallie turned to Nnanji and said, "Four eighteen?"

Nnanji blinked pale eyes in astonishment and obediently began reciting the sutra. Wallie cut him off and said to Boariyi, who was next, "Three twenty-two?"

When he had finished with the Sevenths, he walked down to a nervous, rather young Sixth at the end of the front row and demanded seven twenty-nine . . .

Finally he returned to his place, leaning against the table. "There you are," he said cheerfully. "No sorcerers present!"

There were a few nervous snickers.

"Over the next two or three days, your honors, you are to test every man in the tryst like that! If you find one who does not know his sutras, watch out! Each of you will test his protégés and make sure that they test theirs, and so on."

He glanced around, seeing the nodding heads as they followed his reasoning.

"Anyone here ever seen a sorcerer before yesterday?"

No.

"Well, I'm going to tell you how to fight sorcerers. There are two tricks to it, that's all. What do the sutras say about them?"

Lips moved, brows frowned. Silence. The sutras said nothing at all about sorcerers. Carefully Wallie led them through the logic; sorcerers were not swordsmen, to be greeted with challenge and the ways of honor. Nor were they civilians, to be handled with *kindness, courtesy,* and *firmness,* as the sutras optimistically specified. They had to be treated as *armed* civilians, therefore an abomination. Therefore anything went, anything at all.

He raised his voice as the hammering outside increased. "The first trick is speed. Lord Boariyi, would you assist?" He stood the skinny giant beside him at the table and pointed down the length of the long room, to the door that led into the council chamber. "We are going to have a race, my lord. We shall pretend that a sorcerer has appeared in that doorway, and we shall see who can kill him first."

Boariyi regarded him with disbelief, then amusement. The audience brightened. A race they could understand.

"Lord Tivanixi, will you give us a signal?"

Tivanixi let the suspense build for a moment while the two big men waited, side by side. Then he said, "Now!" Boariyi launched himself forward like a sprinter, pulling his sword . . . and Wallie's knife slammed into the door before he was halfway to it. He skidded to a stop and swung around, face flaming.

"You're dead, my lord," said Wallie. "Sorry."

The audience seethed with silent disgust. Knives—especially concealed knives—were an abomination from the lowest cesspool of the Place of Demons.

Then Zoariyi called out the line that Wallie had been hoping to get. "It's one thing to hit a door, my liege. A man is a much smaller target."

"Nnanji!" Wallie shouted. "Sorcerer!" He pointed as if he were sicking a dog on an intruder.

Nnanji's mind was not as far away as it seemed, and he had crossed his legs so that the knife in his boot was handy. He rose, hurled it, and sat down to continue smiling at nothing. The knife struck within a finger-width of Wallie's. Boariyi dodged, but long after it had gone by him. The audience collectively said: "Ooo!"

"Curiously," Wallie said, gleeful at the lucky shot, "Lord Nnanji is much better with a knife than I am." The Sixths absorbed that thought with interest.

He walked over to get his knife, ostentatiously replacing it in his boot. Then he flipped Nnanji's so that it struck the floor in front of him and Nnanji could pick it up. The hours of practice in the ship were paying off, although not in the way he had expected.

"If you fight sorcerers in the ways of honor," Wallie said, "they will win every time. I was rescued from the sorcerers at Ov by Nnanji and my sailor friends, armed with knives. The sorcerer's thunder weapons are about as accurate and more deadly, but they take time to reload."

Then he said, "Nnanji, you don't need to hear all this. We shall excuse you." Nnanji rose, nodded happily, and sauntered off to attend to the many things that he had been given to do. Whatever his oath brother wanted was fine with him.

When the door had closed behind him Wallie said, "One other thing about testing for spies: Beware of any water-rat swordsmen you may have—they can read lips, some of them, and many of us mouth the words when we're listening to sutras. I suspect that water rats in general may not be very good on sutras, so test water rats with a foil—they'll pass that test!" He dared not look at Tivanixi.

The lecture continued. The second trick, the liege said, was to get the sorcerers out of their gowns—then they were harmless, like the old man he had shown in the temple. Jja's bundle lay on the table, and from that he produced Rotanxi's gown. He showed it off—the long sleeves, the numerous pockets, the cunning slits by which the wearer could reach in any pocket while appearing to have his arms folded within the sleeves. Then he brought out the gadgets, one by one, and explained them, showed them, passed some around. He sent for a stray dog from the street and pricked it with Chinarama's knife. It died quickly and convincingly.

He brought out Rotanxi's glasses and a copper tube—a small telescope—and explained lip reading. He passed them around and everyone marveled at the telescope's inverted, color-blurred, but magnified image.

He told of the sleight of hand he had seen, even the previous day.

He played a few notes on a silver fife and explained how a similar blowpipe had slain Kandoru of the Third.

He produced a small bag of oiled silk fitted with a glass nozzle and told how it sprayed a fiery liquid, how the sorcerers could blind a man or burn his face with a wave of the hand, while mumbling nonsensical spells. He demonstrated this acid spray on the dead dog, filling the room with an acrid stink.

The ink and quill and vellum he did not show, but he mentioned that a pigeon could be used as a signal, and that caged pigeons were an important clue to sorcerer agents.

He struck a match, and that created the biggest sensation yet.

Rotanxi's pockets had yielded two things like firecrackers, but they had become waterlogged in the hold and so rendered useless. Wallie showed them, however. He had cut one open and discovered a mixture of black powder and lead shot. "If you ever see things like these," he warned his audience, "with this wick burning—then run! It may injure you or blind you. It will create a clap of thunder, at least, and much smoke."

They all nodded again, fascinated, half-incredulous, greatly uneasy.

There were other poisoned knives, some so tiny as to be almost skewers. There were petty trick gadgets, like flexible coins and silk flowers that would crumple to nothing and then spring back. There was a compass, which created much more interest among these swordsmen that it had in the sailors, who knew only two directions, upriver and down. There was a pocket lens, and Wallie set one of the Sixths to holding it in sunlight by the window until he made a cloth smoke.

There were several bottles and packets whose purpose even Wallie did not know, labeled in a strange cursive script that tantalized him.

By now he had half his audience terrified and the other half contemptuous, so he ended with the pistol and made them all terrified. He explained it carefully. Then he fired a shot through the table, into the floor. The hammering outside stopped and then gradually picked up once more.

Finally he brought out the "toy for Vixini" that he had made so laboriously on the ship, a model catapult, and he flipped pebbles across the room with it. His listeners were too much in shock to laugh as he had hoped.

"We shall fight sorcerers with knives, with bows and arrows, with battering rams and big catapults to knock down their towers and hurl burning pitch through their windows. They use pigeons as signals, so we need falcons! We shall need men on horseback, who can move quickly. We shall attack by night and without warning and from behind. With these tactics we can win; without them we cannot. If the sorcerers use diabolical weapons, then so must we."

There was a long silence, which happened to match a lull in the racket from the courtyard. He thought it was not going to work.

He said, "Three hundred and thirty men tried to fight sorcerers in the ways of honor. Will you help me avenge them?"

For another moment he was sure that he had failed. Then Boariyi—bless him!—jumped up and said, "Yes!" Then everyone had to rise, and they all cheered. Their cheering probably convinced themselves much more than it did Wallie.

But he could smile, then. He began to pace up and down the long room. "We need to distribute some responsibilities," he said. "Lord Tivanixi has already agreed to look after the cavalry. Someone must be adjutant—I mean he will have to sort out the manpower and assign people and look after finances and relationships with the townsfolk and so on."

The Sevenths all shrank into their stools at that thought.

"That makes two. We need someone to look after building the catapults—three. Slingshots, bows and arrows—I know nothing about those, except that they are used to hunt birds. Do we have anyone who does?"

A couple of Sixths rose, rather shamefacedly.

"Great! I'll assign a Seventh to it anyway, but you can advise him. Lord Nnanji will attend to intelligence and security.

"Lastly," Wallie said and paused. "Lastly, we need some action! All the rest of these things are going to take time; I want action now! They have laughed at us for too long. They must learn to fear us."

Angry mutters of agreement . . .

"I have a small ship. I shall send it over to the left bank to kill some sorcerers. It'll be dirty, nasty work. It'll mean sneaking in by dark, throwing knives, and then running. No honor and much danger! But I want to frighten them. I would like to think that they're scared to walk their streets at night. They ought to know that we can fight.

"Lord Boariyi, I give you your choice."

The tall man had been slumped forward with an elbow on a knee. He straightened up and grinned and said, "The boat!"

That was what Wallie had expected—the attraction of danger outweighed the scruples—but once Boariyi had accepted the most dishonorable job, the other Sevenths would follow more readily.

"Thank you," he said sincerely. "Lord Zoariyi, will you try the catapults? Lord Jansilui, the archery, with the two honorable Sixths? And Lord Linumino, you will be adjutant?"

They nodded, none very happy.

He felt very weary, but he could also feel safer. If the sorcerers killed him now, they could not stop the tryst. The magic had gone away.

Then he realized that they were all waiting for him, so he straightened up and smiled and said, "Dismissed!"

There may be an exam later.

††† †††

Confusion grew into chaos, but it moved back from Wallie. He refused to answer the Sevenths' appeals for help, replying only that they must think for themselves, and soon they stopped asking. Out in the courtyard the hammering gave way to shouting as Linumino sought archers and falconers for Jansilui, water rats and knife throwers for Boariyi, horsemen for Tivanixi, and carpenters for Zoariyi. When the bullfrog chief herald came to call, he was escorted in from the gate by a Fourth. He fumed and raged at this indignity and was promptly escorted back out again —Nnanji had begun organizing security. Fiendori arrived with forty golds purloined from the dock taxes and was directed to Linumino. Forarfi, Wallie's former left-handed fencing partner, came to announce that he had been appointed chief bodyguard. Wallie thought he did not need a Sixth for that job, but he let the assignment stand for the time being.

And so on . . .

At last came the moment when there was no one in the antechamber but Wallie and his bodyguards. He was limp and hoarse and he had a headache, but the tryst was beginning to stagger along without leaning on him. He demanded food and watched in wry amusement as the order went down three ranks before anyone actually left the room. No callers lower than seventh rank, he decreed, and walked through into the square council chamber at the end and closed the door.

Here, also, the cleaning had been perfunctory, but there was improvement. The ashes had gone from the fireplace, the filthy bedding had been replaced by a decent straw mattress and two almost-clean blankets. He removed his sword, sank into the brocade chair, and put his feet up on a stool. His head was still boiling with a hundred ideas that he desperately wanted to write down. But that was impossible—he had tried writing with Rotanxi's quill and it just would not work. He thought in English, and he spoke in the language of the People, and he could not write in either. That portion of his memory had not been passed along.

He missed Nnanji. Nnanji had been an infallible notepad for him until now, but he would be humiliated and affronted if Wallie tried to keep him for that purpose when there was so much else to do—and so much that Nnanji could probably do better than anyone else, too. Nnanji knew how Wallie thought, his memory was a precision instrument, he got along well now with sailors and other civilians, and he was much better at communicating with other swordsmen than Wallie could ever be. Although he was the youngest Seventh on the council, he would probably prove the most effective. His only problem would be the jealousy he must arouse in the older men—and almost every swordsman above second rank was older than Nnanji.

There was a tap on the door. Well, it had been a nice quiet two minutes . . . "Enter!"

Doa entered and closed the door.

Wallie lurched to his feet.

Her wrap was a shimmering satin in cornflower blue. It was very short, the top barely covering her nipples, pulled tight into the curve of her breasts, the hem revealing almost all of her miraculously long and shapely legs. She had scorned the customary sandals of the People in favor of heeled shoes, making her as tall as he. The effect should have been vulgar or obscene or ludicrous, and it was none of those. She triumphed over such trivia by sheer arrogance. There was a thin silver chain around her neck, looping down to the top of her wrap. He thought that she could have worn nothing more than that, yet have succeeded in making it seem entirely proper.

The crazed wildness had gone. No longer did he see her as a madwoman. She was a legendary genius, and her stature and presence again made him thrill with visceral excitement. He was very much aware that she had been Shonsu's mistress and that there was a bed in the corner of the room. Even Jja could hardly rouse him faster than this giant minstrel did. She saw his reaction, or guessed it, or just assumed it, and the plain, almost horsey, face glowed with satisfaction.

She was the answer to one of his problems.

He found his sword and made the salute to a superior. She did not give the ritual reply.

"Flattery?" she murmured.

"Admiration, lady. Yesterday I was present at the birth of something that will live as long as the River flows. You made my name immortal."

She strolled toward the window, showing experienced mastery of the heels. Oh, those legs! Her lute floated on the shining brown cataract of her hair.

"The minstrels refer to it as *The Epic of Rotanxi.*" She seemed not to regard herself as one of the minstrels. She was of another species and she knew it.

"It does not matter. My name will live in it, and yours will be celebrated forever."

Amusement flickered on her rough-hewn features. "The warblers are leaving town in droves. I shudder to think what they will do to it, but it must be well spread already."

"What reward may I give you?" he demanded. He was flushing like an adolescent and his voice was thick. Fool!

She turned from the window and regarded him provocatively. "Whatever is fitting." Her voice had gone husky to match his, or mock it.

He had one sapphire left from the expense money that the god had given him. Even while cursing himself for a lust-maddened idiot, he took it from his pouch and went over to her. She recoiled a step from his advance, then drew in her breath sharply as he placed the blue fire against the chain she wore, holding it with finger and thumb in the hollow between her breasts.

"It is not enough, but it is all I have."

She took the gem hurriedly and backed away a step.

"It will suffice. It is a kingly recompense, my lord." She sighed the words. There was an undertone there that he did not understand, that was intended for Shonsu, and the glance she gave him under lowered lashes would have been in any other woman an invitation to continue his approach. In her, he suspected, it was not; but his hands trembled.

"And you will accompany me to the merchants' ball this evening?"

She nodded as if that were preordained. Who else could the liege lord escort in public but Lady Doa? The greatest swordsman and the greatest minstrel—they were made for each other.

"And let me kiss you?"

She recoiled, claws unsheathed. "Don't touch me!"

He shrugged. And sighed, also. "I do not understand you, Lady Doa. You are a most—"

"You understand very well, Shonsu." Her tone was contemptuous, her stance again seductive.

"I have told you I remember nothing."

"Save those stories for your henchmen!" She headed for the

door, and he dug nails into his palms as he watched the satin moving on her hips. "Tonight, then."

And she was gone.

He did not know where she lived or what the proper procedure was for escorting a lady. Sedan chair? Carriage? He would have to discover all those things, and yet he was supposed to be fighting a war. She roused him like a stallion and simultaneously unmanned him. Where this woman was concerned, Shonsu's glands took total control of Wallie Smith's mind. What would Shonsu have done—thrown her on the bed and raped her?

He sank into his chair with a groan and wondered if rape was what she had expected and wanted. Did she even know that she was constantly inviting him? He was worse than Nnanji had been over Thana—woman refuses, man goes mad with lust. At least Nnanji had the excuse of youth; he was himself, merely a sex-crazed maniac.

But he would have a fitting companion for the evening's festivities, and that was important in case—

The door opened and Nnanji walked in. He was grinning.

"You did it, brother!" he said.

"Did what?"

"You overloaded my memory! I was getting a headache, so I said I needed a break." The headache did not seem to be bothering him. "Two hundred an hour! But we have some curious talents out there: goldsmiths and brickmakers and glassblowers—"

"All very useful, I'm sure," Wallie said, trying hard to match his oath brother's irrepressible cheerfulness. "Any falconers?"

"Not so far, but half the men are away from the lodge. This is *fun*, isn't it?"

He stalked to the window and peered out, while Wallie sat back in his feather-shedding chair and idly pondered a suitable definition for "fun" in that context.

After a few minutes' silence Nnanji said, "Brother, you will tell me the last thirty sutras, when you get a chance, won't you?"

"Of course. But not while you have a headache—and I have a worse one!"

"Good!" Nnanji said. Another pause. "Shonsu?" He had never used that name before. His voice had lost its sparkle. "I'm a fraud!"

"Don't worry about it! You'll pick up the sutras fast enough, and no one can challenge you until the tryst is disbanded. By then you'll be fencing like a Seventh."

Nnanji did not turn from the window. "I hope so."

Nnanji, doubting himself? "I'm sure you'll find time to do some practicing! And practice with many opponents is just what you need now. You've really only ever had me, and one instructor isn't enough. You know all my. . ." Wallie's voice died away.

Ikondorina said, I can teach you no more.

Silence. Of course Nnanji did not know the prophecy about the red-haired brother.

"Easy mark!" Nnanji's voice was full of contempt for himself. In his eyes swordsmanship was paramount. He despised a man who could not fight to his rank. "As soon as the Sixths are free of their oaths, I'm going to be facing thirty-nine tries at promotion! You'll drag the war out for a few weeks, won't you—for me?"

The request was so ludicrous that Wallie laughed aloud and Nnanji turned momentarily to grin at him. Then he went back to staring out the window.

Something else must be bothering him?

"Shonsu?"

"Yes, Nnanji?"

Silence.

Then: "I don't feel . . . I mean I'm not . . ."

"Out with it!"

Nnanji took a deep breath and jabbered: "I know that a tryst can only have one leader, brother, so I just wanted to promise you that I won't . . . I mean I'll try to—*Devilspit!* I mean you *know* so much more than I do . . ."

This was not like Nnanji.

"What are you trying to say?" Wallie demanded, puzzled and suddenly uneasy.

Nnanji swung around, red-faced. "I'll be loyal! You're the real leader! I mean, now we're technically equals . . ."

Goddess! Wallie had not thought of that. Nnanji was a Seventh. He was no longer Wallie's protégé. He was liege lord also. Technically equals! What happened if the two of them disagreed?

"I've never doubted your loyalty, Nnanji."

Nnanji nodded.

Another silence.

"Something else bothering you?" Wallie demanded.

"I was just wondering why the gods arranged this, brother? Why two liege lords? You don't think . . ." He bit his lip and looked even more unhappy.

Now Wallie saw it, and it was a chilling thought. "That you may have to succeed me?"

Nnanji nodded again. "You'll take care, won't you?"

"Damned right!"

"Good!" The old grin came back. Reassured, Nnanji chuckled and headed for the door. He was stopped in his tracks by the spotty mirror. It was a small mirror and he had to crane his neck to see his kilt in it. "How do I look in blue, Shonsu?"

"Absolutely ridiculous! But performance is more important than looks, and you seem to be doing a great job of Seventhing so far."

Nnanji smirked and turned his head one way and his eyes the other.

"Notice the hairclip?" He was wearing a great chunk of blue glass, almost as large as the sapphire that Wallie wore, the one the god had made for him. "You don't happen to have any spare gems left, do you?" he asked hopefully.

"No."

"Pity. It would be safe on me until you needed it, I thought . . . But this will do. It looks quite real, doesn't it?"

To a blind oyster, perhaps. "Yes, it does—and it suits your red hair."

Hairclip?

"Why don't you wear the silver one?" Wallie asked cautiously.

Nnanji flashed him a cryptic, curiously defensive glance. "A blue kilt is bad enough, brother! A griffon?"

True—he was not usually so discreet.

"Besides, I promised Arganari I would wear it when I got to Vul. I'll save it for that."

He smiled less certainly than before and vanished, without closing the door.

Ikondorina said, I can teach you no more, now go and find your kingdom.

Wallie climbed slowly to his feet. A Third appeared in the doorway carrying a small table in one hand, balancing a tray on the other, filling the room with a stench of charred meat.

Vul?

Technically equals?

. . . and his realm was more vast and much greater.

Greater than a tryst?

Impossible!

It had always been impossible—it was gibberish.

He had been betrayed! Deceived!

For the second time that day Wallie lost Shonsu's temper. With a roar that rattled the windows, he threw the swordsman and his food out of the way and went hurtling along the antechamber, bellowing for his bodyguard.

††† † †††

A temple should be a hushed and pious place. This one was not. A small army of slaves was cleaning up glass and stone, the remains of the fallen window. Their chattering and the screech of their shovels echoed along the nave toward the idol.

The brilliant mosaic floor before the dais was almost empty. Worshipers were being tactfully discouraged this day and there were few, anyway, for the city was busy. The wide, tiled space held only one figure, a very small priest of the seventh rank. He had come for meditation and prayer and had stayed longer than he had expected. There had been no specific appeals in his head, only a deep longing for peace, a yearning that seemed to be filling him more and more now. The pains were stilled. Perhaps he would get his answer soon, his release. Kneeling before his Goddess, he had found the wordless comfort he had been seeking. He had remained there, savoring it, waiting without having anything to wait for; in no rush to go anywhere else, for he had nothing left to do, that he knew of. Shonsu was leader of the tryst and whatever else was going to happen would not need Honakura.

Eventually he discovered, to his amusement, that he was hungry. That raised a problem. His old carcass was a problem, and raising it another. He doubted that he could rise to his feet now without help, and there was no one nearby. He pushed himself up to sit on his heels and survey the surrounding emptiness with wry enjoyment of his helplessness. A little fasting would do him no harm, of course.

Two figures came out of one of the rear doors. The first was a priest; he stopped and pointed, then turned on his heel and fled. The other came striding over toward Honakura, a giant swordsman clothed in a black cloud of rage.

Interesting! Having no choice, Honakura stayed where he was. In a moment his view of the Goddess was blotted out by a blue kilt. On its hem was a white griffon, lovingly embroidered by Jja.

There were no preliminaries. The cavernous voice said, "You lied to me!"

It hurt to tilt his head back, so he left it where it was, studying Jja's needlework. He said nothing.

Louder: "You lied to me!"

It was not a question. Why answer? "Tell me what has happened, my lord."

After a moment the kilt moved. The young swordsman sank to his knees and folded huge arms across massive chest. Honakura did not look up at his eyes, he just waited and stared at the tooled leather harness.

"Nnanji has his seventh sword." The voice was a very deep growl, even deeper than usual.

Now the priest looked up at the furious black eyes, seeing the fear and pain under the rage. "Did you ever doubt that he would?"

"It should have been impossible! Under the sutras there was seemingly no way that he could do that, not until the tryst was disbanded."

Nothing was impossible to the Most High, but it would be better not to say so. Better just to wait. Shonsu was so agitated that he could not remain silent, and in a moment Honakura received the story of the spy, and the attempt on Shonsu's life, and the very obscure sutra.

His confusion was pitiable, this enormous, gentle, well-meaning young man . . . Honakura felt a lump in his throat such as had not known in years. Surely the gods would not test like this unless the cause were vital?

"It is a miracle that Nnanji is a Seventh?" he asked quietly.

"Yes!"

"And a miracle that you are still alive?"

"I suppose so." Shonsu hung his head.

"Then you have no cause for complaint, my lord. You each got one this time."

The deadly dark eyes came up to skewer him. Had death been a dread to Honakura, that gaze would have softened every bone in his body. "You lied to me."

He sighed. "Yes."

"Tell me now, holy one! For the sake of your Goddess, tell me now!"

"If you wish, my friend. But it will not make you happier."

"Tell!"

Softly Honakura told him the real prohecy:

> Ikondorina's red-haired brother came to him and said, Brother you have wondrous skill with a sword; teach me, that like you I may wrest a kingdom. And he said, I will. So Ikondorina taught and his brother learned and then Ikondorina said, I can teach you no more, now go and find your kingdom. And he said, But brother, it is your kingdom that I covet, give me that. Ikondorina said, I will not, and his brother said, I am more worthy, and slew him and took his realm.

For a long time there was no sound except the scrape of the slaves' shovels at the far end of the nave, the clash of glass as they filled their wheelbarrows. Doubtless the swordsman was pondering the story of Ikondorina's red-haired brother, but Honakura was thinking of pride.

He had lied, mortal sin for a priest. All his lifetime of service and devotion had been wiped out by that, crashing down as the temple window had crashed down. Pride! He had been too proud of that lifetime. He had been led by his arrogance into mentioning Ikondorina's brothers to Shonsu, and that error had trapped him into telling the lie. Before that, puffed up by awareness of his own sanctity, he had been sure that the Goddess would reward him, that his death would be a victory march, that She would weep tears of gratitude when he came before Her. Now he could only hope that She would be merciful and remember his life's work when She judged his awful sin, that She would in Her mercy allow him to remain on the ladder, according him some lowly place where he could start again, refraining from hurling him off, down into the Place of Demons.

He became aware that he was weeping, weeping for himself, when he should be weeping for this tortured swordsman.

That same swordsman was speaking again: ". . . why you did not tell me before. You were right not to trust me." He was bitter, understandably. "What happens now, holy one? I just wait for him to do it?"

Honakura forced his mind back to Shonsu. Sudden hope surged into his ragtag old frame. That wonderful sense of peace he had felt—would that have been sent to a damned soul? Was it possible that he had been directed to that mortally destructive lie?

"Could it be another of the gods' tests, my lord?" he whispered.

The swordsman recoiled, falling back on his heels. He blanched. *"No!"*

The two men stared at each other in silence.

At last Honakura said, "Is it possible?"

The big man shook his head as if to clear it of crawling horrors. "If the gods will not intervene—yes! He is not a Seventh in fencing—yet! But any match may be an upset, holy one. It is not uncommon—a better man being beaten by a poorer—not uncommon. They would not let me, would they? They would send a miracle?"

Honakura stared over the swordsman's shoulder at the face of the Goddess, but seeing it as it was revealed at Hann, not in this shoddy facsimile; seeing the majesty. The temple was very cold. He was freezing. Why had he not noticed that sooner?

"I am no prophet, my lord. I do not know the answer. But it may be that She wants a . . . that you . . ."

"That I am not enough of a killer for Her needs? Say it, man! Another test? I may be too soft-hearted and Nnanji is a born killer? But if I were to drain him now . . ." His voice tailed off, and agony drove the fear from his eyes.

After a while he whispered, "Kill Nnanji?"

"Would the swordsmen accept you afterward?"

Shonsu jerked, as if he had been lost in hell and had forgotten that Honakura was there. "Yes!" he said. "I went mad this morning. I sold two men into slavery. They are all terrified of me now; they have realized what that oath of theirs means." He laughed without benefit of mirth. "I knew and they didn't! Yes, they will obey."

After another long silence he muttered, "But Jja . . ." and did not say more about that.

"I may be horribly wrong, my lord," Honakura said. "He is an honorable young man. He admires and adores you! He worships you next to the Goddess. It is hard to see him harming you."

"He trusts me!" the big man snarled.

"Then live up to his trust, my lord! Serve the Goddess and She will see that all is well between you."

Shonsu ground his teeth. "I can't!"

"Can't what?"

"Can't beat the sorcerers."

"But you have been telling . . ."

Shonsu stared down at clenched fists and corded forearms. "Yes. What I have been saying is true. I can storm the cities and overthrow the towers and drive out the sorcerers and put the swordsmen back. I believe it and Nnanji believes it and the tryst probably believes it now, or will soon. The sorcerers believe it, or will soon."

"I don't understand."

The deep voice became a whisper, although there was no one near. "They will go away, holy one! If we take the first tower easily, they will depart, abandon the cities, and fade back into their hills."

"Then you will have won!" Honakura said, perplexed at the despair before him.

Shonsu shook his head. "No! I can't take Vul. Not in winter. We don't know where it is. The first Shonsu might have been able to do it—he made a surprise attack. But now they have had half a year to prepare. One tower at a time, yes. At odds of fifty to one, yes. A fortified city, no! Many days' march away from the River? Take catapults into the mountains? Impossible!"

Appalled, Honakura said, "In the spring, maybe?"

"No! We can't wait for spring; we have no money. The tryst must be disbanded! So the sorcerers will come back. In five years, or ten . . ." The whisper became so faint that Honakura could barely hear it. "I can't beat the sorcerers! No one else knows that, holy one!"

Honakura struggled to adjust. This made nonsense of everything. It was incomprehensible.

"Then what are you doing?"

Shonsu groaned. "I am bluffing!"

"Bluffing, my lord?"

"Bluffing both sides."

More confusion. "But why?"

A pause and then another whisper: "To force a treaty!"

Honakura gasped. "Of course! Yes! Yes! That must be the meaning of your parentmarks—swordsman and sorcerer, my lord! It may be that that is Her purpose! That is why She chose you! No other swordsmen would ever think of that! None ever consider it! Can you?"

"Can I what?" the big man snapped. "Force the swordsmen? Yes! They have to obey, right? The sorcerers . . . I don't know! But I was allowed to capture one of their Sevenths. He is probably one of the leaders, perhaps the highest of them all, for he provoked the calling of the tryst. So I must work on him—while I prepare the swordsmen for war."

The priest sighed deeply. "It is a holy cause, my lord! I think you are right!" To patch the ancient quarrel between swordsman and sorcerer—that made sense.

Then he saw the deathly glance on Shonsu's face and stopped. Had he missed something?

"Am I right? I told Jja . . . if I try to do the wrong thing with the tryst, then the Goddess will stop me. I think your Ikondorina story is a warning, holy one! She wants a killer. She will block me."

"How so, my lord?"

"I may convince the sorcerers," Shonsu growled. "They will listen to reason, I think. But swordsmen do not know reason from cowardice. You can't argue with a swordsman."

"But you can command them, you said!"

He bared his teeth. "All except one—he is not my vassal. We are equals. Both liege lords, both Sevenths now. He is not even my protégé anymore! Do *you* think that Nnanji will accept a treaty?"

Silence.

"Well, do you?"

Now it was the priest who whispered. "No."

"Neither do I! You once said he had a head like a coconut. He will have to choose, won't he? I am his brother because we swore the fourth oath—but that is only a sutra. He will say that sorcerers are swordsman killers, and always have been. He will say that a treaty betrays the tryst, and the will of the Goddess. He will say that a treaty is cowardice and shame. We taught him, old man! You and I taught him well—the will of the Goddess takes precedence over the sutras! That story of yours gives the answer —*Slew him and took his realm?* It fits him perfectly! I can hear him saying it: *I am more worthy!*"

Shonsu sprang to his feet. "Maybe he is! Maybe the Goddess thinks so. She has certainly promoted him fast enough!"

Then he was gone, striding away long-legged across the whorls of color in the shiny tiles.

Honakura stayed where he was, staring up at the Most High, haloed now in a rainbow of tears.

BOOK FIVE:

HOW THE SWORDSMAN RETURNED THE SWORD

†

It was the middle of the following morning before Wallie clambered glumly up the rope ladder to *Sapphire*'s deck. Bare-masted and peaceful, the little blue ship lay at anchor on sunlit water, a haven of sanity after the frenzy of the tryst. Yet he was returning only because he had work to do even there, work on the one problem that he could not possibly delegate—Rotanxi. And it would take more than sparkling ripples and wheeling white birds to soften his nagging black mood this morning.

As he stepped on board, Jja came running forward to greet him. He clasped her hands in his and then recoiled in shock at her puffed and discolored face.

"What happened?" he demanded.

She dropped her gaze. "It was an accident."

"Who caused this accident?" he roared. A surge of fury rose like bile in this throat. If this was more swordsman work, then there would be blood to spill . . .

"You did," she said softly.

He gaped at her, suddenly aware that there were many other people on deck, most pretending to be busy, but all of them—from toddlers to old Lina herself—all certainly watching and listening.

"When you were passing judgment on the two swordsmen, master. I tried to plead for them. It was wrong of me."

He had struck her? He thought back into that red mist that had enveloped him in the lodge the day before. Yes, perhaps he had.

"My love!" he wailed. "Oh, Jja!" He took her in his arms and kissed her.

Then he backed off again, puzzled. True, his tongue tasted like an old fur insole, and there were no clinical mouthwashes in the World. He had not been drunk the night before, but he had taken enough of the vile gut-rotting local wine to give himself a pounding hangover. Doubtless he was an unsavory lover this morning. Even so, there had been much lacking in that kiss. And she had called him "master."

"I lost my head, Jja. I did not even know I had done this."

She kept her face down and was silent, but he waited and eventually she spoke.

"I know that, master."

"Then can you not forgive me?"

Now she looked up and studied him dubiously. "Will you make amends, then?"

"How? Tell me how I can!"

"Come down to the cabin and I will show you."

He hugged her again. "I don't dare, my love! I got very little sleep last night and I have work to do."

Little was an understatement. He had barely slept at all. He had returned Doa to her home not long before dawn—and the door had been slammed in his face. He had gone back to the lodge, to find it still a boiling pot of insanity. Adjutant Linumino had certainly not seen bed that night, being engaged in organizing the barracks and the married quarters and food supplies and work assignments, all at the same time. The shouting and the racket of marching boots had never stopped, nor had the endless string of conflicts being referred to the liege himself. The Sevenths were well-meaning and enthusiastic, but Wallie had given them too much to do too soon. The thought of a bed with Jja in it was a vision of paradise, but one that he must resist. Or was that guilt talking?

She bit her lip. "The two men you sold, master. . ."

So her offer had been a bribe? "Stay out of that, Jja! How I run the tryst is not your concern!"

"Yes, master."

"And don't call me that!"

"No, master."

Women!

She turned away. He grabbed her shoulder roughly and spun her round to face him.

"Relations between the swordsmen and the town are bad!" he snapped. "It is important that I keep the elders happy. Do you understand?"

She nodded dumbly.

Liar! said his conscience. *Whatever else Shonsu did when he was castellan, he terrorized the elders. They groveled to you last night.*

"I had to go to that ball!"

Rot! They would much prefer that you stay away and just send Nnanji.

"And they would be grossly insulted if I took a slave as my partner."

You mean the swordsmen would laugh at you.

"And if I choose to take Lady Doa to a dance, then it is none of your business!"

"Of course not, master."

Again she began to turn. This time he grabbed both shoulders and almost shook her.

"You have no cause to be jealous of Lady Doa!"

"*Jealous!*" Now, incredibly, it was Jja who started to shout. "A slave? Jealous? What could possibly make a slave jealous?"

"In this case nothing! I needed an escort to the dance—"

"You think that I care who you take to a stupid dance?"

"And nothing else!"

"You think I care about that, either? Bed whom you like, master. Make no excuses to a slave."

Wallie was astounded. Never had she raised her voice like that before, to him or anyone. He released her. "Then what is bothering you?"

"You are!" she yelled, stamping her foot. "What are you doing to yourself?"

He was a swordsman of the Seventh. He was liege lord of the tryst, the most powerful man in the World. He stammered and then yelled back, "Watch your tongue, woman! For, yes, you are only a slave, remember!"

"And I was happy as a slave! I did as my mistress bid me, for many men. And very few of them struck me!"

He made an effort and lowered his voice. "I said I was sorry. I shall not do that again."

"Perhaps you should! To remind me I am only a slave. You have been telling me to think of myself as a real person!"

Never had she behaved like this! For a moment Shonsu's maniacal temper almost broke loose. Then Wallie forced it down, taking deep breaths and unclenching his fists. He glanced around the deck, seeing the many frightened eyes being hastily averted. Rotanxi, whom he had come to woo and impress, was sitting on the aft hatch cover, impassively listening like the others to this absurd quarrel.

"You said that was what you wanted," she shouted. "A real woman. Now I am a slave again—"

"Yes!" he roared, to silence her. "Go to the cabin!" He turned away and headed over to the sorcerer, passing a cynical, surly Tomiyano and ignoring him. He made formal salute to Rotanxi.

The sorcerer rose and responded, then sat down again. Wallie settled beside him.

"And how are your catapults this fine day?" Rotanxi inquired with acid politeness.

Wallie laughed bitterly. "Lord Zoariyi is in charge of building catapults. I judged him the shrewdest."

"Probably," Rotanxi commented, to show that he knew of the Sevenths.

"He jumped in with all four feet. I stopped by on my way out here; he has a catapult half-built already."

"Remarkable!"

"Yes, but useless—unless he plans to use it to move the tryst across to the other bank. There isn't a hatch on the River that could take it. It will have to be scrapped and a new start made."

Rotanxi made a thin-lipped smile. "I hope he wasted a lot of money on timber."

He had, of course. "Money is no longer a problem," Wallie said, and explained about dock fees.

The sorcerer looked skeptical and said nothing.

"You have heard about Chinarama?" Wallie inquired.

The old man nodded, face unreadable.

"Afterward Nnanji searched his quarters. He found a thunder weapon and the supplies for it. Quill and ink and vellum, of course. And this." Wallie held out a small ivory plaque bearing the image of a girl, wistfully beautiful.

The sorcerer regarded the plaque as it lay on Wallie's palm, but he made no move to take it and he did not speak.

"He and I were on opposite sides, my lord," Wallie said, "but I honor his memory. Courage is not confined to swordsmen. Is this his daughter?" Rotanxi and Chinarama had been about the same age. Vul could not be so huge that they would not have known each other.

The sorcerer hesitated, then said, "His wife. She died in childbirth many years ago."

"Sad!"

"Very. It was not his child. She had been raped by a band of swordsmen."

Wallie winced, then studied the old man, inscrutable now as a mummy. The story was possible, of course, but it might be a ploy to put him on the defensive. "Of course I do not doubt you, my lord, but our sutras expressly forbid any violence toward women, except in two narrowly defined cases—convicted felons, or in retaliation for bloodshed."

He saw at once that he had lost.

"Perhaps 'rape' is the wrong term, then, Lord Shonsu? There was no direct violence by the swordsmen. It happened on a ship. A First importuned her. When she struggled, of course, his friends came to assist. They did not use force on the woman. They began mutilating the sailors. In self-defense, the sailors held the woman for the swordsmen. That would not be rape as your sutras define it, would it?"

The sorcerer's parchment face wrinkled in a sneer of triumph and contempt, and Wallie could only believe. He shuddered.

This was the man whose heart he hoped to win? Again he offered the plaque. "Will you take this, then? Give it to his family, if he has any, when you return?"

Rotanxi accepted it. "He had no family. He did have a brother once, but swordsmen got him, too." He hurled the picture away, and it spun over the rail and vanished.

After a pause, Wallie said, "That is sad also. But there are widows in Sen, my lord, and many orphans on the left bank. The price of power is always others' blood."

The sorcerer sneered, but did not reply.

Wallie changed the subject. "You have heard my story? I told the sailors to answer your questions."

Rotanxi snorted: "Bah! I have accepted that I cannot convince you of magic, Lord Shonsu. Yet you expect me to believe in miracles?"

Wallie was surprised. "Not even the Hand of the Goddess?"

"Not even that. Any time a sorcerer goes on a ship—and that is not rare, as you have guessed—then the ship goes where it is supposed to."

That was interesting, if true. Had not the demigod said that the Age of Legends came before the Age of Writing? Were the sorcerers miracle-proof, being literate? Wallie made a mental note to think about that, when he had time.

"But I confess that I am curious about the source of your knowledge," the sorcerer continued. "Obviously one of the other covens has been subverted or penetrated."

"I am truly from another world, my lord," Wallie said. "What evidence shall I offer? How about the stirrup? That is new to this one."

Rotanxi shook his head. "Impressive, but not convincing. Your stirrup is pretty obvious once you think of it."

"Ah! But all great inventions are like that. Now, take that far-seeing gadget of yours. It inverts the image. That must make it very difficult to use for things like reading lips."

Hesitation . . . and a flicker of excitement. "A matter of practice. Why, can you make a telescope that does not invert?"

Telescope! It was a new word. "Certainly. There are several ways, depending on what lenses you have. You haven't invented the glass lathe for making lenses yet, have you? No matter. The easiest way is to put two telescopes in one tube—four lenses. The first telescope inverts and the second puts the image the right way up again. That's even more obvious than the stirrup, I would say."

The sorcerer tried to keep a straight face, but the pupils of his eyes dilated. Wallie thought he might be making progress. The sailors had wandered away, mostly, now that the shouting was over. A quiet conversation between a sorcerer and a swordsman might be an epoch-making event, but it had no interest for such practical folk as they.

"There are ways of getting rid of the colored fringes, too, but it involves different types of glass in combination and is beyond my knowledge. Of course you can make a telescope with mirrors and that gives no colored fringes."

Now there was eagerness. "Yes? Tell me how you do that."

Wallie produced a piece of charcoal he had brought for just this purpose. "You may have to tell me some terms here." He started sketching on the hatch cover—Tomiyano would be furious. He outlined conic sections. That got him to the parabola, and he explained the reflecting telescope.

Rotanxi became openly excited. "Almost you convince me, my lord! There are other covens than Vul, but I thought none was ahead of us in our knowledge. I do not know where in the World you can have learned such things."

"That is the idea."

"Tell me more, then."

The tiger was at the door of the trap. "Alas, I dare not. Telescopes will not do a great deal of harm, but I am worried about the stirrup. In my world it led to horsemen encased in metal from scalp to toenail, and I fear that I may have opened the door to such horrors in this world. There are other things I could tell you that would do worse damage. I shall try to think of other harmless exceptions while preparing my war. But I am truly from another world, Lord Rotanxi."

He pretended that he was about to leave—and the sorcerer raised a hand to stay him. "That orange thing that flew from your boat?"

Wallie laughed. "Oh, that's harmless." He explained about the effects of heat on gases, hinted at molecular theory, described how a hot-air balloon worked. "Jja has nothing much to do; ask her nicely, and she may even make you one to take home with you. You'll have to get the wax recipe from Swordsman Katanji. He'll only charge you about a hundred golds, I should think."

Now he got a long, hard stare. "I wonder if you intend to let me go home, my lord. You are volunteering a great deal of information."

Wallie smiled innocently. "Trust me," he said.

Rotanxi shook his head. "There is a hook in your bait. What is it?"

Wallie shrugged. For a few minutes he stared across the blue water to the golden city spread along the River's edge, vastly older than the pyramids. He tried to imagine one of the sorcerers' black towers there and mused on what Nnanji had said—sacked and burned many times. If he could win peace with the sorcerers, then he might save many cities from being sacked in the future. If history was only a string of battles, then honor belonged not to those who made history, but to those who prevented it.

"I might trade a few secrets with you. For example, and just out of curiosity, on my world the thunderpower was known for centuries before anyone thought of using it to make weapons. Was that the case here?"

The old man pondered carefully. Finding no trap in the question, he nodded.

Wallie said, "Another question, then: When Katanji managed to sneak into your tower, he reported seeing a big gold ball on a pillar. That sounds to me like something we called . . ." He could not say *electrostatic generator*. It would come out as grunts. "Damn! It sort of collects lightning when you turn a handle and make a belt move. Now, I am guessing that you connect this thing to the metal grid in front of the doors, so any uninvited guest gets zapped. Would you care to comment?"

The sorceer said nothing at all.

"Come on!" Wallie coaxed. "I can't think it would stop an army, because it would take too long to collect more of the lightning between zaps. But it would make a good burglar trap. All right—you tell me that, and I'll give you a secret from my world on the same subject."

Rotanxi glared, but finally admitted that at night the gold ball was connected by a metal rope to the door handles, for the purpose Wallie had guessed. It was a very small concession, but the start of trust.

Wallie told him of the lightning rod—useful to anyone who stored gunpowder in a tall tower.

"You make me nervous," Rotanxi said. "You tell me these

things and all about your plans. I fear that you do not intend to let me go, in spite of your oath."

Wallie said, "We have many days left on the oath. My army will be ready long before then. Boariyi would have been smashed, I admit, but I shall do the smashing now."

Cautiously the old man said, "And what will you do if your fancy catapults and horsemen do not succeed?"

Wallie shook his head. "Hope that they do! Else I must tell the swordsmen how to make thunderpowder. I have been very careful, Lord Rotanxi. I have kept many of your secrets from them—the signs you use to send messages, for example." He did not know the word for writing. "I have made no inquiries about sulfur or saltpeter. Were I to do that, then you are a dead man as soon as your friends catch you. I hope very strongly that I do not have to go to that.

"You see, in my other world the sorcerers invent weapons, but the swordsmen control them; weapons so horrible that I shall not even try to describe them. I am certain that the same thing will happen here. When the first horror wears off, the swordsmen will want those thunderbolt weapons. If I do not give them the secret, then they will get it by other means. Even sorcerers can be overpowered and tortured. You will not long keep the thunderpowder to yourselves, and, when it gets out, then the sorcerers will be servants of the swordsmen, as they were on my world. Think on that, my lord!"

Leaving the sorcerer frowning, Wallie rose and paced away.

His head was still thumping and his eyes still gritty. There was no sign of Jja. Perhaps she had obeyed his peevish command and gone to the cabin. He ought to make up to her—make love to her, even. The tryst would not collapse if he stole a couple of hours' rest. He trotted down the companionway and went to their cabin.

She was waiting there. When he entered she rose to stand before him in silence, eyes downcast, being a well-trained slave.

He lifted her chin with one finger. "Jja!" he whispered.

Her eyes would not meet his. "Master?"

His temper flared again. Damn her! He was carrying too many

burdens to accept another. He needed comfort, companionship, and reassurance; not this stubborn, uninformed reproach.

He tried again. He put his arms around her. "Jja?"

"Master?"

"You're trembling! What are you afraid of?"

He had to wait for her whisper. "You, master."

"Me? My darling, I have said I am sorry! I need love, Jja!"

"Of course, master!" She slipped hurriedly from his grasp and began to pull off her wrap.

Damn her! She was doing this because she knew it would anger him. It was the only weapon she had.

It was a good one.

He left, slamming the door behind him.

††

Midmorning, warm sunshine; Wallie had been inspecting catapult construction and was marching back to the lodge with his bodyguard.

It was day eight of the reign of Shonsu I—or should that be Shonsu II?—and five days since Boariyi had departed in *Griffon*. He should be at Wal by now. The expedition had seemed well outfitted, with water-rat swordsmen to run the ship, with enough supplies for two or three weeks, with a plentiful collection of chains and shackles. Boariyi had been disappointed when Wallie had amended his instructions to kidnapping instead of killing, but he had seen the advantage of being able to parade captives through the streets when he returned. "Kill if you must," Wallie had told him, "but a live captive is more valuable than dead meat, and the more sorcerer gowns you can steal the better." Wal and Aus were the targets this time. He wished he had another ship to send upriver to Sen and on to Cha.

He had grown to like Boariyi. There was something of Nnanji in the beanpole, plus a certain wry cynicism. Wallie approved of all his Sevenths. The Goddess had chosen well.

Money was still pouring in, but it was also pouring out. Horses were absurdly expensive to buy and equip and maintain.

Catapults were going to be worse, and he had to think ahead to the cost of mounting the actual attack. He could sell *Griffon,* of course—if Boariyi did not lose her. It was crazy to send a Seventh into such danger, but at least he had an equivalent prisoner to exchange if necessary.

Then his parade turned into the wide plaza before the lodge, and he called a halt so that he could stand and watch the cavalry at work. The stirrup had been a glorious success. Now all the swordsmen wanted to join the cavalry—was it not always so? Riding in fencing masks was impossible, and thus foil practice too dangerous, so he had invented polo. Of course polo on a paved court was not quite five card stud either, but these were urban fighters he was training. The swordsmen had decided that polo was the greatest breakthrough since the invention of puberty. It had become the tryst's biggest entertainment, after wenching, and most of the pay seemed to go into betting on polo matches.

Even to Wallie's unskilled eye, both men and horses were improving. Now he must think ahead to the next step—mallets were not the best weapons against sorcerers. Polo was good training in horsemanship, but he must start the carpenters making lances. He sent a First off with a luncheon invitation for Tivanixi, and resumed his march.

Closer to the lodge a group of swordsmen was fencing. Wallie did not need to see the green flashes on the shoulder straps to know that they would be Nnanji's men. And there was Nnanji himself, blue kilt and red ponytail, engaging one of Boariyi's Sixths. No one else of his rank ever had time for fencing. Wallie watched for a while. Nnanji was improving—of course. He sighed, trying to ignore his apprehension and doubts. Then he gave the order to move again.

The blank stone face of the lodge, which had once worn only a bronze sword, now bore additional decoration. No one but sorcerers could read, but everyone could use an abacus. On either side of the bronze sword, therefore, there now hung a giant abacus of ropes and straw bundles. One read three hundred and thirty; the other sixteen—one captured and fifteen dead, counting Chinarama. The message was obvious, and so was the motivation it provided. Its construction had kept ten men busy for two days. That was the first rule for running an army: keep it busy. Once

Wallie Smith had run a petrochemical plant efficiently by matching the workforce to the work. Now his manpower was fixed, so he must find things for it to do.

As he reached the archway a troop of men came out carrying foul-smelling buckets—the losers in the daily inspection, those whose dormitory had been the least acceptable. The lodge sparkled now, inside and out, but each day there had to be losers to carry the nightsoil, and the orange flashes showed that these were some of Zoariyi's men. The color coding became complicated on a low rank, for each Seventh had his own color, and each of his protégés, also. A Third wore five flashes. Nnanji knew what every combination meant. Wallie did not care.

He wheeled in through the courtyard, filled now with canvas bathhouses and latrines. At the door to the antechamber he dismissed his entourage and sent them off in search of Forarfi, who could be counted on to keep them busy doing *something*. Then he went in.

The chamber was full of people, as always. At the far end Linumino the adjutant sat at a table because he counted the money. Although Wallie always felt that this room should be full of desks and typewriters and telephones, only Linumino had as much as a table. The money itself stayed in the chest in Wallie's office, which doubled as the council room, and most nights also his bedroom. Everyone else was sitting on a stool or standing. The sitters rose as he entered and all thumped fists to heart in salute. He had abolished formal saluting within the tryst as a waste of time.

He walked on through, nodding and smiling to faces he recognized, making guesses at their business, giving Katanji a wink, frowning at the sight of two sullen, battered-faced Sixths who stood swordless and guarded. When he reached the adjutant's table, Linumino smiled also and gestured toward a group of six. He did not need to speak—three young Thirds with Tivanixi shoulder flashes, each accompanied by a naked boy in his early teens, all six looking nervous.

"How many will that make?" Wallie asked.

"Thirteen, my liege."

Wallie looked over the boys. They all trembled. The Thirds

were almost as jumpy, probably all recent promotions. He turned back to the adjutant. "You've tested them?"

"Honorable Hiokillino has, my liege. He says they'll pass. He turned down four others who couldn't catch a ball if you pushed it in their mouths, he said. Didn't know their right hand from their feet!"

Wallie laughed. "All right." He grudged the time, but this justified some ceremony, so he added, "Present them." Linumino solemnly presented each Third in turn.

"I am Genotei, swordsman of the third rank, and it is my deepest and most humble wish . . ."

"I am Shonsu . . . Present your candidate, swordsman."

"My lord, I have the honor . . ."

"I am Jiulyuio, son of Kiryuio the goldsmith, and it is my deepest . . ."

All three boys were on the young side, Wallie thought, but he solemnly responded to their salutes. He had to listen as each repeated the swordsmen's code and then swore the second oath to one of the swordsmen. The liege lord knelt to give them their swords; for the rest of their lives they would brag about that. Finally he shook each by the hand and welcomed him to the craft. Wallie went into his office, and the recruits rushed away with their new mentors in great excitement.

He threw his sword on the bed and flopped down in the chair, releasing a cloud of dust and more feathers. Linumino closed the door and stood waiting. The pudgy, scar-faced swordsman had proved to be a superb adjutant, with endless patience for detail and an excellent memory. Long hours he sat at his table, seeming to increase in girth daily. Soon he would be too absurdly fat to carry a sword, but that would not matter as long as the tryst lasted, and perhaps he planned to retire at the end of it. Meanwhile he made Wallie's world sane and relatively orderly, not the mad chaos it could so easily have become without him.

"Take a stool," Wallie said. "Something wrong?"

Linumino was frowning. "My liege, am I right in my suspicions? It always seems to be Lord Tivanixi's men who find these promising recruits."

Wallie laughed. "I had noticed. I assumed that you had. And that neither of us had."

"How does it work—six legs per boy?"

"Ten, I believe. Unless four of them are unusually good."

Linumino smiled and said no more. Bribery to induct a recruit was not honorable, but the tryst was desperate for good horses. Their asking price had gone from three golds to twenty or thirty, and finances just could not stand those costs. Yet rich families would pay to have a son become a swordsman. As long as the boys had promise, Wallie turned two blind eyes, and Tivanixi got more of his men mounted, more stablehands, more mouths to feed, more horses.

"All right, let's have it!"

Sitting rigidly on his stool, Linumino closed his eyes as he always did when recalling data. It was an unnerving sight, for the left one did not shut properly, showing a sliver of white. "The holy Lord Honakura replies that what you asked will be possible, up to twelve, and hopes to see you at the masons' dinner this evening. You have been invited to the traders' banquet tomorrow night, the butchers' on the night after, and two balls the following evening, by—"

"Accept the first two on behalf of myself and Lady Doa. Refuse the two that conflict. That sounds like local politics and I won't get involved."

Linumino had opened his eyes to listen. He closed them again. "Lords Tivanixi and Zoariyi have both sent Sixths asking about the leather." The eyes opened.

"Damnation!" Wallie said furiously. "We're going to have to pay! The old bitch threatened to up anchor and leave, taking the sorcerer with her!" Brota had not merely brought a shipload of fine leather to Casr, she had then bought up all the stock in town and cornered the market. Now she was demanding four hundred golds, and nothing Wallie could say would budge her. The two of them had conducted a roaring, screaming row the previous evening, ending with the children in hysterics and the sailors hovering threateningly near the fire buckets. The liege lord's fiat ended at the water's edge.

"Unloading will be tricky," Wallie said "The sorcerer might be tempted when she docks; you look after it yourself. You need some fresh air. Take the money and plenty of men. You ought to meet him, anyway. He's a fascinating old rogue." *And last night he damned nearly got the steam engine out of me.*

The adjutant nodded, then closed his eye once more. "Lord Tivanixi reports another collar bone, and a First had his foot trampled. He'll have the whole tryst in splints soon, my liege. No further cases of belly cramps."

That was good news! Cramming the whole tryst into one building tempted the god of epidemic, who was a far greater threat to any army than its enemies would ever be.

"The new rules about boiling water are being observed?"

"Apparently, my liege. The water in the west well is down another cubit, and the east well about a hand."

That was bad news! Well digging was not in any sutra; it was slaves' work, and Wallie had sold off all the slaves.

"Lord Jansilui reports that he has sent recruiters to Tau and Dri in search of fletchers, falconers, and birds. He asks if he may also send to sorcerer towns and, if so, whether he should seek help from Lord Nnanji."

"Yes, he may send. Not swordsmen, obviously. Try priests, or traders. Tell him to ask Honakura. Bypass Nnanji's network. Recruiting can't be secret."

"Yes, my liege. That's all the messages. Outside there's a deputation . . . of port officers, I suspect."

"If they won't state their business, I won't see them. If they *are* port officers, tell them to come back in a week. A little more fasting won't hurt them."

The adjutant smiled briefly. "The two Sixths accused of brawling . . . Lords Nnanji and Zoariyi have judged the case and sentenced them both to twenty-one lashes with the cat o' seven tails. The sentence awaits your confirmation."

"Damnation!" Wallie said again. He sprang up and wandered over to stare out the window. "I want new drapes here and another lamp. *Both?*"

"Each accuses the other of starting it, I gather." Linumino had risen also, automatically. "The witnesses disagree. The judges concluded that Ukilio started the fistwork and Unamani drew first."

Wallie thought for a moment. "You have a herald handy?"

"No, my liege."

"Call one while I talk with Katanji. Anyone else urgent?"

The adjutant said that the rest could wait. He went out. Wallie strolled back to his chair, glanced at the bed with its brilliant new cover, and sighed. He spent almost all his days and nights in this room. His visits to *Sapphire* were becoming rarer and briefer; he had not slept on board for four nights now. He slept in this room. Alone.

Then he rose and smiled as Katanji entered. They had been meeting socially, but not speaking business, and now Katanji was certainly business. His two new facemarks were barely healed, but he had a passable ponytail, its curls professionally straightened. The clip was a gold griffon. His brown kilt was crafted from expensive suede, his boots shone. He wore a harness, but it supported his cast, not a scabbard. Katanji was prospering.

He glanced around the room approvingly, lifted one of the bright new hangings to chuckle at the ancient sword-cut in the paneling behind it, then made himself comfortable on a stool. "You sent for me, my lord?"

His look of innocence would melt marble.

"I did. It's very clever, Katanji, but it's taking too long. We need them now! I understand you have thirty-seven."

"Thirty-one after these last three, my lord. I'm trying to speed things up—Honorable Trookro just goes and chooses the ones he wants now. That saves arguments. We're getting another ten in today, though. Good ones!"

Wallie admired his brazen impudence. "You know you nearly got thrown in jail, don't you? Tivanixi sent Trookro out to buy horses that first morning, and you'd tripled the price before he saw the first blade of grass. They all assumed that it was Chinarama's foul work. Then they started a witch hunt among the Sixths who'd overheard me telling Tivanixi to bring a saddler out to the ship. They didn't know I'd mentioned horses earlier, when you were around. Then they wouldn't believe that a First—even when he got a sudden promotion—was capable of organizing it. I had to argue that you weren't sworn to the tryst, and therefore what you were doing was not treason, only good business!"

Katanji smiled tolerantly and said nothing.

"Who's your partner?"

Without a blush, Katanji said, "Ingioli of the Fifth, my lord.

Normally he deals in rugs, but he knew some good horse traders."

"Obviously! Was he surprised to see you again?"

Katanji grinned and nodded.

"Another thing," Wallie said. "It's getting too obvious! To start with you kept it out of sight. Now, I'm told, you just turn up with a bunch of kids, and the swordsmen flock round you like . . . like . . ." He thought of ice-cream carts, but they would not translate.

"It's love at first sight!" Katanji protested, swinging his legs. "Very touching!"

"Love?" Wallie echoed in horror.

Katanji's innocence became even more heart-warming. "Did you not know about the girls, my lord? There were four weddings last night and five the day before . . ."

Now Wallie could not hold back a roar of laughter. "Horses for dowry? What sort of marriages will they be, Katanji? How long will they last after the tryst is disbanded?"

Katanji's shrug was a reminder that he never worried other people's troubles for them. "I ran out of sons."

"You're running a slave market!"

Katanji's eyes narrowed at this intrusion of morals into a business discussion. "The swordsmen want mounts. Tivanixi gets a man mounted and a spare horse. The ranchers get twenty golds, more for something special, like a four-year gelding with good legs. The tryst pays nothing—well below cost! Parents are getting sons in the craft and daughters well married. All those rich folk go creepy at the thought of swordsmen grandsons. Who loses?"

"Not Swordsman Katanji, I'm sure."

"If you want to speed things up, my lord . . . you've been rejecting too many! I admit that Olonimpi is poor material, but I thought that the others would pass."

"They won't," Wallie said firmly.

"Three horses apiece?" Katanji said hopefully. "That would be two dozen of the thirty-odd, right there. I'll make it four for Olonimpi. He couldn't be any worse a swordsman than I was."

The nerve of the kid! Wallie had no idea which candidate this inept Olonimpi had been, but obviously his family was rich.

"No," he said. "I'm not going to lower our standards. How much just to buy the thirty-one horses?"

"More than you can afford!"

Wallie jumped up—and Katanji did not even flinch. Anyone else would flinch for Wallie nowadays, but Katanji had summed up Lord Shonsu a long time ago.

"You know that Tivanixi wants to go and help himself? A cavalry outing?"

Quietly Katanji said, "Pitch?"

Wallie sat down again. Pitch? He had not even thought about pitch yet, but it would be essential for the catapults.

The boy had read his face and was trying not to look smug. "There are two thousand, four hundred and eighty-one barrels of pitch in Casr, my lord. Brota has eight hundred and twelve of them. The rest are mine."

"And barrels of pitch are easier to hide than horses?"

Katanji smiled.

"We have a torture chamber under this lodge."

Katanji shrugged. "You promised the sorcerer . . . do you only torture your friends?" He turned his charm on again. "I didn't think you would stoop to stealing our horses, but Ingioli was nervous and wanted insurance. Just as well, because that was how we discovered what Brota was doing. We were too late on the leather, but she's going to burn her fingers on the pitch." He gloated.

Now Wallie was apprehensive, as he was supposed to be. "How much are you going to charge us for pitch?"

"I'll throw it in with the horses," Katanji said generously, "if you'll take those rejected candidates, and if the elders will grant a certain trader a ten-year monopoly on importing rugs into Casr. Thirty-one horses and sixteen hundred-odd barrels of pitch! And Brota can eat all of hers!"

That was a tempting thought after the previous evening's battle, as Katanji had known it would be.

"These rejected candidates?" Wallie said thoughtfully. "Would they make priests?"

Katanji's pupils dilated. "I didn't know you could—"

"Honakura might manage it. A monopoly on *silk* rugs for *five* years wouldn't hurt the poor."

A frown came over Katanji's face as he calculated. Then he said, "The pitch, all forty-one horses, eight priests, six priestesses, all rugs for five years, and Olonimpi a swordsman."

Honakura had said twelve—he would have to manage fourteen.

"Done!" Wallie said. "Except for one other thing."

Katanji raised a wary eyebrow.

"You tell me—on your honor—how much Olonimpi's family will pay you."

"We have a deal?"

"Yes. I've already spoken to Honakura," Wallie admitted, "and I can certainly bully the elders."

"You won't tell Nanj?"

"Gods, no!" That would create a riot . . . or worse?

"It's more than the others . . ."

"How much?"

It took longer to get that information than it had to get the horses, but eventually Katanji reluctantly muttered, "Twelve hundred."

"Get out of here!" Wallie roared, trying not to laugh and not succeeding very well. "Arrange with Trookro to pick up the ponies—and this Olonimpi lunk had better go in the cavalry."

Katanji understood, and chuckled. He paused at the door. "It would help if you would pull in your scouts, my lord. They drive up prices—the ranchers are whipsawing us."

"Go! And tell your brother I want to see him."

Wallie rose and followed Katanji out to the antechamber, feeling as if he'd been wrestling bulls. Twelve hundred! Olonimpi alone had covered the syndicate's expenses. All the rest would be profit—thousands! But forty-one mounts at no cost to the tryst . . .

Linumino followed as the liege lord marched along to where a twitchy young herald of the Third was waiting beside the two captive Sixths.

Two Sixths, wearing black eyes and swollen lips and surly expressions. It had very nearly been a murder charge for one or the other of them. Ukilio had led his own troop of frees, a large one. Unamani had been reeve of a big city. Good men both, yet they had reacted with hate at first sight, for no known reason.

Wallie could sense their antagonism, when he looked at one, the other snarled.

He wasted no time on formalities. "Who's Ukilio? So you're Unamani? You've heard the sentence?" They nodded impassively. How could a man be impassive when facing that sort of demolition? "Do you know what twenty-one lashes will do to you?" Wallie did not, but he could guess. They nodded again.

"I don't like it," he said. "You'll both be useless for a year, perhaps evermore. I'd rather have one whole Sixth than two half Sixths."

There were still two dozen people waiting in the room. They all stiffened in apprehension.

"What I want from a Sixth is leadership, so I'm going to give you a leadership test, a competition. The winner will get one lash from the loser. The winner may then lay as many strokes on the loser as he chooses, he can flog him to death if he wants."

The victims were startled. Then they looked at each other. The puffed eyes narrowed, and the swollen lips curled in mirror image.

"Lord Linumino," Wallie said, "will give you back your swords and two golds apiece as expenses. You're going to dig wells. Here are the rules. Herald, you will proclaim these at the next two meals. Lord Linumino will chose sites for digging and sites for dumping, all dirt must be removed from the courtyard. You may buy the tools you need and recruit no more than twelve men each. You may take any man below the rank of Sixth. You may not interfere with each other's teams or excavations, or you will be disqualified and declared the loser. One day's penalty for every injury. The holes must be shored all the way. I shall appoint one judge and you may appoint two each. The first team to recover a full barrel of water is the winner." He turned to Linumino, who was grinning—a horrible sight. "What other rules do we need?"

"Incentives or threats?"

"Right!" That was tricky, though. Free swords despised money; some were even refusing the daily pittance they were offered for entertainment. "We need more harlots. The winning team will be sent to Dri as talent scouts to recruit in the brothels and bring back the most enjoyable girls. All expenses paid. Do you think that will do it?"

The adjutant chortled. "That ought to get the blood pounding, my liege! The waiting lines are bad, you know."

So Wallie had been told. "And you must not threaten, or injure, or punish your men. You are to *inspire* them to dig for you. If you can do that, you have real leadership. Any questions?"

"When do we start, my liege?" asked Ukilio, the larger.

"Now."

"At the end, my liege," Unamani said, "can we have a day off before the flogging? I'd like to be well rested so I can do a good job on him." The two exchanged glares.

"That's fair enough. Add that, herald. Their swords, Lord Adjutant?"

I am a god, Wallie thought. *I play games with men's lives*. Yet a sporting chance was better than no chance. Being flogged to death was little worse than twenty-one lashes with the cat, and maybe—please, gods!—just maybe, the winner would be merciful. It would entertain all those other bored men out there. The betting would be ferocious.

Unamani and Ukilio took their swords and collided in the doorway with a duet of oaths. Then they were gone, almost running into Thana, who was accompanied by a tall and imposing woman in a richly embroidered blue gown. The two women stared in surprise after the departing Sixths.

Wallie sighed. Obviously today was Family Night, but Thana must be accorded precedence, although other callers were now piling up. She was not a vassal, so she made a formal salute, and he responded. Then she presented the scraggy, white-haired matron . . . Olonanghi, weaver of the seventh rank. Curious, Wallie escorted them along to the office and bade them to be seated, giving Lady Olonanghi the chair.

Thana still brazenly continued to wear her riverfolk bikini, the two yellow sashes, but no male was going to complain about that. With her usual confidence she took charge of the conversation.

"We shall not detain you long, my lord. I happened to hear from Nnanji that you were concerned over winter clothing. Wool cloaks, in particular, I think?"

So now Thana was getting into the graft?

"That is true."

"Fifteen silvers, I think he mentioned?"

Wallie nodded. Nnanji was his oath brother, so Thana was his oath sister-in-law and—Great Gods!—was Brota his oath mother-in-law?

"Lady Olonanghi believes that she can make a better offer, my lord."

But why to Thana?

The dowager raised a finger to her right eye. "My father was a swordsman, my lord, so I have a special place in my heart for swordsmen."

Wallie muttered a politeness, thinking that many women had, although not usually so late in life.

Then revelation! "You are not, by chance, related to young Olonimpi, are you?"

The wrinkled face beamed. "My grandson!"

Now Wallie understood and hastily coughed to cover a smile. "A most promising lad. He is close to the front of our list of recruits, but of course we do have constraints on numbers . . ."

"Perhaps we should discuss the cloaks, my lord," Thana said in a cold voice—the intrigue was slipping out of her hands.

"We might be able to go as low as ten silvers per item," Lady Olonanghi suggested.

"I was hoping to find a place in the cavalry for him," Wallie mused. "Of course the competition there is outrageous—that is the prestige division, you understand . . . I beg your pardon, my lady, my mind was wandering. Did you say six?"

Lady Olonanghi bit her lip. "Eight, I said, my lord."

"Then the contract is yours! And I do think we can find a spot for a lad of such obvious ability."

"In the prestige division?" Lady Olonanghi purred.

"Certainly. I am told that he is well qualified for the work."

He took them out to Linumino to arrange details, while he wondered who was going to come out best in the resulting confusion. Thana and Katanji had both sold Olonimpi. Probably Katanji. Thana was not in his class when it came to money.

And tomorrow Wallie would meet this maladroit Olonimpi

and kneel to the boy to give him his sword. For a First in the prestige division, he ought to make it a shovel.

More petitioners had now arrived, but again there was no doubt who took precedence. He forgot all about Thana as he watched Doa's stately approach. He followed her into the office and closed the door carefully.

Then she smiled. As usual his loins almost burst into flame.

Today was the long hemline again; it varied. But the neckline fell audaciously low, and the pale-blue silk was as close to transparent as any fabric he had ever seen, clinging like lacquer. She was not wearing her lute, and her only adornment was the sapphire he had given her, dangling on its silver chain.

The finances of the tryst desperately needed that gem now.

Doa sauntered across to close the drapes, and his eyes hung on every movement of that superlative body. Time and failure had not blunted his craving. Almost every night be squired her to some function or other, and always she would be asked to sing during the evening. Her dancing was superb, but intimate encounters like the waltz were unknown, so he rarely had a chance to touch more than her hand. They were a striking couple, he knew, towering over everyone else. She was the recognized prima donna, the star of Casr, a figure of awe to the epic-loving swordsmen. Even the liege lord could boost his prestige by being seen with such a companion.

He told her of the invitations he had accepted earlier.

"Fine," she said, the first word she had spoken. She went to lean against the fireplace, her favorite spot, to regard him with languorous amusement, her favorite occupation.

"What did you think of Mistress Sola's exhibition the other night?" Doa said. "Did you notice what her husband . . ."

She was a scurrilous gossip, and a merciless mimic. Each day she came calling at about this time. She would review the most recent festivities, savaging the high society of Casr and the senior swordsmen. Wallie had very little interest in the topic, but he admired the skill of the performance. Sometimes he was moved to genuine laughter—Doa's impersonation of Nnanji was unbearably funny—but usually he just sat in silence, smiling politely and dreaming lecherous thoughts.

And her real purpose in coming was to enjoy taunting him, teasing and luring like a hungry harlot.

She was mad, and so was he.

Today he felt no desire to indulge in the usual pretence. Last night he had visited Jja, in their cabin. The encounter had been a disaster, as his visits with Jja always were now. Oh, she had submitted, a slave had no choice. She had even pretended that she was trying to please, but her efforts had been those of a well-trained and skillful night slave. The woman he had known, the friend and lover, had vanished, and his attempts to call her back merely reduced Jja to tears and him to fury. He had no patience with her stubborn, silent recrimination. Doa, now—Doa knew how a senior swordsman must behave.

So he had Doa for social companionship and status, Jja for his physical needs. Why should he complain? Most men would have been more than satisfied with either.

He moved toward Doa, and her voice died away. She regarded him warily, and he stopped, knowing that any closer approach would bring on flashing eyes and claws, threats of violence and of screaming. Screams from Doa would be audible all the way to Vul.

"Why do you come here?' he said.

"I thought you enjoyed our little chats, my lord."

He shook his head. "Be honest for once."

She regained confidence and chuckled mockingly. "Because your bodyguard knows where you sleep at night, darling. And whom you sleep with. Or should I say 'without'? Right now, they believe, you are making up for it. Would you prefer that they knew the truth? The other boys would laugh at you!"

"They might laugh at you, also?"

She smiled. "I think not."

He thought not, as well. Suddenly his hands were shaking, but how much from anger and how much from frustrated lust, he did not know. "What is the price, my lady? What does it take to buy a kiss? Or more than a kiss?"

"You know your promise, Shonsu."

She had referred to that before. She had always refused to explain.

"I recall no promise."

Now the eyes flashed, but before she could speak, he said, "I told you to be honest! You are an acute observer of people, Doa. Even if you won't admit it, you do know that I am not the other Shonsu."

She stared at him in angry silence.

"You do know! And I do not know what the other Shonsu promised you. So enlighten me."

Reluctantly she said, "To make me a queen."

"A *what?*"

"A queen, Shonsu! Queen of Vul! You swore upon your sword! That was what you promised, and I expect you to deliver."

Wallie went back to his chair and sat down, stunned. Queen of Vul? Had that been why Shonsu had attacked the sorcerers? Not to avenge the swordsmen, but to bed this woman? Forty-nine dead?

"Vul is a tall order, my lady. How about a smaller kingdom to start with? Tau, say?"

She smiled her feline smile. "That might suffice, at least for openers . . ." Then she saw that he was not serious and she flared in rage. "But I think I need a lesser present, to hold my interest in the meantime."

He had showered her with gifts. "You own half the gems in Casr, Doa. What more?"

"A slave."

"What slave?"

She stalked to the window and threw open the drapes. "It is well known that Shonsu owns the most beautiful concubine in the city. I saw her on the ship, briefly."

He jumped up. "Never! You would mutilate her!"

"Maybe a little!" Doa swept to the door. "But I want her. Very soon!" She paused, as if to recover her poise. He had never seen her lose it so obviously. "I must go and practice some new songs. They will think you have been exceptionally speedy today, my lord. A new record!"

And then she was gone.

Wallie stared at the closed door. Queen of Vul? She must have been lying . . . And yet, whatever Shonsu's motives had been in attacking the sorcerers, he would certainly have thought about making himself king of Vul. What else could he have done with a captured sorcerer city, except just raze it? So he might very well have offered Doa a place on his future throne.

The promise itself would not have got him very far, though. *New songs*, she had said—a threat. Wallie had fallen into the same trap as Shonsu had. One thing was now certain: Shonsu had never raped Doa. She undoubtedly derived a great, perverted pleasure from skirting the edge of violence with her constant invitations, but any man who attempted further intimacy would be immortalized at once in one of her satirical masterpieces, his reputation ruined forever, a public laughingstock.

He could not even jilt her, or the same thing would happen.

Give her Jja? The idea was unthinkable. But many married men kept concubines. It was one of the advantages of a slave-owning society. Perhaps Doa would settle for being queen of Tau?

And tonight, the masons' dinner . . . business as usual.

Yes, back to business. Forcing thoughts of Doa to the back of his mind, he stepped forward and opened the door. Outside there was loud laughter. Nnanji was perched on the edge of Linumino's table, doubled over with mirth. He rose, saluted without losing his grin, and then started laughing again. "Flogged to death by the winner? Our liege knows how to motivate a man, doesn't he, Lord Adjutant?"

He stepped past Wallie into the office, pausing to inspect his healing facemarks in the mirror. "What can I do for you, brother?" As usual, he was in very good spirits.

Ever since Honakura had told him the true prophecy, Wallie had felt uneasy in Nnanji's presence. On the face of it, he was a soft-spoken, likable youth, as honorable as his brother was devious, totally without guile. He was good company and an incomparable subordinate. Yet he was also—as Wallie well knew—a completely unscrupulous killer. With the tale of Ikondorina's brother hanging between them, the combination was disturbing in the extreme.

Closing the door, Wallie pointed to the bruises and scrapes on his ribs. "How does a Seventh get so battered?" he asked.

Nnanji pouted. "A fraudulent Seventh? He takes on thirty-nine Sixths in order, starting at the bottom—they all being his vassals, so they can't refuse. By the time he gets to twenty-two he's battered! By the time he gets to thirty-nine, he's going to be doing the battering, I think." He grinned hopefully.

The Sixths were butchering him? That was not too surprising. The Boy Wonder was not popular with the older men. "You're not scared that they'll do serious injury?"

Nnanji shrugged. "I warn them—bruise all they like, but real hurt to a liege is a capital offense. They're all terrified of you, brother." Then he grinned again. "And when they hear about this well-digging contest . . ."

Wallie sank back in his chair and waved toward a stool, but Nnanji continued to mooch idly around the room.

"How do you have the time?"

Nnanji gave him a hurt look. "I've done everything you asked, haven't I?"

He began to count, raising fingers. Thumb: "I've memorized all the skills. Linumino was asking for dowsers just now. I gave him three names. Zoariyi wants wheelwrights; we have none."

Index finger: "The River is patrolled, night and day, and especially *Sapphire*, of course. No ship approaches the city without showing swordsmen aboard."

Middle finger: "Katanji has his irregulars checking the ships when they dock, especially if Fiendori's collectors are suspicious. So far we've located four pigeon fanciers and are watching them. Yes, they do buy vellum, as you suspected."

Ring finger: "Tomiyano and the other sailors are collecting gossip all the time, and we have offers going out to traders in Sen and elsewhere to be our agents. There hasn't been time to get replies."

Little finger: "The streets around the lodge are guarded night and day. Visitors are escorted. All boxes and packages coming in are checked for that thunderpowder that bothers you so much. Any wagon that stops is challenged."

Thumb: "I have two boats surveying the opposite bank for sorcerer activity. Nothing at Gob or Ag, the two closest hamlets, and we're working up and down from there."

Index finger: "I found—Tomiyano found—four men who know the Sen and Wal areas well, and the villages near them. I have all that information when you want it.

"I have to stay by the lodge, brother! They need to be able to find me. Now, is there something I've missed?"

Probably Wallie had really wanted only to drag him away from fencing, so he smiled apologetically. "No! I'm just jealous, I think. You're very good at delegating, better than I am. Well, I was wondering about poisoning pigeons . . ."

He explained—bribe some sailors to visit the sorcerer towns and scatter poisoned grain around the towers. Nnanji pointed out that civilians were reluctant to approach the towers by night, but he promised to discuss it with Tomiyano.

"By the way, brother," he added. "I need some expense money! I'm broke."

Wallie rose and went to the chest in the corner. "You ought to keep your own separate," he said. Yet it was impossible, in the absence of ledgers and bookkeeping. He himself bought gifts for Doa from the tryst's funds.

"I suppose so," Nnanji said. "But Katanji needed some. When he gave me your message just now, he cleaned me out."

"Katanji?" Then Wallie said no more. He handed Nnanji a bag of coins and slammed the lid of the chest.

Nnanji laughed. "Yes, Katanji! I'm going soft in my old age, aren't I? He seems to be doing very well, whatever he's up to." He paused and turned slightly pink. "He says that some of the boys he's using as irregulars are good material, brother. I said he could promise to induct them afterward—not more than five, I said. That's all right, isn't it?"

Wallie sighed. "Yes, as long as they're not utter cripples."

Nnanji started. "You don't think—he couldn't be taking money from their parents, could he?"

This was getting tricky. Nnanji himself was very sensitive on this subject.

"We'll test his recruits, don't worry!"

Nnanji scowled and turned away. "He might get five or ten golds apiece, mightn't he? Little blackguard!" Then he chuckled again. "Whatever he's doing, it's paying well. And when Thana leaves *Sapphire*, her share will be thousands, did you know that? Funny, isn't it, brother? I never cared for money. All I ever wanted from life was cool beer and warm girls, and I'm going to have a rich wife and a rich brother. And if I needed money, Katanji would give me everything he's got!"

Some of it, Wallie thought. "And your goods are my goods?"

"Of course!" Nnanji said, obviously meaning it.

Then the lunch bugle sounded in the courtyard.

"I'm dining with Tivanixi," Wallie said. "Care to join us?"

Nnanji looked regretful. "Sorry! This is Masons' Day, my birthday."

Wallie had not known that. He bit back the obvious question—nineteen? Maybe twenty. But to ask that question was a gross discourtesy among the People, the reason being that most would not know the answer. Like Nnanji, they would know the day, but only because they must keep it holy, with fasting and an all-night vigil in the temple.

"I wonder what Shonsu's birthday was? I'll have to choose one! The day I came to the World, I suppose. That would be three days before we met."

"Teachers' Day, then!" Nnanji said with a smile.

Mark it on the calendar, Wallie thought. "In my other life, Nnanji, it was usual to give one's friends presents on their birthdays. Is there anything you want?"

"Funny custom!" Nnanji said. He thought about it and then laughed. "If you'd asked me that when we first met, brother, I'd have said I needed new boots. My old ones leaked. But now?" He gestured at his blue kilt. "What's left? What in the World could you possibly give me that you haven't given me already?"

†††

The days passed.

On Sailors' Day, Honorable Ukilio's digging team hit rocks and broke all the picks. Odds were adjusted and bets increased.

The prototype catapult self-destructed on its third shot.

Lord Nnanji, whose ribs were adorned with the colors of all ranks, completed his collection of Sixths and started over on the difficult ones.

On Charcoalburners' Day, Honorable Unamani's team had a cave-in and broke both its wheelbarrows. Odds were adjusted and bets increased. On that day, also, the sailor spy network reported that thunderbolts had been heard in Wal by night.

On Minstrels' Day, a fifth pigeon fancier was identified and placed under surveillance.

Exhausted men tore at rocks with their bare hands and staggered through the night with buckets of dirt. Bets were increased. Cheering and booing were banned during hours of darkness. Four workers collapsed from exhaustion and were taken to the house of healing. Penalties were assessed.

On Cobblers' Day, Lord Nnanji brazenly ordered Lord Linumino to bring his foil out to the plaza. The portly adjutant poked his head into Lord Shonsu's office to explain where he was going. Lord Shonsu went out in his stead and drove Lord Nnanji all around the plaza backward, giving him three red welts on the *left* side of his chest to show that it could be done. But Lord Nnanji put a bruise on Lord Shonsu.

The redesigned catapult went into mass production.

No evidence of sorcerer activity was found on the left bank opposite the city.

Several wealthy matrons married handsome young cavalry officers after whirlwind courtships, presenting them with horses as dowries. Swordsman Katanji was invited to all the weddings.

The elders declared a financial crisis and imposed a hearth tax. The liege lord informed them that no swordsmen were available to accompany the collectors. The tax was canceled.

Shortly before lunch on Lacemakers' Day, Honorable Unamani's team reported seepage. During lunch, so did Honorable Ukilio's. Bets were increased. One hour later a cloudburst ended a three-week drought and put six cubits of water in both holes. The judges declared a draw.

The price of pitch in Casr dropped precipitously.

Lord Jansilui, leaving the lodge after reporting to liege Shonsu on the problems of finding suitable wood for both arrows and bows, was accosted by liege Nnanji and handed a foil. Lord Nnanji won.

Lord Shonsu, even with the aid of large quantities of ensorceled wine and a promise of two talent-scouting teams, could not persuade Ukilio and Unamani to accept the gods' verdict. Finally he made an exception to the rules and allowed them to fight it out with fists—as he should have done in the first place. They pounded each other to custard and became the best of friends.

The sailors reported that thunderbolts had been heard in Aus.

Lord Shonsu accepted a gift of a magnificent silk rug, emblazoned with silver pelicans.

On Healers' Day, *Griffon* returned.

The prisoners were safe in the dungeons, the crowds dispersed, the giant's abacus suitably adjusted. The tryst had a day off to celebrate. The cheering and the booing were over, the minstrels toiled at their epics—*How Boariyi of the Seventh Smote the Sorcerers in Wal and Aus*, or some equally catchy title.

The office-bedroom was a council chamber again. The Sevenths were gathered on the circle of stools around the brilliant silk rug in the center. A noisy fire crackled in the fireplace. Wallie stood before it, enjoying the warmth against his legs and pondering his strategy. This meeting would be crucial. Square-jawed Jansilui was expounding at length to Linumino on the shortage of fletchers; Tivanixi was describing to Boariyi the finer points of couching a lance; Nnanji was humped on his stool, scowling truculently at the floor. They were waiting for Zoariyi.

The room had been transformed; Boariyi had recoiled in astonishment on seeing it. The paneling shone with wax, its worst blemishes hidden by brilliant tapestries, matching the drapes. The shabby old stools had been replaced by fine oak, the bed and chair similarly upgraded. But the showpiece was undoubtedly the silk rug given by Ingioli, glowing with resplendent silver pelicans and bronze river-horses.

Tivanixi remarked suddenly, "I have a warning for you, Lord Boariyi. We have seven real Sevenths in the tryst now."

Nnanji glanced up and grinned.

Boariyi raised his eyebrow, wrinkling the red scar above it. "I had better get back in practice, you feel?"

"Definitely! Lord Jansilui will confirm that—and so will thirty-nine Sixths. You can top them all now, my liege Nnanji?"

Turning faintly pink, Nnanji nodded and grinned again.

"I dread the summons," Tivanixi said. "I have been expecting it for days."

"You flatter me, my lord."

The castellan shook his head. "No, I have been watching you closely. I shall be surprised if I can beat you now, my liege."

Wallie smiled to himself—flattery, but close to the truth, as good flattery should be. Jansilui was a borderline Seventh, but so now, obviously, was Nnanji. Then Zoariyi came scurrying in, sprinkling apologies, and the meeting came to order, the seven Sevenths of the tryst of Casr.

Wallie passed around goblets for toasts. "Lord Boariyi," he said, "we have heard of your exploits and inspected your prisoners. We congratulate you again on a magnificent beginning to the tryst. I think we should now bring you up to date on what has been going on in your absence. Brief progress reports, if you please. Nnanji?"

Making himself as comfortable as he could on his stool, he let them do their bragging: Nnanji on his espionage, Zoariyi on his catapults, Tivanixi on his cavalry, Jansilui on his archers and the only two operational falcons he had managed to find. Boariyi's Sixths, in his absence, had developed his troop into a force of guerrillas, knife-throwing, garrote-wielding assassins, who might sneak ashore black-faced by night and seize a dock.

Wallie could feel a great satisfaction. He had brought the tryst forward a thousand years, from Greek phalanx to the Middle Ages. While the sorcerers would class as early Renaissance, a few centuries ahead still, he had significantly closed the gap. He could concentrate his forces, the sorcerers could not. At odds of fifty to one the outcome seemed certain.

Yet it was all in vain. That was the devastating news he must soon impart. How would they take it? How would Nnanji take it?

Wallie himself was secretly jubilant. The thought of going through with the assault horrified him. The pitch-pitching catapults would inevitably start fires, as would the sorcerers' cannons. Whichever city was attacked would be left half ruined, the population decimated. Boariyi had captured eight sorcerers alive and killed six, losing only one man. He had brought back ten sorcerer gowns, with a treasury of gadgets that Wallie had not yet had time to study. Yet seven men had died! Add that to the fourteen at Ov and the toll was mounting. Add also Tarru and his renegades, add the pirates . . . Wallie Smith was starting to rank with the great killers. But however these swordsmen might dislike the thought of a treaty, he could show that it was the only hope.

They had done. "Thank you," he said. But he had not called on Linumino and the adjutant was staring at him, glum and puzzled.

"I congratulate you all," Wallie continued. "Perhaps we should have invited the sorcerers to attend this meeting and hear all that!" They laughed obediently, little guessing how serious he was. "Now, my lords, how would you proceed?"

Again he sat back and he let them plan. They were not stupid. Now that he had jerked their thinking into unconventional paths, they could design the campaign as well as he could, or better. Of course Tivanixi wanted to emphasize cavalry and the others their own specialties, but after a long discussion they more or less came to an agreement. The guerrillas would land at night, when pigeons could not fly, and take over the closest village to the city, whichever one was chosen. They would round up the entire population. The cavalry would disembark at the jetty, ride into the city, secure the docks, and bottle up the sorcerers in their stronghold before they knew the attack was coming. Then the catapults could be unloaded and the real attack begun.

Wallie rose and brought the wine for refills. He remained standing by the fireplace again, because he was going to need all the dominance he could find.

"That was the good news. Now, Lord Linumino? Tell them about finances." That was a dirty trick to play on a loyal adjutant.

The pudgy swordsman scowled down at his knees. "Finances are very bad and getting worse, my lords. We can cover our running costs from day to day, but we have no money to mount an attack!"

Five faces registered shock. Six sets of eyes swung to look at Wallie.

"I am afraid that this is true," he said. "Indeed, things are worse than that. I don't think we can even continue to cover our day-to-day expenses much longer. I have agreed to reduce our sequestration of dock fees."

Nnanji said, "Why?" indignantly.

"Because the poor are close to starvation!"

He got six blank stares. Economics was beyond them, and he did not fully understand, himself. "Yes, that money is graft, in the sense that it is not authorized by law and does not go into the city coffers. It goes to the collectors, and some of it under the table to the elders. Yes, they are parasites. But they are rich parasites, my lords. They employ servants, keep slaves, and buy services and goods in the city. We have forced them to cut back, so the poor earn less."

Still bewilderment showed on six faces.

"Put it another way, then," he said. "The city of Casr buys food from the countryside, right? It sells the country folk things it manufactures—pots, tools, ropes, and so on. Then the tryst brought thousands of extra mouths to feed, but did not increase production. In fact we have been buying horses and lumber and stuff like that—again from the countryside. Gold has been flowing out of the city and not coming back."

"What has that to do with the poor?" Zoariyi asked angrily. "They never see gold."

Wallie sighed. "And silver and tin and copper! The price of food has quadrupled since we arrived." He looked at the disbelieving Nnanji. "Ask Lina—she knows! Prices of other things are falling as desperate people sell their possessions. I repeat: The poor are going to starve unless we take the tryst away quickly."

They did not understand and they did not overmuch care. Wallie began to feel exasperated. "That rug that you are snarling at, brother. Yes, it was a gift."

Nnanji turned red and said nothing.

"But I gave no favors in return and I intend to sell it before we leave. The same is true of most of these things. I accepted them on behalf of the tryst, because the tryst is temporary. They will help our finances in the end. Is that acceptable, *brother*?"

Nnanji mumbled an apology.

"Perhaps I was foolish," Wallie said—and here he must be very careful not to bruise Boariyi's prickly swordsman honor, or he would be storing up a challenge for after the tryst was disbanded. "But I did promise the sailors that we would pay for our transportation. They ought to contribute it as a service to the Goddess, of course, but I know sailors! Our swords would rust away first. And if we anger them, they would leave us stranded in Sen or Wal, or wherever; we would never get to the other six cities. There is the worst problem: We do not have the money to charter ships!"

Five faces stared at him in mingled anger and despair. the sixth face was merely furious; Nnanji was never good at hiding his feelings. "How much would the first assault require, brother?"

Wallie shrugged and looked to Linumino.

"I estimate almost four thousand golds, Lord Nnanji. For supplies and transportation, and of course we shall be cut off from our income as soon as we sail."

"He said five!"

"Who said five?"

"Katanji."

"What the hell has Katanji got to do with this?" Wallie barked.

"He's offered to finance our assault."

"You didn't tell me that!"

"You didn't tell me it would be needed! I wouldn't believe him!"

"Perhaps I should put your brother on my council?"

"Perhaps you should!"

Wallie took a very deep breath, then returned to his stool as a gesture of appeasement. Certainly the last thing he must do was to quarrel with Nnanji. The other Sevenths were now frowning, worried and uncertain.

"All right, brother," Wallie said. "I'm sorry, I should have kept you better informed. I just thought you had your own problems. Now, what is your financial genius suggesting?"

"He'll give us five thousand golds for the assault." Nnanji was still surly. Money was not a fit subject for swordsmen to worry about. "And the same for each successive assault, as long as we keep winning. All except Ov. He isn't sure about Ov."

"And what does he expect in return?"

Nnanji scowled and dropped his glare to the silver pelicans again. "The tower."

"What?"

"The sorcerers pulled down a lot of buildings to make their towers and leave open spaces around them, right? Katanji wants the land. He'll sell it and give us money to go on to the next city. He says land in a town is worth more than farmland. Is that right? It seems backward! You can't grow things on flagstones."

From rugs, to jewels, to livestock, to real estate? Katanji was making a logical progression to . . . to immense wealth! The Goddess had rewarded all those who had helped him, Wallie knew, and now he saw another example, very plainly. Was the lad himself already worth five thousand golds, or had he put together a syndicate? Did it matter?

What did matter was that the main support for Wallie's arguments had just collapsed. This was going to be trickier than he had expected.

The other Sevenths were all grinning. They had a right to, Wallie conceded to himself. He had overlooked the possibility of looting the sorcerers. Katnaji had not, although he might not have considered the devastation an attack would bring, or what that might do to real estate values.

"Very well," he said grudgingly. "So we could finance the attacks that way. But there is another problem. Suppose we attack Sen or Wal—or any of the cities on the left bank. Suppose we take the tower. What happens then?"

Honakura had not thought of what happened then. It was unlikley that the swordsman would, even with sutras on strategy to help. They looked blankly at him, so he explained. The sorcerers would return to the hills.

Then they saw.

"Attack Vul?" Zoariyi muttered uneasily.

They talked that over and they did not like it. It would certainly have to wait until spring, perhaps even next summer. Vul —wherever or whatever it was—would be well fortified by then.

When they had all smelled that bad egg, Wallie laid another. "Forarfi has been doing a little research for me." He avoided looking at Nnanji, who was supposed to be Chief of Intelligence. "He has talked to all the Sixths and many Fifths. We have swordsmen here, my lords, from all over the World. He asked about other sorcerer cities, like Vul. There is one near Plo . . . and others. He compiled a list of eleven. I recited it to Rotanxi. He admitted that there are thirteen in all. Covens, he called them. He says that Vul is the greatest, but he may be bragging."

The Sevenths scowled at the mention of Rotanxi.

"Are you suggesting that we should have to attack all thirteen?" Zoariyi asked waspishly.

"I am suggesting that they may attack us! So far, apparently, only Vul has these thunderbolt weapons, or only Vul has used them. The others may well be waiting to see what happens here. We may be able to scotch Vul, my lords—although I am not confident—but we can hardly hope to kill all the sorcerers there. The survivors will flee to the other cities . . ."

The smarter ones nodded—Zoariyi, Tivanixi, Nnanji.

Outside, the day was blustery, even in the courtyard, and the miniature canvas city there flapped and rattled in the wind.

At last Nnanji put the matter into words. "Sometimes when you try to clean a stain you spread it?"

Wallie had been thinking of cancer cells, but that would do. As a child, Nnanji had cleaned rugs for his father.

"Exactly! In truth, my lords, there is no way that the tryst can triumph completely over the sorcerers. The best we can do is drive them away for a year or two. The worst we can do is to make things much worse than they are now."

"What are you suggesting, brother?" Nnanji demanded, his eyes glinting dangerously.

Here it came: "Try to make a treaty."

Their hiss of anger faded away into the flapping noises from beyond the windows and the crackling of the fire.

Then they began to exchange glances, and their eyes converged at last on Nnanji. The old suspicions of Shonsu had erupted again. He had a feathermark on his eyelid, he kept a sorcerer on his ship, there was always something strange about him. But Nnanji was the known sorcerer-killer of Ov, and it was impossible to suspect Nnanji of being anything but what he claimed to be, a simple swordsman.

They were bound to obey their liege lord, but the tryst could not last forever. Wallie could force these men to violate their own sense of honor, for they must obey his commands—until the tryst was disbanded. Then they would all be at liberty to challenge him, one after another to exhaustion. Yes, they would obey, but Nnanji was a liege lord, too, and if he were to try to take the tryst away from Wallie—young as he was—the other Sevenths in their present mood would probably not argue.

Nnanji was scarlet with rage. Wallie should have warned him in advance; that had been a stupid oversight.

Finally Nnanji said, "A treaty with assassins?" as if the words burned his mouth.

"We know that they will keep their oaths," Wallie said quietly.

"Three cities for them and four for us? Or the other way?"

"Seven for us, seven for them. I want to end the quarrel between our two crafts."

Stunned silence.

"And what does your tame sorcerer say to this?" The older men were all going to leave it to Nnanji.

"I haven't asked Rotanxi," Wallie said. "I was hoping to get your agreement first. He may well dislike the idea as much as you do. I just think that it is worth trying—the best thing for both sides. If we do attack Sen, say, we shall kill hundreds of innocent civilians. I don't think that's very honorable behavior."

"I think a treaty is worse!"

Almost imperceptibly, the others were nodding.

Wallie sighed. "It is a novel idea. You need time to think about it. But remember that the sorcerers know about our cavalry and our catapults and our archers; we could not have kept them secret had we tried. They are not fools. They know the odds.

They must be worried. Now is the time to to offer terms."

"What terms?" Nnanji spat the words.

"They get rid of their thunderbolt weapons. We extend to them the same protection we give to all other crafts. The towers remain, but we put garrisons back in the cities."

Nnanji's jaw dropped. He glared incredulously at Wallie, then around at the others. Then he slumped forward, staring at the silver pelicans for along time, shaking his head, tugging at his ponytail as he did when he was thinking hard. No one else spoke. No one would meet Wallie's gaze.

Suddenly a log in the hearth collapsed in a shower of sparks, and Nnanji looked up with a curious gleam in his eye. "What do you propose to do next, Shonsu?"

"I thought I might go—we might go and talk to Rotanxi."

"I may come, then?"

What was amusing him? Still, that was a very good idea. Nnanji would be representative for the swordsmen. If Wallie could somehow convince him, then the other Sevenths must follow.

"Certainly! Let's do that, then. Lord Nnanji and I will go and sound out the sorcerer Seventh, my lords, and report back to you. If he turns us down flat, then my proposal is hopeless."

They took that as a welcome dismissal. They all sprang to their feet, saluted fist on heart, and marched to the door. The last one out was Boariyi. He slammed it behind him deafeningly.

Nnanji chuckled. "I think you upset them, brother!"

"I thought I'd upset you, too."

Nnanji wrinkled his nose in amusement. "That was when I thought you were serious! You fooled me there for a minute! Now, brother, your secrets are my secrets. What's your real plan?"

†† ††

The tryst had established its own loading dock on the waterfront. There were always swordsmen there, but the arrival of the two liege lords with their combined bodyguards made it seem like an armed encampment. An icy wind was whipping in from the

River, blowing spray. Lady Olonanghi's factory had begun delivery of swordsmen cloaks—strange garments that left sword hilt and sword arm free—but Wallie had insisted that the lowranks be outfitted first, for juniors spent more time out in the cold. Thus many white and yellow capes roiled in the wind around him, and a few browns, also, but the highranks and most of the middleranks shivered. Wallie was no exception. It was all he could do to keep his teeth from chattering.

Nnanji was managing to combine blue lips and a very black expression. He had finally been convinced that Wallie was serious in wanting a treaty. His disgust was bottomless. Just as the swordsmen arrived, so did Thana, bringing in one of *Sapphire*'s dingies. She stared in astonishment at Nnanji's obvious anger and ephemeral kiss. She regarded the baggage with curiosity—bundles and two stools—then offered to take the visitors out. Wallie agreed, to save calling in a patrol boat.

Thana's questions began as soon as the dinghy was underway. She received no answers. Nnanji was in a speechless sulk, while she and Wallie had been on poor terms since the Olonimpi incident. Apparently Katanji had won the cigar.

The sun was bright enough, but could force no warmth through a white overcast. High above, creating this haze, three long plumes of cloud streamed toward the city from RegiVul. The Fire God was exceedingly enraged. Perhaps he disapproved of Boariyi's victory, or else he did not want a treaty, either. The River was choppy in the gusty wind, bouncing the boat roughly. The air bore a faint stink of sulfur.

Wallie was very conscious of Nnanji's anger and was miserably trying not to think about the Ikondorina prophecy: *it is your kingdom that I covet*. If the sorcerers would accept a treaty and Wallie tried to force it on the swordsmen, then Nnanji might very well be driven to that idea. The other Sevenths had no legal vote, but in practice their views must be considered. They might even encourage him to mutiny.

Then what? Nnanji's swordsmanship was certainly approaching seventh rank now, and the gods might not allow a fair match. The gods? The gods would not need to intervene! With foils Wallie was still the better man, but if he and Nnanji pulled swords, the result would be a forgone massacre. He had been reluctant to injure even Boariyi, whom he had disliked. He could never exert himself against Nnanji. Where honor was concerned, Nnanji would have no such milksop scruples.

A long tack brought them alongside *Sapphire* and Wallie scrambled up the rope ladder to the deck. It seemed larger than usual because it was almost deserted. Anchored by the bow, the ship faced toward far-off RegiVul. The old sorcerer in his blue gown was huddled in Brota's trading chair in the lee of the fo'c'sle. The golden city lay aft. Faint shouts from that direction showed that the children were romping in the deckhouse, out of the wind. Jja was just emerging, swathed in sweater and pants of thick black wool. Tomiyano and Holiyi, on hands and knees amidships, were holystoning the deck, and still defiantly wearing only skimpy breechclouts, to demonstrate macho indifference to cold.

Wallie flashed Jja a brief smile and then turned to catch the stools and bundles as Nnanji tossed them up from the dingy. Jja was a problem. It was two days since he had last been out to *Sapphire*, so his physical reaction to her would be overwhelming —Shonsu's glands would roar—but this visit was too important to waste time on mere bodily processes. He must try to find some free time in the near future to deal with such personal trivia.

The last bundle delivered, he turned and found her standing beside him. For an instant her deep, dark eyes searched his face, then she inclined her head and waited in silence.

"We only came to talk with Lord Rotanxi, love," he said. "You go back inside, out of the wind."

But Tomiyano was there, also, arms akimbo, blocking Wallie's path. So we were back to formalities, were we? He began the salute to a superior—and the captain cut him off.

"Never mind that bilge, Shonsu! I want to talk business."

"Be quick about it!"

"I'm told the tryst is short of cash."

"What is that to do with you, sailor?"

"I thought a thousand golds might interest you?"

Startled, Wallie paused to think, moving aside as Nnanji and Thana came on board. Tomiyano flashed them a smile and went back to scowling at Wallie. Nnanji was the popular swordsman on *Sapphire* now. He was one of the family. He slept on board every night, no matter how late the banquets and balls ended; Nnanji seemed able to dispense with sleep for weeks at a time when he wanted to. But what was the sailor after? Wallie did not doubt that the money was available. He was sure that Brota had far more than that hidden away aboard somewhere, the family's savings. Then he noticed that Brota herself had emerged from the fo'c'sle door and was standing beside it, red robe rippling, watching the exchange with a worried stare. Expecting trouble?

"A thousand golds for what, Captain?"

Tomiyano indicated Jja with a jerk of his head. "Her."

Jja gasped.

"Been entertaining the crew, have you?" Wallie roared.

She shook her head wildly. "No, master! I know nothing of this!"

Tomiyano had his hand very close to his dagger. "You should know better than that, Shonsu!"

"Then what the hell do you mean?"

"I mean that she's a desirable property and she isn't getting the use she deserves. She's pining. I've heard her weeping in her cabin. If you don't want her, then I'll take her. A thousand? It's a fair offer."

It was an absurd offer. No slave, no matter how attractive, would ever fetch more than twenty. It was also an offer that made murder feel like a very good idea. Wallie's hand trembled with the conflicting signals it was being sent.

"You stay away from my slave, sailor, or by the gods, I'll fillet you!"

"Twelve hundred?"

Nnanji grabbed Wallie's arm just in time. "Easy, brother!"

Wallie jerked free, sending Nnanji staggering backward. "No!" He glared at the horror-struck Jja. "You're coming ashore with me when I go! Get your things ready!"

She nodded fearfully. "Vixini, master?"

Having Jja underfoot would be bad enough. He certainly did not want a slave baby with a blacksmith fathermark running after him, calling him Daddy in front of the swordsmen. "He stays here!"

Jja paled even more. He had promised her once . . .

"And stay out of my business, sailor!"

Wallie nodded to Nnanji, grabbed up one of the bundles, and headed forward. Thana had gone to join Brota. The two of them retreated into the fo'c'sle.

Twelve hundred golds! Wallie struggled to drag his mind back to business. The insolence! But Rotanxi was more important at the moment. What game was the sailor playing? He must have known that Wallie would not accept. Had Rotanxi overheard? A supreme trader like Tomiyano would never open negotiations that way. . .

Nnanji clattered the two stools down in front of the sorcerer. Nnanji was back to scowling. The sorcerer raised his shaggy white eyebrows. Wallie made formal salute, and the old man pushed himself to his feet to respond. Nnanji glowered at Wallie, saluted peremptorily, and barely waited for Rotanxi's response before sitting down.

"The wind is chill, my lord," Wallie said. "Would you prefer to go below?"

"This is fine."

Wallie sat. The old man was better dressed, and that put him about ten points ahead already. On the deck near his feet lay a sheet of vellum, weighted down by a marlinespike. His quill and ink bottle lay beside them. He had asked for those—almost humbly—many days before. Wallie had granted them, trusting him not to send messages. Probably he was recording all the curious knowledge he had extracted from Lord Shonsu.

"We came to give you a progress report on the tryst, my lord."

"You came to gloat?" Any slight relaxation that had crept into their relationship over the past weeks had vanished now. The sorcerer could smell business, and business at the moment was war. His always-craggy face was stony.

The deck was empty except for the three of them and Tomiyano, who had gone back to his scraping. The others had all gone below. A haze of volcanic dust was sweeping by in the wind.

Ignoring Rotanxi's question, Wallie began to summarize what had been reported at the meeting—the catapults, the archers, the guerrillas, the cavalry. He described Boariyi's success—six dead, eight captured. Nnanji ground his teeth in silence. Finally

Wallie assured the sorcerer that he could finance his attack. The tryst was almost ready for battle.

"So you want me to go back and tell my friends to give up?" Rotanxi was needle-sharp. Swordsmen won promotion by prowess with their blades. Sorcerers must do so by intelligence test.

"I wanted to show you that we can win."

"Against our thunder weapons? It will be bloody."

"We have much more blood available than you do, my lord."

The sorcerer's wrinkles writhed, displaying skepticism. "We shall see."

"I should rather not," Wallie said. "We shall wreck the cities and kill innocent bystanders."

"Since when have swordsmen worried about civilians?"

Wallie vowed a silent oath that he was not going to lose his temper. "This tryst was called to restore the honor of the swordsmen's craft, my lord. Killing civilians is not honorable and never has been. To be quite honest, I am not sure that killing sorcerers is, either. Do you know the origin of the quarrel between our two crafts?"

"No. It goes back even before our records."

"Then let us two stop it."

That won a reaction. The sorcerer stared at him unbelievingly.

"I came to suggest a treaty," Wallie said. "Before the serious killing starts."

"Bah! Why should we? You cannot win, Shonsu! One tower or even two, perhaps, but then we shall go away! Had you not thought of that? Admit it—the tryst must be disbanded. You cannot hold your superiority in numbers. In five years we shall be back." He smiled a cruel, thin-lipped smile. "Of course you are welcome to attack Vul again. I hope you try! You may win in the short run, but we win in the end. Admit it, swordsman!"

"I admit nothing!" Wallie lifted the bundle and tipped out twelve pistols—Rotanxi's own, Chinarama's, and the ten that Boariyi had brought. Then there was a lull in the conversation, while *Sapphire* wrestled with her cable and a straggle of geese flew by, far overhead. The sorcerer was frowning at this new threat.

"We win in the short run," Wallie said. "You may win in the middle run—perhaps. In the end we both lose."

"How so?"

"The swordsmen now know that your thunderbolts are not spells, that they are weapons. They will seek to obtain such weapons so that they may fight you on equal terms. And swordsmen are much better fighters! If I do not give them the secret, they will gain it by other means. In five years, my lord, you will be facing swordsmen armed with the same weapons you have now. I could make better, if I chose."

Another pause. Then Wallie added: "Nor will it stop there. Such weapons cannot be kept secret. Civilians will start getting them also. Then any old grandmother is a match for the toughest swordsman. Brigands will keep sorcerers captive in their cellars to manufacture weapons. It will mean ruin for both our crafts, my lord."

This was his argument-for-sorcerers. He had not presented it to the swordsmen and he wondered what Nnanji was making of it, but he kept his eyes on Rotanxi.

"I have no power to negotiate anything," the sorcerer said at last, and Wallie knew that he was making progress.

"You could take a message. And I cannot believe that the wizard of Sen is without influence."

The bitter old man studied him carefully. "What exactly are you proposing, Shonsu?"

"That we end the needless hostility between swordsman and sorcerer. It was always foolish and now it will lead to a growing, spreading struggle . . ." It was hard to find words to describe an arms race. Eventually he thought the sorcerer understood. "So you must agree to destroy your weapons and make no more. In return we treat your craft as we do all others, and you would be under the protection of the swordsmen."

Rotanxi laughed scornfully. "The protection of that gang of killers, thieves, and rapists you have in Casr? I had sooner be guarded by rabid wolves!"

Nnanji cursed and half rose from his stool, reaching for his sword. Then he sank back, muttering.

But Wallie managed to control his own temper. "I do not defend what happened when the swordsmen began arriving, my lord. It was shameful. But it was also unusual. There has been no tryst in many centuries to warn us—hundreds of free swords, all expecting to be treated like kings and heroes, all of them with nothing to do! As soon as the tryst was sworn, Lord Boariyi imposed discipline. The elders say that Casr has never been more peaceful than it is now. Maidens walk the streets at midnight unmolested. Thieves and cutpurses have vanished. I offer you this for your seven cities, and all others!"

Rotanxi scoffed. "You think you have such power?"

"I have unlimited power. The swordsmen are sworn to obey me to the death and without question." *All except that angry young man beside me*. "If I say that sorcerers are friends, then they will be treated like friends. I can make the swordsmen swear an oath to that effect."

The sorcerer stared coldly at him, but he was very intent. "'And all others,' you said?"

Wallie smiled. "I am being optimistic. The fourteen cities of the loop, certainly. The rest of the World will obviously be a little harder, and take time. But I could impose a new sutra on the men we have here. I could make them swear to work for its adoption everywhere. The Goddess brought them, and She will return them to their homes. They can tell the others. We do not have all the World's swordsmen here, my lord, only a tiny fraction of them. But in time, with goodwill on both sides . . .

"I believe that you sorcerers have much to offer the World." He pointed to the vellum and the quill. "That alone is desperately needed, by priests and merchants . . . even by swordsmen!"

The sorcerer was thinking, pulling his lip and not looking at Wallie. After a moment he said, "This is a strange idea, Lord Shonsu! You have surprised me many times, but never like this! Let me ponder awhile." He rose stiffly and paced off along the deck.

Wallie became aware that he was trembling with the cold. But he was also feeling a stir of hope. He glanced cautiously at Nnanji.

Nnanji was grinning.

Astounded, Wallie said, "What do you think?"

"I think he's going to go for it, brother!" Nnanji was excited. Nnanji was pleased! His black rage had vanished. So the argument-for-sorcerers had worked on him, also? Wallie would have to try it on the other Sevenths. He was astonished, but he also felt a great surge of relief.

"A new sutra would have to be number eleven forty-five, I suppose," Wallie said, "although that is at the wrong end of the list. But I can't meddle with the others."

Nnanji laughed. "Thirteen?"

Of course! There was no sutra thirteen. Knowing the sutras without ever having learned them, Wallie had not been aware of that—and yet somehow he knew as soon as Nnanji spoke that it was a trick question for Firsts. Twelve was on duties to priests, fourteen on the rights of civilians. Had there once been a sutra thirteen that dealt with sorcerers, a sutra abandoned after the great quarrel?

"Then we shall make a sutra number thirteen!" Wallie said, feeling that he had stumbled on something significant.

Rotanxi returned to his chair without a word and picked up his writing equipment. He pulled his glasses from a pocket, and put them on, causing Nnanji to snicker. He uncorked the ink bottle, laid it carefully on the seat beside him, and began to write. Nnanji watched in astonishment and then turned to look inquiringly at Wallie.

"That is the sorcerers' greatest magic, Nnanji. Lord Rotanxi is being very trusting in showing you."

"But what is he doing?" Nnanji whispered.

Wallie tried to explain, and his young companion's invisible eyebrows rose impossibly high, crumpling the seven swords on his forehead. Storing words?

"What sutra would you impose, Shonsu?" demanded Rotanxi, peering over his glasses. Wallie told him and he wrote it down.

"And on your side?" Wallie asked.

"How about this? 'Violence is the prerogative of the swordsmen. The sorcerers' arcane knowledge shall not be used to harm or kill or to make weapons.'"

"That would do very well," Wallie said.

The sorcerer put away his writing equipment and leaned back in thought again, gazing up at the rigging.

"I should go and get some blankets, brother!" Nnanji said through chattering teeth.

Wallie shook his head. To leave now would break the spell. A stench of sulfur filled the air and the unladen ship rocked uneasily, but history was being made on this spot, at this moment. His life as Shonsu would be judged by what happened here.

"Swordsmen have been killing sorcerers for thousands of years," Rotanxi murmured. "Now that we have the power to retaliate, they want peace?" He was rehearsing an argument.

"More than three hundred swordsmen have died here in the last fifteen years. My side is howling for blood, also."

The sorcerer nodded, then went still again, as if he had frozen to death.

At long last his vulpine old eyes came back to Wallie. "It might work! I can testify that the leader of the swordsmen is a man of honor, my lord. I admit that you have done well at winning me over, these last few weeks."

There was praise indeed.

"I speak for the swordsmen," Wallie said. "Who speaks for the sorcerers? Is there a Grand Wizard of Vul?"

Rotanxi shook his head. "We have a council of thirteen. There are factions, those who wish to drive out the barbarous swordsmen, and those who say that our mission is the quest for knowledge, that government is not our business."

"The hawks and the doves?"

"Mm? Good metaphor! I admit that I was a hawk, my lord. If I change sides, I may carry some votes—if I am allowed a hearing, that is." He frowned once more.

"Why should you not be?"

The shrewd old eyes smiled cynically. "I shall have the same problem you had. I shall be regarded as a turncoat."

"I have been very careful," Wallie said, "not to reveal anything that I might have learned from you."

Rotanxi shrugged. "I sneer at your swordsman brutality, my lord, but I admit that we sorcerers are not without a few barbarities of our own. If I fail, then I shall be given to the tormentors."

"Then . . . your honor shall be the greater," Wallie stammered.

"Mm? Honor is a fine reward, but a poor consolation. And I can do nothing about the other covens, you understand. Only Vul."

"But Vul could advise them?"

Rotanxi nodded. "As you say, the World will take time and be harder. But if it worked here, we could hope that the example would encourage others."

Wallie glanced again at Nnanji. The grin was wider than ever. Apparently sorcerers would listen to reason, as Wallie had hoped, and apparently Rotanxi was going to cooperate. He might, of course, be utterly untrustworthy, seeking only to return to his own side and report on the swordsmen's plans, but that risk was worth taking. And Nnanji, incredibly, was now in favor. Could Nnanji persuade the other swordsmen?

Happy ending?

"What exactly do you propose, Shonsu?" the sorcerer demanded abruptly, switching from thought to action.

"You and I must swear an oath, I suppose," Wallie said—he had hardly got this far in his thinking. "We will swear to work for this peace we envisage. I shall return you to the left bank, and you will put it to your council. If they agree, then we shall make a formal treaty. Of course the tryst will need victory parades, with bands, so that they can say they won, but not more than fifty men per town. I shall put garrisons back into the cities, and I shall choose good men, no young hellions—"

"Vul is excluded! No swordsman has ever entered Vul."

"Certainly! But the sorcerers will remain as honored citizens and will be admitted to the other seven cities of the loop also. Then we shall worry about the rest of the World, working together, sending forth swordsman and sorcerer side by side to spread the word."

"It is a staggering concept!" the sorcerer muttered. "But worth striving for. To do our best—that is all that we two can swear to."

"In my other world, a god once said *Blessed are the peacemakers*."

Rotanxi nodded. "However..." His tone changed. "I see one immediate problem. You have an army in place. I believe that you are a man of honor, but my comrades will naturally suspect a trap. Many of the city wizards are members of the council. For there to be a meeting, they must travel to Vul."

Wallie saw what was coming, like a great black bird descending.

"At this time of year the roads may be difficult. We shall need time, at least twenty days, there and back again."

Winter was near. The longer the swordsmen's attack could be delayed the better—for the sorcerers.

"How many?" Wallie demanded harshly. "Who?"

Rotanxi looked thoughtfully at Nnanji. "I think one would suffice—a Seventh and co-leader of the tryst, oath brother to Lord Shonsu. He would be ideal."

Appalled, furious that he had not foreseen this, Wallie turned to Nnanji.

Nnanji shrugged. "I shall wear my sword, though!"

Rotanxi hesitated and then said, "I suppose so. You will be the first swordsman ever to enter Vul, Lord Nnanji—assuming that we are allowed so far."

Wallie said, "He would not be expected to negotiate?"

"No, merely a hostage for your good faith. He may be asked about you, of course, and how the other swordsmen feel." The sorcerer smiled faintly. "My colleagues will be surprised by his youth, but by then the meeting will be in session."

"What guarantees do you give for his safe return?"

"Only my own word, my lord. If my plea is rejected, then he will suffer the same fate as myself. Being younger, he will take longer to die."

Nnanji seemed unconcerned, even pleased, at the prospect. *How Nnanji of the Seventh Went to Vul . . .*

"Come with me!" Wallie said. Grabbing him by the shoulder, he hauled Nnanji off his stool and almost dragged him along the deck, out of earshot. "I can't allow this!"

Nnanji chuckled. "You can't stop it."

"Oh! Can't I? I'm not going to swear that oath, Nnanji, not on those terms! This council of his may be a gang of mad dogs. Rotanxi himself may be treacherous—as long as all I was gambling was a couple of weeks' delay, then the wager was worth it! But I'm not going to gamble you, oath brother. You were seen killing sorcerers in Ov—"

"I repeat: You can't stop it! It is preordained."

"What?"

"Don't you see? We always said that I would have a part to play in your mission. This is it, at last! This is why I was made your oath brother, why I became a Seventh! Better than counting pigeons! And I promised Arganari I would wear his hairclip to Vul! Of course I didn't know I would be going as a hostage . . ." He laughed. "It's destiny, Shonsu, the will of the Goddess!" Then he added with relish, "The first swordsman ever to enter Vul!"

He leaned back against the rail and smirked mockingly. "Unless you want to go yourself?"

The idea was enough to make Wallie's gut heave. He would be thrown into the nearest torture chamber and laid on the rack, producing a secret a day for the sorcerers like a battery hen, a one-man industrial revolution. He could easily imagine that sour old Rotanxi wielding his hot irons—and that thought made him realize how very little he really trusted the sorcerer.

"Nnanji! Your oaths are my oaths! Suppose they make you swear to disband the tryst?"

Even Nnanji could pause at that prospect. Then he said, "I promise you that they will not succeed, brother."

"You won't enjoy it while they're trying!"

Nnanji shrugged, then his smile returned.

"We'll send two of the other Sevenths!" Wallie insisted.

Nnanji's smile vanished. "Send vassals into danger? To do my duty?"

Perhaps it was only Wallie's imagination, but he thought then that he saw something change in Nnanji's eyes, saw something he had been dreading he might one day see. The killer look? *It is your kingdom that I covet*? He knew then that Nnanji would not be denied this chance for honor and fame.

Once he had joked that Nnanji was an egg that was going to hatch something extraordinary. Now, suddenly, he saw what it was. Take a lanky, red-haired, jovial young man of courage and honor, add swordsmanship and a few miracles, marinate in all those epics and sagas . . .

Wallie had always denied being an epic hero. Even Doa's epic was not named after him. But he knew one when he saw one.

"Right, brother?" Nnanji thumped Wallie's shoulder and grinned.

"I . . ." He could not find words.

Chuckling, Nnanji went swaggering back toward the sorcerer. Wallie followed, his mind whirling. Why had he not been more insistent? Was he trying to rid himself of a threat?

Had the gods created Nnanji to be nothing more than a sacrificial martyr, whose death would inspire the tryst?

Rotanxi looked up at them appraisingly. "I have my hostage, Shonsu?"

Wallie nodded. "Twenty days. But if he is harmed in any way, then I swear that I will bring the tryst to Vul and raze it, no matter what the cost! And I have eight sorcerers in my dungeons, remember!"

The sorcerer shrugged. "Of course. Now we need to swear our oaths, we two?"

"I suppose so." Wallie sat down limply. His brief euphoria was wearing thin. He could see complications springing up like thorns all around him. He felt ashamed and horrified at betraying Nnanji. "I should put this to my own council first, my lord. They must obey, but I would prefer to have willing agreement."

The sorcerer nodded shrewdly. "Yes. I should have assurance that the liege lord will not meet with an unexpected accident."

"Let us go and meet them, then." Wallie glanced around and saw that Tomiyano was still on deck, leaning on the rail, openly watching. Wallie rose and went over to him warily.

"If you have a crew handy, Captain, it would be all right to take the ship in now. I waive dock fees!"

The sailor studied him in silence for a moment. Then he said, "You're crazy."

"What now?" Wallie asked angrily.

"Him!" Tomiyano gestured, but which of the two he meant Wallie was not sure: the tall, imposing sorcerer or the lithe, taller, red-haired swordsman. They were deep in conversation already, the bitter enmity of an hour ago apparently discarded. Oh, let that be an omen!

"You were spying, were you?" Wallie had forgotten that sailors could read lips.

"A council of thirteen Rotanxis?" Tomiyano sneered. "Can you imagine it?"

"Barely."

"And you're going to send that boy to them? The first thing they'll ask him is how many sorcerers he's killed."

And Nnanji would tell them.

"I don't think I can stop him." It sounded weak even to Wallie as he said it, but it was the truth.

Tomiyano was furious, his voice rising. "You know what they'll see when they look at him? A trained killer! A boy monster! I don't suppose sorcerers reach seventh rank until they're sixty at least. They'll be a bunch of frightened old men, Shonsu, and you're suggesting something totally new. You want them to trust you—and you send *Nnanji*? You're making my sister a widow, damn you! Do you suppose they'll send some bits of him back to her as souvenirs?"

†† † ††

The circle of seven had now become a circle of eight. Seven swordsmen sat on stools, the solitary sorcerer in a chair. The fire crackled and sparked, sometimes blowing out clouds of smoke as the wind gusted. Likely the chimney had not been swept in a century.

Yet the group of eight held subgroups. Rotanxi was a conspicuous minority of one in his cowled gown. The old man was understandably wary, a solitary cat in a doghouse, being cautious and courteous.

Wallie himself felt strangely isolated, the other swordsmen's suspicion walling him in like thick glass. As he described the tentative agreement he had made with the sorcerer, he could feel his words bouncing off it. They did not want to hear.

And Nnanji was another group all to himself. He was staying silent, sinewy arms folded and ankles crossed, gazing at his boots with a secret smile teasing the corners of his mouth. Even the silver pelicans on the rug did not upset him now.

The other five Sevenths were implacable. They had been given time to think about a treaty, and they thought even less of it afterward than they had before. Be nice to sorcerers? Shameful! A twenty-day truce with winter coming? Insanity! Liege Nnanji as hostage? Outrageous! All their war preparations to be thrown away? Treason! They were not saying so, but their opinion was obvious. Rotanxi could not help but notice. He would surely withdraw from the agreement if he felt that Shonsu could not count on the willing support of even his senior officers.

Then Wallie played what he thought was his trump card, his argument-for-sorcerers that had apparently converted Nnanji—if this struggle goes ahead, then swordsmen and even civilians will get hold of the sorcerers' weapons. It did not work. It was too farfetched and hypothetical for the Sevenths. Their icy disapproval did not thaw in the slightest.

Nnanji caught Wallie's eye, grinned faintly, and shook his head. Nnanji was being uncharacteristically telepathic this day and he was saying that this was not the argument to use.

But what was? Why had he come around so dramatically? Even Wallie did not know, and the other Sevenths certainly did not. Nnanji had them all baffled—they kept staring at him, trying to understand his inexplicable change of heart.

Finally Wallie asked for comments or questions. A pall of silence fell, like earth on a coffin lid. As it dragged on, Rotanxi turned and gave him a quizzical and cynical glance—this is your support?

Wallie's temper began to stir. Stupid iron-age barbarians! Ignorant savages! Why had he been given this impossible task? For the first time since his early days in the temple at Hann, he felt a great longing for his old life on Earth come washing over him and a bottomless contempt for this primitive culture and its muleheaded swordsmen. Almost he could want to wash his hands of the whole affair, of the tryst, of the gods' mission. He could take Jja down to the River and find a ship and sail away to be a water rat for the rest of his days . . .

Which would be few and nasty, if he defied the Goddess.

"Shonsu," Nnanji said, "perhaps we should allow the valiant lords a chance to discuss this without the sorcerer present?" He could not portray innocence nearly as well as his duplicitous brother could. He was plotting something. Wallie hesitated and then concluded that he had no choice. He would have to trust Nnanji.

"Very well! My lord?" Wallie rose and escorted Rotanxi to the door. As he had expected, Nnanji stayed where he was. The door closed behind them, Rotanxi turned to say something . . .

But Wallie had already gone.

There were only a few bodyguards remaining in the long antechamber—and Jja. He had set her on a stool and told her to wait, certain that she would be safe there, after what had happened the last time she had visited the lodge. Safe from swordsmen—but now she was standing with eyes downcast in front of a very tall woman in blue. Wallie hurtled along the room with giant strides.

"Doa!"

"Ah, there you are, my dear!" the minstrel said in a voice that would have swarmed bees.

"I am very busy today, my lady!"

"That's quite all right, *darling*. I was just interviewing this slave."

"Interviewing?"

Doa's large mouth showed all her teeth in a smile. "This is Jja, is it not? The one you promised to give me?"

For a moment her audacity left Wallie speechless. Jja was being as silent as a rock.

He had never seen them together before—and the glint in Doa's eye said plainly that he had better choose which one he wanted.

Then Jja looked up at him, and the appeal he saw there would have hauled the sun god down from his heaven.

He stepped between them and put an arm around Jja, wondering what rubbish Doa had been saying. The swordsmen were listening and trying to appear otherwise. He must not lose his temper.

Jja moved against him, seeking contact. He remembered his momentary dream of sailing away into the sunset, and remembered who had been included in that dream. Not Doa.

"Yes, this is Jja. Jja, my love, this is Lady Doa. I am not planning to give you to her. Whatever she told you, she was lying."

Doa's face flamed scarlet. The swordsmen were being very quiet.

"Honorable Forarfi!" Wallie was keeping his voice calm only by immense effort. "Escort Lady Doa from the lodge. See that she is not admitted in future. My lady, I shall not be available this evening to escort you to the healers' banquet."

He thought for a moment that Doa was going to spring at him. He rather hoped she would.

"I shall go to the banquet anyway! They want me to sing. I have some new songs to try."

"Watch your tongue, minstrel, or you will sing them to rats in the dungeon."

Doa gasped, then she wheeled around and stalked toward the door.

Wallie put his other arm around Jja also. "I am sorry, my love, so very sorry! Don't believe her, whatever she said."

Jja just stared up at him, searching.

"Wallie?" she whispered.

"Who else?"

The door to the council chamber flew open and Nnanji's voice sang out. "Brother!"

But Wallie was busy and did not hear. It was Jja who finally broke the embrace. "They are waiting for you, my love," she whispered.

"Let them!" Wallie said, and kissed her again, for several more minutes. When he eventually released her and headed back to the meeting, he was feeling lightheaded and so aroused that he wondered if he even cared what happened to the tryst.

He had made a dangerous enemy in Doa.

Who cared? He saw at once that the mood of the meeting had changed. The five Sevenths were all beaming. Rotanxi, standing in their midst, was attempting to hide his lack of understanding under an aristocratic sneer.

And Nnanji was grinning from shoulder to shoulder. "I think the valiant lords have come around, brother!"

"It is a noble cause, my liege!" Zoariyi proclaimed. As the oldest, he was the natural spokesman. "Lord Nnanji has indeed persuaded me."

The others nodded, smiling and apparently excited.

How?

Why?

Who cared? Wallie looked to Rotanxi and shrugged. "Then we can go ahead and swear our oaths, my lord?"

The sorcerer nodded uneasily. "What arguments did you use, Lord Nnanji, exactly?"

Nnanji smirked. "Exactly? Exactly the arguments that Lord Shonsu gave you, my lord, and that you accepted. Word for word, and nothing else, I swear." He was enjoying himself enormously. Being able to mystify Wallie was a new experience for him. "Shonsu, for an oath like this you ought to summon the priests!"

"I suppose so."

"Then why not take Lord Rotanxi to the dungeons while we wait?" He sniggered at Wallie's expression. "To show him how swordsmen treat prisoners? And meanwhile—" He swung around in high glee to the castellan. "—Lord Tivanixi and I have time for our fencing match!"

Dungeons were dungeons—dark, dank, and damp, smelling of urine and rats. Wallie had been insistent that the prisoners were to be well treated. By the standards of the World, he had been obeyed. He let Rotanxi speak to them in private, assuming that the old man would explain that they were now counterhostages and therefore not in immediate danger. It would have been interesting to hear what they thought of the proposed treaty and its chances.

Yet dungeons were dungeons, and it was a relief to emerge once more into fresh air, even the fresh air of the lodge courtyard, tainted by the numerous outhouses and bathhouses now filling it. Their canvas still flapped and thumped, but over that noise Wallie heard a distant cheer.

"We still have some time to kill, my lord," he suggested. "How about viewing a little fencing? Not your favorite sport, I should imagine, but another interesting tale to take back."

The sorcerer was still blinking in the bright daylight. "Indeed!" he said. "But first tell me what happened with Lord Nnanji? How did he persuade the others?"

"If he says he used the same arguments, my lord, then I must believe him. I admit I don't understand."

Rotanxi frowned, worried. "If it were anyone else—even, with respect, yourself, Lord Shonsu—I should suspect treachery. But him . . ." He shook his head. During his captivity on *Sapphire*, he had come to know Nnanji. Even a sorcerer could not expect duplicity from Nnanji. Nnanji would commit murder with a smile, but he would not lie about it.

Wallie led the way, through the tunnel and the archway to the steps before the lodge, evicting a half-dozen middleranks to make room. The polo matches were over, and now the assembled swordsmen were watching fencing. Almost every man seemed to have an arm around a woman as he celebrated this holiday. Few noticed the sinister sorcerer standing with their liege.

In the center of this huge circle of onlookers, Nnanji and Tivanixi were dancing to and fro among the dung heaps, flashing foils.

"Ooo!" said the crowd, and Nnanji capered to show that he had a hit.

"The score?" Wallie demanded of a nearby Third.

"Two nothing, my liege. Best of five."

Then the fencers closed again, whirling foils too fast to follow, leaping forward and back, impersonally masked, ponytails jumping. The crowd roared at a narrow escape, but neither man claimed a point and the battle continued. Wallie had never watched a match between Sevenths before. High-speed ballet with steel—it was magnificent, the grace of born athletes in motion. He noted how tall Nnanji was, compared to Tivanixi, and how fast. Here and there he recognized some of his own favorite moves, but most were too quick for even him to analyze. Superb experts, inspiring each other . . .

"*Ahh!*" That was it, the match point. Nnanji's mask spun high in the air, his whoop of triumph lost in the roar as the crowd surged forward. Tivanixi's face appeared, flushed and grinning, and he raised his foil in salute, while Nnanji was swept up on shoulders to be marched around the plaza.

Wallie stared in astonishment. So now Nnanji was a believable Seventh, not a convenient fiction, and a very good Seventh if he could beat Tivanixi. That just did not seem possible! Nnanji was a lightning-fast learner, but to reach such a level so quickly? Four weeks ago, he had barely made Sixth. Surely the castellan had thrown that match, faking it as a tribute to Nnanji's display of courage in agreeing to go as hostage to Vul? If he had, would Nnanji have been able to detect the fraud?

The display of popularity was even more surprising. The

smart-aleck kid had gained acceptance by sheer perseverance, with sweat and innumerable bruises. A short while ago he had won over the Sevenths and now, apparently, the rest of the swordsmen, also.

Wallie turned to speak to the sorcerer and saw satisfaction on his face. A popular hostage was a valuable hostage.

Before they could speak, however, two sedan chairs appeared at the side of the steps. Honakura and Kadywinsi disembarked in a fluster of attendant priests and priestesses.

Wallie's first reaction to Honakura was delight. A ruddiness had replaced the ominous pallor. Then the old man came creeping up the steps, leaning on a younger priest. At close quarters his skin had a strange transparency to it, and the brightness in his eyes was febrile. Sometimes a candle will flare up momentarily, just before it gutters out?

Wallie saluted and presented Rotanxi, all of them having to shout above the continuing roar of the crowd.

"You are in good health, holy one?"

The old eyes sparkled up at him. "Not especially. But I see that you are—and you have your treaty!"

His face asked a question.

Wallie nodded meaningfully. *He is enthusiastic*!

Honakura raised an eyebrow. *Why?*

Wallie shrugged. *I don't know!*

"We were just watching some fencing, my lord," he said. "Lord Nnanji has just beaten Lord Tivanixi, the third best man in the tryst."

Honakura nodded, understanding. "We priests have a saying, Lord Shonsu: *The pupil may be greater than the teacher*."

And Wallie, in turn, understood that. It could only be the epigram from the same sutra as the story of the red-haired brother. The epitome would deal with mentors' obligations, of course. Well, he did not think Nnanji was quite there yet—but he had no desire to find out, certainly not with blades.

Then Kadywinsi arrived, and the salutes began again. The crowd noise billowed louder. Wallie glanced over heads in time to see Boariyi's grinning face vanish inside a mask. Nnanji was being borne shoulder-high toward him, waving his foil and laughing. Would Boariyi also throw a match for him?

The liege lord could not stay to watch. He must escort his guests indoors. He did not really want to watch, anyway.

When they reached the council chamber, they found it full of busy swordsmen. Jja was there, also, and Honakura greeted her with warmth and affection, shocking the other priests by demanding a kiss.

Linumino had been efficient, as usual. The bed had gone; chairs had appeared from somewhere for the guests; tables bore white cloths and refreshments. There was even a small brazier by the fireplace so that Rotanxi might swear over fire without setting his gown ablaze.

Important oaths were sworn before priests. Oaths of great significance required seven of them, one of each rank, to combine status and longevity. Wallie had to meet them all. He already knew a few of them, including the surly priestess of the Third who had brought him Honakura's message on his first day in Casr. Eventually he settled the old man on a chair, fetched him a glass of wine, and had a moment for a private word.

"Nnanji approves?" Honakura whispered.

Wallie told how Nnanji had not merely approved of the treaty, but had also convinced the others.

The old man shook his head in wonder. "We did indeed teach him well, my lord!" But he was as puzzled as Wallie. A treaty with swordsman killers? It was totally out of character.

Then other Sevenths came streaming in—Tivanixi, Zoariyi, Jansilui—and the salutes began again. Eventually Boariyi and Nnanji appeared also, hot and sweaty, grinning like children—and Thana, more catlike than ever.

When Nnanji arrived at Wallie his eyes were dancing.

"You won again?"

"Straight points again!" He was so pleased with himself that he was almost giggling. "Sure you can't spare a few minutes, Shonsu?"

"Quite sure! We'll do it when you return!"

Disappointed, Nnanji nodded. "Get lots of practice, then!"

Wallie smiled tolerantly.

"Brother?" Nnanji said softly. "Tell me the exact words you are going to swear?"

"Why?"

"Because I am bound also."

"True! Sorry!" Wallie told him the oath he had prepared. Nnanji smiled cryptically and nodded again.

"Remember—lots of practice!" he said and moved on.

It had to be a setup, did it not? Tivanixi and Boariyi had cooked it up between them?

Never!

They put too much value on their status as top fencers. They would not throw that away, even for Nnanji. Certainly neither would have faked a straight-points defeat. Three–two, just maybe, but three–nothing was humiliation. So no trickery; Nnanji had trashed them both. Nnanji and Shonsu were the two best.

Which left only one question.

Three–nothing, against *Boariyi*!

The meeting had come to order. The priests and priestesses were lined up and waiting, all except Honakura, who had stayed in his chair, insisting he had come only to watch. Wallie stepped to the center and drew his sword, glancing around at the company—priests and swordsmen, heralds and minstrels. Jja was there, also, at his insistence, trying to be invisible in one corner, staying close to Thana.

Then Wallie swung back for another look at the cluster of minstrels. Doa! She smirked at him over the others' heads. How had she managed to return? He had given orders—but he had only given them to Forarfi, who had now been sent to charter a ship. Of course Linumino would have specified that Lady Doa be included with the minstrels. Angrily he turned his back on her, facing toward the priests.

He raised the seventh sword to the oath position, at arm's length, pointing over the witnesses' heads. *I, Shonsu, swordsman of the seventh rank, liege lord . . .*

History was made then. The senior swordsman of the World swore to work for peace with sorcerers. No miracle intervened. No thunder rolled. No earthquake threw down the lodge on his head. It was almost an anticlimax.

He stepped back, and Rotanxi came forward to extend one hand above the brazier and swear his oath, also.

And still the World did not move.

Wallie shook Rotanxi's hand. The witnesses cheered and applauded.

That was it? Epochs end so quietly? Wallie had a whirling sensation of unreality. He had expected more, somehow.

He noted that the Sevenths were looking puzzled again, and worried.

"My lords . . ." He gestured toward the table of refreshments.

"Shonsu?"

Wallie stiffened. "Yes, Nnanji?"

"I also wish to swear an oath." Nnanji smiled apologetically.

"I trust that you will share it with me first?"

Nnanji nodded, then could no longer restrain a huge and childlike grin. "I have solved the god's riddle for you, brother! I know how you must return the sword. And I know its destiny!"

The audience waited. Jja, Honakura, Tivanixi seemed startled, the rest only puzzled. Wallie was thinking furiously.

Old Kadywinsi spoke first. "The seventh sword? The sword of the Goddess? She sent it to lead the tryst against the sorcerers, didn't She?"

"Not really, holiness," Nnanji said. "The sorcerers have nothing to do with it. The sorcerers are not important at all."

What in the World was going on under that red hair? What had Nnanji seen that Wallie could have missed? "So how do I return the sword, brother Nnanji?"

"You go to Quo, where it was made."

Wallie stared at him, apprehensive, totally baffled. "Quo?"

"Perhaps you would like to have a private word, brother?"

Wallie said he thought that would be a very good idea.

††† †††

There were swordsmen in the anteroom and swordsmen standing around the door. "Upstairs!" Nnanji said. Wallie trotted up after him; but there were two dormitories on the next floor, and vacationing swordsmen there, also.

"Top floor—race you!" Nnanji sprinted off up the stairs like an excited child. Wallie followed more slowly, worrying his problem as a puppy worries a slipper. Whatever Nnanji was thinking, he was very sure of himself. Always he had deferred to Shonsu, but that had been because Shonsu was the greatest swordsman in the World, thus a hero. Now who was greatest?

And why Quo?

Why Quo?

He reached the top and was surprised to see that the museum door was open, the great bar leaning against the wall. A slim, red-haired swordsman was wandering along beside the tables, studying the wall of swords. He turned at the end and came back on the other side, looking now at the litter on the tables themselves. Wallie stood just inside the room, waiting with folded arms.

"Nothing moved!" Nnanji said, beaming. "Just as we left it, on Merchants' Day, when you gave me my sword. We forgot to have the bar put back, brother! I forgot!" He snickered. "But no one's taken a thing. That's very good!"

Wallie waited.

"Right!" Nnanji folded his arms also. "Now, let's make sure I understand. We all swear to the new sutra. You put two hundred men or so into the seven cities as garrisons. You make everyone swear to spread the word about sorcerers being nice boys. Then you disband the tryst. Do I have it right?"

Wallie nodded.

Nnanji swung around and began to pace. "And the sorcerers will destroy their fire weapons—but we have to take that on trust, don't we?"

He took down a sword and hefted it. "That is tricky, isn't it? The sorcerers won't be outnumbered any more. They can hold a massacre any time. Splash? Two hundred splashes."

Wallie found his voice. "But we went over all that this morning. We must have a treaty; and it's for the good of the sorcerers, too. It's a risk, yes, but we must trust them, just as they must trust us."

Still studying the sword, Nnanji said quietly, "The sorcerers are not the problem."

Wallie gaped. Then it was obvious. Sooner or later some idiot swordsman would pick a fight with a sorcerer—in a bar, over a girl, or just to show how tough he was. The wizard would demand justice from the reeve, and . . . and what?

"Oh, hell!" Wallie said. "Damn! Damn! Damn!"

He leaned against a table and put his hands over his face. He had been judging the swordsmen by their sutras and the Sevenths of his council, who were exceptional. He had overlooked Hardduju and Tarru, the rapists of Yok, the drunks at Wo, the fossil at Tau, even the initial chaos in Casr—all the bad swordsmen he had met and should have remembered. Swordsmen swore their superhuman oaths, and perhaps most of them tried their best, but in reality they were a very mixed bag—often corrupted by power, unsupervised, laws unto themselves—better than anarchy, but far from perfect. It would take near-perfection to make his plan work. Nnanji had always understood the swordsmen better than he, and if Nnanji said it would not work, then it would not. Wallie had promised Rotanxi the World. He could not even deliver the seven cities.

Failure as a bottomless pit! Wishful thinking—he had been so reluctant to fight a war that he had invented an impossible peace. And now he had sworn an oath and thrown away the tryst.

Disaster!

"But why now?" he wailed, looking up. "Why not say so in the council?"

Nnanji replaced the sword and shrugged. "Swordsmen don't say such things about their own craft. We all know it, but we don't talk about it." He continued his wanderings.

"But Rotanxi swore—"

"Ah, yes! But he didn't bind his friends, did he? They know about the fourth oath, so I go into the first convenient dungeon. He'll start with my toenails, I expect, as I suggested that approach to him."

"What! You're joking!"

"True!" Nnanji admitted. "But we should remove the temptation!"

Wallie shivered. "You're right! I should have thought of that. So you're planning to swear that the tryst will not be disbanded, not until the garrisons are in place?"

Nnanji was back in front of him.

"Why then?" he said.

"Huh?"

Nnanji grinned. "It's funny; you've got an odd way of saying things, sometimes, Shonsu. I understand you now, but... Rotanxi said, 'Admit it—the tryst must be disbanded.' Remember? And you said, 'I admit nothing.' What he *thought* you promised was that you—the liege lord—would make the cities safe for sorcerers. That the tryst would keep order, as it does in Casr. He was willing to accept that, and when I repeated your words to the Sevenths, that was what they understood, too." He smirked. "Perhaps I changed the emphasis a little, but I used the same words. Then you didn't put it in your oath; we must keep the tryst in being!"

Relief washed over Wallie like a spring thaw.

"Of course!" he said. "That would work! We keep the garrisons sworn by the third oath!"

Nnanji nodded and grinned again. "And we hold a group of good swordsmen here in Casr. If there is any nonsense in any of the cities, we go and . . . educate them!"

"And it wouldn't cost much more, just a few extra men!" Now Wallie could smile. "You had me scared, Nnanji! But I think that will work." He had wondered what he would do after the tryst was disbanded. Now he had job security.

Then his mood went black again.

"But that only solves the problem of the seven cities. I promised the World."

"Ah!" Nnanji set off on his rambling once more. "The god's riddle—return the sword. That's why you have to go to Quo, brother, where Chioxin lived."

"Why? What's special about Quo?"

"Think strategy!" Nnanji said from the middle of the room. "Nine ninety-three, ten seventy. The loop is closed, almost. You can't go upstream from Ov or down from Aus, right? Not easily. Quo is our front door, our door to the World. Not only a permanent tryst, Shonsu, but a universal tryst!" His voice rose with excitement. "*Do you see now?* We send the Sevenths out from Quo, to every city on the River. They will swear the garrisons to the tryst! By force, if necessary."

Wallie roared with laughter. "Steady there, laddie!" he said. "We can't make every swordsman in the World into our vassal!"

Nnanji was not laughing.

"We have to! It's the only way to make the World safe for sorcerers—which was what you just swore that we would do, oath brother! And it will safeguard the garrisons—we'll have a huge tryst to call on if the sorcerers play false. Even Vul would be no problem then."

If you must dream, dream big! Liege lords of all swordsmen?

Nnanji's eyes gleamed. "More important, at the same time we'll clean up the whole craft—dispose of the crooks and the bullies and the sadists. Weed out the bad swordsmen and leave the good. Then every city and town can have a decent, honest, honorable garrison!"

Here was the juvenile reformer, shining with enthusiasm, the young idealist set to remake the World. That was why he had seemed so pleased!

"Tell me why it won't work!" Nnanji said, pacing restlessly, excited by his vision. His boots tapped and the boards squeaked.

There was a ship waiting. This would have to be quick. "Money!"

"Money?" Nnanji echoed scornfully. "The swordsmen ate before—they can eat in future. We'll find a way."

"Nnanji!" Wallie spoke very gently, as if talking to a child. "Not all swordsmen will want to be your vassal. What do your henchmen do if a man refuses to swear?"

"*Blood needs be shed* . . . but the honorable ones will swear quite happily."

"*Courage is the highest honor* . . ."

"Only in a good cause!"

This was more than idealism. This was fanaticism! Wallie felt the beginnings of fear.

"And what if Boariyi, say, runs into a better man? What if it's your man who gets killed, Nnanji?"

Nnanji was by the door, inspecting a jumble of standards stacked against the wall. He pulled one out and coughed in the dust. Then he grinned at Wallie. "I thought that bit would bother you! You send me. I'm the greatest swordsman in the World—except you. Maybe you? But I'll look after that job for you, brother!"

So this was the destiny he had seen on the ship: Nnanji the

Avenger, terror of the ungodly. No wonder he had looked so pleased! Katanji was being led to great wealth—was this Nnanji's reward? Chief Enforcer for the Goddess . . . he would like nothing better.

Wallie shivered. He had created a monster.

"What about geography?" he asked, as calmly as he could. "What happens if you try to go to Hither and the Goddess sends you to Yon?"

"She will support us!" Nnanji said, surprised. "Surely you see how the gods have been helping me? I got miracles, too!"

Megalomania!

Nnanji the messiah—he would set up a military dictatorship. Like Caesar. Like Cromwell. It could lead only to tyranny.

Wallie was sweating, wondering if he could bring himself to do whatever would be needed to stop this. "And the free swords?"

But Nnanji had worked out all the answers. "The same with them. If necessary we'll ride them down with your cavalry. They can keep their jobs, but we'll assign each group an area, and regional headquarters over them, eventually. Just like the cities —any complaints come back here, to me . . . us, I mean."

It was not only megalomania. Impossible courage, no scruples—Nnanji was a psychopath, and that should have been obvious from the beginning. He liked to play with babies, and he had wept at Gi. He was a fond husband and brother . . . but he was also a truly remorseless killer. He had enjoyed killing pirates and sorcerers. Wallie had thought that Nnanji had mellowed, from the debaucher of the barracks to the troubadour who had courted Thana so patiently. Not so!

"What about the council?" he asked, playing for time to think.

"They love the idea! Swordplay and honor? Better than building catapults, brother!" He thumped the flagstaff on the floor enthusiastically and was showered by dust again.

The tryst had carried him shoulder high.

"There will be resistance!" Wallie warned. "Refugee swordsmen setting up countertrysts."

"If it comes to battles, we shall have the numbers—and soon all the best men, too."

There must be a flaw! Now Wallie started to pace, groping for some logical way to end this madness peacefully, to convince Nnanji before Nnanji convinced him. "Thousands of swordsmen —their performances and histories and reliability—hundreds of cities and garrisons. How do you keep track of it all?"

Nnanji just laughed.

"Communications, then? After a few weeks the distances will become impossible."

Nnanji spread the flag to look at the faded emblems. "Fast boats, horse posts, and pigeons! The sorcerers will support the tryst because it protects them. I saw what Rotanxi was doing with that feather, remember!"

He was right again. A permanent and universal tryst must seem a mortal threat to the sorcerers. Vul itself would be in jeopardy. Wallie had convinced Rotanxi with an argument he had not even known he was presenting—small wonder that the old man had grabbed at the chance of the treaty! The sorcerers could provide communications and record keeping. They would seek to make themselves indispensable, and in so doing, they would perpetuate the dictatorship.

Wallie had proposed peace between the swordsmen and the sorcerers. He had not seen that the gods might have been keeping them apart for very good reasons.

But it was possible.

Wallie thought: *It would work. I will have to do it, or Nnanji will try, and I may not have the power to stop him anymore. Nnanji is an illiterate barbarian, who knows nothing but killing. I am an educated and a peace-loving man. I know the dangers and could avoid them. . . . Is this my reward, omnipotence? I can be a benevolent despot, Emperor of the World, with a government and a palace . . .*

His head swam with the vision. He could imagine the court, the honor guards of kilted swordsmen, the courtiers standing on both sides of the great aisle, and the petitioners creeping forward, bowing to the throne, to the Son of Heaven sitting there, holding the sword of the Goddess as symbol of his authority. . .

It could be done! There was nothing in the World to stop him. Nnanji would happily be chief of the army and Shonsu could be emperor.

And on the other throne, at his side . . .

The vision was so clear that he could almost turn his head and see her . . .

Who?

Nnanji leaned on the pole and waited, smiling.

And waited . . .

And waited . . .

Wallie looked up sadly. "The last thing the god told me," he said, "was that the guard on my sword hilt was a griffon, and that the griffon meant *Power wisely used*. He said that if I remembered that, I would not fail. It was a warning, Nnanji! He foresaw this temptation! The Goddess has given me power. I do not think that using power to gain more power is wise."

"Well, I do! In a good cause."

"Then I should have the greater problem of using the greater power wisely. An hour ago I threatened to throw Doa in the dungeons if she made fun of me—I'm not good enough, Nnanji."

Nnanji frowned. "Then you must step aside and let me do it."

The prophecy: *It is your kingdom that I covet*.

Wallie straightened up. Argument was always useless against fanaticism, and there were no words for despot or tyranny or dictatorship anyway.

"No," he said. "The tryst was called against the sorcerers. You are planning to turn it against the swordsmen! You don't know what it will lead to, Nnanji. I won't do it!"

"The tryst was called to restore the honor of the craft. The sorcerers are not important! I told you!"

"No!" Wallie insisted. "Do you remember the first lesson I ever gave you? We sat together on a wall in the temple grounds, in the shade of a tree. I told you then—power corrupts!"

"Not me!"

I am more worthy.

Stalemate.

Nnanji smiled hopefully. "You once said you would like to be reeve of Tau, didn't you? I will give it to you! And I will keep the tryst away, because I know you will be honorable."

Tyranny—already he was giving away cities? Wallie shook his head in silence.

Now Nnanji was becoming exasperated. "We agreed that the tryst can only have one leader. I have always deferred to you, have I not? Till this. Must we have the combat for leadership, round three, brother? But let's use foils and swear to abide by that."

An hour ago Wallie would have jumped at that offer.

They stared at each other, eyes level—black eyes and pale brown eyes and neither would yield.

It was Wallie who turned away. He stalked slowly down the long room, wrestling with the problem. How to stop this? If he could not, then no one could. He could no longer trust his sword against Nnanji. Could he bring himself to commit murder? Throw his knife, say?

He had reached the broken fragment of the Chioxin fifth, another desolate memorial to human stupidity. He stared at it bleakly. Murder?

"No!" he said loudly. "I am leader. You are going to Vul. I shall go down there and swear to disband the tryst as soon as the garrisons are in place. If they provoke a massacre later, it will be their own fault."

Nnanji slammed the door with a noise like thunder and dropped the flagpole into the brackets across it. Then he went pounding down the stairs. He was almost at the bottom before he heard the door exploding, seven floors above him.

"Jja?" Lord Honakura called in his cracked old voice.

Jja hurried over to him.

"Bring me another cake, would you, my dear?"

She slipped carefully through the munching, sipping guests to the nearest table and managed to capture a plate of cakes without jostling anyone. Thana was there.

"Whatever can they be doing?" Jja whispered.

"No idea!" Thana said with her mouth full. "Not fighting, I shouldn't think. Not unless Shonsu's gone crazy."

Jja did not like the expression on Thana's face. She went back to Lord Honakura and knelt by his chair. He thanked her and selected the creamiest cake on the dish.

"Stay here!" he commanded when she was about to rise. "Have one yourself!"

Smiling, she obeyed. She was happy to remain; she felt safe

beside him. The horrid minstrel woman had been eyeing her ever since Wallie left.

The sorcerer's voice cut suddenly through the uneasy chatter. "Your divided leadership perplexes me. What do you do if they disagree?"

Jja watched as the swordsmen glanced at one another. Somehow they selected Lord Tivanixi to carry the burden.

"We don't know, Lord Rotanxi. There are no precedents. In fact, I have never heard of the fourth oath ever being sworn before. I don't know why the Goddess made that sutra."

"Perhaps just for this occasion?" Lord Honakura mumbled, wiping cream from his chin. Probably no one but Jja heard.

"Why should a tryst need two leaders anyway?" one of the other lords asked.

"It has three, I think," Honakura remarked quietly, and now he was certainly speaking to Jja.

"Three, my lord?"

The little bald head nodded. "Shonsu, Nnanji—and Wallie-smith. Would you not say so?"

Jja nodded, surprised. Yet it was not quite true. Wallie had been missing since the day she had been stripped by the two Seconds, here in the lodge. That had been Shonsu who had lost his temper and sold the swordsmen, Shonsu who had struck her. When he returned to *Sapphire* the next day, he had still been Shonsu. He had been Shonsu on the ship this morning when he almost drew against the captain. She had not seen Wallie until later today, when he had rescued her from the minstrel woman. Wallie had been there then. Her heart had told her.

She thought it had been Wallie swearing that oath before the priests, but she suspected that it had been Shonsu again who had gone off with Lord Nnanji.

There was shouting in the anteroom. The door flew open and men scattered as Nnanji burst in, red-faced and waving his sword. He skidded wildly on the silk rug, recovered his balance, and came to a panting halt. Jja's heart sank. Where was her master? Nnanji peered around until he located little Lord Kadywinsi, then stretched out his blade in the oath position, facing the priest.

Without preamble he began: *I, Nnanji, swordsman of the seventh—*"

Honakura threw a cake at him.

"Young man," he snapped from his chair, "there are certain rituals that must be observed for oaths. If you wish my holy friends to be witnesses, then the least you could do is to ask their consent."

Nnanji spluttered and asked if they would witness his oath.

"I suppose we could manage that," Honakura said. "What do you think, Lord Kadywinsi?"

The priests had to be lined up. Lord Honakura asked Jja to help him rise, then went to join in, telling Lord Kadywinsi that he would like to do this one. He went to the wrong place. Lord Nnanji was twitching with impatience and very red, almost jumping from one foot to the other. The priest of the Fifth tried to help, but only muddled everyone worse than before. In spite of her worry, Jja almost smiled at that.

But at last they were ready. Lord Nnanji raised his sword again.

"I, Nnanji, swordsman . . ."

There was sound of a major disaster in the anteroom.

". . . liege lord of the tryst of—"

Two Fourths came hurtling bodily through the door and rolled. Shonsu was right behind them, stumbling over them, drawing his sword, stopping behind Lord Nnanji, flashing it down on his shoulder—and staying it, steel just touching flesh.

Screams and cries of outrage were stifled. The onlookers froze in horror. Shonsu was scarlet with fury, eyes bulging, the veins on his face swollen, but the seventh sword did not waver, just hung there.

Nor did Lord Nnanji's sword waver. But his voice died away and his eyes moved to look at that deadly edge alongside his neck, so close to those so-vital tendons. The two Fourths scrambled up and fled, closing the door silently.

"Drop that sword!" the big man growled, in a voice like grinding millstones.

Jja cringed. It was Shonsu, not Wallie. But he should know that Lord Nnanji would never yield to a threat. She could remember Wallie teaching him that principle, and if *she* remembered . . .

Turning his eyes straight ahead again, toward the line of petrified priests, Lord Nnanji softly said: "No."

"Drop it! Or I'll make you drop it!"

"Holy ones, I shall start over. *I, Nnanji, swordsman of the . . .*"

"You'll never lift that arm again!"

". . . seventh rank, liege . . ."

"I shall count to three."

Jja whispered a little prayer to the Goddess.

". . . lord of the tryst of Casr, do solemnly swear . . ."

"On three I cut! *One!*"

Someone in the minstrels' corner was whimpering quietly.

". . . that the tryst of Casr . . ."

"Two!"

". . . shall not be disbanded until . . ."

Lord Nnanji paused, as if daring his tormentor to act, as if waiting for the deadly "Three." But Shonsu was silent now, staring at the back of Lord Nnanji's head. His rage was fading, Jja thought. Her hands hurt. She had dug her nails into her palms.

". . . it shall have completed the task for which it was called; and this I swear upon my honor, and in the name of the Goddess."

Silence.

Lord Nnanji slowly lowered his sword and again he moved his eyes to study the Chioxin blade beside his neck.

Wallie? Jja dug her nails into her palms again. Was it Wallie? He had gone very pale. The rage had vanished; he seemed stunned. He was staring fixedly at Lord Nnanji's ponytail. She thought it was Wallie.

Lord Nnanji ducked his shoulder a fraction, and the seventh sword did not move. He slid gently out from under it, then slowly turned to look at. . . . Yes, it was Wallie back again. What was wrong with him? He was rigid, every muscle knotted, and sweat shone on his face.

"I shall sheath my sword now," Lord Nnanji said quietly. He did so, moving very slowly and deliberately, not taking his eyes off . . . off Wallie.

And Wallie lowered his sword until the point touched the floor. He stared down at it as if he had never seen it before, or did not know why it was there. The spectators began to relax, very slightly, but no one yet dared speak. He turned his head and gazed toward Jja. She tensed, wondering if he wanted her to go to him, dismayed at the inexplicable pain she could see in his face. Was he asking her something? Before she could move, though, he switched his gaze back down to his sword . . . to her briefly . . . to the sword again . . . almost as if he were comparing them.

Then he raised his head and looked at Nnanji. For a moment he seemed unable to find his voice. He licked his lips.

"You were wrong, brother!"

Obviously as puzzled as any, Lord Nnanji put his fists on his hips. "I waited. You could have stopped me."

"Not the oath. You were wrong about returning the sword. I must return it, yes. But not to a place. Not to Quo. To a person —to the man who gave it to me."

"A god gave it to you!"

Wallie shook his head. "Gods do not kneel to mortals. The god made the sword appear on a rock, and I picked it up. He did not dedicate it . . ."

Lord Nnanji said, "Then . . ." and was silent.

"I suppose I should have asked the first swordsman I met to dedicate it, to give it to me properly. I didn't think of it. I didn't ask you—you were the first swordsman I met. But when I went ashore in Aus, I left the sword in your care. And when I came back to the ship—"

"I said the words! I knelt! But what I meant was—"

"I know what you meant, brother." Wallie swallowed hard, as if his throat hurt. "And so you gave it to me then—as swordsmen understand giving a sword. *You* gave me the seventh sword, Nnanji! You! Now I must return it."

The other swordsmen muttered in amazement as he sank to one knee and held out the Chioxin sword in both hands. "Live by this. Wield it in Her service. Die holding it."

The onlookers fell silent, and there was a long pause.

"But why, brother?" Nnanji whispered. "The Goddess wanted you to have Her sword!"

"Not anymore. Take it."

"You're leader of the tryst . . ."

"Not anymore. You are. Take it!"

Still Nnanji hesitated, staring as if hypnotized at the weapon being proffered to him.

"Damnation!" Wallie roared, suddenly loud. Everyone jumped. "Do you think this is easy for me? Boariyi! Upon your honor—who is the best swordsman in this room?"

"My liege . . . Lord Nnanji."

"Oh!" Nnanji smiled. "Well, in that case . . . say it again, brother!"

"Live by this! Wield it in Her service! Die holding it!"

Still Lord Nnanji wavered for a moment. Then he reached out his hand and softly said, "It . . . it shall be . . . my honor and my pride." And took the seventh sword.

Then he looked at Thana and uttered a great whoop of joy.

††† † †††

Wallie leaned back against the wall with Jja leaning back against his chest. She had no choice, for his arms were tight around her. Her head was on his collarbone and he could smell the sweet, familiar scent of her hair. Perhaps he was trying to hide behind her, to hide from the consequences of what he had done. He had assured her that he was all right now, but in truth he was still confused and uncertain about his sudden decision.

He had been ready to cripple Nnanji, to prevent his oath by severing the tendons in his shoulder. Then he had seen the Arganari hairclip, a silver griffon. *Power wisely used!* He had read it as a message—the gods wanted Nnanji to have the power. So Wallie had given him the tryst.

It is your kingdom that I covet . . . and Ikondorina agreed . . .

Honakura had said that he had made the right choice. Thana had rushed forward to hug Nnanji and congratulate him; then the swordsmen and priests had added their own congratulations, while casting sideways glances of wonder at Lord Shonsu, for any man who would voluntarily give up the sword of the Goddess must seem strange to them beyond imagining. But it was to Wallie that Honakura had gone to offer his congratulations, and tears of joy had trickled down his wrinkled old cheeks while he did so.

But why? Why would the Goddess turn over control of Her swordsmen to a bloody-minded juvenile like Nnanji? And not just the swordsmen—the World itself! He did not know that, of course, not yet. He was thinking only of reforming substandard city garrisons, he did not see what must follow.

Gradually order was being restored in the council chamber. The priests had been thanked and dismissed. Nnanji had presented his own sword to Wallie in exchange for the Chioxin.

Then, joyfully gathering confidence as he went along, he had issued a proclamation for the heralds and sent them off to tell the swordsmen about the truce—employee relations. He had dismissed the minstrels with a stern warning not to mention any transient disagreement between the two liege lords—press censorship. Tyrants were good at that, Wallie reflected.

That left only the swordsmen and the sorcerer. Nobody sat down in Nnanji's tryst, apparently. The council chamber was an untidy jumble of chairs and stools, but everyone was standing. It stank of wine and woodsmoke and people; the rumpled silk rug had not been straightened. No one cared. There was a ship waiting, but Nnanji paced restlessly around among the furniture, every now and again glancing warily toward Wallie for signs of approval or disagreement. Whenever he turned his back, Wallie saw the sapphire of the seventh sword glittering beside the red ponytail, and then he wanted to weep.

Now Nnanji was shooting out orders to the Sevenths. He was good at delegating.

He had begun with gray-haired Zoariyi. "Honorable Milinoni is outside. He knows the identities of the spies we have been watching. I want them arrested!"

Rotanxi frowned. "Have we not a truce, Lord Nnanji?"

"Aha!" Nnanji wheeled round to him triumphantly. "Are you testifying that they are sorcerers, my lord? If so, then they are wearing the wrong facemarks and are felons! However, that was not what I had in mind. Lord vassal, you speak to them when they are brought in. Frighten them a little! Make their teeth rattle!

Then tell them about the truce and Lord Rotanxi's return—and let them go!"

Zoariyi looked puzzled, but thumped fist to heart in acknowledgment and headed for the door. Nnanji sneaked a glance at Wallie. He got a nod of approval and grinned. The spies, of course, would report by pigeon. Sen would be warned to prepare a reception, and Vul, also, but there was a hidden message there, too: "I understand your communications and will use them." Clever! Nnanji was doing all right so far.

Then he beckoned to the wildly happy Thana and put an arm around her when she went to him. "Lord Rotanxi?" he demanded. "How many members of this council-of-thirteen are women?"

The sorcerer blinked. He was finding these violent swordsmen proceedings unnerving. "But two, Lord Nnanji."

"Then, if you do not object to a second hostage, my wife wishes to accompany me."

Sensation! Rotanxi choked in astonishment. The swordsmen gasped, and a couple of them looked to Wallie to see if he would move to prevent such an outrage.

But Wallie would not. He understood—and again he was impressed. He wondered whose idea it was. Probably Thana's, but it might have come from Tomiyano, or even Nnanji himself. Thana could restrain Nnanji's suicidal tongue. She could charm the eleven men, if not the two women. The council of frightened old people would not see a boy monster, they would see a storybook prince and princess. Nnanji and Thana together were an ideal of young love, handsome youth and beautiful maiden, and it would take a very embittered old sorcerer to send those two to the tormentors. Taking Thana along would be bravado, of course, but probably a very shrewd move. The pupil may indeed be greater than the teacher!

The other Sevenths did not comprehend that and they disapproved. But Nnanji's next innovation shocked them far more.

"Lord Linumino? Take the eight prisoners down to the dock and buy passage for them, also—on the same ship as myself if possible."

Boariyi turned fiery red. "You are releasing them, my liege?"

Nnanji looked up at him coldly, unabashed. "You object?"

And of course his vassal could not object, although he had risked his own life and those of his men in collecting those prisoners, had even lost a man. Return the counterhostages: a generous gesture, a clever tactic to throw the enemy off balance, and also more bravado. Wallie had his doubt about this one, but he still stayed silent, hugging Jja tighter.

Undeterred by the reaction, Nnanji told Linumino to summon a sedan chair for Rotanxi, and pulled his sword for formal farewell as the two departed. Then he surveyed the dwindling company with glee, with the air of a man about to enjoy himself very much.

"Lord Boariyi? The next two cities downriver are Ki San and Dri. You have twenty days before I return. Take whatever force you deem necessary. Go and investigate the garrisons. Punish the guilty, if any, and put good men in their place."

"*Yes*, my liege!" The tall swordsman's scowl had already become a broad grin. That sounded like honorable work—better than sneaking around by night with clubs. Free swords rarely got the chance to meddle in the affairs of large cities.

"Swear the garrisons to the tryst and inform the King of Ki San and the elders of Dri that any swordsmen trouble they may have in future should be reported to me, or to Lord Shonsu, here in Casr."

Boariyi nodded vigorously in approval.

"I do know," Nnanji continued, baring his teeth, "that the reeve of Ki San, the Honorable Farandako, is a thief. He stole my slave. Depose him! Sell his possessions for the benefit of the tryst. Bring him back to Casr in chains. I will deal with him myself."

No proper denunciation? No trial? Of course Nnanji would give the man a sword and issue a formal challenge, but it would be as much an execution as if the man's head were on a block. Wallie's doubts began rattling the bars of their cage.

"Swordsmen who refuse to swear, my liege?" asked Boariyi.

Nnanji shrugged. "Let them choose—head or thumbs. But leave no able-bodied swordsman unsworn!"

Boariyi saluted, fist on heart. Nnanji was turning away when Thana stepped close and whispered something in his ear. He grinned at her and swung around to Wallie, eyes alight. "How much has Casr contributed to the tryst, brother?"

It took some hard thought before Wallie could say that he thought about five thousand golds, if the dock fees were included.

Nnanji nodded and looked back to Boariyi. "Dri and Ki San are both much larger and richer, but five thousand from each will do for now. We shall assess them more exactly later."

He smirked triumphantly at Wallie; the swordsmen would eat.

Boariyi was smarter than he looked. "If they refuse to comply, my liege?"

Nnanji bit his lip, then said, "You will carry out your orders within the ways of honor, vassal."

Horror-struck, Wallie blurted: "Nnanji!"

In all times and places, probably in all worlds, tyrants had found that same escape. Boariyi had been told to be zealous, without limit, but whatever atrocities he might commit in obeying his orders could be disavowed by Nnanji. It was a classic evasion of responsibility, and the very stuff of despotism. Almost Wallie could smell the burning homes already.

Nnanji flinched and looked defensive. "Brother?"

And Wallie shrank back from the confrontation. He had made his decision and must live with it. To dispute the new leader's orders so soon and in public would be crass disloyalty. Some day he would have to bring up the matter in private and hope to make Nnanji see reason.

"Even a rich city may not be able to raise so much at the flash of a sword, Nnanji," he said weakly.

Nnanji pouted, but he was obviously relieved that the objection was no more serious than that. "Of course you may give them time to remit the exaction, vassal. Lord Jansilui? Upriver, Wo and Tau are smaller. Swear the swordsmen there, also, but . . . two thousand golds from each will suffice for the present. You will not have time to go on to Shan, I fear."

Jansilui saluted, and the thought of action had made him grin, also.

Then Nnanji looked to Tivanixi—and he was already grinning.

"Quo, my liege?"

Nnanji nodded.

Inside Wallie, something died. The stirrup he had introduced would have its first taste of warfare in the World—but not against sorcerers. The cavalry would ride against a friendly city and loot in the name of law. He felt sick.

"How big is Quo?" Nnanji asked. "Never mind—use your own judgment about money."

Wallie choked back another protest. Carte blanche! Tivanixi was a fine man, but no swordsman could be totally trusted to be sympathetic to civilians. Eager to display his enthusiasm and efficiency in this new order, he might well rape the hapless city, pillage it for its own good. *Goddess! Forgive me!*

Tivanixi saluted and Wallie knew that he was next. He eased Jja away from him, straightening up in more swordsmanlike fashion to hear his fate.

"The catapults have served their purpose, brother, I think," Nnanji said. "They were enough to scare the sorcerers into your treaty . . ."

His tone was more gentle than it had been with his vassals, and the words were grouped in requests, but those requests were supposed to be obeyed. Probably that was how Wallie had spoken to him before their positions were reversed, so Wallie should not quibble. Catapult building, archery, knife throwing—all were to be spat out like grape seeds. From now on sutras and swordsmanship were what the tryst would need, Nnanji said. Instruction should not be left to incompetent middleranks . . . there were some variants among the sutras and the tryst should have a uniform cannon . . . any man who had not tried for promotion since arriving at Casr must explain . . . any man who had jumped two ranks before Nnanji returned from Vul could become his personal protégé . . . make a start on converting temporary arrangements, like the women's quarters, into permanent . . . maintain strict discipline at all times . . .

When he had finished, Wallie thumped fist on heart in silence as the vassals had done. Nnanji had the grace to blush slightly. Then, with the juvenile naïveté that was so much of his charm, he grinned hugely and said, "How'm I doing so far, Shonsu?"

Wallie concealed his despondency, manufactured a smile, and said, "Straight points so far, brother."

Already? his conscience inquired. *Already we are into flattery? Why not tell him that the gods are pleased with him?*

The problems would have to wait, Wallie thought; there was a ship standing by. But they would not wait long. The King of Ki San would reportedly pay a hundred golds for a well-rounded concubine. That did not sound like benevolent monarchy. What were these newly immaculate garrisons supposed to do when ordered to administer unjust laws? Or gather gluttonous taxes? Who would do this assessing of tribute? Who collect it? Guard it? Account for it? Distribute it?

Nnanji's simple view of a perfect World did not include any of those questions. Even Wallie's did not contain the answers.

"Right! We have a ship to catch, wife," Nnanji said. He took two steps, stumbled, and regained his balance. Then he looked down at the rumpled rug that had tripped him—silver pelicans and bronze river-horses. He glanced around at the wall hangings, the drapes, the shiny furniture.

No tyrant in any world could have bettered the look he then turned on Wallie. Wallie recoiled before it.

"You will not be needing this trash anymore, will you, Shonsu? As soon as you have disposed of it, issue a proclamation: From now on, any acceptance of bribes by a swordsman will be a capital offense—without exception!"

That was not a request.

Nnanji swung around and marched out with his arm around Thana. Wallie watched the seventh sword depart. His eyes misted, and he quickly gestured for the others to precede him.

Finally return that sword. Finally? Either he had completed his mission for the Goddess, or he had just resigned as Her champion without completing it. Either way, he was finished. The adventure was over.

The sound of boots receded. Only Jja remained, standing with a hand on his arm, studying him, concerned, sensing the dismay he had hidden from everyone else, or hoped he had.

He took her in his arms and hugged her in silent misery.

He could not explain, even to her. There was still no word in the language for "despot." But there soon would be! Nnanji had taken less than twenty minutes to become one.

EPILOGUE:
THE LAST MIRACLE

The wind flapped awnings and gowns, blustering among the wagons and pedestrians on the riverside plaza, chasing a few remaining leaves. Traders strode homeward, with their slaves dragging wearily behind. Most of the ships had fallen silent as sailors prepared to enjoy an evening in the law-abiding sanctuary of Casr.

Wallie drooped despondently on a bollard, watching the lengthening shadows creep over the bronze stones. The day that had begun with *Griffon*'s return was drawing to a close, and the World would never be the same again.

Nnanji had gone, marching up the plank as the band played *The Swordsmen in the Morning*, standing on deck with Thana and nine sorcerers as the ship had sailed away. He had no doubts that he would return safely, with treaty sworn. For him the sorcerers were now but a minor nuisance to be tidied up before he got down to his serious work of reforming the swordsmen of the World.

The bodyguards and bandsmen and minstrels had gone. Seeing no danger now, Wallie had sent Forarfi and his troops off to enjoy what was left of the holiday. He ought to go back to Jja—but he had been thinking that for quite a while and he was still on the bollard.

Where had he gone wrong? It was almost half a year since he had promised the Goddess that he would be a swordsman. He had tried. If his mission had been to defeat the sorcerers, then he had failed, for now they would spread freely across the World. Their disruptive technology would follow.

If his mission had been to save the swordsmen, then he had still failed. The sorcerers could be no threat to Nnanji's universal tryst, but he was sure that Nnanji's universal tryst would soon be killing off swordsmen at a far greater rate than the sorcerers ever had. The fiercely independent free swords would not readily submit to a central authority, nor garrisons yield their autonomy.

Or had his mission been Nnanji himself? The demigod had said that the task would be revealed, and Nnanji had been the first person Wallie had met afterward. Nnanji had received his share of miracles. Yet, if Nnanji had been his mission, then Wallie had still failed, for he had loosed a power-mad psychopath on a helpless World. Dri and Ki San, Wo and Tau, Quo—those unsuspecting cities would be the first to fall, and there would be hundreds of others before he could be stopped. Every day his power would grow. Who or what could ever stop him?

Not Wallie, certainly. He was still deputy leader of the tryst, and for the next twenty days he was going to be run ragged, he and Linumino and Zoariyi. Nnanji had made sure of that. Wallie had taught him that an army must be kept busy.

But after Nnanji returned? Wallie had now concluded that he must then leave. He would not be able to bear to watch what his folly had created. He would quarrel with Nnanji, and there could only be one ending to such a quarrel. So he would accept the sinecure he had been offered—retire to Tau and be reeve of that smelly little Tudor town. In his spare time he could help Jja make babies. His work was done—bungled, but finished. Failure!

He was about to rise when a crowd of small, naked children ran giggling by him. One little brown boy stopped and flashed a gap-toothed grin . . . pixie face . . . every bone showing like a bundle of sticks, hair dark and tightly curled, eyes glittering like gems.

Wallie made to drop to his knees, and the boy said, "Stay where you are. You've had a hard day."

So Wallie stayed on the bollard and said nothing, but his skin crawled with fear. Punishment, the god had said before, would be death, or worse than death.

"Oh, no!" the demigod said. "I came to thank you, Mr. Smith! You have done everything required of you, and more."

The sudden sense of astonishment and relief was like falling into a cold bath. "I have?"

"Certainly!" The boy laughed. "You trained him. You taught him compassion. You gave him the tryst. You made the treaty with the sorcerers and, finally, you gave him the sword, unasked. A task well done, indeed!"

Wallie snorted with bitter disbelief. "Compassion? He would kill a man as soon as eat a peanut."

"That is a job requirement," the god replied sadly. "Genghis Khan was just the same. But he is a polite, quiet-spoken young man and he has learned much from you. He still admires you beyond words. You have done well!"

"I don't understand, Master!"

The boy laughed. "That's why I came. You see, Walliesmith, not all worlds follow quite the same path, but always the invention of speech begins the Age of Legends. The invention of writing ends it."

Revelation! "You mean that the swordsmen were a curse on the sorcerers, like the curse on Nnanji?"

"More or less! Because after the Age of Legends comes the Dark Age, like a birth canal, and then the Age of Wisdom—although some worlds never seem to get out of the Dark Age."

A hawker pushed his cart slowly past. The boy held out a hand and two apples jumped from the cart into it. He gave one to Wallie. They bit simultaneously and the boy grinned.

"But he will be a tyrant! The gods will support tyranny?" Wallie almost dared to sound disbelieving.

The pixie face turned sad. "The gods will not be interfering much anymore—I just told you. And think of 'empire,' not tyranny! Of course there has never been an empire, so he cannot conceive of one. He will discover that by ruling the garrisons he is also ruling the cities. That will annoy him hugely! Thana invents the empire."

Wallie shook his head. "I thought he was mad."

"Oh, not at all!" the boy said. "It is not madness to think the gods are on your side when you have received so many blessings. You thought the same of yourself. No, he knows now that he is a man of destiny. He has supreme power. He is ruthless, fearless, zealous, and incorruptible. He cares nothing for money. He seeks power only for his ideals."

An empire? Easy for gods, who need not live in it. Wallie believed in democracy. Could he ever learn to support an empire?

"You have one thing left to do," the demigod said with a teasing smile.

"Yes, Master."

"The last line of my riddle—you must accept the destiny of the sword!"

"Yes, Master."

The boy shook his head reprovingly. "More enthusiasm! He will be Nnanji the Great, founder of the first dynasty. For almost a thousand years, the symbol of his house will be the sapphire sword."

Wallie remembered that day when he had first seen the seventh sword—he had at once thought of crown jewels. He should have guessed! Now he regarded the god warily. "Nnanji never met Shonsu, but You let me think I was being given the same task that Shonsu had failed at. Was that fair?"

Another gap-toothed grin. "I did not lie to you! You knew that the words of gods or their oracles must be considered very carefully. The objective was not sorcerers, or Nnanji, or Shonsu . . . always the objective was an empire. That was why I could not tell you! But you predicted what chaos the sorcerers' knowledge might produce as it escaped. Only an empire can control that.

"Shonsu's surprise attack very nearly succeeded—it would have done, had he thought to use horses to speed his approach. He would have made himself king of Vul, then king of everywhere else, using firearms. You would not have been brought into play at all, and Nnanji would have lived and died in obscurity—and died young, for his is one of the great souls, and would have been needed elsewhere.

"Your treaty keeps the firearms under control, which is much better. It will shorten the Dark Age. Nnanji could not have made that treaty."

"And I could not make an emperor," Wallie said sadly.

The boy gave him a steady look. "No. You could not hurl your legions at Quo and Ki San as he just did. But it was offered to you! You turned down a world for the love of a slave girl, Mr. Smith—and all the halls of heaven rang with joy!"

Wallie blinked. It still hurt a little. Had that been the only reason for Jja—to distract him? "There will be much bloodshed!"

"Not as much as you think," the god said. "The swordsmen are very civilized about that, much more so than your other world was. And it is the Dark Age now."

There was another long silence while Wallie pondered and chewed apple. A troop of swordsmen clattered by on horses on the far side of the plaza. His melancholy seemed to amuse the little god more than annoy him.

"You have done well. You have all done well—Brota, Tomiyano. You will all be rewarded."

"Honakura?"

"Of course. You must say farewell to him tomorrow, but his reward will be glorious."

Wallie nodded and could not speak.

"Come!" the boy said. "For my time is short and I have something to show you. We can talk on the way."

Wallie rose and walked alongside. He still could not feel convinced. "Master," he said. "Explain the prince to me. Did he have to die just to send me a signal with that hairclip?"

The skinny little boy had a terrifying frown. "If you are going to judge the gods, Walliesmith, you must know what the gods know. However, since you have done so well this day . . . know that there are some souls brighter—older, more effective. Higher on the ladder! Like Nnanji's. Had Shonsu made his empire, then about fifteen years from now there would have been a crisis—a node, a cusp—at Kra, which is the sorcerer city south of Plo. A strong ally, a swordsman king . . . now can you understand what Arganari was to be?"

"I think so."

"There will be no such need under Nnanji, for the sorcerers are on his side. But he is founder of a dynasty, so there will be a different crisis, later."

"The succession?" Wallie asked, beginning to see.

"Right! Do you remember the night Arganari died?"

"Nnanji's wedding night?"

The boy nodded and smiled, which was much more comforting than the frown. "Thana conceived a son that night. She does not waste time. Nnanji surely did not! Now do you understand what Arganari is to be? Don't try to be a god, Mr. Smith. You could not even be an emperor!"

They left the dockside plaza and headed up one of the wider streets. The few pedestrians parted readily for the big swordsman. The boy they did not notice.

"Nnanji will make a much better emperor than Shonsu would have done," the god remarked. He looked up with a sly smile. "And Thana a better empress than Doa!"

Wallie snorted. "I certainly do not understand what Doa is!"

"Hardly surprising! Genius on her scale comes rarely to any world!" He chuckled at the vagaries of mortals and led the way around a corner. "Forget Doa! She has lost interest in you and she can smell history in the making. She is on that ship!"

"Going to Vul?"

"She will try. You will never meet her again. You have exorcised Shonsu, Mr. Smith!" The boy's tone said that the subject was closed.

Doa had served her purpose, also, Wallie decided, by rousing Shonsu in him—but a quick frown from the little god warned him not to put the thought into words.

Now he could see that their destination was the lodge, and he had many questions to ask before they got there.

"So Nnanji is right when he says that the swordsmen will submit to him?"

"Most of them."

"But what of the cities, the civilians? As soon as he controls the garrisons he will have to adjudicate their disputes—internal politics and taxes and trade. The tryst's finances are going to be a madhouse of corruption. The whole economy of the World will tremble. I just can't see Nnanji coping with those problems! He can't and he won't!"

"Of course not!" The demigod's scorn made Wallie break out in goosebumps. "But he has Thana, and he has Katanji, Ikondorina's black-haired brother! With a crippled arm he will not alarm the civilians, but to the swordsmen he is one of them, and brother to the liege. Of course he is a scoundrel! He will be the richest man in the World before he is twenty. But he is loyal to Nnanji, which is all that matters."

Katanji for Prime Minister?

"Chancellor," the boy said.

The gods had made their plans well. Lost in thought, Wallie almost walked into a horse, standing between the shafts of a parked wagon. He gave it his apple core and went on.

"So Nnanji seizes power, Thana turns it into an empire, and Katanji keeps it profitable? It will be a force for good?"

"They will make mistakes, of course," the god said. "But Nnanji is a fast learner. They need wise counsel to minimize their follies."

Wallie's heart jumped. Did that mean . . .

"Certainly!" The boy vanished around a group of gossiping women and rejoined Wallie beyond them. "You don't really want to spend the rest of your life wrestling drunks in Tau, do you? You have been Merlin to Nnanji's Arthur. Now you can be Aristotle, Alcuin, or Imhotep—loyal friend, advisor, and sometimes conscience; resident wizard. The power behind the scabbard!"

"Will he listen?"

"Most of the time. I do not say it will be easy. But he knows that you know things he never can, just as he can do things you can't."

"Nnanji and me? Like the sword—sharpness and flexibility?"

"Like the griffon—a lion and an eagle!"

And suddenly Wallie felt better. No, he was not yet ready to retire to Tau. How could he be happy there, knowing that Nnanji was trampling unchecked through the life of the People? He followed his divine master through the alley and into the wide plaza, growing dim now in twilight . . . and stopped in surprise at the huge and rowdy party in progress. The tryst was vacationing. Oxen were being roasted over bonfires. Swordsmen and their ladies were everywhere, laughing and singing and whirling in dance. Minstrels and heralds were being drowned out in the hubbub and the music.

Then he realized that they must be celebrating more than Boariyi's victory. Nnanji's accession was already known. The young hero of Ov was more acceptable than the ambiguous, unorthodox Shonsu. Sutras and swordsmanship had returned. Perversions like archery could be forgotten. Nnanji had known.

Feeling wounded by their ingratitude, Wallie looked down and saw the demigod studying him with amusement, his face indistinct in the shadow, but his eyes gleaming bright.

"Wealth for Katanji, power for Thana, glory for Nnanji," he said softly. "But you chose love, did you not?"

Wallie nodded.

"You shall have it, then . . . unless you wish to change your mind? If you want to try being emperor, the Goddess can still arrange for Nnanji to die in Vul."

"No!" Wallie said hastily. "I . . . I'll settle for love!"

The boy chuckled. "I thought so! Power does not appeal to you, Shonsu, just as the People do not interest Nnanji or the other two. You would rather right a wrong, would you not?"

That was true, Wallie admitted thoughtfully. And an empire could do so much: impose uniform laws, stamp out injustice and torture and perhaps even slavery, install good drainage. . . . It would need hundreds of junior sorcerers to be scribes and accountants; city elders ought to be elected, not self-appointed; taxes should be fairly assessed and honestly collected. . . . Ideas and plans began to romp through his mind until at last he saw the little god grinning at him. They both laughed.

"Your reward!" the boy said. "The World seems old to you, Shonsu, but in truth it is very young. To all the ages that are to be, this day will seem like the dawn of history, the Coming of Nnanji. *The Swordsmen in the Morning!*"

He gestured for Wallie to move again. They wound their way across the plaza, between the dancers and the bonfires. No one noticed the passing of the deputy liege lord; that was a trick that the demigod had demonstrated once before, and Wallie was grateful for this temporary invisibility.

"But you will need a house for your lady," the boy said. "Real estate in Casr is an excellent investment just now. Talk to Katanji."

Wallie choked. "I have to get rid of that damned rug before Nnanji gets back! You think he will stand for my getting a house? A furnished house, I suppose?"

"But you will give Katanji *Griffon*, which is yours. Fair exchange, so Nnanji will not mind."

"A leaky old tub like that? What sort of hovel would that buy?"

The god laughed shrilly. "A modest mansion! Nnanji will not know any better—he does not care about money. You will be amazed at the palace that Thana builds—with the money she gets from *Sapphire*, of course! You must learn to manage him, just as his brother and Thana have learned. He is an autocrat, remember. You are a courtier now."

"Am I no better than those two, then?"

"Don't judge! You taught Nnanji that every man must be arbiter of his own honor. You will be as true to him as you can. You can't be a god, Walliesmith, you can't be an emperor, and you can't live by Nnanji's standards! But you can be a good friend and helper."

"And what does Katanji get out of this mansion-for-ship deal? Katanji and his friends?"

"Offer to make him treasurer of the tryst and see what he says! If you don't, Nnanji will anyway. And warn him about the gold coming in from Ki San and Dri—he is sharp enough to see what it will do to prices and he will make another fortune on that alone. Tomorrow will be time enough. Swordsman Katanji has just heard the news, and at the moment he is still delirious over the prospects of a permanent tryst. This is a primitive World still, Shonsu. Don't expect payroll deductions and medical insurance and pension plans. . . . Ah! Here we are."

He stopped and pointed at the lodge entrance ahead. A woman in blue was coming down the steps with a small, naked boy at her side.

Wallie looked twice and then again at his companion.

"That's you, isn't it?" he said.

"Of course! Could I ever get all my work done if I were only in one place at a time? And the lady with me, the seamstress of the Seventh?"

Wallie's eyes misted over, and he could not see.

"Some swordsman you are!" The boy chuckled. "Shonsu, the gods are grateful! Your rewards will be wonderful: long life and happiness, power, and accomplishments." He snickered. "And loving, of course! You will rule when Nnanji is absent. You will plot the atlas of the World and watch the circles close. You will force justice on Katanji, reason on Thana, and mercy on Nnanji. You will travel the World as his ambassador and ride at his side when he returns to Hann to thank the Goddess and visit his parents.

"The others will have the honor and fame, but you get the love of the People. And when at last you die, with your grandchildren's children beside you and a multitude in vigil at the gates, then a World will weep. Until then, Jja's love is yours and her beauty unfading. She minded little being a slave, but you minded, so she and Vixini have been freed. No one but you and she will even notice the change—it is a retroactive miracle, and the last. I have just explained to her."

Wallie rubbed his watering eyes angrily. The little boy had run off to meet the other little boy, and then they were running side by side, except there was only one of him, and then he had vanished altogether in the darkness between the dancers and the bonfires . . .

And Lady Jja was standing at the bottom of the steps, smiling and waiting for her swordsman.

ABOUT THE AUTHOR

Dave Duncan was born in Scotland in 1933 and educated at Dundee High School and the University of St. Andrews. He moved to Canada in 1955 and has lived in Calgary ever since. He is married and has three grown-up children.

Unlike most writers, he did not experiment beforehand with a wide variety of careers. Apart from a brief entrepreneurial digression into founding—and then quickly selling—a computerized data-sorting business, he spent thirty years as a petroleum geologist. His recreational interests, however, have included at one time or another astronomy, acting, statistics, history, painting, hiking, model ship building, photography, parakeet breeding, carpentry, tropical plants, classical music, computer programming, chess, genealogy, and stock market speculation.

An attempt to add writing to this list backfired—he met with enough encouragement that he took up writing full time. Now his hobby is geology.